# BLUE
# SMOKE

## *Nora Roberts*

# Series

## Irish Born Trilogy

BORN IN FIRE
BORN IN ICE
BORN IN SHAME

## In the Garden Trilogy

BLUE DAHLIA
BLACK ROSE
RED LILY

## Dream Trilogy

DARING TO DREAM
HOLDING THE DREAM
FINDING THE DREAM

## Circle Trilogy

MORRIGAN'S CROSS
DANCE OF THE GODS
VALLEY OF SILENCE

## Chesapeake Bay Saga

SEA SWEPT
RISING TIDES
INNER HARBOR
CHESAPEAKE BLUE

## Sign of Seven Trilogy

BLOOD BROTHERS
THE HOLLOW
THE PAGAN STONE

## Bride Quartet

VISION IN WHITE
BED OF ROSES
SAVOR THE MOMENT
HAPPY EVER AFTER

## Gallaghers of Ardmore Trilogy

JEWELS OF THE SUN
TEARS OF THE MOON
HEART OF THE SEA

## Three Sisters Island Trilogy

DANCE UPON THE AIR
HEAVEN AND EARTH
FACE THE FIRE

## The Inn BoonsBoro Trilogy

THE NEXT ALWAYS
THE LAST BOYFRIEND
THE PERFECT HOPE

## Key Trilogy

KEY OF LIGHT
KEY OF KNOWLEDGE
KEY OF VALOR

## The Cousins O'Dwyer Trilogy

DARK WITCH
SHADOW SPELL
BLOOD MAGICK

# eBooks by Nora Roberts

## Cordina's Royal Family

AFFAIRE ROYALE
COMMAND PERFORMANCE
THE PLAYBOY PRINCE
CORDINA'S CROWN JEWEL

## The Donovan Legacy

CAPTIVATED
ENTRANCED
CHARMED
ENCHANTED

## The O'Hurleys

THE LAST HONEST WOMAN
DANCE TO THE PIPER
SKIN DEEP
WITHOUT A TRACE

## Night Tales

NIGHT SHIFT
NIGHT SHADOW
NIGHTSHADE
NIGHT SMOKE
NIGHT SHIELD

## The MacGregors

THE WINNING HAND
THE PERFECT NEIGHBOR
ALL THE POSSIBILITIES
ONE MAN'S ART
TEMPTING FATE
PLAYING THE ODDS
THE MACGREGOR BRIDES
THE MACGREGOR GROOMS
REBELLION/IN FROM THE COLD
FOR NOW, FOREVER

## The Calhouns

SUZANNA'S SURRENDER
MEGAN'S MATE
COURTING CATHERINE
A MAN FOR AMANDA
FOR THE LOVE OF LILAH

## Irish Legacy

IRISH ROSE
IRISH REBEL
IRISH THOROUGHBRED

BEST LAID PLANS
LOVING JACK
LAWLESS

SUMMER LOVE
BOUNDARY LINES
DUAL IMAGE
FIRST IMPRESSIONS
THE LAW IS A LADY
LOCAL HERO
THIS MAGIC MOMENT
THE NAME OF THE GAME
PARTNERS
TEMPTATION
THE WELCOMING
OPPOSITES ATTRACT
TIME WAS
TIMES CHANGE
GABRIEL'S ANGEL
HOLIDAY WISHES
THE HEART'S VICTORY

THE RIGHT PATH
RULES OF THE GAME
SEARCH FOR LOVE
BLITHE IMAGES
FROM THIS DAY
SONG OF THE WEST
ISLAND OF FLOWERS
HER MOTHER'S KEEPER
UNTAMED
SULLIVAN'S WOMAN
LESS OF A STRANGER
REFLECTIONS
DANCE OF DREAMS
STORM WARNING
ONCE MORE WITH FEELING
ENDINGS AND BEGINNINGS
A MATTER OF CHOICE

## Nora Roberts & J. D. Robb

## Anthologies

FROM THE HEART
A LITTLE MAGIC
A LITTLE FATE

MOON SHADOWS
*(with Jill Gregory, Ruth Ryan Langan, and Marianne Willman)*

## The Once Upon Series

*(with Jill Gregory, Ruth Ryan Langan, and Marianne Willman)*

ONCE UPON A CASTLE      ONCE UPON A ROSE
ONCE UPON A STAR      ONCE UPON A KISS
ONCE UPON A DREAM      ONCE UPON A MIDNIGHT

SILENT NIGHT
*(with Susan Plunkett, Dee Holmes, and Claire Cross)*

OUT OF THIS WORLD
*(with Laurell K. Hamilton, Susan Krinard, and Maggie Shayne)*

BUMP IN THE NIGHT
*(with Mary Blayney, Ruth Ryan Langan, and Mary Kay McComas)*

DEAD OF NIGHT
*(with Mary Blayney, Ruth Ryan Langan, and Mary Kay McComas)*

THREE IN DEATH

SUITE 606
*(with Mary Blayney, Ruth Ryan Langan, and Mary Kay McComas)*

IN DEATH

THE LOST
*(with Patricia Gaffney, Mary Blayney, and Ruth Ryan Langan)*

THE OTHER SIDE
*(with Mary Blayney, Patricia Gaffney, Ruth Ryan Langan, and Mary Kay McComas)*

TIME OF DEATH

THE UNQUIET
*(with Mary Blayney, Patricia Gaffney, Ruth Ryan Langan, and Mary Kay McComas)*

MIRROR, MIRROR
*(with Mary Blayney, Elaine Fox, Mary Kay McComas, and R. C. Ryan)*

## Also available . . .

THE OFFICIAL NORA ROBERTS COMPANION
*(edited by Denise Little and Laura Hayden)*

# BLUE SMOKE

# NORA ROBERTS

BERKLEY BOOKS, NEW YORK

BERKLEY

An imprint of Penguin Random House LLC
375 Hudson Street, New York, New York 10014

Berkley trade paperback ISBN: 978-0-425-27842-0

The Library of Congress has catalogued the G. P. Putnam's
Sons hardcover edition of this book as follows:

Roberts, Nora.
Blue smoke / Nora Roberts.
p.       cm.
ISBN 0-399-15306-3
1. Arson—Investigation—Fiction.   2. Women—Maryland—Fiction.
3. Baltimore (Md.)—Fiction.   4. Psychopaths—Fiction.
I. Title.
PS3568.O243B55        2005        2005043009
813'.54—dc22

PUBLISHING HISTORY
G. P. Putnam's Sons hardcover edition / October 2005
Jove mass-market edition / June 2006
Berkley trade paperback edition / July 2015

PRINTED IN THE UNITED STATES OF AMERICA

10   9   8   7   6   5   4   3   2   1

Cover photos: "Baltimore" by Scruggelgreen / Shutterstock; "Smoldering Scene"
by Spirit of America / Shutterstock.
Cover and endpaper design by Rita Frangie.
Endpaper photos: "Building Fire Escape" by Bob Keenan Photography / Shutterstock; "Street
Lighting" by Morgan Studio / Shutterstock; "Metal Deco" by Nadezhda Bolotina / Shutterstock.
Text design by Laura K. Corless.
Title page and part opener art © Triff / Shutterstock.

Penguin
Random
House

*For my own Carpenter Guy*

# POINT OF ORIGIN

*The specific location at which a fire was ignited.*

*Things bad begun make strong themselves by ill.*
—WILLIAM SHAKESPEARE

# PROLOGUE

Fire became in heat and smoke and light. Like some preternatural beast clawing its way from the womb, it burst to life with a cackle that rose to a roar.

And changed everything in one magnificent instant.

Like that beast, it slithered, snaked its way over wood, and scored what had been clean and bright with its black and powerful fingers.

It had eyes, red and all seeing, and a mind so brilliant, so complete, it memorized everything in its orbit.

He saw it as a kind of entity, a gilded, crimson god that existed only to destroy. And it took what it wanted without remorse, without mercy. With such *ardor*.

Everything fell before it, kneeling supplicants that worshipped even as they were consumed.

But he had made it, created it. So he was the god of fire. More powerful than the flames, more canny than the heat, more stunning than the smoke.

It hadn't lived until he gave it breath.

Watching it become, he fell in love.

The light flickered over his face, danced in his fascinated eyes. He took a beer, savored its sharp coolness in his throat as his skin streamed with the heat.

There was excitement in his belly, wonder in his mind. Possibilities flashing through his imagination as the fire streaked up the walls.

It was beautiful. It was strong. It was *fun*.

Watching it become, he became. And his destiny was scored into him, branding heart and soul.

# 1

Catarina Hale's childhood ended on a steamy August night a few hours after the Orioles demolished the Rangers at Memorial Stadium, kicking their Texas butts—as her dad said—nine to one. Her parents had taken a rare night off to haul the whole family to the game, which made the win all the sweeter. Most nights one of them, often both, put in long hours at Sirico's, the pizzeria they'd taken over from her mother's father. And the place where, eighteen years before, her parents had met. Her mother, a young, vibrant eighteen—so the story went—when the twenty-year-old Gibson Hale had swaggered in for a slice.

Went in for pizza, he liked to say, and got myself an Italian goddess.

Her father talked weird that way, a lot. But Reena liked to hear it.

Got himself a pizzeria, too, ten years later when Poppi and Nuni decided it was time to put their traveling shoes on. Bianca, the youngest of five and their only daughter, took it over with her Gib, as none of her brothers wanted the place.

Sirico's had stood in the same spot in Baltimore's Little Italy for over forty-three years. Which was even older than Reena's father, a fact that amazed her. Now her father—who didn't have even a single drop of Italian blood in his whole body—ran the place, along with her mother—who was Italian all the way through to the bone.

Sirico's was almost always busy, and a *lot* of work, but Reena didn't mind, even when she had to help. Her older sister, Isabella, complained because sometimes she had to work there on Saturday nights instead of going out on a date, or with her friends. But Bella complained almost all the time anyway.

She especially complained that their oldest sister, Francesca, had her own bedroom on the third floor while she had to share with Reena. Xander got his own room, too, even though he was the youngest, because he was the only boy.

Sharing with Bella had been okay, it had even been fun until Bella got to be a teenager and decided she was too old to do anything but talk about boys or read fashion magazines or play with her hair.

Reena was eleven and five-sixths. The five-sixths was an essential addition because it meant she had only fourteen months until *she* was a teenager. This was currently her most fervent ambition, overtaking previous ambitions such as becoming a nun or marrying Tom Cruise.

On this hot and heavy August night when Reena was eleven and five-sixths, she awoke in the dark with hard, cramping pains in her belly. She curled up, trying to make herself into a ball and biting her lip to hold back a moan. Across the room, as far as could be managed now that Bella was fourteen and more interested in having big hair than in being a big sister, Bella snored gently.

Reena rubbed at the ache and thought of the hot dogs and popcorn and candy she'd gobbled up at the ball game. Her mother told her she'd be sorry.

Couldn't her mother be wrong, even once?

She tried to offer it up, like the nuns were always saying, so some poor sinner could benefit from her bellyache. But it just hurt!

Maybe it wasn't from the hot dogs. Maybe it was from when Joey Pastorelli hit her in the stomach. He'd gotten in bad trouble for it. For knocking her down and ripping her shirt and calling her a name she didn't understand. Mr. Pastorelli and her father had gotten into a fight when her dad went to his house to "discuss the situation."

She'd heard them yelling at each other. Her father never yelled—well, hardly ever yelled. Her mother was the yeller because she was one hundred percent Italian and had a temper.

But boy had he yelled at Mr. Pastorelli. And he'd hugged her so hard when he got home.

And they'd gone to the ball game.

Maybe she was being punished for being glad Joey Pastorelli was going to get punished. And being a little glad he'd knocked her down and torn her shirt because then they'd gone to the game and watched the O's stomp all over the Rangers.

Or maybe she had internal injuries.

She knew you could get internal injuries and even *die* because she'd seen it on *Emergency!*, one of her and Xander's favorite shows.

The thought brought on another vicious cramp that had her eyes welling with tears. She started to get out of bed—she wanted her mother—and felt something wet between her thighs.

Sniffling, embarrassed she might have wet her pants like a baby, she crept out of the bedroom, down the hall toward the bathroom. She stepped inside the room with its pink tub and tiles and pulled up her *Ghostbusters* T-shirt.

Hot waves of fear rolled through her as she stared at the blood on her thighs. She was *dying*. Her ears began to ring. When the next cramp seized her belly, she opened her mouth to scream.

And understood.

Not dying, she thought. Not suffering from internal injuries. She had her period. She was having her first period.

Her mother had explained it all, about the eggs, and cycles and about becoming a woman. Both her sisters had periods every month, and so did her mother.

There was Kotex in the cabinet under the sink. Mama had shown her how to use it, and she'd locked herself in one day to practice. She cleaned herself up and tried not to be a sissy about it. It wasn't the blood that bothered her so much, but where it came from was pretty gross.

But she was grown-up now, grown-up enough to take care of what her mama told her was a natural thing, a female thing.

Because she was no longer sleepy, and she was now a woman, she decided to go down to the kitchen and have some ginger ale. It was so hot in the house—dog days, Dad called them. And she had so much to think about now that she'd *become*. She took her glass outside, to sit and sip and think on the white marble steps.

It was quiet enough that she heard the Pastorellis' dog bark in that hard, coughing way he had. And the streetlights were glowing. It made her feel like she was the only one in the world who was awake. For right now, she was the only one in the world who knew what had happened inside her body.

She sipped her drink and thought about what it would be like going back to school next month. How many of the girls had gotten their period over the summer.

She would start to get breasts now. She looked down at her chest and wondered what *that* would be like. What it would feel like. You didn't feel your hair grow, or your fingernails, but maybe you could feel breasts growing.

Weird, but interesting.

If they'd start to grow now, she'd have them by the time she was *finally* a teenager.

She sat on the marble steps, a still flat-chested girl with a tender tummy. Her crop of honey-blond hair going frizzy in the humidity, her long-lidded tawny eyes getting heavy. There was a little mole just above the right corner of her top lip, and braces on her teeth.

On that sultry night the present seemed absolutely safe, the future a misty dream.

She yawned once, blinked sleepily. As she rose to go back in, her gaze swept down the street toward Sirico's, where it had stood since even before her father was born. At first she thought the flickering light she saw in the big front window was some kind of reflection, and she thought, Pretty.

Her lips curved as she continued to study it, then her head cocked in puzzlement. It didn't really look like a reflection, or like someone had forgotten to turn off all the lights at closing.

Curious, she stepped down to the sidewalk, the glass still in her hand.

Too intrigued to consider just how her mother would skin her for walking out alone in the middle of the night, even on her own block, Reena wandered down the sidewalk.

And her heart began to thud when what she saw began to filter through the dreamy sleepiness. Smoke poured out the front door, a door that wasn't closed. The lights she saw were flames.

"Fire." She whispered it first, then screamed it as she ran back to the house and flew through the front door.

She would never forget it, not for all of her life, standing with her family while Sirico's burned. The roar of the fire as it stabbed through broken windows, shot up in quick gold towers, was a constant thrum in her ears. There were sirens screaming, whooshing gusts of water pumping out of the big hoses, weeping and shouting. But the sound of the fire, the voice of it, overpowered everything else.

She could feel it inside her belly, the fire, like the cramping. The wonder and horror, the awful beauty of it, pulsed there.

What was it like inside the fire, inside where the firemen went? Hot and dark? Thick and bright? Some of the flames looked like big tongues, lapping out, curling back like they could taste what they burned.

Smoke rolled, pluming out, rising. It stung her eyes, her nose, even as the whirling dance of flame dazzled her eyes. Her feet were still bare, and the asphalt felt like heated coals. But she couldn't step away, couldn't take her eyes off the spectacle, like some mad and ferocious circus.

Something exploded, and there were more screams in response. Firemen in helmets, faces blackened by the smoke and ash, moved like ghosts in the haze of smoke. Like soldiers, she thought. It sounded like a war movie.

And yet even the water sparkled as it flew through the air.

She wondered what was happening inside. What were the men doing? What was the fire doing? If it was a war, did it hide, then leap out to attack, bright and gold?

Ash floated down like dirty snow. Mesmerized, Reena stepped forward. Her mother caught her wrist, drawing her back, hooking an arm around her to bring Reena close against her.

"Stay here," Bianca murmured. "We have to stay together."

She just wanted to *see*. Her mother's heart was an excited drumbeat against her ear. She started to turn her head, to look up, to ask if they could get closer. Just a little closer.

But it wasn't excitement on her mother's face. It wasn't wonder that shone in her eyes, but tears.

She was beautiful; everyone said so. But now her face looked like it had been carved out of something very hard, leaving sharp lines dug deep. The tears and the smoke had reddened her eyes. There was gray ash in her hair.

Beside her, Dad stood with his hand on her shoulder. And to Reena's horror, she saw there were tears in his eyes, too. She could see the fire reflected in the shine of them, as if it had somehow crept inside him.

It wasn't a movie, it was real. Something of theirs, something that had been theirs all of her life, was burning away right in front of her. She could look beyond the hypnotic light and movement of the fire now, she could see the black smears on the walls of Sirico's, the grime and wet soot staining the white marble steps, the jagged shards of glass.

Neighbors stood on the street, the sidewalk, most in their nightclothes. Some held children or babies. Some were crying.

She remembered all at once that Pete Tolino and his wife and baby lived in the little apartment above the shop. Something squeezed her heart when she looked up, saw the smoke pouring out of the upper windows.

"Daddy! Daddy! Pete and Theresa."

"They're all right." He lifted her when she pulled away from her mother. Lifted her as he used to when she'd been little. And he pressed his face against her neck. "Everyone's all right."

She hid her face against his shoulder, in shame. She hadn't thought of the people, she hadn't even thought of all the things—the pictures and the stools, the tablecloths and the big ovens.

She'd only thought of the fire, its brilliance and its roar.

"I'm sorry." She wept now, with her face buried against her father's bare shoulder. "I'm sorry."

"Shh. We'll fix it." But his voice was raw, as if he'd drunk the smoke. "I can fix it."

Comforted, she rested her head on his shoulder, scanned the faces and the fire. She saw her sisters holding each other, and her mother holding Xander.

Old Mr. Falco sat on his steps, his gnarled fingers working a rosary. Mrs. DiSalvo from next door came over to put an arm around her mother's shoulders. With some relief she saw Pete now, sitting on the curb with his head in his hands, his wife huddled beside him clutching the baby.

Then she saw Joey. He stood, his thumbs hooked in his front pockets, his hip cocked as he stared at the fire. His face was full of something like joy, the kind in the faces of the martyrs on her holy cards.

A something that made Reena hold on tighter to her father.

Then Joey turned his head, looked at her. Grinned.

She whispered, "Daddy," but a man with a microphone strode up and began asking questions.

She tried to cling when he set her down. Joey was still staring, still grinning, and it was more frightening than the fire. But her father nudged her toward her sisters.

"Fran, take your brother and sisters home now."

"I want to stay with you." Reena grabbed at his hands. "I have to stay with you."

"You need to go home." He crouched until his red-rimmed eyes were level with hers. "It's almost out now. It's almost done. I said I'd fix it, and I will." He pressed a kiss to her forehead. "Go on home. We'll be there soon."

"Catarina." Her mother drew her back. "Help your sisters make coffee, and some food. For the people who're helping us. It's what we can do."

Food was always something they could do. Pots of coffee, pitchers of cold tea, thick sandwiches. For once there was no arguing in the kitchen between the sisters. Bella wept steadily throughout the process, but Fran didn't slap at her for it. And when Xander said he'd carry one of the pitchers, no one told him he was too small.

There was a stink in the air now, one she would always remember, and the smoke hung like a dirty curtain. But they set up a folding table on the sidewalk for the coffee, the tea, the sandwiches. Passed out cups and bread to grimy hands.

Some of the neighbors had gone back home, out of the smoke and stink, out of the drifting ash that settled on cars and ground in a thin, dirty snow. There was no brilliant light now, and even from a distance Reena could see the blackened brick, the rivers of wet soot, the gaping holes that had been windows.

The pots of flowers she'd helped her mother plant in the spring to sit on the white steps lay broken, trampled, dead.

Her parents stood in the street outside Sirico's, their hands locked, her father in the jeans he'd grabbed when she woke him, her mother in the bright red robe she'd gotten for her birthday only last month.

Even when the big trucks drove away, they stood together.

One of the men in a fireman's helmet walked over to speak to them, and they spoke for what seemed a long time. Then her parents turned away, still hand in hand, and walked toward home.

The man walked toward the ruin of Sirico's. He switched on a flashlight and went into the dark.

Together, they carried the leftover food and drink back inside. Reena thought they all looked like survivors in those war movies, dirty hair, tired faces. When the food was put away, her mother asked if anyone wanted to sleep.

Bella started to sob again. "How can we sleep? What are we going to do?"

"What comes next. If you don't want to sleep, go clean up. I'll fix breakfast. Go. We'll think better when we're clean and have some food."

Being third in line in age meant Reena was always third in line for the bathroom. She waited until she heard Fran come out and Bella go in. Then she slipped out of her room to knock on her parents' bedroom door.

Her father had washed his hair, and it was still wet. He'd changed into clean jeans and a shirt. His face looked the way it did when he got sick with the flu.

"Your sisters hogging the bathroom?" He smiled a little, but it didn't reach his eyes. "You can use ours this time."

"Where's your brother, Reena?" her mother asked.

"He fell asleep on the floor."

"Oh." She pulled her damp hair back into a band. "That's all right. Go, have your shower. I'll get you clean clothes."

"Why did the fireman go in when the others went away?"

"He's an inspector," her father told her. "He'll try to find out why it happened. They got here faster than they would have if you hadn't seen it. Pete and his family are safe, and that's most important. What were you doing up so late, Reena?"

"I—" She felt the flush heat up the back of her neck as she remembered her period. "I need to just tell Mama."

"I won't be mad."

She stared down at her toes. "Please. It's private."

"Can you go start some sausage, Gib?" Bianca said casually. "I'll be down soon."

"Fine. Fine." He pressed his hands to his eyes. Then he dropped them, looked at Reena again. "I won't be mad," he repeated, and left them alone.

"What is it you can't tell your father? Why would you hurt his feelings at a time like this?"

"I didn't mean . . . I woke up because I— My stomach hurt."

"Are you sick?" Bianca turned, laid a hand on Reena's forehead.

"I started my period."

"Oh. Oh, baby girl." Bianca drew her in, held her hard. Then began to weep.

"Don't cry, Mama."

"Just for a minute. So much, all at once. My little Catarina. So much loss, so much change. My *bambina*." She eased back. "You changed tonight, and because you did, you saved lives. We'll be grateful for what was saved, and we'll deal with what was lost. I'm very proud of you."

She kissed Reena on both cheeks. "Does your tummy still hurt?" When Reena nodded, Bianca kissed her again. "You'll take a shower, then a nice warm bath in my tub. It'll make you feel better. Do you need to ask me anything?"

"I knew what to do."

Her mother smiled, but there was something sad in her eyes. "Then you take your shower, and I'll help you."

"Mama, I couldn't say it in front of Dad."

"Of course not. That's all right. This is women's business."

Women's business. The phrase made her feel special, and the warm bath eased the achiness. By the time she got downstairs, the family was in the kitchen, and she could tell by the gentle way her father touched her hair he'd been told the news.

There was a somberness around the table, a kind of exhausted quiet. But at least Bella seemed to have used up all her tears—for the moment.

She saw her father reach over, lay his hand over Mama's, squeeze it before he began to speak. "We have to wait until we're told it's safe. Then we'll start cleaning up. We don't know yet how bad the damage is, or how much time it's going to be before we can open again."

"We're going to be poor now." Bella's lip trembled. "Everything's ruined, and we won't have any money."

"Have you ever not had a roof over your head, food on your table, clothes on your back?" Bianca asked sharply. "Is this how you behave when there's trouble? Crying and complaining?"

"She cried the whole time," Xander pointed out as he played with a piece of toast.

"I didn't ask you what I can see for myself. Your father and I have worked every day for fifteen years to make Sirico's a good place, an important place in this neighborhood. And my father and mother worked to build all that for more years than you can know. It hurts. But it's not the family that burned, it's a place. And we'll rebuild it."

"But what will we do?" Bella asked.

"Be quiet, Isabella!" Fran ordered when her sister started to speak.

"I mean, what do we do first?" Bella asked again.

"We have insurance." Gibson looked down at his plate as if surprised to find food on it. But he picked up his fork, began to eat. "We'll use it to rebuild or repair or whatever we need to do. We have savings. We won't be poor," he added with a stern look at his middle daughter. "But we'll need to be careful, for as long as it takes. We're not going to be able to go to the beach like we planned over Labor Day weekend. If the insurance isn't enough, then we'll have to go into our savings, or take out a loan."

"Remember this," Bianca added. "The people who work for us have no job now, not until we can reopen. Some of them have families. We aren't the only ones hurt by this."

"Pete and Theresa and the baby," Reena said. "They might not have any clothes or furniture or anything. We could give them some."

"Good, that's a positive thing. Alexander, eat your eggs," Bianca added.

"I'd rather have Cocoa Puffs."

"Well, I'd rather have a mink coat and a diamond tiara. Eat. There's going to be a lot of work to do. You'll all do your part."

"Nobody. Nobody," Gibson added with a jab of his finger toward Xander, "goes inside until you have permission."

"Poppi," Fran murmured. "We have to tell him."

"It's too early to call him with news like this." Bianca pushed food around her plate. "I'll call him soon, and my brothers."

"How could it have happened? How can they tell how?" Bella asked.

"I don't know. It's their job. Ours is to put it back together." Gibson lifted his coffee cup. "And we will."

"The door was open."

Gibson turned his gaze to Reena. "What?"

"The door, the front door, was open."

"Are you sure?"

"I saw. I saw the door was open, and the lights—the fire in the window. Maybe Pete forgot to lock it."

This time it was Bianca's hand that reached out and covered her husband's. Before she could speak, the doorbell rang.

"I'll get it." She rose. "I think it's going to be a very long day. If anyone's tired, they should try to sleep now."

"Finish eating," Gibson ordered. "Take care of the dishes."

Fran rose as he did, came around the table to put her arms around him. At sixteen she was slim and graceful, with a femininity Reena recognized and envied.

"It's going to be all right. We'll make it even better than it was before."

"That's my girl. Counting on you. All of you," he added. "Reena? Come with me a minute."

As they walked out of the kitchen together, they heard Bella's irritated, "Saint Francesca." Gibson merely sighed, then nudged Reena into the TV room. "Um, listen, baby, if you don't feel well, I can spring you from KP."

A part of her wanted to jump at the chance, but guilt was just a little heavier. "I'm okay."

"Just say something if you're . . . not."

He gave her an absent pat, then wandered off toward the front of the house.

She watched him. He always looked so tall to her, but now his shoulders were bowed. She wanted to do what Fran had done—say the right thing, put her arms around him, but it was too late.

# 2

She meant to go right back into the kitchen, to be good. Like Fran. But she heard Pete's voice, and it sounded like he was crying. She heard her father, too, but couldn't understand the words.

So she moved quietly forward toward the living room.

Pete wasn't crying, but he looked like he might, any second. His long hair fell over the sides of his face as he stared down at the hands he clenched in his lap.

He was twenty-one years old—they'd given him a little party at Sirico's, just the family. Because he'd worked there since he was fifteen, he *was* family. And when he'd gotten Theresa pregnant and had to get married, her parents had let them have the upstairs apartment dirt cheap.

She knew *that* because she'd heard Uncle Paul talking about it with her mother. Eavesdropping was something she had to do penance for—a lot. But it always seemed worth a couple extra Hail Marys.

Now she could see her mother sitting beside Pete, her hand on his leg. Her father sat on the coffee table—which they were *never* allowed to do—facing him. She still couldn't quite hear what her father said, his voice was so low, but Pete kept shaking his head.

Then he lifted it, and his eyes glimmered. "I swear, I didn't leave anything on. I've gone over it a thousand times in my head. Every step. God, Gib, I'd tell you if I screwed up. You have to believe me, I'm not covering. Theresa and the baby—if anything had happened to them—"

"Nothing did." Bianca closed her hand over his.

"She was so scared. We were so scared. When the phone rang." He looked at Bianca. "When you called, said there was a fire and to get out, it was like a dream. We just grabbed the baby and ran. I didn't even smell the smoke until you were there, Gib, running up to help us get out."

"Pete, I want you to think carefully. Did you lock up?"

"Sure, I—"

"No." Gib shook his head. "No, don't just knee-jerk it. Go through the steps. Lots of times routines get so automatic, you can skip something without remembering it later. Just go back. Last customers?"

"Ah. God." Pete pushed a hand through his hair. "Jamie Silvio and a girl he's seeing. New one. They split a pepperoni, had a couple of beers. And Carmine, he hung out till closing, trying to talk Toni into going out with him. Um, they left about the same time, about eleven-thirty. Toni and Mike and I finished the cleanup. I did the drawer— Oh God, Gib, the bank envelope's still upstairs. I—"

"Don't worry about that now. You and Toni and Mike left together?"

"No, Mike left first. Toni hung out while I finished up. It was about midnight, and she likes if one of us watches while she walks home. We went out—and I remember, I remember hauling out my keys, and her saying how cute my key ring is. Theresa had this picture of Rosa made into a key ring. I remember her saying it was sweet while I locked the door. I locked the door, Gib. I swear. You can ask Toni."

"Okay. None of this is your fault. Where are you staying?"

"With my parents."

"You need anything?" Bianca asked. "Diapers for the baby?"

"My mom, she keeps some stuff there for her. I just wanted to come, to tell you. I want to know what I can do. I just went by. You can't get in, they've got it blocked off. But it looks bad. I want to know what I can do. There must be *something* I can do."

"There's going to be plenty to do once we're cleared to get in there and clean up. But right now, you should go be with your wife, your baby."

"You call me at my mom's, you need anything. Anytime. You guys have been good to me, to us." He reached out to hug Gib. "Anything you need."

Gib walked to the door before turning to Bianca. "I need to go down, take a look."

Reena dashed into the room. "I want to go with you. I'm going with you."

Gib opened his mouth, and Reena could see the denial on his face. But Bianca shook her head at him. "Yes, go with your father. When you get back, we'll talk, again, about listening to private conversations. I'll wait until you get back before I call my parents. Maybe we'll have more to tell them. Maybe it isn't as bad as we think."

It looked worse, at least to Reena's eye. In the daylight, the black brick, the broken glass, the sodden debris looked horrible, smelled worse. It seemed impossible that fire could have done so much, so fast. She saw the destruction inside through the gaping hole where the big window with its painted pizza had been. The burned mess of what had been the bright orange benches, the old tables, the twisted mess that was once chairs. The sunny yellow paint was gone, as was the big menu sign that had hung in the open kitchen area where her father—and sometimes her mother—tossed dough to entertain customers.

The man with the fireman's helmet and the flashlight came out carrying a kind of toolbox. He was older than her father; she could tell because there were more lines on his face, and the hair she could see under the helmet was mostly gray.

He'd given them a quick study before stepping out. The man—Gibson Hale—had the long, lanky build that rarely went stocky. A little worse for wear with the night he'd put in. He had a lot of curling hair, sandy with some bleached-out tips. Got out in the sun when he could, didn't wear a hat.

John Minger didn't just study the fire, but the people involved in it.

The kid was pretty as a picture, even with the hollow, sleep-starved look in her eyes. Her hair was darker than her father's but had the curl in it. Looked to John as if she was going to get his height and build along with it.

He'd seen them last night when he arrived on scene. The whole family, grouped together at first like shipwreck survivors. The wife, now she was a looker. The sort of bombshell you didn't see often outside the movie screen. The oldest daughter favored her the most, he recalled. With the middle one missing that wow factor by a fraction. The boy had been handsome, with the sturdy look of childhood still on him.

This kid looked whippy, and there were some bruises and scrapes on the long legs that made him think she probably spent more time running around with her little brother than playing with dolls.

"Mr. Hale. I'm not going to be able to let you go in yet."

"I wanted to see. Did you . . . could you find out where it started?"

"Actually, I'd like to talk to you about that. Who's this?" he asked with a smile for Reena.

"My daughter Catarina. I'm sorry, I know you told me your name, but—"

"Minger, Inspector John Minger. You mentioned one of your daughters saw the fire, woke you."

"I did," Reena piped up. She knew it was probably a sin to be proud of her status. But maybe it was just a venial sin. "I saw it first."

"I'd like to talk about that, too." He glanced over as a police car pulled up to the curb. "Can you give me a minute?" Without waiting for an answer, he went to the car, spoke quietly to the policemen inside. "Is there someplace you'd be comfortable talking?" he asked when he came back.

"We live just up the block."

"That's fine. Just another minute." He went to another car and stripped off what Reena saw now were like coveralls. Beneath he wore regular clothes. He put them, and his helmet, in the trunk, along with the toolbox and, after locking it, nodded to the policemen.

"What's in there?" Reena wanted to know. "In the toolbox?"

"All kinds of things. I'll show you sometime if you want. Mr. Hale? Can I have a second? Could you wait here, Catarina?"

Again, he didn't wait, simply stepped off a short distance.

"If there's anything you can tell me," Gib began.

"We'll get to that." He took out a pack of cigarettes, a lighter. He took the first drag as he pushed the lighter back in his pocket. "I need to talk with your daughter. Now your first instinct might be to fill in details for her, prompt her. It'd be better if you didn't. If you just let the two of us talk it through."

"Okay. Sure. She's, ah, observant. Reena."

"Good." He stepped back to Reena. Her eyes, he noted, were more amber than brown and, despite the bruises under them, looked sharp. "Did you see the fire from your bedroom window?" Minger asked as they walked.

"No. From the steps. I was sitting on the steps of my house."

"A little past your bedtime, huh?"

She thought about this, about how to answer it without revealing the embarrassing personal details and avoiding a lie. "It was hot, and I woke up because I didn't feel very good. I got a drink of ginger ale in the kitchen and came out to sit on the steps and drink it."

"Okay. Maybe you can show me where you were sitting when you saw it."

She dashed ahead and obediently sat on the white marble steps as close to her original position as she could remember. She stared down the block as the men approached. "It was cooler than upstairs in my room. Heat rises. We learned that in school."

"That's right. So." Minger sat beside her, looked down the block as she did. "You sat here, with your ginger ale, and you saw the fire."

"I saw the lights. I saw lights on the glass, and I didn't know what they were. I thought maybe Pete forgot to turn the lights off inside, but it didn't look like that. It moved."

"How?"

She lifted a shoulder, felt a little foolish. "Sort of like dancing. It was pretty. I wondered what it was, so I got up and walked a little ways." She bit her lip, looked over at her father. "I know I'm not supposed to."

"We can talk about that later."

"I just wanted to see. I'm too nosy for my own good, Grandma Hale says, but I just wanted to know."

"How far'd you walk down? Can you show me?"

"Okay."

He got up with her, strolled along beside her, imagined what it would be like to be a kid walking down a dark street on a hot night. Exciting. Forbidden.

"I took my ginger ale, and I drank some while I walked." She frowned in concentration, trying to remember every step. "I think maybe I stopped here, close to here, because I saw the door was open."

"What door?"

"The front door of the shop. It was open. I could see it was open, and I thought, first I thought, Holy cow, Pete forgot to lock the door, and Mama's going to skin him. She does the skinning in our house. But then I saw there was fire, and I saw smoke. I saw it coming out the door. I was scared. And I yelled as loud as I could and ran back home. I ran upstairs and I think I was still yelling because Dad was already up and pulling on pants, and Mama was grabbing her robe. And everybody was shouting. Fran kept saying, What, what is it? Is it the house? And I said, No, no, it's the shop. That's what we call Sirico's mostly. The shop."

She'd thought this through, John decided. Gone back over it in her head, layered the details.

"Bella started crying. She cries a lot because teenage girls do, but Fran didn't cry so much. Anyway, Dad, he looked out the window, then he told Mama to call Pete—he lives above the shop—and tell him to get out, get his family out. Pete married Theresa and they had a baby in June. He said to tell Pete there was a fire in the shop and to get out right away, then to call the fire department. He was running downstairs when he told her. And he said to call nine-one-one, but she already was."

"That's a good report."

"I remember more. We all ran, but Dad ran the fastest. He ran all the way down. There was more fire. I could see it. And the window broke and it jumped out. The fire. Dad didn't go in the front. I was afraid he would and something would happen to him. He'd get burned up, but he ran to the back steps, up to Pete's."

She paused a moment, pressed her lips together.

"To help them get out," John prompted.

"Because they're more important than the shop. Pete had the baby, and my dad grabbed Theresa's arm and they all ran down the stairs. People were starting to come out of their houses. And everybody was shouting and yelling. I think Dad was going to try to run inside, with the fire, but Mama grabbed him hard and said, Don't, don't. And he didn't. He stood with her and he said, Oh Christ, baby. He calls my mother that sometimes. Then I heard the sirens, and the fire trucks came. The firemen jumped out and hooked up hoses. My dad told them everyone was out, that there was nobody inside. But some of them went inside. I don't know how they could, with the fire and smoke, but they did. They looked like soldiers. Like ghost soldiers."

"Don't miss much, do you?"

"I've got a memory like an elephant."

John flicked a glance up at Gib, grinned. "You got a pistol here, Mr. Hale."

"Gib. It's Gib, and, yeah, I do."

"Okay, Reena, can you tell me what else you saw? Just when you were sitting on the stairs, before you saw the fire. Let's go back and sit and you can try to remember."

Gib glanced toward the shop, then back at John. "It was vandalism, wasn't it?"

"Why do you say that?" John asked.

"The door. The open door. I talked to Pete. He closed last night. I took the family to the ball game."

"Birds trounced the Rangers."

"Yeah." Gib managed a small smile. "Pete closed, along with one of my other kids—employees. He locked up, he remembers specifically because he and Toni—Antonia Vargas—had a conversation about his key ring when they locked up. He's never left a door unlocked. So if it was open, somebody broke in."

"We'll talk about that." He sat with Reena again. "It's a nice spot. Nice place to have a cold drink on a hot night. Do you know what time it was?"

"Um, it was about ten after three. Because I saw the clock in the kitchen when I got the ginger ale."

"Guess most everybody in the neighborhood's asleep that time of night."

"All the houses were dark. The Castos' outside light was on, but they mostly forget to turn it off, and I could see a little bit of light in Mindy Young's bedroom window. She sleeps with a night-light even though she's ten. I heard a dog bark. I think it was the Pastorellis' dog, Fabio, because it sounded like him. He sounded excited, then he stopped."

"Did any cars go by?"

"No. Not even one."

"That late at night, that quiet, you'd probably hear if a car started up down the block, or a car door closed."

"It was quiet. Except for the dog barking a couple times. I could hear the air-conditioning humming from next door. I didn't hear anything else, that I remember. Not even when I was walking down toward the shop."

"Okay, Reena, good job."

The door opened, and once again John was struck by beauty.

Bianca smiled. "Gib, you don't ask the man in? Offer a cold drink? Please, come inside. I have fresh lemonade."

"Thank you." John had already gotten to his feet. She was the sort of woman men stood for. "I wouldn't mind something cold, and a little more of your time."

The living room was colorful. He thought bold colors would suit a woman like Bianca Hale. It was tidy, the furniture far from new, but polished recently enough that he caught the drift of lemon oil. There were sketches on the walls, pastel chalk portraits of the family, simply framed. Someone had a good eye and a talented hand.

"Who's the artist?"

"That would be me." Bianca poured lemonade over ice. "My hobby."

"They're great."

"Mama had drawings in the shop, too," Reena added. "I liked the one of Dad best. He had a big chef's hat on and was tossing a pizza. It's gone now, isn't it? Burned up."

"I'll draw another. Even better."

"And there was the old dollar. My Poppi framed the first dollar he made when he opened Sirico's. And the map of Italy, and the cross Nuni had blessed by the Pope and—"

"Catarina." Bianca held up a hand to stop the flow. "When something's gone, it's better to think of what you still have, and what you can make from it."

"Somebody started the fire, on purpose. Somebody didn't care about your drawings or the cross or anything. Or even that Pete and Theresa and the baby were inside."

"What?" Bianca braced a hand on the back of a chair. "What're you saying? Is this true?"

"We're jumping a little ahead. An arson inspector will—"

"Arson." Now Bianca lowered herself into the chair. "Oh my God. Oh sweet Jesus."

"Mrs. Hale, I've reported my initial findings to the police department's arson unit. My job is to inspect the building and determine if the fire should be investigated as incendiary. Someone from the arson unit will inspect the building, conduct an investigation."

"Why don't you?" Reena demanded. "You know."

John looked at her, those tired and intelligent amber eyes. Yeah, he thought. He knew. "If the fire was deliberate, then it's a crime, and the police take over."

"But you know."

No, the kid didn't miss a trick. "I contacted the police because when I inspected the building, I found what appears to be signs of forced entry. The smoke detectors were disabled. I found what appear to be multiple points of origin."

"What's a point of origin?" Reena asked.

"That means that the fire started in more than one place, and from the burn patterns, from the way the fire marked certain areas of the floor, the walls, the furnishings, and the residue, it appears that gasoline was used as a starter, along with what we call trailers. Other fuel, like newspaper or waxed paper, books of matches. It looks as though someone broke in, set trailers through the dining areas and back to the kitchen. You had more fuel back there: pressurized cans, wood cabinets. The framing throughout, the tables, chairs. Gasoline, most likely, was poured over the floor, the furnishings, splashed on the walls. The fire was already involved by the time Reena went outside."

"Who would do that? Deliberately do that?" Gib shook his head. "I could see a couple of stupid kids breaking in, messing around, having an accident, but you're talking about deliberately trying to burn us out—with a family upstairs. Who would do that?"

"That's what I'm asking you. Is there anyone who has a grudge against you or your family?"

"No. No, God, we've lived in this neighborhood for fifteen years. Bianca grew up here. Sirico's is an institution."

"A competitor?"

"I know everyone who runs a restaurant in the area. We're on good terms."

"A former employee, maybe. Or someone who works for you who you've had to reprimand."

"Absolutely not. I can swear to it."

"Someone you or one of your family, or one of your employees, argued with? A customer?"

Gib rubbed his hands over his face, then pushed up to walk to the window. "No one. No one I can think of. We're a family place. We get some complaints now and then, you can't run a restaurant without them. But nothing that would send off something like this."

"Could be one of your employees had an altercation, even outside the job. I'll want a list of their names. They'll need to be interviewed."

"Dad."

"Not now, Reena. We've tried to be good neighbors, and to run the place the way Bianca's parents did. Modernized the system, some, but it's the same heart, you know?" There was grief in his voice, but smoking through it was anger.

"It's a solid place. You work at it hard enough, you make a good living. I don't know anybody who'd do this to us, or to it."

"We've had calls from neighbors all morning," Bianca put in as the phone rang again. "I have our oldest girl answering the phone for us. People telling us how sorry they are, offering to help. To clean up, to bring food, to help rebuild. I grew up here. I grew up in Sirico's. People love Gib. Especially Gib. You'd have to hate to do this, wouldn't you? No one hates us."

"Joey Pastorelli hates me."

"Catarina." Bianca passed a weary hand over her face. "Joey doesn't hate you. He's just a bully."

"Why do you say he hates you?" John wanted to know.

"He knocked me down and hit me, and tore my shirt. He called me a name, but nobody will tell me what it means. Xander and his friends saw, and they came to help, and Joey ran away."

"He's a rough kid," Gib put in. "And it was . . ." He looked into John's eyes, and something passed between them Reena didn't understand. "It was upsetting. He should have counseling at the least. But he's twelve. I don't think a twelve-year-old broke in and did what you said was done."

"It's worth looking into. Reena, you said you thought you heard the Pastorellis' dog when you were sitting outside."

"I think it was him. He's kind of scary, and has a hard bark. Like a cough that hurts your throat."

"Gib, I'm thinking if some kid roughed up my daughter, I'd have a few words with him, and his parents."

"I did. I was at work when Reena and Xander and some of the kids came in. Reena was crying. She hardly ever cries, so I knew she was hurt. Her shirt was ripped. When she told me what happened . . . I was pretty steamed. I . . ."

Slowly, he looked over at his wife, a hint of horror in his eyes. "Oh my God, Bianca."

"What did you do, Gib?" John brought his attention back.

"I went straight over to the Pastorellis'. Pete was hanging out, and he went over with me. Joe Pastorelli answered the door. He's been out of work for most of the summer. I lit in."

He squeezed his eyes shut. "I was so pissed off. So upset. She's just a little girl, and her shirt was torn, her leg was bleeding. I said I was tired of his kid bullying mine, and it was going to stop. That this time Joey had gone too far, and I was thinking of calling the cops. If he couldn't teach his kid any better, the cops would. We yelled at each other."

"He said you were a fucking do-gooder asshole who should mind his own goddamn business."

"Catarina!" Bianca's tone was razor sharp. "Don't you ever use that kind of language in this house."

"I'm just saying what *he* said. For the report. He said Dad was raising a bunch of snotty, whining brats who couldn't fight their own battles. But he said more swears. Dad said some, too."

"I can't tell you exactly what I said, or he said." Gib pinched the bridge of his nose. "I don't have a tape recorder in my head like Reena. But it was heated, and it was close to getting physical. Might have, but the kids were standing out in front of the shop. I didn't want to start a fistfight in front of them, especially since I went over there about violence in the first place."

"He said somebody ought to teach you a lesson, you and your whole family. With swears," Reena added. "And he made swear signs when Dad and Pete walked away. I saw Joey when we were all out because of the fire. He smiled at me. A nasty smile."

"Do the Pastorellis have any other children?"

"No. Just Joey." Gib sat down on the arm of his wife's chair. "You want to feel sorry for the kid because it looks like Pastorelli's pretty hard on him, but he's such a bully." He looked at Reena again. "Maybe worse."

"Like father, like son," Bianca murmured. "He beats his wife, I think. I've seen her with bruises. She keeps to herself, so I don't know her well. They've lived here nearly two years, I think, and I've rarely had a conversation with her. The police came once, right after he was laid off. Their next-door neighbors heard shouting and crying and called the police. But Laura, Mrs. Pastorelli, told them nothing was wrong, and that she'd walked into a door."

"He sounds like a charmer. The police will want to talk to him. I'm sorry this happened."

"When can we get in, start cleaning up?"

"Going to be a little while yet. Arson team's got to do their job. Structurally, the place held up pretty well, and your fire doors stopped it from spreading to the upper floors. Your insurance company's going to need to look at it. These things take time, but we'll do what we can to expedite. I'll tell you, it would've been worse without Eagle Eye here." He gave Reena a wink as he rose. "Sorry about all this. I'll make sure you're kept informed."

"Will you come back?" Reena asked him. "So you can show me what's in your toolbox and what you do with it?"

"I'll make a point of it. You've been a really big help." He held out a hand, and for the first time her eyes went shy. But she put hers in it for a shake.

"Thanks for the lemonade, Mrs. Hale. Gib? You mind walking me back to my car?"

They walked out together.

"I don't know why I didn't think of Pastorelli. I still have a hard time believing he'd have gone this far. In my world, you're that pissed off at a guy, you take a swing at him."

"Direct approach. If he was involved in this, it could be he wanted to hit you where you live. Your foundation, your tradition, your livelihood. He's out of work, you're not. Hey, who's out of work now?"

"Well, God."

"You and your employee confront him. Your kids are standing out in front of the restaurant watching you confront him. Neighbors, too, I imagine."

Gib closed his eyes. "Yeah. Yeah, people came out."

"Attack and destroy your place of business, it sure teaches you a lesson. You want to point out his house?"

"There, on the right." Gib nodded. "The one with the drapes drawn. Hot day to close the curtains. Son of a bitch."

"You're going to want to steer clear of him. Push down that urge you're feeling to confront him over this. He got a car?"

"Truck. That old Ford there. The blue one."

"About what time did the two of you go a round?"

"Ah, sometime after two, I guess. Lunch crowd was about done."

As they walked, several people stopped, or opened doors, or stuck their head out a window to call out to Gib. At the Pastorelli house, the curtains stayed closed.

There was a small crowd gathered on the sidewalk near the restaurant, so John stopped while they were still out of earshot. "Your neighbors are going to want to talk to you, ask questions. Be best if you didn't mention what we've talked about."

"I won't." He let out a long breath. "Well, I've been thinking about doing some redecorating. Guess this would be the time."

"When the scene's cleared, you're going to see a lot of damage, a lot that was done during suppression. But the bones of your place, they held strong. Give us a few days, and when it's cleared, I'll come back and take you through myself. You've got a nice family, Gib."

"Thanks. You haven't met all of them, but I do."

"I saw all of you last night." John took out his keys, jingled them in his hand. "Saw how your kids set up food and sandwiches for the firefighters. People who think of doing something positive in their hard times, they've got good bones, too. There's Arson now." He inclined his head as a car pulled up. "I'm going to have a word with them. We'll be in touch," he said and offered his hand.

John walked to the car as the detectives got out of either side, and he gave them a steely grin.

"Yo, Minger."

"Yo back," he said. "Well, looks like I've done about all your work for you." He took out a cigarette, lit it. "Let me bring you up-to-date."

# 3

It didn't take a few days. The police came the following afternoon and took Mr. Pastorelli away. Reena saw it happen with her own eyes as she walked home with her best friend since second grade, Gina Rivero.

They stopped when they reached the corner where Sirico's stood. Both the police and the fire department had put up tape and warnings and barricades.

"It looks lonely," Reena murmured.

Gina put a hand on her shoulder, expressing support. "My mom said we'll all light candles before Mass on Sunday for you and your family."

"That's nice. Father Bastillo came to see us, at the house. He said stuff about strength in adversity and God working in mysterious ways."

"He does," Gina said piously, and touched a hand to the crucifix she wore.

"I think it's okay to light candles and pray and all that, but it's better to do something. Like investigate, and find out why, and make sure some-body gets punished. If you just sit around praying, nothing gets done."

"I think that's blasphemy," Gina whispered, and looked around quickly in case an Angel of God was about to strike.

Reena just shrugged. She didn't see how it could be blasphemy to say what you thought about something, but there was a reason Gina's older brother Frank called her Sister Mary these days.

"Inspector Minger and the two detectives *do* stuff. They ask questions and look for evidence, then you know. It's better to know. It's better to do something. I wish I'd done something when Joey Pastorelli knocked me down and hit me. But I was so scared, I could barely fight."

"He's bigger than you." Gina's free arm linked around Reena's waist. "And he's mean. Frank says he's nothing but a little punk who needs his a-s-s kicked."

"You can say ass, Gina. Donkeys are asses, and it's even in the Bible. Look, it's the arson detectives."

She recognized them, and the car. They wore suit coats and ties like businessmen today. But she'd seen them in the coveralls and helmets when they'd worked inside Sirico's.

They'd come to the house and talked to her just like Inspector Minger. And a spurt of excitement hit her belly when they got out of their car and walked to the Pastorellis'. "They're going to Joey's house."

"They talked to my dad, too. He came down to look at Sirico's and talked to them."

"Shh. Look." She wrapped her arm around Gina's waist, too, and cased them both back, just around the corner, when Mrs. Pastorelli opened the door. "She doesn't want to let them in."

"Why not?"

It took a mighty strength of will not to tell, but Reena only shook her head. "They're showing her a paper."

"She looks scared. They're going inside."

"We're going to wait," Reena stated. "We're going to wait and see." She walked down to sit on the curb between parked cars. "We can wait right here."

"We were supposed to go straight back to your house."

"This is different. You can go up, tell my dad." She looked up at Gina. "You should go tell my dad. I'm going to wait and see."

While Gina ran up the sidewalk, Reena sat, her eyes trained on the curtains that hadn't opened again today—and watched.

She got to her feet when her father came back alone.

His first thought when he looked at her eyes was that it was no longer a child looking back at him. There was a chill in them, a ferocity of chill that was completely adult.

"She tried not to let them in, but they showed her a paper. I think it was a warrant, like on *Miami Vice*. So she had to let them in."

He took her hand in his. "I should send you home. That's what I should do because you're not even twelve, and this is the kind of thing you shouldn't have to be part of."

"But you won't."

"No, I won't." He sighed. "Your mother handles things the way she handles them. She has her faith and her temper, her rock-hard sense and her amazing heart. Fran, she has the faith and the heart. She believes that people are innately good. That means it's more natural for them to be good than bad."

"Not for everybody."

"No, not for everybody. Bella, right now she's pretty centered on Bella. She's walking emotion, and whether people are good or bad isn't as important to her at the moment, unless it affects her. She'll probably get over most of that, but she'll always feel before she thinks. And Xander, he's got the sunniest nature. A happy kid, who doesn't mind scrapping."

"He came to help when Joey was hurting me. He scared Joey away, and Xander's only nine and a half."

"That's his nature, too. He wants to help, especially if somebody's being hurt."

"Because he's like you."

"That's nice to hear. And you, my treasure." He bent down, kissed her fingers. "You're most like your mother. With something extra all your own. Your curious nature. Always taking things apart, not just to see how they work but how they fit. When you were a baby, it wasn't enough to tell you not to touch something. You had to touch it, to see what it felt like, to see what happened. It's never been enough for you to be told some-thing. You have to see for yourself."

She leaned her head against his arm. The heat was thick and drowsy. Somewhere in the distance thunder grumbled. She wished she had a secret, something deep and dark and personal so she could tell him. She knew, in that moment, she could tell him anything.

Then across the street, the door opened. They brought Mr. Pastorelli out, one detective on either side of him. He was wearing jeans and a dingy white T-shirt. He kept his head down, as if he was embarrassed, but she could see the line of his jaw, the set of his mouth, and she thought, Anger.

One of the detectives carried a big red can, and the other a large plas-tic bag.

Mrs. Pastorelli was crying, loud sobs, as she stood in the doorway. She held a bright yellow dishcloth and buried her face in it.

She wore white sneakers, and the laces of the left shoe had come untied.

People came out of their houses again to watch. Old Mr. Falco sat on his steps in his red shorts, his skinny white legs almost disappearing into the stone. Mrs. DiSalvo stopped on the sidewalk with her little boy Chris-topher. He was eating a grape Popsicle. It looked so shiny, so purple. Ev-erything seemed so bright, so sharp, in the sunlight.

Everything was so quiet. Quiet enough that Reena could hear the harsh breaths Mrs. Pastorelli took between each sob.

One of the detectives opened the back door of the car, and the other put his hand on Mr. Pastorelli's head and put him inside. They put the can—gas can, she realized—and the green plastic bag in the trunk.

The one with dark hair and stubble on his face like Sonny Crockett said something to the other, then crossed the street.

"Mr. Hale."

"Detective Umberio."

"We've arrested Pastorelli on suspicion of arson. We're taking him and some evidence into custody."

"Did he admit it?"

Umberio smiled. "Not yet, but with what we've got, odds are he will.

We'll let you know." He glanced back to where Mrs. Pastorelli sat in the doorway, wailing into the yellow dishcloth. "She's got a black eye coming up, and she's crying for him. Takes all kinds."

He tapped two fingers to his forehead in a little salute, then crossed back to the car. As he got in, pulled away from the curb, Joey streaked out of the house.

He was dressed like his father, in jeans and a T-shirt that was gray from too many washings and not enough bleach. He screamed at the police as he ran to the car, screamed horrible words. And he was crying, Reena saw with a little twist in her heart. Crying for his father as he ran after the car, shaking his fists.

"Let's go home, baby," Gib murmured.

Reena walked home with her hand in her father's. She could still hear the terrible screams as Joey ran hopelessly after his.

N ews spread. It was a fire of its own with hot pockets and trapped heat that exploded when it hit air. Outrage, an incendiary fuse, carried the flames through the neighborhood, into homes and shops, along the sidewalk and into the parks.

The curtains on the Pastorelli house stayed tightly shut, as if the thin material were a shield.

It seemed to Reena her own house was never closed. Neighbors streamed in with their covered dishes, their support and their gossip.

Did you know he couldn't make bail?

*She* didn't even go to Mass on Sunday.

Mike at the Sunoco station sold him the gas!

My cousin the lawyer said they could charge him with attempted murder.

In addition to the gossip and the speculation was the oft-repeated statement: I knew that man was trouble.

Poppi and Nuni came back, driving their Winnebago all the way from

Bar Harbor, Maine. They parked it in Uncle Sal's driveway in Bel Air because he was the oldest and had the biggest house.

They all went down to Sirico's to look, the uncles, some of the cousins
and aunts. It looked like a parade, except there were no costumes, no
music. Some of the neighbors came out, too, but they stayed back out of
respect.

Poppi was old, but he was robust. It was the word Reena had heard
most to describe him. His hair was white as a cloud, and so was his thick
mustache. He had a big wide belly and big wide shoulders. He liked to
wear golf shirts with the alligator on the pocket. Today's was red.

Beside him, Nuni looked tiny, and hid her eyes behind sunglasses.

There was a lot of talk, in both English and Italian. The Italian was
mostly from Uncle Sal. Mama said he liked to think he was more Italian
than manicotti.

She saw Uncle Larry—he was only Lorenzo when someone was teasing
him—step over to lay his hand on Mama's shoulder, and how she lifted her
hand to his. He was the quiet one, Uncle Larry, and the youngest of the uncles.

Uncle Gio turned and stared holes through the closed curtains of the
Pastorelli house. He was the hothead, and she heard him mutter something
in Italian that sounded like a swear. Or a threat. But Uncle Paul—Paolo—
shook his head. He was the serious one.

For a long time, Poppi said nothing at all. Reena wondered what he
was thinking. Was he remembering when his hair wasn't white and his
belly not so big, and he and Nuni had made pizza and put the first dollar
in a frame for the wall?

Maybe he remembered how they'd lived upstairs before Mama was
born, or how once the mayor of Baltimore had come to eat there. Or when
Uncle Larry had broken a glass and cut his hand, and Dr. Trivani had
stopped eating his eggplant Parmesan to take him to his office down the
street and stitch it up.

He and Nuni told lots of stories about the old days. She liked to listen
to them, even when she'd heard them before. So he must remember them.

She wiggled through the cousins and aunts to put her hand in his. "I'm sorry, Poppi."

His fingers squeezed hers, then to her surprise, he pushed one of the barricades aside. Her heart beat fast and quick as he led her up the steps. She could see through the tape, the burned black wood, the puddles of dirty water. The tray of one of the high chairs had melted into a strange shape. There were scorching marks everywhere, and the floor had bubbled up where it hadn't burned away.

To her amazement, she saw a spray can embedded in a wall as if it had been shot out of a cannon. There were no cheerful colors left, no bottles with candle wax dripped down the sides, no pretty pictures on the wall drawn by her mother's hand.

"I see ghosts here, Catarina. Good ones. Fire doesn't scare ghosts away. Gibson?" When he turned, her father stepped through the opening in the barricade. "You have your insurance?"

"Yes. They've been down to look. There won't be a problem with it."

"You want to use the insurance money to rebuild?"

"There's no question of that. We may be able to get in and get started as soon as tomorrow."

"How do you want to begin?"

Uncle Sal started to speak—because he always had an opinion—but Poppi lifted a finger. He was the only one who could, according to Reena's mother, make Uncle Sal swallow words. "Gibson and Bianca own Sirico's. It's for them to decide what's to be done and how. What can the family do to help?"

"Bianca and I own Sirico's, but you're the root it grew from. I'd like to hear your advice."

Poppi smiled. Reena watched the way it moved over his face, lifting his thick, white mustache, and stopped his eyes from being sad. "You're my favorite son-in-law."

And with this old family joke, he stepped down to the sidewalk again. "Let's go back to the house and talk."

As they walked back, another parade, Reena saw the curtains on the Pastorelli house twitch.

Talk" was a loose word to describe any event that brought the bulk of the family into one place. Massive amounts of food were required, older children were put in charge of younger ones, which resulted in squabbles or outright wars. Behavior was scolded or laughed over, depending on the mood.

The house filled with the scent of garlic and the basil Bianca cut fresh from her kitchen garden. And noise.

When Poppi told Reena she was to come into the dining room with the adults, butterflies batted wings in her belly.

All the leaves had been put in the table and still it wasn't big enough for everyone. Most of the children were outside using the folding table or blankets, while some of the women ran herd. But Reena was in the dining room with all the men, her mother and Aunt Mag, who was a lawyer and very smart.

Poppi scooped pasta out of one of the big bowls and put it on Reena's plate himself. "So this boy, this Joey Pastorelli, he hit you."

"He hit me in the stomach and he knocked me down and hit me again."

Poppi breathed through his nose—and he had a big one, so the sound reminded her of the one a bull makes before it charges. "We live in an age when men and women are meant to be equal, but it's never right for a man to hit a woman, for a boy to hit a girl. But . . . did you do something, say something, to this boy so he thought he had to hit you?"

"I stay away from him because he starts fights in school and in the neighborhood. Once he took out his pocketknife and said he was going to stab Johnnie O'Hara with it because he was a stupid mick, and Sister took it away from him and sent him to Mother Superior. He . . . he looks at me sometimes and it makes my stomach hurt."

"The day he hit you, what were you doing?"

"I was playing with Gina, at the school playground. We were playing kickball, but it was so hot. We wanted ice cream, so she ran home to see if her mother would give her some money for it. I had eighty-eight cents, but that's not enough for two. And he came up and said I should come with him, that he had something to show me. But I didn't want to and I said no, that I was waiting for Gina. His face was all red, like he'd been running, and he got mad and grabbed my arm and was pulling me. So I pulled away and said I wasn't going with him. And he hit me in the stomach. He called me a name that means . . ."

She broke off, looked toward her parents sheepishly. "I looked it up in the dictionary."

"Of course you did," Bianca murmured, then she waved a hand in the air. "He called her a little cunt. It's an ugly word, Catarina. We won't speak it again in this house."

"No, ma'am."

"Your brother came to help you," Poppi continued. "Because he's your brother and because it's right to help someone in trouble. Then your father did what was right, and went to speak to this boy's father. But the man was not a man, he didn't stand up and do what was right. He struck out to hurt your father in a cowardly way, to hurt all of us. Was this your fault?"

"No, Poppi. But it was my fault I was too scared to fight back. I won't be next time."

He gave a half laugh. "Learn to run," he said. "And if you can't run, then you fight. Now." He sat back, picked up his fork. "Here's my advice. Salvatore, your brother-in-law has a construction business. When we know what's needed, you can get this for us, at a discount. Gio, your wife's cousin is a plumber, yes?"

"I've already talked to him. Whatever you need, Bianca, Gib."

"Mag, will you talk to the insurance company, see what hoops we can avoid jumping through to get this check?"

"More than happy to. I'd like to look at the policy, see if there might be anything we'd want to change or adjust for the future. Then there's the matter of the criminal action against this . . ." She lifted her eyebrows at Reena. "This person. If it goes to trial, Reena will most likely be required to testify. I don't think it will," she continued. "I've put out some feelers. Typically arson cases are very difficult to prove, but they appear to have this one locked."

She wound pasta around her fork as she spoke, ate economically. "Your investigators were very thorough, and the firestarter very stupid. The prosecutor feels he's going to take the plea bargain to avoid the possibility of being tried for attempted murder. They've got evidence up the yin-yang, including the fact that he was questioned twice before regarding other fires."

Mag twirled more pasta as voices erupted around the table.

"He was laid off earlier this summer from his job as a mechanic," she continued. "There was a suspicious fire in the garage a few nights later. Minimal damage, as another employee had plans to use said garage for a tryst with his girlfriend. They talked to people, including Pastorelli, but couldn't determine arson. A couple of years ago, he had an altercation with his wife's brother in D.C. The brother managed an electrical supply house. Somebody pitched a Molotov cocktail through the window. A . . ."

She sent another look down at Reena. "A lady of the evening saw a truck speeding away, even got a partial on the plate. But Pastorelli's wife swears he was home all night, and they took her word over the other woman's."

Mag picked up her wine. "They'll use this as a pattern and nail him down."

"If Inspector Minger and our arson detectives had been in charge, they'd have stopped him."

Mag smiled at Reena. "Maybe. But he's stopped now."

"Lorenzo?"

"You've got my strong back," he said. "And I've got a friend in the flooring business. I can get you a good price on replacements."

"Got dump trucks and labor at your disposal," Paul added. "Got a friend's brother-in-law in restaurant supplies. Get you a good discount."

"With all this, and the neighborhood, Bianca, the kids and I can take most of the money and have a vacation in Hawaii."

Her father was joking, but his voice was a little shaky, so Reena knew he was touched.

When the leftovers had been doled out or put away and the kitchen put to rights, and the last of the uncles, aunts and cousins had trailed out the door, Gib got a beer and took it out on the front steps. He needed to stew, and preferred stewing with a cold beer.

The family had come through, and he'd expected no less. He'd gotten a "Gee, that's terrible" from his own parents. And had expected no more.

That's the way it was.

But he was thinking now that for two years he'd been living on the same block with a man who set fires to solve his personal problems. A man who could have chosen to burn his house instead of his business.

A man whose twelve-year-old son had attacked—Christ, had he meant to rape her?—his youngest daughter.

It left him sick, and brought home to him that he was too trusting, too willing to give the benefit. Too soft.

He had a wife and four children to protect, and at the moment felt completely inadequate.

He took a pull on a bottle of Peroni when John Minger parked at the curb.

Minger wore khakis and a T-shirt with canvas high-tops that looked older than dirt. He crossed the sidewalk.

"Gib."

"John."

"Got a minute?"

"Got plenty of them. Want a beer?"

"Wouldn't say no."

"Have a seat." Gib tapped the step beside him, then got up and went into the house. He came back with the rest of the six-pack.

"Nice evening." John tipped back a bottle. "Little cooler."

"Yeah. I'd say it's merely approaching the fifth level of hell instead of hitting it square on."

"Rough day?"

"No. No, not really." He leaned back, bracing one elbow on the step above. "My wife's family came today. It was hard watching her mother and father look at that." He jerked his chin toward Sirico's. "But they're handling it. More than. Ready to shove up their sleeves, dig in. Going to have so much help I can pretty much sit here with my thumb up my ass and have the place up and running in a month."

"So you're feeling like a failure. That's what he wants you to feel."

"Pastorelli?" Gib lifted his bottle in toast. "Mission fucking accomplished. His kid came after mine, laid hands on mine, and I'm thinking about it now, looking at it now, really looking, and I think, Sweet Jesus Christ, I think he was going to try to rape my little girl."

"He didn't. She got scrapes and bruises, and it doesn't help to worry about what might've happened."

"You've got to keep them safe. That's the job. My oldest is out on a date. Nice boy, nothing serious. And I'm terrified."

John took a long, slow drink. "Gib, one of the things a man like Pastorelli's after is your fear. It makes him feel important."

"Never going to forget him, am I? That makes him pretty fucking important. Sorry. Sorry." Gib straightened, shoved at his hair. "Feeling sorry for myself, that's all. I've got an entire family—with members too numerous to count—ready to help me out. I've got the neighborhood ready. Just got to shake this off."

"You will. Maybe this will help. I came by to tell you you're cleared to go in, start putting your place back together. Doing that, it's taking it back from him."

"It'll be good, good to actually do something."

"He's going away, Gib. I'm going to tell you that a fraction of arson cases result in arrest, and we've got him. Son of a bitch had shoes and clothes stuffed in his shed, stinking of gas, gas he bought locally from a kid at the Sunoco who knew him. He had a crowbar wrapped up in the clothes, what we figured he used to break in. He was stupid enough to help himself to beer out of your cooler before he torched the place. Drank one while he was in there. We got his prints off the bottle."

He held up the Peroni, tipped the bottle to the side to catch the sun on the glass. "People think fire takes everything, but it leaves the unexpected. Like a bottle of Bud. He broke into your cash register, took your petty cash. You had extra ones in a bank envelope and we found it on him. We got his prints inside the drawer, off the cooler in your kitchen. There's enough his public defender took the deal."

"There won't be a trial?"

"Sentencing hearing. I want you to feel good about this, Gib. I want you to feel just. A lot of people see arson as a property crime. Just a crime against a building, but it's not. You know it's not. It's about people who lose their home or their business, who see their hard work and their memories burned away. What he did to you and yours was malicious and it was personal. Now he pays."

"Yeah."

"The wife couldn't scrape the money together for bail, or for a lawyer. She tried. Word's out on the kid. Last time the cops were in there, he threw a chair at one of them. Mother begged them not to take him away, so they let it go. You're going to want to keep your eye on him."

"I will, but I don't think they'll stay here. They rent the place, and they're behind, three months." Gib shrugged. "Word gets out in the neighborhood, too. Maybe this was my wake-up call, pay more attention to what I've got."

"You've got the most beautiful woman I've ever seen in my life for a wife. You don't mind me saying."

"Hard to mind." Gib opened another beer, leaned back again. "First time I saw her, I was lightning struck. Came in with some pals. We were thinking about doing The Block later, maybe picking up some girls, or going to a bar. And there she was. It was like somebody pushed their fist through my chest, grabbed hold of my heart and squeezed. She was wearing jeans, bell-bottoms, and this white top—peasant top they called them.

If anybody had asked me before that moment if I believed in love at first sight, I'd've said hell no. But that's what it was. She turned her head and looked at me, and bang. I saw the rest of my life in her eyes."

He laughed a little, seemed to relax. "I still do, that's the amazing thing. Heading toward twenty years, and I still see everything there is when I look at her."

"You're a lucky man."

"Damn right. I'd've given up everything, anything, to be with her. Instead I got this life, this family. You got kids, John?"

"I do. A son and two daughters. A grandson and granddaughter, too."

"Grandkids? No kidding?"

"Lights of my life. I didn't do all I should've done when my kids were coming up. I was nineteen when the first came along. Got my girl pregnant, we got married. Next one came two years later, and the third three years after that. I was fighting fires back then. That life, those hours, can be hard on a family. I didn't put them first, and that's my fault. So we got a divorce. Nearly ten years ago now."

"Sorry."

"Funny thing is, after, we got along better. We got closer. Maybe the divorce burned away the bad stuff, made room for some good. So." He tipped back his bottle. "I'm free if your wife's got an older sister available."

"Just brothers, but her cousins are legion."

They were silent for a moment, companionably. "This is a good spot." John sipped and smoked and studied the neighborhood. "A good spot, Gib. You need another pair of hands putting your place back together, you can have mine."

"I'd appreciate it."

Upstairs, Reena lay on her bed and listened to their voices carry up to her open window as the sky went soft with summer twilight.

I t was full dark when the screams woke her. She tumbled out of bed with thoughts of fire chasing her. He'd come back. He'd come back to burn their house.

It wasn't fire, and it was Fran who'd screamed. Fran who stood on the sidewalk now with her face buried against the shoulder of the boy who'd taken her to the movies.

The television was on in the living room, with the sound turned down low. Both of her parents were at the doorway already. When she pushed between them, she saw why Fran had screamed, why her mother and father stood so stiffly in the open doorway.

The dog was burning, its fur smoldering, smoking, as was the pool of blood that had come from its throat. But she recognized the hard-barking mutt Joey Pastorelli called Fabio.

She watched the police take Joey Pastorelli away, much as they had his father. But he didn't keep his head lowered, and his eyes had a vicious glee in them.

It was one of the last things she remembered with absolute clarity during those long, hot weeks of August when summer was ending and her childhood was over.

She remembered the glee in Joey's eyes, the strut in his walk as they took him to the police car. And she remembered the smears of blood, his own dog's blood, staining his hands.

# 4

The glossy pink goo of Mariah Carey's overorchestrated *Emotions* oozed through the wall of the adjoining room. It was a never-ending stream, like frothy lava. Inescapable and increasingly terrifying.

Reena didn't mind music when she studied. She didn't mind partying, small petty wars or the thunder of God's judgment. After all, she grew up in a house with a big, loud family.

But if her dorm mate spun that track just one more time, she was going in and jabbing a pencil through her eye. When that was done, she was going to make her *eat* that damned CD, jewel case and all.

She was in the middle of finals, for God's sake. And the load she was taking this semester was a killer.

Worth it though, she reminded herself. It was going to be worth it.

She pushed back from her computer, rubbed her eyes. Maybe she needed a short break. Or earplugs.

She got up, ignored the flotsam of two college students sharing one small room and opened the little refrigerator for a Diet Pepsi. She found an open pint of low-fat milk, four Slim-Fasts, a Diet Sprite and a bag of carrot sticks.

This was just wrong. Why did everyone steal her stuff? Of course, who the hell was going to pilfer Gina's I'm-on-an-endless-diet food, but still.

She sat on the floor, Mariah's voice swimming in her overtaxed brain like evil mermaids, and stared at the piles of books and notes on her desk.

Why did she think she could do this? Why did she think she *wanted* to do this? She could have followed Fran's lead, into the family business.

She could be home right now. Or out on a date like a normal person. Once, becoming a teenager had been her life's ambition. Now she was nearly out the other side of the era, and she was sitting in a crowded dorm room, with *no* Diet Pepsi, buried under a course load for the insane masochist.

She was eighteen years old and hadn't had sex yet. She barely had what passed for a boyfriend.

Bella was getting married next month, Fran was practically beating guys off with a stick, and Xander plowed happily through what their mother called his bevy of beauties.

And she was alone on a Saturday night because she was as obsessed with finals as her dorm mate was with Mariah Carey.

Oh no, now it was Celine Dion, she realized.

Just kill me now.

It was her own fault. She was the one who'd studied her brains out in high school, and worked more weekends than dated. Because she'd known what she wanted. She'd known since that long hot week in August.

She wanted the fire.

So she'd studied, with her eye focused on more than learning. On scholarships. She worked, tucking her money away like a squirrel with nuts in case the scholarships didn't come.

But they had, so she was here, at the University of Maryland, sharing a room with her oldest friend, and already thinking about the grad courses down the road.

When the semester was over she'd go back home, work in the shop, carve away most of her free time down at the fire station. Or talking John Minger into letting her do ride-alongs.

Of course, there was Bella's wedding. There'd been little on the menu but Bella's wedding for the last nine months. Which, come to think of it, was a really good reason to be here, alone in her room on a Saturday night.

It could be worse. She could be back at Wedding Central.

If she ever got married—which meant she'd need an actual, *official* boyfriend first—she was going to keep it simple. Let Bella have the endless fittings of the elaborate dress—though it was gorgeous—and the endless, often weepy debates about shoes and hairstyles and flowers. The plans— more like a major war campaign—for the enormous reception.

She'd rather have a nice family wedding at St. Leo's, then a party at Sirico's.

Most likely, she'd just end up being a bridesmaid, perennially. Hell, she was already an expert in the field.

And for God's sake, how many *times* could Lydia listen to the theme from *Beauty and the Beast* without going into a coma?

On a sudden inspiration, Reena sprang up, kicked her way over to the portable CD player and pushed through the masses of jewel cases.

With her teeth set in a fierce grin, she plugged in Nirvana and blasted "Smells Like Teen Spirit."

While the war raged between diva and grunge, the phone rang.

She didn't turn down the music—it was a matter of principle now—just shouted into the phone.

A third blast of music assaulted her ear as Gina shouted back.

"Party!"

"I told you I have to study."

"Party! Come on, Reene, it's just starting to roll. You gotta live."

"Don't you have a lit final Monday?"

"Party!"

She had to laugh. Gina could always make her laugh. The religious phase she'd gone through during the summer of the fire had morphed into a poetry phase, into a rock star phase, then a fashion diva phase.

Now it was all party, all the time.

"You're going to tank it," Reena warned.

"I'm putting it all in the hands of a higher power and am reviving my brain with cheap wine. Come on, Reena, Josh is here. He's asking where you are."

"He is?"

"And looking all sad and broody. You know you're going to ace every damn thing anyway. You better come save me before I let some guy take advantage of my drunken self. Hey, on second thought . . ."

"Jen and Deb's place, right?"

"Party!"

"Twenty minutes," Reena said on another laugh, then hung up.

It took her nearly that long to change out of ancient sweatpants, wiggle into jeans, decide on a top and deal with the hair that was currently an explosion of curls down to her shoulder blades.

She kept the music blasting while she dressed, added blusher to relieve the cramming-for-finals pallor.

Should study, should get a good night's sleep. Shouldn't go. She flicked on mascara, lectured herself.

But she was so tired of being the one who always did the sensible thing. She'd just stay for an hour, have a little fun, keep Gina from getting into too much trouble.

And see Josh Bolton.

He was so good-looking with the sun-swept hair, the dazzling blue eyes, that sweet, shy smile. He was twenty, a lit major. He was going to be a writer.

And he was asking where she was.

He was going to be the one. She was ninety-nine percent sure of it. He was going to be her first.

Maybe tonight. She set the mascara down and stared at herself in the mirror. Maybe tonight she'd finally know what it was like. She pressed a hand to her belly as it jittered with anticipation and nerves. This could be the last time she looked at herself as a virgin.

She was ready, and she wanted it to be with someone like Josh. Someone dreamy and sweet, and with some experience so there wasn't a lot of embarrassing fumbling.

She *hated* not knowing what to do. She'd studied the basics, of course. The anatomy, the physicality. And she'd absorbed the romance of the act in books and movies. But the doing of it, the getting naked and fitting two bodies together, would be an absolute first.

It wasn't something you could practice or diagram or experiment with until you worked out the kinks in your technique.

So she wanted an understanding and patient partner who'd guide her over the rough spots until she found her own way.

It didn't matter so much that she didn't love him. She liked him a lot, and she wasn't looking for marriage like Bella.

Not yet, anyway.

She just wanted to know, to feel, to see how it worked. And, maybe it was stupid, but she wanted to shed this last vestige of childhood. Having it all in the back of her mind was probably why she'd been restless and distracted the last few days.

And, of course, she was overthinking it again.

She grabbed her purse, shut off the music and rushed out of the dorm.

It was a beautiful night, warm and star-studded. Ridiculous to waste it buried in chem notes, she told herself as she walked toward the parking lot. She tipped her face up to the sky, started to smile, but a chill tickled down her spine. She glanced over her shoulder, scanned the grass, the paths, the glow of the security lights.

Nobody was watching her, for God's sake. She gave herself a little shake, but quickened her pace. It was just guilt, that was all. She could live with a little guilt.

She hopped into her secondhand Dodge Shadow and, giving in to paranoia, locked the doors before driving away.

The group house was a five-minute drive off campus, an old three-story brick that was lit up like Christmas. Partiers spilled out onto the lawn, and music spilled out of the open door.

She caught the sweet drift of a burning joint and heard snatches of high-toned debates on the brilliance of Emily Dickinson, the current administration and more comfortable discussions on the Orioles' infield.

She had to squeeze her way through once she was inside, narrowly avoided having a glass of some alcoholic beverage splashed down her front, and felt some relief that she actually knew some of the people crammed into the living room.

Gina spotted her and wiggled through the bodies to grab her shoulders. "Reene! You're here! I have such news!"

"Don't tell me any more until you eat an entire box of Tic Tacs."

"Oh, shit." Gina dug into the pocket of jeans so tight they must be causing organ damage. The Slim-Fast hadn't whittled off all the twelve pounds she'd gained in their first semester.

She pulled out the little plastic box she always carried and tapped several orange Tic Tacs in her mouth. "Been drinking," she said, chewing.

"Who'd have guessed? Look, you can leave your car and I'll drive you back. I'll be the DD."

"It's okay, I'm going to throw up soon. I'll be better then. Anyway, news!" She pulled Reena through an equally jammed kitchen and out the back door.

There were more people in the yard. Did the entire campus at College Park decide to blow off studying for finals?

"Scott Delauter's totally flunking out," Gina announced, and did a little butt boogie to accompany the statement.

"Who's Scott Delauter and why do you boogie on his misfortune?"

"He's one of the housemates. You met him. Short guy, big teeth. And I dance because his misfortune is our jackpot. They're going to be one short next semester and another of the group graduates next December. Jen says they can squeeze both of us in next term if we bunk together. Reena, we can get out of the pit."

"Move in here? Gina, come back to my world. We can't afford it."

"We're talking about splitting the rent and stuff four ways. It's not that much more, Reena." Gina gripped her arms, her dark eyes dazed with excitement and cheap wine, her voice reverent. "There's three bathrooms. Three bathrooms for four people. Not one for six."

"Three bathrooms." Reena spoke it like a prayer.

"It's salvation. When Jen told me, I had a vision. A vision, Reena. I think I saw the Blessed Mother smiling. And she was holding a loofah."

"Three bathrooms," Reena repeated. "No, no, I must not be drawn to the dark side by shiny objects. How much is the rent?"

"It's . . . when you consider the split, and how you won't need the food allowance on campus because we can cook here, it's practically free."

"That much, huh?"

"We're both working this summer. We can save. Please, please, please, Reena. They have to know pretty quick. Look, look, we'll have a yard." She swept her arm out toward it. "We can plant flowers. Hell, we'll grow our own vegetables and set up a stand. We'll actually *make* money living here."

"Tell me how much, Gina."

"Let me get you a drink first—"

"Spit it out," Reena demanded. And winced when Gina blurted out the monthly rent.

"But you have to factor in—"

"Shh, let me think." Reena closed her eyes, calculated. It would be tight, she decided. But if they made their own meals, cut out some of the money they blew on movies, CDs, clothes. She could give up new clothes for the wonder of three bathrooms.

"I'm in."

Gina let out a whoop, caught Reena in a hug that danced them both over the grass. "It's going to be awesome! I can't wait. Let's go get some wine and drink to Scott Delauter's academic failures."

"Seems mean, but oddly appropriate." She swung around with Gina, then stopped dead. "Josh. Hi."

He closed the back door behind him then gave her that slow, shy smile that curled her toes. "Hi. Heard you were here."

"Yeah, I thought I'd take a break from studying. My brains were starting to leak out my ears."

"Got tomorrow for the final push."

"That's what I told her." Gina beamed at both of them. "Listen, you two get cozy. I'm going to go throw up now, in what will shortly be one of my own bathrooms." She gave Reena a last boozy hug. "I'm so happy."

Josh watched the door slap shut behind Gina. "Should I ask why Gina's so happy to puke?"

"She's happy because we're going to move in here next semester."

"Really? That's great." He moved in a little, and with his hands still in his pockets dipped his head to kiss her. "Congratulations."

Nerves sizzled over her skin, a sensation she found fascinating and wonderfully adult. "I thought I'd like living in the dorm. The adventure. Me and Gina from the neighborhood, doing the coed thing. But some of the others on our floor make me crazy. One's trying to destroy my brain with round-the-clock Mariah Carey."

"Insidious."

"I think it was starting to work."

"You look great. I'm glad you came. I was about to head out when I heard you were here."

"Oh." Pleasure fizzled. "You're leaving."

He smiled again, and took a hand out of his pocket to take one of hers. "Not anymore."

B o Goodnight wasn't sure what he was doing in a strange house with a bunch of college types he didn't know. Still, a party was a party, and he'd let Brad rope him into it.

The music was okay, and there were plenty of girls. Tall ones, short ones, round ones, thin ones. It was like a smorgasbord of females.

Including the one Brad was currently crazy about, and the reason they were here.

She was a friend of a friend of one of the girls who lived in the house. And Bo liked her fine—in fact, he might have gone for her himself if Brad hadn't seen her first.

Rules of friendship meant he had to hang back there.

At least Brad had lost the toss and had to serve as designated driver.

Maybe neither of them should've been drinking, as they were still shy of the legal age. But a party was a party, Bo thought again as he sipped his beer.

Besides, he was earning his own living, paying his own rent, cooking his own meals—such as they were. He was as much, hell more of an adult than a lot of the college boys knocking them back.

Considering his options, he scanned the room. He was a long, lanky boy of twenty with a wavy mop of black hair and eyes that were green and somewhat dreamy. His face was on the narrow side, like his build, but he thought he'd built up some pretty good biceps swinging a hammer and hauling lumber.

He felt a bit out of place with the snippets of conversation he made out—bitching about finals, comments about poli sci and female studies. College hadn't been for him. He'd never been happier than on the last day of high school. He'd been working summers up until then. First as a laborer, then an apprentice, and now, at twenty, he was a carpenter who made a decent wage.

He loved making things out of wood, and he was good at it. Maybe he was good at it because he loved it. He'd gotten his education on the job, with the smell of sawdust and sweat.

That's how he liked it.

And he made his own way. He didn't have Daddy paying the bills like most of the people here.

The kernel of resentment surprised him, even embarrassed him a little. Flicking it aside, he made a deliberate attempt to loosen his shoulders. And taking a long, slow sweep of the room, he homed in on a couple of girls huddled together on a couch, chattering at each other.

The redhead looked very promising, and if not, the brunette was a strong backup.

He took a step toward them, and Brad blocked him. "Out of my way, I'm about to brighten a couple of female hearts."

"Told you you'd have a good time. Listen, I'm about to have a better one. Cammie and I are heading out, to her place. And I believe it's not presumptuous to say, Score."

Bo looked at his pal, noted the about-to-get-laid gleam behind the lenses of Brad's glasses. "You're ditching me in a houseful of strangers so you can go get naked with a girl?"

"Absolutely."

"Well, that's reasonable. She kicks your ass out though, don't call me. Find your own way home."

"Won't be a problem. She's just gone to get her purse, so—"

"Wait." Bo's hand curled hard around Brad's arm as he saw the blonde— just a glimpse at first—through the crowd. A sexy tumble of wild curls the color of good, natural oak. She was laughing, and her skin—it looked like porcelain—was flushed along the high curve of her cheekbones.

He could see the shape of her lips and the little mole above them. It was as if his vision had sharpened, had telescoped, and he could see the details of her through the haze of smoke, the crowd of faces. Long eyes he thought were almost exactly the same shade of her hair, a long, slim nose. And that luscious curve of lips. Gold hoops at her ears. Two in the left, one in the right.

She was tall—maybe she was wearing heels, he couldn't see her feet. But he could see the chain around her neck holding some sort of stone or crystal, the outline of her breasts against a dark pink top.

For an instant, maybe two, the music stopped for him. The room went silent.

Then someone stepped into his line of vision and it all came roaring back.

"Who is that girl?"

"Which girl?" Absently Brad looked over his shoulder, then shrugged it. "Place is crawling with them. Hey, next time you take a side trip, take me along."

"What?" Still dazzled, Bo looked down. He could barely remember his friend's name. "I gotta . . . here." He pushed the beer into Brad's hand and started shoving his way through the crowd.

By the time he got to where she'd been, there was no sign of her. A kind of panic bubbled in his throat as he maneuvered his way into the kitchen, a dining room where people sat at, on and under the table.

"Did a girl come through here? Tall blonde, curly hair, pink shirt."

"Nobody's come in but you." A girl with a short wedge of black hair sent him a sultry smile. "But I can be blond."

"Maybe some other time."

He searched the house, all the way to the third floor, and all the way down again where he circled both the front and back yards.

He found blondes, he found curls. But he never found the one who'd made the music stop.

She was driving with her heart in her throat. She thought it was good that she was driving herself. It showed that she wasn't being swept along, that she was making a choice. She was in control of her actions, the consequences.

Making love the first time, every time, should be a choice.

She only wished she had thought ahead enough to have bought some sexy underwear.

Josh lived in an off-campus apartment, and his roommate was pulling an all-nighter with a study group. When he'd told her that—he'd been kissing her when he told her that—she'd been the one to say, Let's go there.

She was the one who'd made the move. And she was the one beginning a new phase of her life. But it didn't stop her hands from trembling a little.

She parked a few spaces down from where he pulled in, carefully turned off the engine, picked up her purse. She knew exactly what she was doing, she reminded herself, illustrating it by locking her car, placing her keys in the little inside pocket where she always kept them.

She smiled when she held her hand out to his. They crossed the lot, stepped through the front door of the building when another car pulled in. And parked.

"Place is a little messy," Josh said as they started up the stairs to the second floor.

"At the moment, ours is about to be condemned by the health department."

She waited until he'd unlocked the door, then stepped inside. He was right about the mess—clothes, shoes, an empty pizza box, books, magazines. The sofa looked like it had been salvaged from the dump, then haphazardly covered with a Terps blanket.

"Homey," she said.

"Fairly disgusting, actually. I should've told you to give me ten minutes before coming up. I could've shoved stuff in closets."

"It doesn't matter." She turned and let herself go into his arms. He smelled like Irish Spring and tasted like cherry Life Savers. His hand skimmed over her hair, down her back.

"You want some music?"

She nodded. "Music's good."

He ran his hands down her arms before he stepped back, walked over to a stereo. "I don't think we have any Mariah Carey."

"Praise Jesus." With a laugh, she pressed a hand to her racing heart. "I'm nervous. I've never done this before."

His mouth opened and closed again as his eyes widened. "Never . . ."

"You're my first."

"God." He stared another moment, blue eyes serious. "Now I'm nervous. Are you sure about—?"

"I am. I really am." She crossed to him, then looked down at the pile of CDs. "How about this?" She picked out Nine Inch Nails.

"*Sin?*" He gave her that sweet smile. "Is this a Catholic girl thing coming out?"

"Maybe a little. Anyway, I like their cover of Queen's *Get Down, Make Love*. And, well, it seems appropriate."

He put it in the changer, turned back just to look at her. "I've been hung up on you since the beginning of the semester."

Warmth spread in her belly. "You didn't ask me out until after spring break."

"Started to, dozens of times. I kept choking. And I thought you were with that guy, that psych major."

"Kent?" At the moment, she couldn't even bring Kent's face into her mind.

"We went out a few times. Mostly we just study together now and then. I was never with him."

"Now you're with me."

"Now I'm with you."

"If you change your mind—"

"I won't. I never do." She laid her hands on his face, her lips on his lips. "I want this. I want you."

He touched her hair, twining his fingers through the mass of it while he kissed her, long, slow. Bodies drew together, magnetized by lust.

Hers felt electric, and alive.

"We can go into the bedroom."

This is it, she thought. Held her breath; let it go. "Okay."

He held her hand. She wanted to remember that, remember every little detail. The way he smelled like Irish Spring and tasted like cherry Life Savers, and how his hair curtained over his temples when he dipped his head.

The room, his bedroom, with its messy twin bed—blue-striped sheets and a denim-colored spread, a single pillow that looked flat as a pancake. He had a bulky old metal desk, with a muscular computer and a jumble of books and floppies and papers. A corkboard with more notes, photographs, flyers.

The bottom drawer of his dresser—small enough to make her think it had been his through childhood—was open and crooked. There was a film of dust on it, more books, and a big clear jar half full of change. Mostly pennies.

He turned the lamp by the bed on low.

"Unless you'd rather have it off," he said.

"No." How could she see if it was dark? "Um. I don't have protection."

"I've got that covered. I mean—" He actually flushed, then laughed. "I mean, it's not covered at the moment. But I have condoms."

It was easier than she'd thought it would be. The way they turned to each other, into each other. The lips, the hands, the thrill that leapfrogged over nerves.

The kisses went deep and breath came quick as they sat on the bed. As they lay back. She had a moment to wish she'd thought to take her shoes off first—wouldn't it be awkward?—then there was so much heat and movement.

His mouth on her neck, his hands on her breast. Over her shirt, then under it. She'd been here before, but never with the knowledge that this was only the beginning.

His skin was so warm, so smooth, his body so slight it brought on a flood of tenderness. She'd imagined this, the rising excitement, the sensation of her skin sliding along another's, the sounds desire pushed out of her. Gasps and moans and hums of pleasure.

His eyes were so vivid and blue, his hair so silky. She loved the way he kissed her, wished he would simply kiss her forever.

When his hand moved between her legs, she tensed. This is where she'd always stopped in the past. This privacy she'd never allowed to be invaded. Then he stopped, this sweet boy, whose heart was hammering against hers, and pressed his lips to the side of her throat.

"It's okay, we can just—"

She took his hand, brought it back to her center, pressed. "Yes." She said yes, then closed her eyes.

The shudder ran through her. Oh, this was new! This was beyond what she'd known before, or felt before, or understood. The body was a miracle and hers was quickening with heat and aches. She clutched at him, tried to find her balance. Then again, let it go.

He said her name, and she felt him shudder, too. Then his mouth was on her breast, all wet and hot, pulling racking sensations up from her belly. She reached for him, and he was so hard. Fascinated, she explored. When he sucked in his breath and reared up, she released him as if she'd been burned.

"I'm sorry. Did I do something wrong?"

"No. No." He gulped in another breath. "I, ah, I need to suit up."

"Oh. Okay." Everything in her was quivering, so she must be ready.

He got a condom out of the drawer by the bed. Her first instinct was to look away, but she shook it off. He was going inside her, that part of him would be inside her. It was better to see, to know, to understand.

She braced, but when he'd put it on, he rolled back to her to kiss her once more. To kiss and stroke until the hard ball of nerves dissolved again.

"It's going to hurt a little. I think it's going to hurt for a minute. I'm sorry."

"It's all right." It should hurt, a little, she thought. A change so big shouldn't come without some pain. Or else it didn't matter.

She felt him pushing at her, into her, and struggled not to fight against it. He kept kissing her.

Soft on her lips, hard between her legs.

There was pain, a shock of it that took the dreamy edge off the moment. Then it eased into a kind of ache, and the ache—as he began to move inside her—into a confusing mix of excitement and discomfort.

Then he pressed his face into her hair, his slim, smooth body fused to hers. And it was only sweet.

# 5

It was strange moving back home for the summer, hauling her things from the dorm, knowing for the next three months she wouldn't have classes, or Gina moaning every morning when the alarm went off.

Still, once it was done, and she was back in her old room, it was as natural as breathing.

It wasn't the same. She was different now. She had taken several deliberate steps away from childhood. Maybe the girl who'd packed her things the previous summer was still inside her, but the one who'd come back knew more, had experienced more. And was ready, more ready than ever to see what was next.

Even the house had changed in her absence. She'd be sharing with Fran for the next few weeks. Bella needed her own room for all the wedding paraphernalia, and Fran, in her easygoing way, had turned over her own bedroom for the duration.

"Easier," Fran said when Reena asked her. "Keeps the peace and it's only for a couple more weeks. She's all but moved into the house Vince's parents bought for them."

"I can't believe they bought them a *house*." Reena arranged tops in her second drawer the way she liked best. According to color.

The single thing she wouldn't miss about dorm life was the constant disorder.

"Well, they're rich. This is a great dress," Fran added as she hung some of Reena's clothes in the closet. "Where'd you get it?"

"Hit the mall after finals. Shopping's a great stress reliever." And she'd wanted some new things, for her new self. "It's sort of strange, Bella being the first of us to move out. I thought it would be you or me. She's always been the most needy."

"Vince is giving her what she needs." Fran turned, and though she knew her sister's face and form as intimately as her own, Reena was struck. In the streams of afternoon light, Fran looked like a painting. Gilded and gorgeous.

"I don't know him all that well, but he seems nice—steady. And God knows he's handsome."

"Crazy about her. Treats her like a princess, which is what she's always wanted. Rich doesn't hurt either," Fran added with a tiny smirk. "Once he finishes law school and passes the bar, he'll go straight onto the fast track at his father's firm. Rightfully so, from what I hear. He's brilliant. Mama and Dad like him a lot."

"How about you?"

"I do. He's got style, which Bella likes, but he's easy around the family, and slips into the rhythm when we're here, or down at the shop." Something wistful came into her face as she kept her hands busy unpacking Reena's things. "He looks at Bella like she's a work of art. I don't mean that in a bad way," she added. "It's like he's stunned by his good fortune. Most of all, he rolls with her moods. Which are legion."

"Then he has the seal of approval." Reena walked over to the closet herself, drew out the mint green confection of a bridesmaid dress. "Could be uglier."

"Sure." Studying it, Fran leaned on the jamb, folded her arms. "She could've gone with the puce. We'll all look a bit sallow and silly next to her elegant radiance. Which is exactly the plan."

With a grin, Reena let the dress fall back. "Better than the pumpkin orange with the million flounces and puff sleeves cousin Angela decked us out in last year."

"Don't remind me. Even Bella's not that mean."

"Let's make a pact. When our turns come around, we pick dresses for each other that don't make us look like homely runners-up."

Fran put her arms around Reena, pressed cheek to cheek and swayed. "It's so good to have you home."

She walked down to Sirico's at lunchtime, straight into the familiar scents and sounds.

They'd done more than clean up and repair after the fire. They'd kept traditions—the kitchen area open to the dining area, the bottles of Chianti serving as candleholders, the wide glass display holding the desserts still purchased from the Italian bakery every day.

But they'd made changes, too, as if to say they not only weren't leveled by adversity, but would use it to thrive.

The walls were a dusky Tuscan yellow now, and her mother had done dozens of new drawings. Not only of the family, but of the neighborhood itself, of Sirico's as it had been, as it was now. The booths were a defiant red, with the traditional red-and-white-checked cloths covering the tables.

New lighting kept the place cheerful even on gloomy days, or could be dimmed to add atmosphere for the private parties they'd begun booking over the last two years.

Her father was at the big work counter, ladling sauce on dough. There were touches of gray in his hair now that had started weaving in during those weeks after the fire. He also needed reading glasses, which annoyed the hell out of him. Especially if anyone told him they made him look distinguished.

Her mother was back at the stove, minding the sauces and pastas. Fran had already donned her bright red apron and was serving plates of lasagna that were today's lunch special.

On the way to the kitchen, Reena stopped by tables, greeted neighbors and regulars, laughed each time she was told she needed to *eat*, get some *meat* on her bones.

Gib was sliding one pizza into the oven, taking another out by the time she got to him.

"There's my girl." He set the pie aside and gathered her in for a rib-crusher. He smelled of flour and sweat. "Fran said you were home, but we were swamped. Couldn't get away to come up."

"Came by to pitch in. Bella in the back?"

"You just missed Bella. Wedding emergency." He picked up the pizza cutter, divided the pie with quick, practiced strokes. "Something about rose petals. Or maybe it was bud vases."

"Then you're short-handed. Who gets the sausage and green pepper?"

"Table six. Thanks, baby."

She delivered the pizza, took two more orders. It was like she'd never been away, she thought.

Except she was different. There was not only a year of college under her belt, but everything she'd learned crowded in her head. Familiar faces, familiar smells, routines and movements that were automatic. Yet she was just a little more than she had been the last time she'd worked here.

She had a boyfriend. It was official now. She and Josh were a couple. A couple who slept together.

She liked sex, which was a relief to know. The first time had been sweet and adventurous, but she'd been so new at it, her mind and body scrambling to understand. She hadn't reached orgasm.

*That* was something new and wonderful she'd discovered about the act, and herself, the second time they'd been together.

Now she could barely wait to be with him again, to learn the next new thing.

Not that sex was all they did together, she reminded herself as she grabbed the phone to take an order for delivery. They talked, often for hours. She loved listening to him talk about his writing, how he wanted to tell stories about small towns, like the one where he grew up in Ohio. Stories about people, and what they did to and for each other.

And he listened. He seemed equally interested when she told him that she wanted to study and train, to understand fire and why.

Now she didn't just have a date for Bella's wedding. She was bringing her boyfriend.

She was still grinning over the idea when she swung into the prep area for the first time. Her mother was taking vegetables out of one of the big, stainless steel refrigerators. Pete, now the father of three, stood at the prep counter cutting dough from holding bowls to weigh for pizza crust.

"Hey, college girl! Give us a smooch."

Reena threw her arms around his neck, gave him a noisy kiss dead on the lips.

"When'd you get back?"

"Fifteen minutes ago. Walked in the door, they put me to work."

"Slave drivers."

"You don't get that dough weighed, I'm getting the whip. Now let go of my girl before I tell your wife." Bianca threw open her arms. Reena went into them.

"How do you stay so beautiful?" Reena asked her.

"It's the steam in the kitchen. Keeps the pores clean. Oh, baby girl, let me look at you."

"You saw me two weeks ago at Bella's Bridal Shower of the Century."

"Two weeks, two days." Bianca pulled back. Her smile faltered for a moment, and something came and went in her eyes.

"What? What?"

"Nothing." But Bianca pressed a kiss to her brow, like a benediction. "I've got all my children home again. Pete, go switch with Catarina. She'll take over for you in here. We want to be girls."

"More wedding talk. I'm already getting a headache." Waving his hands, Pete scooted out.

"Am I in trouble?" Only half joking, Reena got a bottle of water out of the cooler. "Did the crack I made about the bridesmaid dress making me look like an anemic scallion get back to Bella?"

"No, and you'll look beautiful, even if the dress is . . . unfortunate."

"Oooh, diplomacy."

"Diplomacy is my last tool of survival in this wedding business. Otherwise, I'd have snapped Bella's neck like a twig by now." She lifted a hand, shook her head. "She can't help it. She's excited, terrified, wildly in love, and she wants Vince to be proud of her—all while impressing his parents, looking like a movie star and trying to furnish a big new house."

"Sounds like she's in her element."

"True enough. Your dad needs dough for two large and a medium," she added, and watched as Reena competently cut and weighed. "You don't forget how."

"I was born weighing dough."

She put the extra dough back in the cooler, took out what her father needed. Then joined her mother at the work counter to pitch in with salad.

"Two house for table six. I'll take the Greek for station three. This wedding is the biggest dream of her life," Bianca continued as they chopped. "I want her to have exactly what she wants. I want all my children to have exactly what they want."

She loaded a tray, moved it to the pick-up area. "Order up," she called out, then moved back to fill another.

"You've been with a boy."

The water felt like a hard little ball when Reena managed to swallow. "What?"

"You think I can't look at you and see?" Bianca kept her voice low, gauging her husband's proximity and the noise element that would cover her words. "That I couldn't see with each of my children? You were the last."

"Xander's been with a boy?"

To Reena's relief, Bianca laughed. "So far he prefers girls. Do I know the boy?"

"No. It just . . . We started seeing each other a while ago, and it just happened. Just last week. I wanted it to happen, Mama. I'm sorry if you're disappointed, but—"

"Did I say that? Did I ask you about your conscience, or your choice? You were careful?"

"Yes. Mama." Reena put the knife down, turned to wrap her arms around her mother's waist. "We were careful. I like him so much. You will, too."

"How do I know if I'll like him when you don't bring him home to meet your family? When you don't tell me anything about him."

"He's a lit major. He's going to be a writer. He keeps a sloppy apartment and has the sweetest smile. His name is Josh Bolton, and he grew up in Ohio."

"What about his family?"

"He doesn't talk much about them. His parents are divorced, and he's an only child."

"He's not Catholic, then?"

"I don't think so. I didn't ask. He's gentle, and he's very smart, and he listens when I talk."

"All important things." Bianca turned, took Reena's face in her hands. "You'll bring him to meet the family."

"He's going to come to Bella's wedding."

"Brave, too." Bianca raised her eyebrows. "Well, if he lives through that, he may be worth keeping awhile."

When the lunch crowd thinned out, Reena sat—at her father's insistence—with an enormous plate of spaghetti. With Pete taking over for him, he started making the rounds. She'd seen him do it all her life, and knew her grandfather had done the same before him.

With a glass of wine, a bottle of water, a cup of coffee—depending on the time of day—he would go by each booth or table, have a word, sometimes a full conversation. If it was a regular, he would sometimes sit down for a few minutes. Talk ranged from sports, food, politics to neighborhood news, births, deaths. The subject didn't matter, she knew.

It was the intimacy.

Today it was water, and when he sat across from her, he took a long pull. "It's good?" He nodded at her plate.

"The best."

"Then put more of it in your stomach."

"How's Mr. Alegrio's bursitis?"

"Acting up. He says it's going to rain. His grandson got a promotion, and his roses look good this year." Gib grinned. "What did he have for his meal?"

"The special, with minestrone and the house salad, a glass of Peroni, a bottle of sparkling water, bread sticks and a cannoli."

"You always remember. It's our loss you're taking those criminal justice courses, the chemistry, instead of restaurant management."

"I'll always have time to help out here, Dad. Always."

"I'm proud of you. Proud you know what you want and you're working for it."

"Somebody raised me that way. How's the father of the bride?"

"I'm not thinking about it yet." He shook his head, drank more water. "I'm not thinking about the moment when she comes toward me in her dress. When I walk her down the aisle and give her to Vince. Blubber like a baby if I do. It's easy to tuck that away while we're dealing with the insanity of preparing for that moment."

He glanced over, smiled. "Somebody else must've heard you were home. Hey, John."

"Gib."

With a cry of pleasure, Reena scooted up, flung her arms around John Minger. "I missed you! Haven't seen you since Christmas. Sit down. Be right back."

She dashed off, got another setup. When she plopped down again, she scooped up half the spaghetti and put it on the second plate. "You're eating some of this. Dad thinks I starve myself at college."

"What can I get you to drink, John?"

"Anything soft's good. Thanks."

"I'll have it brought right out. Gotta get back to work."

"Tell me everything," Reena demanded. "How are you, your kids, the grandkids, life in general?"

"Doing good, keeping busy."

He looked good, Reena thought. A little heavier under the eyes, and his hair was nearly stone gray now. But it suited him. The fire had made him part of the family. No, more than the fire, she corrected. What he had done since. Pitching in to work, answering the endless questions she'd posed.

"Any interesting cases?"

"They're all interesting. You still up for ride-alongs?"

"You call, I'm there."

His face softened with a smile. "Had one start in a kid's bedroom. Eight-year-old boy. Nobody home at the time it engaged. No accelerants, no matches, no lighter. No sign of forced entry or incendiary components."

"Electrical?"

"Nope."

She began to eat again as she considered. "Chemistry set? Kids that age often like playing with chemistry sets."

"Not this one. Told me he's going to be a detective."

"What time of day did it start?"

"Around two in the afternoon. Kid's in school, parents at work. No previous incidents." He twirled spaghetti, closed his eyes in appreciation of the taste. "Not fair to quiz you when you can't see the site, or pictures."

"Wait a minute, wait a minute, I'm not giving up yet." Puzzles, she'd always thought, were made to be solved. "Point of origin?"

"Kid's desk. Plywood desk."

"Bet he had a lot of fuel on it. Construction paper, glue, the desk itself, school papers and binders maybe, toys. Near the window?"

"Right under it."

"So he's got curtains, probably, they catch, keep it going. Two in the afternoon." Now she closed her eyes, tried to see it. She thought of Xander's desk when he'd been that age. The careless jumble of boy toys, comic books, school papers.

"What way did the window face?"

"You're a pistol, Reena. South."

"Sun should be coming in strong that time of day, unless the curtains were closed. Kid isn't going to close his curtains. What was the weather that day?"

"Clear, sunny, warm."

"Kid wants to be a detective, probably has a magnifying glass."

"Bull's-eye. Yeah, you're a pistol. Glass is sitting right on the desk, canted up on a book, over a bunch of papers. Sun beats through, heats the glass, fires the papers. Wood desk, cloth curtains."

"Poor kid."

"Could've been worse. Delivery guy saw the smoke, called nine-one-one. They were able to contain it in the bedroom."

"I've missed being able to talk shop. I know, I know, I'm just a student, and most of the courses I'm hungry for I can't take until my junior year when I transfer to the Shady Grove campus. But it feels like talking shop."

"Something else I need to talk to you about." He set down his fork, looked in her eyes. "Pastorelli's out."

"He—" She drew herself in, glanced around to see if any of her family could overhear. "When?"

"Last week. I just got word."

"It had to happen," Reena said dully. "He'd have been out before this if he hadn't gotten extra time for punching a guard."

"I don't think he's going to give you any trouble, or even come back around here. He's got no ties to the neighborhood anymore. His wife's in New York still, with her aunt. I checked. The kid's already done a stint up there for assault."

"I remember when they took him away." She looked out the window, across the street. There were pots of geraniums on the steps of what had been the Pastorelli house, and the curtains were open.

"Which?"

"Both. I remember how they brought Mr. Pastorelli out, in handcuffs, and how his wife buried her face in a yellow dish towel, and one of her shoes was untied. I remember Joey running after the car, screaming. I was standing with my father. I think watching that together strengthened something we already had between us. I think that's why he let me go with him when they took Joey. After he killed that poor dog."

"He was closing a chapter for you, one that started when the little bastard attacked you. No reason to think it's not still closed, but you and your family need to know he's out."

"I'll tell them. Later, John, later, when we're all at home."

"Good enough."

She looked out the window again, and the frown vanished. "It's Xander. I'll be right back." She scooted out of the booth, hurried to the door, then raced across the street and launched herself at her brother.

B eing home was like being a child again in so many ways. The scents and sounds of the house were so much what they'd always been. The furniture polish her mother always used, the cooking smells that seemed as much a part of the kitchen as the old butcher-block table. The music that pumped out of Xander's room, whether he was in there or not. The watery tinkle from the toilet in the powder room that ran unless its handle was jiggled.

It was rare for an hour to go by without the phone ringing, and since the weather was fine, the windows were open to the shoosh of street traffic, and the voices of pedestrians who stopped to chat.

She could've been ten again, sitting cross-legged on her sister's bed while Bella reigned at the little vanity, primping for an evening out.

"There's just so much to do." Bella blended tones of eyeshadow with the skill of an artist. "I don't know how I'll get everything done before the wedding. Vince says I worry too much, but it has to be perfect."

"It will be. Your dress is gorgeous."

"I knew exactly what I wanted." She shook back glamorous clouds of blond hair. "After all, I've been planning for this my whole life. Remember when we used to play bride, with those old lace curtains?"

"And you were always the bride." But Reena smiled when she said it.

"Now, it's not make-believe anymore. I know Dad was freaked about how much the dress cost, but the bride's the showpiece on her wedding day, after all. And I can't be the showpiece in some knockoff. I want Vince dazzled when he sees me in it. Oh, wait until you see what he gave me for my something old."

"I thought you were wearing Nuni's pearls."

"No. They're sweet, but they're old-fashioned. Besides, they're not real pearls." She opened the drawer of the vanity, took out a small box. She brought it over, sat on the side of the bed. "He bought them for me at an estate jeweler."

Inside were earrings, sparkling drops of diamonds and filigree so delicate they might have been spun by magic spiders.

"God, Bella, are those real diamonds?"

"Of course." The square-cut solitaire on her finger flashed as she gestured. "Vince wouldn't buy me paste. He's got class. His whole family has class."

"And ours doesn't?"

"I didn't mean it that way." But Bella spoke absently as she held up one of the earrings so it could catch the light. "Vince's mother flies to New York and Milan to shop. They have a household staff of *twelve*. You should see his parents' house, Reena. It's a mansion. They have full-time grounds-keepers. His mother's so sweet to me—I'm calling her Joanne now. She's taking me to her salon on the morning of the wedding, for the works."

"I thought we—you and Mama and Fran and I—were going to Maria's."

"Catarina." Bella smiled gently, patted Reena's hand before she rose to put the earrings back in the drawer. "Maria's doesn't make the cut for me now. I'm going to be the wife of an important man. I'm going to have a different lifestyle now, different obligations. To meet them I have to have the right haircut, the right wardrobe, the right everything."

"Who says what's right?"

"You just *know*." She fluffed at her hair. "Vince has a cousin, he's really cute. I thought you might like for him to be your escort at the reception. I think you'd hit it off. He's a junior at Princeton."

"Thanks, but I have a boyfriend. He'll be coming to the wedding. I cleared it with Mama."

"A boyfriend." Forgetting her primping for the moment, Bella dropped down on the bed. "When, where, how? What's his name? What does he look like? Tell me everything."

The seeds of resentment blew away, and they were sisters again, huddling together over the serious priority of boys.

"His name's Josh. He's so sweet and he's a major hottie. He wants to be a writer, and I met him at college. We've been seeing each other a couple of months now."

"Months? And you didn't tell me?"

"You've been a little preoccupied."

"Still." Bella pouted a moment. "Is he from around here?"

"No, he grew up in Ohio. But he's living here now. He's got a job in a bookstore for the summer. I really like him, Bella. I've slept with him. Five times."

"Jesus!" Bella's eyes went saucer-wide as she bounced her butt on the bed. "Reena, this is *huge*. Is he good at it?" She popped up, closed the door. "Vince is amazing in bed. He can go for *hours*."

"I think he's good at it." Hours? Reena wondered. Was that really possible? "He's the only one I've ever been with."

"Make sure you always use protection. I stopped."

"Stopped what?"

"Birth control," she whispered. "Vince said he wants to have a family right away, so we tossed away my pills. It's so close to the wedding, it won't matter if I get pregnant. We threw them away last weekend, so I might already be pregnant."

"God, Bella." It gave Reena a jolt, a hard one, to think of her sister going from bride to wife to mother in one big rush. "Don't you want some time to get used to being married first?"

"I don't need time." When she smiled, everything about her went dreamy. Lips, eyes, voice. "I know just how it's all going to be. And it's going to be perfect. I have to finish getting ready. Vince will be here any minute, and he hates when I'm late."

"Have a good time."

"We always do." Bella sat down at the vanity again when Reena went to the door. "Vince is taking me to a fabulous restaurant tonight. He says I need to relax and take my mind off the details of the wedding."

"I'm sure he's right." She went out, closing the door just as her brother came up the stairs.

He glanced at the door, back at Reena and grinned. "So how many times did she say 'Vince thinks'?"

"I lost count. He's pretty crazy about her."

"Good thing, otherwise by now he'd have been driven crazy by her. I know one thing, I'll be glad when it's over."

She walked to him. He'd edged over her in height, so she bounced up on her toes to kiss his cheek. "You'll miss her when she isn't in the next room."

"I guess I will."

"You got plans tonight?"

"On your first night home? What kind of brother am I?"

"My favorite kind."

She waited until Bella was out to her fancy dinner and the rest of the family was around the dining room table sharing steak Florentine in honor of Reena's return from college.

"I have some news," she began. "John told me today, and I asked him to let me tell everyone else. Pastorelli's out. He was released a week ago."

"Son of a bitch."

"Not at the table, Xander," Bianca said automatically. "Do they know where he is, where he went?"

"He served his time, Mama." She'd had time to reconcile to that, and to sound calm about it. "John doesn't think we need to worry, and I agree.

He doesn't have any ties to the neighborhood, no reason to come back here. What happened was long ago."

"And yesterday," Gib said. "Seems like yesterday. But I think we have to accept this. What else can we do? He was punished for what he did. It's done, and he's out of our lives."

"Yes, but it wouldn't hurt to be a little watchful, at least for a while." Bianca drew a long breath. "And it's probably best not to say anything to Bella until after the wedding. She'll just have hysterics."

"She can have hysterics over a chipped nail," Xander put in.

"My point exactly. So we know, and we'll be a little more careful. But we'll believe, as John does, that there's nothing to worry about. So . . ." Bianca lifted her hands. "Eat, before the food gets cold."

# 6

Bo wasn't a hundred percent regarding the plans for the day, but he was usually willing to go along. His pal Brad was now officially one half of the Brad and Cammie show. And since that show was in its first act, everybody was happy. To spread the joy, the new couple arranged for a double date, and that was fine. The all-day and into the evening term of the date was a little worrying.

A big commitment, to Bo's way of thinking.

What if he and this friend of Cammie's took an instant dislike to each other? It happened. She was supposed to be pretty, but that was Cammie's opinion. And you just couldn't trust the opinion of a girlfriend.

Even if she looked like Claudia Schiffer, she might talk all the time, or giggle. He really hated gigglers. Or she might be one of those humorless types. He'd rather take the giggling over the super-serious, I've-got-to-save-the-world-from-itself-and-so-do-you sort.

On top of that, he was still hung up on a girl whose face he'd seen for about ten seconds, and whose name he didn't know.

Stupid, but what could you do?

This was, he knew, one of Brad's methods of getting him back to the real world. A pretty girl—at least that was the billing—a day out with a convivial group at Baltimore's Inner Harbor. Do the aquarium, hang out, catch some music, eat some seafood. Have a few laughs. He ordered himself to get into the spirit of it as he followed Cammie's directions.

She and Brad took the backseat of his car, mostly, in his opinion, so they could make out.

He pulled into the lot, waited while his passengers completed their latest lip-lock.

"We'll all go in." Cammie unwrapped herself from Brad, grabbed her purse. "This is going to be fun! It's a totally awesome day."

She had him there, Bo thought. Blue sky, puffy clouds, steaming sunshine. Better to be out and about than sitting home brooding about some fantasy girl or even fooling around in his foreman's workshop.

What he was aiming for was a workshop of his own. Once he had enough money to rent a house—or, more fantasy, actually buy one—he was going to have a shop of his own. A nice little shed he'd outfit with worktables and power tools. Maybe get his own side business going.

He walked into the apartment building, which looked exactly like every other off-campus apartment building to him. And was just the sort of place he wanted to say good-bye to. What he needed to do was talk Brad into parting with some of his money, going in with him to buy a place for rehab.

"She's right here on the first floor." Cammie walked to a door, knocked. "You're really going to like Mandy, Bo. She's a lot of fun."

Cammie's big smile reminded Bo why he hated being fixed up. Now if he didn't like her friend, he'd have to pretend he did. Otherwise, Cammie would poke at Brad until Brad poked at him.

But some of his worry lifted when the little redhead with the big blue eyes and curves nicely packed into jeans and a snug gray T-shirt opened the door.

Packed nicely enough he was going to reserve judgment on the eyebrow ring. Maybe it was sexy.

"Hey, Mandy. You know Brad."

"Sure. Hi, Brad."

There was just the slightest hint of a lisp—a sexy one.

"And this is Bo. Bowen Goodnight."

"Hi, Bo. Just gotta get my bag, and I'm ready to roll. Place is wrecked. Don't come in." She laughed as she said it, and shooed them back. "My room-mate left yesterday for a wild weekend in OC, and tore the place up looking for a pair of sandals. Which I found after she'd gone. I'm not cleaning it up. That's her deal."

She talked nonstop, but in a funny, bouncy way, while she grabbed a shoulder bag and a black O's fielder's cap.

Ah, baseball, Bo thought. There was hope.

She scooted out, shut the door behind her, then offered Bo a quick, easy smile. "Got a camera in here." She patted the bulging shoulder bag. "I'm a pain in the ass with it. Fair warning."

"Mandy's an awesome photographer," Cammie put in. "She's interning at the *Baltimore Sun*."

"Horrible hours, no pay. I love it. Hey, look at you."

Before Bo could comment, she'd turned completely around to study a guy coming down the stairs. He was wearing a suit and tie, and looked a little flustered.

"Dude," she said with a chuckle. "Looking hot."

"Going to a wedding." He lifted a hand to the knot of his striped tie, tugged. "Is this thing on right?"

"Cammie, Brad, Bo, this is Josh. Upstairs neighbor, fellow student and amateur tie knotter. Let me fix it. Who's getting married?"

"Girlfriend's sister. I'll be meeting her whole family. I feel a little sick."

"Oooh, the gauntlet." She straightened his tie, gave his lapel a little pat. "There, you're perfect. And don't worry, hon, people are either crying or getting drunk at weddings."

"They're mostly Italian."

"Then they'll be doing both. Italian weddings are big buckets of fun. Just lift your glass and say—what is it?—*salute!*"

"*Salute.* Got it. Nice to meet you guys. See you later."

"He's a sweetie," Mandy said when he went out. "Been hung up on this
girl in his lit class most of the term. Looks like it's finally working out. So."
She adjusted her cap. "Let's go see some big-ass fish."

Bella had ordered perfect, and in Reena's opinion, she'd gotten her wish.
The weather was spectacular, the balmy blue and gold of early summer,
with the flowers both bright and delicate, and the humidity mercifully low.

She looked like a princess, everyone said so, in her frothy white gown, her
hair gleaming gold under her sparkling veil. She carried a spectacular creation
of pink roses accented with miniature white lilies.

The church was bedecked with her choice of flowers in white baskets.
She'd rejected the more traditional organ in favor of a harp, flutes, cello
and violin. Reena had to admit the sound was lovely.

And classy.

No more lace curtains and Kleenex bouquets, Reena thought as her
eyes stung and her throat went hot. Isabella Hale swept down the aisle of
St. Leo's on their father's arm looking like royalty. Her train a sparkling
white river behind her, her face glowing, diamonds firing at her ears.

She'd gotten her wish all around, Reena thought, as Vince—elegant
and handsome in his formal morning coat—looked dazzled by her.

His eyes, deep and dark, lit on her face and never moved from it. Her
father's were damp as he carefully lifted Bella's veil, gently kissed her cheek
and answered the priest's question about who gives this woman to this
man with a tenderly spoken, "Her mother and I do."

For once Bella didn't weep, but stayed dry-eyed and luminous through
the Mass and ceremony. Her eyes like stars and her voice clear as a bell.

Because she knows this is exactly what she wants, Reena thought.
What she's always wanted. Just as she knows this is her spotlight, and all
eyes are on her.

It no longer mattered that the bridesmaid dress was a little less than
flattering. Here was another kind of fire, she realized. It was strong and
bright and hot. It was her sister's joy flaming through the air.

So Reena wept when the vows were exchanged, and the rings given, knowing that this was the end of a part of their lives. And the beginning of the next part of Bella's.

The reception was held at Vince's parents' country club, where his father was some sort of officer or board member. Here, too, there were flowers in abundance, and food and wine and music.

Each table was draped with the same shade of pink as Bella's signature roses, sprinkled with white rose petals and centered with yet more flowers and glossy pillars of pure white candles.

Reena was required to sit at the long head table along with the bridal party. She was grateful her mother had the foresight to seat Josh at the same table as Gina, who could be counted on to keep him entertained. She was nearly as grateful that Fran—as maid of honor—and Vince's brother, who served as best man, were the ones who would make the traditional toasts.

She ate rare prime rib, talked and laughed with the other members of the wedding party, worried about Josh. And when she took time to gaze around the big ballroom, wondered what kind of world her sister was now a part of.

The two families were mingling, as people do at such events. But even if she didn't know them, she'd have been able to separate them into groups. The working class, the upper class. City neighborhood, suburban wealth.

The bride wasn't the only one wearing diamonds, or draped in a dress that cost more than a week's take at Sirico's. But she was the only one of her blood who'd managed it.

Probably, Reena admitted, the only one of her blood who could pull it off as if she'd been born wearing Prada.

As if reading her thoughts, Xander leaned close to her ear. "We're now the poor relations."

She snickered, then picked up her champagne. "Screw it. *Salute.*"

It was easier when she could escape the formal duties and find Josh. "You doing okay? I should be clear now, at least for a while."

"Fine. It was some wedding."

"Some wedding," she agreed. "I didn't know the pictures would take so long. I feel like I deserted you. And I wanted to warn you that—"

"Catarina!" Her aunt Carmela swept up to envelop her in clouds of White Shoulders. "How beautiful you look! Like a bride yourself. But so thin! We'll fatten you up now you're home. And who is this handsome young man?"

"Aunt Carmela, this is Josh Bolton. Josh, my aunt, Carmela Sirico."

"It's nice to meet you, Mrs. Sirico."

"Polite, too. It's a wedding, today I'm Carmela. My niece." Carmela wrapped a strong arm around Reena's shoulders. "She looks so pretty, doesn't she?"

"Yes, ma'am, she—"

"Francesca's the beauty, and Isabella, she has the style, the passion. Our Catarina, she's the smart one. Aren't you, *cara*?"

"That's right. I got the brains."

"But today, you look beautiful! Maybe your young man will get ideas when you catch the bouquet." She winked broadly. "Do I know your family?" she asked Josh.

"You don't," Reena said quickly. "I know Josh from school. I need to introduce him around."

"Yes, yes. You save a dance for me," she told Josh as Reena dragged him away.

"That's what I was going to warn you about," Reena began. "You're going to get a lot of that *and* some third degree. Who are your family, what do they do, what are you doing, where do you go to church. Everyone in my family thinks it's their business to know. Don't take it personally."

"It's okay. Gina gave me the heads-up. It's a little scary, but okay. And you do look beautiful. I've never been to a big Catholic wedding. It was something."

"And really long," she said with a laugh. "Okay, I'm going to have to show you off to the uncles, and the rest of the aunts. Stay strong."

And it was okay, she saw as the party went on. Josh might have been peppered with questions, but there was so much talking going on he only had to answer about half of them.

The music kept things lively with something for everyone, from Dean Martin to Madonna. She'd relaxed into the moment when she took her dance with the groom.

"I've never seen my sister look happier. The ceremony was beautiful, Vince. Everything's beautiful."

"She worried every day. But that's our Bella."

He moved so smoothly over the floor, stayed so focused on her face as he did that Reena was sure there'd been lessons along the way. Dance and charm.

"Now we can start our lives, make our home, have our family. We'll have you over for dinner once we're back from our honeymoon and settled."

"I'm there."

"I'm a lucky man to have such a beautiful wife, such an enchanting woman. And she cooks." He laughed and kissed Reena's cheek. "And now I have another sister."

"I have another brother. *Una famiglia.*"

"*Una famiglia.*" He grinned and swept her around the dance floor.

Later, snuggled in bed with Josh, Reena thought of her sister's long-awaited day. The grandeur of the ceremony, all the solemn words, the elegant flowers. The initial formality of the reception that had, thankfully, broken down into a boisterous party.

"Tell me, did my aunt Rosa actually do the Electric Slide?"

"I can't remember which one was Rosa, exactly, but yeah, I think. Or maybe it was the Hokey Pokey."

"No, it was my second cousins Lena and Maria-Theresa who got that one going. Jeez."

"I liked the dancing, especially the tarenbella."

"Tarantella," she corrected, giggling. "You held up, Josh, and it's not easy. Big points for you."

"I had fun, serious fun. Your family's really cool."

"Also big and loud. I think Vince's family was a little wigged, maybe especially when my uncle Larry grabbed the mike and started belting out 'That's Amore.'"

"Sounded good. I like your family better. His are kind of snobby. He's okay," Josh said quickly. "And he's over the moon about your sister. They looked like a movie couple."

"Yeah, they did."

"And your mom. Is it okay to say your mom's really beautiful? She just doesn't look like a mom. My family never did stuff like this, you know, the big events. I liked it."

She rolled over, smiled down at him. "Then you'll come to dinner tomorrow? Mom told me to ask you. You can see what we're like when we're not all dressed up."

"Sure. Maybe you can stay tonight? My roommate's not getting back until tomorrow night. We can go out if you want, or just stay here."

"I wish I could." She bent her head to kiss his chest. It was so smooth and warm. "I really do. But I think an overnight's a little more than my dad could take tonight. He's going to be feeling blue. On top of it, people were giving him the business about how soon he'd be doing this again for Fran."

"You did shove her right at the bouquet when Bella tossed it."

"Reflex." She laughed again, and sat up to shake back her hair. "I want to keep Dad busy tonight. Otherwise he's going to be thinking about Bella's wedding night, and that's iffy territory for him." She touched his cheek. "I'm glad you had fun today."

He sat up, hugged her in a way that warmed her heart. "I always do when I'm with you."

She dressed, freshened her makeup. No good going home looking like she'd just rolled out of bed with a guy. At the door she let Josh draw her into several lingering kisses.

"Maybe, next day off, we could go somewhere," he suggested. "The beach or something."

"I'd like that. I'll see you tomorrow." She stepped out, then turned back and pulled him into the doorway for another kiss. "That'll have to hold me."

She all but danced down the stairs and into the warm night.

Bo drove into the lot as she was putting her key into the ignition.

He'd dropped Brad and Cammie off at Cammie's place. It had been a good day, he thought, the kind that promised more. He liked Mandy. It was impossible not to. She *was* a pain in the ass with the camera, but in a way that made him laugh, or impressed him.

"I'm going to want to see some of the six million pictures you took today," he told her as they got out of his car.

"You couldn't escape it. I'm nearly as annoying with prints as I am with the lens. This was fun. I'm glad Cam nagged me into it. And saying that just proves I forget to engage brain before tongue."

"It's okay, I got nagged into it, too. I figured if it turned out to be a nightmare, I could hold it over Brad for years. I'll have to find something else to hold over his head. Okay if I call you?"

"Really okay." She pulled a scrap of paper out of her pocket. "I already wrote down my number. If you hadn't asked for it, I was going to plant it on you while I was doing this."

She grabbed his shirt in both hands, gave a quick yank and rose onto her toes at the same time. The kiss was hot and promising.

"Nice." She rubbed her lips together. "You know, if something works between us, *they're* going to hold it over our heads."

"Life's full of risks." He'd decided the eyebrow ring was sexy. "Maybe I could come in."

"Tempting, very tempting. But I think we'd better hold off on that." She unlocked her door, backed in. "Call me."

He put her number in his pocket and was grinning as he walked out to his car.

Since he had the evening free, and no roommate to blare music, Josh sat down to write. He decided it would be fun to try to build a short story around the wedding.

He wanted to get some of it down before the impressions—there were so many of them—got jumbled up or started to fade away.

As much as he would've liked having Reena stay the night, he was sort of glad she'd gone home. Having the place to himself meant he could really think. Really work.

He had most of a quick draft roughed out when the knock on the door interrupted him. With his mind still on the story, he went to answer. When he opened the door, he cocked his head in greeting. "Can I help you?"

"Yeah, I'm from upstairs. Have you heard— See, there it is again."

Instinctively Josh glanced over his shoulder in the direction his visitor pointed. Pain exploded in his head, a red bloom over his eyes.

The door was shut before he hit the floor.

. . .

*Skinny kid. No trouble hauling his stupid ass into the bedroom. The sock full of quarters would leave a mark. Maybe they'd find it later. Leave him on the floor, so it looks like he hit his head falling out of bed.*

*Keep it simple, keep it quick. Light the cigarette, wipe it clean, put it between the dumb fuck's lips. Just in case. Get his prints on the pack, on some matches. Just in case. Now lay the burning cigarette on the bed, lay it on the sheets. Smolder good there. Add a little paper—College Joe's school papers. Leave the pack of smokes, leave some matches.*

*Go find a beer in the kitchen. Might as well have a drink while it starts.*

*Nothing like watching a fire being born. Nothing in the world. Power is like a prime drug.*

*The smoldering fire. The sneaky fire. Sly and cunning. Building, building, quiet and secret, toward that first flash of flame.*

*Gloves on, take the battery out of the smoke detector. People are so careless. Just forget to replace the batteries. Damn shame.*

*Kid could come to. Comes to, just smack him again.*

*Hope he comes to. Come on, you skinny bastard, come around so I can hit you again.*

*Hold it in, hold it down. Watch the smoke—sexy, silent, deadly. Smoke's what gets them. Dazes them. Paper's catching, there's the flame.*

*First flame's the first power. Hear how it speaks, whispers. Watch how it moves, dances.*

*Now the sheets. Good start, got a start. Drape the sheet down, over the asshole. Beautiful! Look at the colors of it. Gold and red, orange and yellow.*

*Here's how it looks: Lights up in bed, falls asleep. Smoke gets him, he tries to get out of bed, falls, hits his head. Fire takes him while he's out.*

*Bed's going up. Pretty, isn't that pretty? A little more paper won't hurt. Get his shirt caught. That's the way!*

*Keep going, keep going. It takes so damn long. Drink some beer, keep your cool. Who knew a skinny bastard could burn that way? Carpet's caught now—what you get for buying cheap!*

*Toast, that's what he is. Fucking toast. Smells like roasting pig.*

*Better go. Hate to leave, miss the show. It's so interesting to watch people crackle and melt while the fire eats them.*

*But it's time to say our good-byes to dumbass College Joe. Take it slow, take it easy. Check the hall. Too damn bad you can't stay and watch, but gotta go. Stroll away, no hurry. Don't look back. Nice and easy, got no worries.*

*Drive away. Keep to the posted limits like any law-abiding son of a bitch.*

*He'll be crisp before they get to him.*

*Now that's entertainment.*

# 7

Bo woke with a hangover that rang like cathedral bells. He was face-down on a bed that smelled more like gym socks than sheets, and was just miserable enough to consider staying like that, breathing in the rank, for the rest of his natural life.

It wasn't his fault that his downstairs neighbor's party had been at full blast when he got home from dropping off Mandy. Stopping in had been polite, and an entertaining way to spend the rest of his Saturday night.

And since he'd only had to walk up the stairs to his own place, he hadn't seen the harm in drinking a couple of beers.

But it was his fault, and he was willing to admit it once his head stopped screaming, that he'd hung out until after two in the morning and sucked down a six-pack.

But it wasn't completely his fault, because the beer had been there, along with the nachos. And what were you supposed to do when you were eating nachos but wash them down with beer?

Oceans of beer.

He had aspirin. Probably. Somewhere. Oh, if only there was a merciful God who would remind him where the hell he'd stashed the bottle of

Advil. He'd crawl to it himself, if only he knew where to drag his poor, abused body.

And why hadn't he pulled the shades? Why couldn't that merciful God turn down the sunlight so it wasn't blasting like a red furnace against his aching eyes?

Because he'd worshipped the god of beer, that's why. He'd broken a commandment and worshipped the false and foamy god of beer. And now he was being punished.

He thought the aspirin, which now took on the weight of his salvation, was most likely in the kitchen. He prayed it was as he covered his eyes with one hand, eased himself out of bed. His moan was heartfelt, and turned into something more like a scream when he tripped over his shoes and fell flat on his face.

He barely had the strength to whimper, much less swear.

He made it to his hands and knees, balanced there, prayed there until he got most of his breath back. Never again. He swore it. If he'd had a knife he'd have drawn his own blood and used it to write the vow on the floor. He managed to get to his feet, while his banging head spun and his stomach churned. His last hope was that he wouldn't puke on his own toes. He'd rather have the pain than the puking.

Fortunately, his apartment was about the size of a minivan, and the kitchen only a few short steps from the pull-out sofa. Something in the kitchen smelled like dead rat, and wasn't that just perfect? He ignored the sink full of dishes, the counter junked with boxes of takeout he'd yet to throw away, and fumbled through his cabinets.

Crap wood, he thought as he always did. Next thing to plastic. Inside were open boxes of Life, Frosted Mini Wheats, Froot Loops and Cheerios. A bag of sour cream and onion potato chips, four boxes of macaroni and cheese, Ring-Dings, assorted cans of soup and a box of raspberry and cheese coffee cake.

And there, *there* between Life and Cheerios, was the Advil. Thank you, Jesus.

Since he'd already tossed the cap after his last hangover, all he had to do was dump three little pills in his clammy hand. He shoved them in his mouth, turned on the faucet and, since there was no room for his head among the dishes, scooped running water into his palm and sucked it in to down the pills.

He choked when one stuck in his throat, stumbled to the fridge and grabbed a bottle of Gatorade. He drank, leaning weakly against the counter.

He wove his way through the pile of clothes, the shoes, his stupid keys and whatever else had hit the floor, into the bathroom.

Bracing his hands on the sink, he gathered his courage. And lifted his head to look at himself in the mirror.

His hair looked like the dead rat in his kitchen had danced through it overnight. His face was pasty. His eyes were so full of blood he wondered if there was any left in the rest of him.

"Okay, Goodnight, you stupid son of a bitch, this is it. Your ass is going to straighten up."

He turned on the shower, stepped under the stingy piss trickle. And casting his eyes to the ceiling, dragged off his boxers and the single sock he still wore. He leaned forward so the water that dribbled out of the showerhead dribbled on his hair.

He was getting out of this dump, first chance. Meanwhile he was going to clean it up. It was one thing to save money living in a piece of shit apartment, and another to let it become a freaking cesspool because he didn't bother to take care of it.

It was no way to live, and he was tired of himself for settling. Tired of busting his hump all week, then blowing off the steam with too much beer so he suffered on Sunday mornings.

It was time to make a move.

It took him an hour to shower, brush the taste of over-partying out of his mouth, then force something into his stomach he hoped would stay there. He pulled on ripped sweats and started shoveling out his living room.

He made piles of laundry. Who knew he had so many clothes? He stripped the revolting sheets off the bed and considered just burning them.

But in the end, his frugal nature had him using them as a sack for the rest of the clothes and towels. From the looks of it, he decided he'd be spending a good chunk of his Sunday in the Laundromat.

But for now, he pulled out the rattiest of his towels, ripped it into pieces and used one to clear the dust off the crate table. He'd made the piece, damn good work, and look how he was treating it.

He dug out his spare sheets, and one whiff had them going in the laundry pile.

He hit the kitchen, discovered he actually did have dish detergent and an unopened bottle of Mr. Clean. He loaded bags with trash, found it wasn't a dead rat stinking up the place but some really ancient sweet-and-sour pork. He dumped detergent in the sink. Dumped more. The dishes looked pretty grungy.

He stood, legs spread like a gunslinger's, and washed dishes in an ocean of suds.

By the time he'd scrubbed counters off so he had a place to pile the dishes once they were clean, he was feeling almost normal.

Since he was in the groove, he emptied out his refrigerator, scrubbed it down. He opened the stove, found a pizza box containing what might have been, at one time in the dim past, the remains of a Hawaiian pizza.

"God, you're a pig."

He wondered where he could rent a Hazmat suit before tackling the bathroom.

Nearly four hours after he'd crawled out of bed, he had two bundles of laundry stuffed in the plastic hamper he'd been using as a catch-all, three Hefty bags of trash and garbage that defied description and a clean apartment.

It was a righteous man who hauled the trash out to the Dumpster.

Upstairs, he stripped off the sweats, added them to the laundry, then pulled on his cleanest jeans and least offensive T-shirt.

He gathered the change he'd found in the bed, under the bed, in his single chair and out of various pockets. He put on the sunglasses he thought he'd lost weeks before, grabbed his keys.

Someone knocked just as he was about to haul up the laundry basket. Brad walked in when he opened the door.

"Hey. I tried to call . . ." He trailed off, gaped. "What the hell! Did I walk into an alternate universe?"

"Did some housekeeping."

"Some? Dude, a human could actually live here. You have a chair."

"I've always had a chair. It was just buried. I'm heading to the Laundromat if you want to hang out. Sometimes hot chicks do laundry."

"Maybe. Listen, I tried to call you a couple hours ago, kept getting a busy signal."

"I must've knocked the phone off the hook last night. What's up?"

"Heavy shit." Brad walked into the kitchen, stood dazed a moment, then got a Coke out of the fridge. "There was a fire at Mandy's place last night."

"Fire? Jesus, what kind of fire? She okay?"

"She's okay. Really shaken up. She came over to Cammie's. I just left there. I figured she needed to chill, you know? It's been on the news."

"Haven't turned the TV on. I cleaned to Black Sabbath. It kept me focused. How bad was the fire?"

"Major bad." Brad dropped down in the chair. "Started in an apartment upstairs. They're saying it looks like smoking in bed." He ran a hand over his face, sliding his fingers under his glasses to press them against his eyes.

"Jesus, Bo, a guy died. I mean he burned up, along with most of his place. Lost a lot of the second floor, part of the third. Mandy got out, and they let her in to get some of her stuff, but she's a wreck. It was the guy in the tie. Ah, Josh. Remember, the guy from upstairs?"

"God, he's *dead*?" Bo sank down on the sofa.

"It was bad. Mandy could hardly talk about it. The guy died, and there are a couple others in the hospital with burns or smoke inhalation. She said it must've started right after you dropped her off. She was still up, watching some tube when she heard people screaming, and smoke alarms going off."

"He was going to a wedding," Bo murmured. "And he couldn't get his tie right."

"Now he's dead." Brad took a long drink from the can of Coke. "Makes you think, makes you realize how short the trip can be."

"Yeah." Bo got a picture of the dead guy in his head, standing in his suit with a sheepish smile on his face. "Yeah, it makes you think."

Business tended to be slow on Sunday afternoons. There were some who traditionally came in after Mass for a meal, but most went home to make their own Sunday dinners. Reena and Xander took the after-Mass shift with Pete's young cousin Mia waiting tables and Nick Casto on delivery and dish duty.

They had Tony Bennett on the little stereo because the Sunday regulars liked it, but Xander made the pizzas and calzones at the big worktable with Pearl Jam playing low in his headset.

It was a treat for Reena to man the kitchen when the demand was light, and to wander into the dining area from time to time to work the tables as her father did.

Fran would carry this on—that was understood—but Reena would always put time in here. If they weren't having company for dinner, she and Xander might wander down after their shift and watch the latest boccie tournament, or hook up with some of their friends for a pickup game of ball.

But since they were having company—and that company happened to be her boyfriend—she'd go home and give her mother a hand with dinner.

In just a couple of hours, she'd walk home and set the table with the company dishes and linens. Her mother was making her special rosemary chicken with prosciutto, and there'd be tiramisu for dessert.

There were flowers from Bella's wedding.

He'd be shy, she thought as she arranged risotto on a plate. But her family would bring him around. She'd coach Fran, have her ask Josh about his writing.

Fran was great at bringing people out of themselves.

Humming along with Tony, Reena carried the plates out to serve them herself.

"So, your sister's a married woman."

"That's right, Mrs. Giambrisco."

The woman nodded, sent a look toward her husband, who was already digging into his risotto. "Caught a rich one, I hear. As easy to fall in love with a rich man as a poor one."

"It might be." Personally, Reena wondered what it felt like to fall in love with any kind of man. Maybe she was falling in love with Josh and didn't know it.

"Just you remember." Mrs. Giambrisco wagged her fork. "Maybe the boys, they do their sniffing around your sisters, but your day will come. This husband of your sister's, he's got a brother?"

"Yes. A married one, with a child and another on the way."

"Maybe a cousin, then."

"Don't worry, Mrs. Giambrisco," Xander called out from his work counter. "Catarina's got a boyfriend." He kissed his fingers in her direction. "He's coming to dinner tonight so Dad can give him a good grilling."

"As it should be. An Italian boy?"

"No. And he's coming to dinner to eat chicken," she called back to Xander. "Not to be grilled. Enjoy your meal."

She shot Xander a dark look on her way back to the kitchen, but she was secretly pleased she was in a position to be teased about her boyfriend.

She watched the clock, baked penne and was serving spaghetti puttanesca when Gina rushed in.

"Reena."

"You need anything else?" She grabbed a water pitcher, refilled glasses. "We've got some of Mama's zabaglione today, so save room."

"Catarina." Gina grabbed her arm, pulled her away from the table.

"Jeez, what's the problem? I'm off in a half hour."

"You haven't heard?"

"Heard what?" The intensity of Gina's grip, the teary eyes got through. "What happened? What's wrong? Is it your grandmother?"

"No. Oh God, no. It's Josh. Oh, Reena, it's Josh."

"What happened?" Her fingers went numb on the handle of the pitcher. "Did something happen?"

"There was a fire, at his apartment. In his apartment. Reena . . . Let's go in the back."

"Tell me." She jerked away from Gina's hold, and water slopped over the rim of the pitcher and splashed cold on her hand. "Is he hurt? Is he in the hospital?"

"He . . . Oh, Blessed Mary. Reena, they didn't get there in time, didn't get to him in time. He's dead."

"No, he's not." The room swam in front of her eyes. A slow, sick circle of Tuscan yellow walls, colorful sketches, red-and-white-checked cloths. Dean Martin was singing "Volare" in his creamy baritone.

"No, he's not. What's wrong with you, saying that?"

"It was an accident, some kind of horrible accident." Tears rolled fat down Gina's cheeks. "Reena. Oh, Reena."

"You're wrong. There's a mistake. I'll call him and you'll see. I'll call him right now."

But when she turned, Xander was there, smelling of flour, like her father. His arms came hard around her. "Come on, come into the back with me. Mia, call Pete, tell him we need him in here."

"No, let go. I have to call."

"You come and sit." He snatched the water pitcher before she dropped it, shoved it at Mia.

"He's coming to dinner. He might even have left already. Traffic—" She began to shake as Xander pulled her into the prep room.

"Sit down. Do what I tell you. Gina, are you sure? There's no mistake?"

"I heard from Jen. A friend of hers lives in the same building. She—her friend lives right down the hall from Josh. They took her to the hospital." Gina wiped at tears with the back of her hand. "She's going to be all right, but she had to go to the hospital. Josh . . . It started in his apartment, that's what they said. They couldn't get to him before . . . It was on the news, too. My mother heard it on the news."

She sat down at Reena's feet, laid her head in Reena's lap. "I'm sorry, I'm so sorry."

"When?" Reena stared straight ahead, saw nothing now. Nothing but gray, like smoke. "When did it happen?"

"I'm not sure. Last night."

"I need to go home."

"I'm going to take you in a minute. Here." Xander handed her a glass of water. "Drink this."

She took the glass, stared at it. "How? Did they say how it started?"

"They think he must've been smoking in bed, fell asleep."

"That's not right. He doesn't smoke. That's not right."

"We'll worry about that later. Gina, call my mother, and can you wait here until Pete gets down? We're going home, Reena. We'll go out the back."

"He doesn't smoke. Maybe it wasn't him. They made a mistake."

"We'll find out. We'll call John. When we get home," Xander said as he drew her to her feet. "We're going to go home now."

The sunlight and June heat struck her. Somehow she was walking, putting one foot in front of the other, but she couldn't feel her legs.

She heard children playing as she turned the corner, calling out to one another the way children do. And car radios, turned up loud, to stream music out as cars drove by. And her brother's voice murmuring to her.

She'd always remember Xander taking her home, both of them still wearing their aprons. Xander smelling of flour. The sun was bright and hurt her eyes, and his arm stayed strong and firm around her waist. There were some little girls playing jacks on the sidewalk, and another sitting on the white marble steps holding an intense conversation with her Barbie doll.

Opera—*Aida*—poured out of an open window and sounded like tears. She didn't cry. Gina's tears had been so big, so fast, but her own eyes felt painfully dry.

Then there was Mama, rushing out of their house, leaving the door open wide behind her. Mama, running down the sidewalk to her, as she had once when she fell off her bike and sprained her wrist.

And when her mother's arms came around her, tight, tight, tight, it all became real. Standing on the sidewalk, held by her mother and brother, Reena drowned in tears.

She was put to bed, and her mother stayed with her through the next storm of tears. And was there when she awoke from a thin and headachy sleep.

"Did John call? Did he come?"

"Not yet." Bianca stroked Reena's hair. "He said it would take some time."

"I want to go see. I want to go see for myself."

"And what did he say about that?" Bianca asked gently.

"That I shouldn't." Her own voice sounded thin to her ears, as if she'd been sick a very long time. "That they wouldn't let me go inside. But—"

"Be patient, *cara.* I know it's hard. Try to sleep a little more. I'll stay with you."

"I don't want to sleep. It could be a mistake."

"We'll wait. It's all we can do. Fran went to church to light a candle and pray so I could stay with you."

"I can't pray. I can't think of words."

"It's not the words, you know that."

Reena angled her head, saw the rosary her mother held. "You always have the words."

"If you need words, you can say them with me. We'll start a rosary." She put the dangling crucifix in Reena's hand. Taking a breath, Reena crossed herself with it, then moved up to the first tiny bead.

"I believe in God, the Father Almighty, Creator of heaven and earth."

They prayed the rosary, her mother's quiet voice blending with hers. But she couldn't pray for Josh's soul, or the grace to accept God's will. She prayed it was a mistake. She prayed she'd somehow wake up and find it all a horrible dream.

When Gib came to the bedroom door, he saw his daughter lying with her head in his wife's lap. Bianca still held the rosary, but she was singing softly now—one of the cradle songs she'd sung to all the children when they were fretful at night.

Her eyes met his, and he knew she saw what was in his because grief passed over her face.

"John's here." He waited, felt the pang when Reena turned her head, looked at him with such naked hope. "Do you want him to come up, baby?"

Reena's lips trembled. "It's true?"

He said nothing, just crossed to her, laid his lips on her head.

"I'll come down. I'll come down now."

He was waiting in the living room with Xander and Fran. If she'd read sorrow on her father's face, it was grim sympathy she saw in John's. She would stand it, somehow she would stand it, because there was nothing else to be done.

"How?" It came out in a croak, and she shook her head before he could speak. "Thank you. Thank you for doing this, for coming to talk to me. I—"

"Shh." He stepped forward to take her hands. "Let's all sit down."

"I made coffee." Fran busied herself pouring. "Reena, I got you a Pepsi. I know you don't like coffee, so . . ." She stopped, lifted her hands helplessly. "I didn't know what else to do."

"You did just fine." Bianca led Reena to a chair. "Please, sit, John. Reena needs to know whatever you can tell her."

He pulled his thumb and finger down his nose, sat. "I spoke with the company officer, and the investigator called in, and some of the firefighters, and the police. The fire's being considered accidental, caused by a cigarette."

"But he didn't smoke. Did you tell them I said he didn't smoke?"

"I went over that with them, Reena. People who don't smoke habitually might have a cigarette from time to time. Maybe someone left a pack at his place."

"But he *never* smoked. I—I *never* saw him smoke."

"He was alone in the apartment, with no sign of forced entry. He was . . . It appears he'd been sitting or lying in bed, possibly reading or writing. A dropped cigarette on the mattress. The point of origin and the progress of the fire is pretty clear and straightforward. Started with a smoldering fire, in the mattress, caught the sheets. He must've woken up, been dazed and confused by the smoke. He fell, honey. Fell or rolled out of bed, taking the sheets with him. It worked as a trailer. The, ah, medical examiner will be running tests, and the fire examiner will take another look as a professional courtesy, but at this point there's no reason to suspect it was anything but a tragic accident."

"They'll look for drugs. Do a tox screen looking for drugs or alcohol. He didn't do drugs, and he didn't drink all that much. And he didn't smoke. What time did the fire start?"

"Around eleven-thirty last night."

"I was with him. At his apartment. I was there until nearly ten. I went there with him after the wedding. We—I'm sorry, Daddy—we made love. He asked if I could stay the night because his roommate was out of town, but I thought I should be home. If I'd stayed—"

"You don't know anything would have happened differently if you'd stayed," John interrupted. "You don't smoke."

"No."

"Odds are he knew that, and it's possible he didn't want to smoke around you."

"Did you examine the scene? Did you—"

"Reena, it's out of my jurisdiction. It's Prince George's County, and the people in charge are competent. I took a look at the scene pictures, the sketches, the reports—again because they gave me professional courtesy. I'd have come to the same conclusions on this. Honey, you've dealt with arson firsthand, and you know about malicious fire-setting. But you're studying this kind of investigating and you know that sometimes this sort of tragedy is just an accident."

"Pastorelli—"

"Is in New York. Just to cover bases, I asked the local cops to check. He was in Queens last night. He's got a job as a night janitor, and it looks like it checks out. He couldn't have been in Maryland and gotten back to New York to clock in at twelve-oh-six. Which he did."

"So it just . . . happened? Why does that make it worse?"

"You're looking for answers, and there aren't any."

"No." She stared down at her hands and felt a little piece of her heart break off and shrivel to dust. "Sometimes the answers aren't the ones you're looking for."

# 8

How tough could it be? Reena circled the innocuous-looking trailer, dubbed "the maze." Maybe it had earned an almost mythical rep within the department, but it didn't strike fear in her heart. Sure, she'd heard the stories, the jokes, the warnings about what a recruit faced inside that box, but really, wasn't it just a matter of staying focused?

She'd handled the training in burn buildings right here at the Academy. She'd dealt with the physical stress. Climbing ladders, rappelling walls— in full gear. She'd worked shifts—mostly ride-alongs, true—but she'd done stints as a nozzleman in two residential fires.

And manning a live hose wasn't for the weak or the faint of heart.

She was a cop now, wasn't she? And proud to wear the uniform. But if she wanted to climb up to arson investigator, to carry a shield for that unit, she wanted to understand fire from the inside out. Until she could do what a firefighter did, until she *had* done it, she wouldn't meet her personal goal.

Not just in the lab, not just simulations. She wouldn't be satisfied with less than hands-on.

She was in good shape, she reminded herself. She'd worked hard to sculpt muscle onto a bony frame. The kind that could carry her in full turnout gear up and down five stories at a jog.

She'd earned this rite of passage, and the respect she'd gain from the men and women on the front line of the battle with fire.

"You don't have to do this, you know."

She turned, looked at John Minger. "Yeah, I do. For me. And it's more to the point that I can do it."

"Hell of a way to spend a pretty Saturday morning."

He had her there. But this was her mission, and in a way she couldn't explain, her reward.

"Sun'll still be shining when I get out. Birds'll still be singing." But she'd be different. At least she hoped. "I'll be okay, John."

"You're not, your mother's going to have my head." He shifted his stance, studied the maze. He was nearing sixty.

The squint lines around his eyes were deep.

He trusted the girl, had a father's pride in her accomplishments and her dogged pursuit of her goals. But with pride came concern.

"I've never seen anyone train as hard as you."

Surprise flickered over her face, an instant before her smile. "That's nice to hear."

"You've crammed a lot into these past few years, Reena. The training, the study, the work." And he wondered if what had lit in her eleven years before had gone active and hot the day the boy she'd cared for died in a fire. "You move fast."

"Any reason I should move slow?"

Hard to explain to a girl of twenty-two how much life there was, not just to live but to savor. "You're young yet, hon."

"I can handle the maze, John."

"I'm not just talking about the maze."

"I know." She kissed his cheek. "That was a metaphor for the life I'm heading into. It's what I want. What I've always wanted."

"Well, you've made plenty of sacrifices to get it."

She didn't think of it that way. Summers spent working, studying, training were investments in the future. Added to it was the rush, the adrenaline spill she experienced when she put on her uniform, or when she heard someone call her Officer Hale. The heart-hammering, stomach-tightening thrill she knew when she was surrounded by fire, pitched in that battle.

Or the absolute exhaustion that came after the war.

She'd never be Fran, serenely content to run a restaurant, or Bella, juggling salon appointments and luncheons.

"I need this, John."

"Yeah, I know that, too." Hands in pockets, he nodded toward the maze. "Okay. It's rugged in there, Reena. You don't want to go in cocky."

"I won't. I'll just come out cocky. Here come a couple of smoke eaters." She lifted a hand in greeting, and regretted she hadn't bothered with makeup.

Steve Rossi, dark and wiry with eyes like a cocker spaniel, was Gina's current hot item. That simmer had been coming to a boil since Reena had introduced them six weeks before. But his companion, the buff, bronzed Adonis in jeans and a BFD T-shirt, had a great many possibilities.

She'd shared a meal with Hugh Fitzgerald—and a kitchen full of other firefighters—at the station. They'd played poker, had a couple of beers. And, after some major league flirting, had done the pizza and a movie routine, followed by several very juicy kisses.

Even so, it seemed to her that more than half the time he thought of her as one of the guys.

Hell, in turnout gear and Fire Line boots, *she* thought of herself as one of the guys.

"Hey," she said to Steve, "what did you do with my roommate?"

"She's sleeping like a baby. Couldn't budge her to come out for this. You up for it?"

"Ready to go." She looked at Hugh. "Did you come to watch?"

"Just finished my shift, thought I'd swing by in case you need CPR."

She laughed, began to don her turnout gear, stepping into the protective pants, adjusting the suspenders. "The two of you got through it, so can I."

"No doubt about it," Hugh agreed. "You're as tough as they come."

Not exactly the sort of description a woman pined for from a potential lover, Reena thought. But if you were going to work in the boys' club, you often ended up one of the boys. She tied her long, curly hair back into a tail, donned her hood.

No, she'd never have the innate femininity of her sisters, but, by God, she'd have a firefighter's certification before the end of summer.

"Maybe we can catch a meal after you're done," Hugh suggested.

She fastened her coat, heavy in the heat of August, and lifted her eyes. His were like lake water, she thought, somewhere fascinating between blue and gray. "Sure. You buying?"

"You get through the maze, I spring." After helping her on with her tank, he gave her shoulder a friendly pat. "You bail, you buy."

"Deal." She sent him a smile as sunny as the day, put on her mask and helmet.

"Radio check," John ordered.

She checked her radio, her gear, gave John a thumbs-up.

"I'll be guiding you through," he reminded her. "Remember to regulate your breathing. Panic's what gets you in trouble."

She wouldn't panic. It was a test, just another simulation. She breathed steady and normal, waited for John to click his stopwatch. "Go."

It was dark as a tomb and hot as the seventh layer of hell. It was fantastic. Thick black smoke smothered the air so she could hear her own breath, wheezing just a little as she drew oxygen from her tank. She oriented herself, put the points of the compass in her head before she felt her way along, hands, feet, instinct. Found a door.

She eased through it. Already, sweat slicked over her face.

There was some sort of blockage. She tried to see it through her gloved fingers, located the low, narrow gap and bellied under.

There could be people trapped inside. That was the purpose of this exercise. She was to search the "building," find any survivors or victims and work her way out again. Do the job. Save lives. Stay alive.

She heard John's voice, strange and foreign in this black hole, asking for her status.

"Good. Fine. Five-by-five."

She felt her way up a wall, then was forced to squeeze through a narrow opening. She was losing her bearings, paused to try to orient herself again.

Slow, steady, she ordered herself. Get in, get through, get out.

But there was nothing but black and smoke and unspeakable heat.

She dead-ended, felt the first trickle of panic in her throat, heard it in her quick, gasping breaths.

John's voice told her to keep calm, to keep centered. Watch her breathing.

Then the floor dropped away beneath her.

She grunted on impact, lost her breath, felt her control slip another notch.

She was blind, and for a terrifying moment, she was deaf as the blood buzzed in her ears. Sweat was rivers now, pouring off her face, down her body under the smothering turnout suit. Her gear weighed a thousand pounds, and the mask was gagging her.

Buried alive, she thought. She was buried alive in smoke. Survivors? No one could survive this suffocating black hell.

For a moment, she fought a desperate need to rip away the gear, free herself.

"Reena, check your breathing. I want you to slow your breathing and give me your status."

*I can't.* The words were nearly out. She couldn't do it. How could anyone do it? How could she *think* when she couldn't see or breathe, when every muscle in her body was screaming from the strain? She wanted to claw her way out, through the floor, the walls. Just get out into the light, into the air.

Her throat was on fire.

Had it been like this for Josh? Tears burned her eyes now because she could see him. No compass points in her mind now, but that sweet face, that shy smile, that curtain of hair when he dipped his head. Had he been conscious long enough to be blinded and choked by the smoke before the fire took him? Had he panicked like this, struggling, struggling to find enough air to call for help?

Oh God, had he known what was coming?

That, of course, was one reason she was here, in this hideous hole of heat and misery. To know what it was like. To understand. And to survive it.

She got shakily to her hands and knees. She wasn't dying, she told herself, even if it seemed like she was in her own coffin.

"I'm okay. Hit one of the drop floors. I'm okay. Moving on."

She pulled herself up, crawled. There was no sense of direction now, just movement. Another door, another dead end.

How could the place be so damn big?

She climbed through a window opening. Every muscle trembled now and poured sweat like water. Time and space clogged. Her eyes strained to see—to see anything. Light, shape, shadow.

Smoke and disorientation, panic and fear. They killed as insidiously as the burn. Fire wasn't just flame, hadn't she learned that? It was smoke and vapor, weakened floors, caving ceilings. It was smothering, blinding panic. It was exhaustion.

She hit another drop floor—the same one?—and was too tired to curse.

She felt another wall. What sadist had designed this thing? she wondered. She pushed her body through yet another opening, found yet another door.

And opening it, stumbled out into the light.

Dragging down her mask, she pulled in air, braced her hands on her knees as her head spun.

"Nice job," John told her, and she managed to lift her head enough to see his face.

"Nearly broke a few times in there."

"Nearly doesn't count."

"Taught me something."

"What's that, hon?"

She took the bottle of water he offered, drank like a camel. "Any doubts I had about going into investigation instead of smoke eating have been put to rest. That's not how I want to spend my time."

He helped her off with her tank, patted her on the back. "You did good."

She drank again, then set the bottle on the ground to once again brace hands on knees. A shadow crossed her, bringing her head up again as Hugh joined her. He mimicked her position, grinned into her face.

She grinned back, and though she heard her own breath huffing, felt the laugh bubble out. One as much from relief as triumph.

He laughed with her, and caught her helmet when she shoved it off.

"She's a bitch, isn't she?"

"A big one."

"Looks like I'm out the price of the breakfast special at Denny's."

She laughed again, and let her head dangle between her knees.

T hen I get inside, into the showers, and see myself in the mirror." Reena winced, shifted the shopping bag—a score from the personal reward of an afternoon at White Marsh Mall with Gina. "My hair is nothing but frizzy strings smelling of sweat. My face is black from the smoke. And I stink. Seriously stink."

"He still asked you out," Gina reminded her.

"More or less." She paused, distracted by a pair of sexy red shoes in a display window. "Breakfast at Denny's, and we had some laughs. And we're going to go hit some balls tomorrow. It's not that I don't like an hour in the batting cages, Gina, but I wouldn't mind a fancy dinner now and then. The kind where I could justify buying those shoes."

"Oh, they're fabulous. You have to."

As was her duty as best friend, Gina dragged Reena into the store.

"They're eighty-seven dollars," Reena said as she looked at the price on the sole.

"They're shoes. They're sexy, *red* shoes. They have no price."

"They do on a rookie cop's salary. But I want them. They should be mine." Reena clutched the shoe to her breast. "No one else should have them. But they're just going to sit in my closet."

"So?"

"You're right." She found a clerk, gave him the shoe and her size, then sat with Gina and their bags. "They'll be my reward for surviving the maze. And don't say the outfit I just bought was supposed to be my reward."

"Why would I?" And the genuine surprise in Gina's voice had Reena grinning. "That was your reward twenty minutes ago. This is your current reward."

"I love you."

She cocked her head to look at her friend. Gina had let her hair grow, and it was now a tumbled mass of ebony waves. "You look all dewy."

"I feel all dewy." Gina hunched her shoulders up, wrapped herself in a hug. "Steve is all . . . He's tough and strong and sweet and smart. Reena, he's the one."

"*The* one?"

"And only. I'm going to marry him."

"You— Gina! When? We've been shopping over an hour, and you just drop this now?"

"He hasn't asked me yet. But I'll work him around to it," she added with an airy wave. "I think we should get married next May. Or maybe wait until September. I'm thinking maybe September because then I could use all those wonderful fall colors. You'd look great in burnt gold. Or russet."

It was, in Reena's mind, a big leap from hot guy to choosing bridal colors. But she could see Gina was taking it in stride. "You really want to get married."

"I really do. I know it might be hard, a firefighter's wife." She dug a box of spearmint Tic Tacs out of her bag, shook some out, offered them to Reena. "The hours are so long, and the work's so dangerous. But he makes me so happy. Oooh, red shoes. Put them on!"

Obediently, Reena slipped on the shoes the clerk brought her. She stood, testing them out, admiring them in the low mirror.

She was trying on red shoes she couldn't afford and would probably never wear. Gina was planning a future. Even while she preferred the shoes, there was a little clutch of envy in her belly.

"Is Steve thinking about marriage?"

"No, not yet. I wasn't until this morning when he came in and kissed me good-bye. I thought, Oh my God, I'm in love, and I can see myself waking up every morning with this guy. I never saw that with anyone before. You're buying those shoes, Reene. I give you no choice."

"Well, in that case." She sat, took them off again. And gulped when she took out her beleaguered credit card to pay. "I'm being irresponsible."

"No, you're being a girl. It's okay."

"I'm compensating." She sighed at herself. "I know it. My best friend's in love and I can't even get a serious date."

"Oh, you can, too. Look at you! You're all tanned and toned and beautiful. It takes you under five minutes to slap yourself together in the morning. It takes me an hour, if I'm lucky."

"I'm putting on a uniform," Reena reminded her. "No-brainer wardrobe-wise." She shook her head. "I'm stopping this right now. I really like Steve, that's what I should be saying. And if he doesn't have the good sense to snap you up quick, he needs a good butt kicking."

"Thanks."

"Maybe I'll ask Hugh out to a fancy dinner. Except, oh God, I just spent ninety-one dollars and thirty-five cents on shoes."

"We'll all go out to dinner. I'll get Steve to fix it."

"There's my best friend in the world."

"Which means I get to borrow your new shoes."

"They're a full size too big for you."

"Like that matters. You know, you could ask Hugh to Fran's wedding."

"It's not till October." Reena gathered her bags and ordered herself not to spend another penny in the mall. "I may be done with him by then."

"Slut."

"Oh, if only. I freely admit I'm not looking for Mr. Right. I'm not even sure I want Mr. Right Now. It's just that this one has such a body. And we definitely have a little heat going."

They strolled out of the store, into the throng of Saturday shoppers. "I'm not dewy," Reena added.

"You look moist and tasty to me."

"Oh, I am. I am, but not dewy. Not love dewy." She stopped by another display window. "Not the way you're looking today, or the way Fran's looked every day since she met Jack."

"He's such a sweetie."

"He really is, and perfect for her. They're going to be ridiculously happy. I don't think I want to meet the perfect guy yet. What would I do with him?"

"Be ridiculously happy?"

Reena shook her head. "I don't know. I've got things I need to do first. The perfect guy and dewy love would just get in the way."

D ragging his feet didn't do a damn bit of good, but Bo dragged them anyway.

"I don't wanna go shopping. I don't wanna."

"Oh, quit your whining." Mandy used her hand on his arm like a shackle as she pulled him along. "Are you, or are you not, my best pal and sometime booty buddy?"

"Why am I being punished? Why would you drag your best pal and sometime booty buddy into the hell of a Saturday mall?"

"Because I need this birthday present today. How was I supposed to know the last couple of weeks would be insanely busy and I'd forget about the surprise party tonight? Oh! Look at that outfit."

"No! No outfits. You promised."

"I lied. See, that color green's made for me and me alone. And look how the jacket's cut. I'm on staff at *The Sun* now. I have to dress like a professional. Just going to try it on. Two seconds."

He mimed a gun to his head, then a rope around his neck as she dashed off to the dressing room.

He could run, he considered. He could just run away. There wasn't a man in the world who would blame him.

But, of course, he needed a present, too, for their mutual friend's stupid-ass surprise party. Mandy had stomped on his notion of just picking up a bottle of wine on his way to the celebration.

But she could buy the gift, and he'd go halves. What was wrong with that?

Where the hell was she? What was taking so long?

"It's perfect." Mandy all but sang it as she danced back to Bo with her shopping bag. "I'm going to wear it tonight. I just need to find the right shoes."

"I'll kill you where you stand."

"Oh, stop." She gave his hand a pat with a hand glittering with four rings. The eyebrow ring was history. Bo sort of missed it. "You can sit in the food court while I find shoes. Present first, though. Before my credit card starts smoking."

She pulled him out of the department store, into the belly of the beast. Everything echoed, everything moved. Bo thought, not fondly, of the House of Horrors he'd paid five bucks to endure at the age of twelve.

"What do you think? Fun or practical?"

"I don't care. Just buy something and get me out of here."

Mandy strolled, like a woman who not only knew her ground, but who would be content to hike over it for hours. Possibly days.

"Candles maybe. Some big, fancy candles. That's sort of fun and practical."

She started to sound like Charlie Brown's mother to him. Just a nasal *wah-wah-wah*. He loved her, he really did, but he imagined Charlie Brown loved his mother, too. It didn't make her any more comprehensible.

He thought maybe he could try praying, and cast his eyes up.

Sound cut off. Voices, piped music, whining children, giggling girls.

His vision telescoped, as it had once before. He saw her with perfect clarity.

She was standing on the second level, arms loaded with bags, that mass of dark gold curls spilling over her shoulders. His heart did one long, slow roll in his chest.

Maybe some prayers were answered before you thought to ask.

He started to run, trying to keep her in sight.

"Bo! Bowen!" Mandy shouted, sprinting after him. She caught him after he'd narrowly missed plowing into a thicket of teenagers.

"What is *wrong* with you?"

"It's her." He couldn't quite get his breath, couldn't quite feel his own feet. "She's here. Up there. I saw her. Where's the damn stairs?"

"Who?"

"*Her.*" He spun a circle, saw stairs and ran for them with Mandy at his heels. "Dream Girl."

"Here?" Her voice spiked up with surprise and interest. "Really? Where? Where?"

"She was just . . ." He stopped at the top of the steps, panting like a hound on the hunt. "She was there, down there."

"Blonde, right?" She'd heard the story often enough, and craned her neck, searching through the crowds. "Curly hair. Tallish, slim?"

"Yeah, yeah. She's wearing a blue shirt. Um . . . without sleeves, with a collar. Damn it, where'd she go? This can't be happening again."

"We'll split up. You go that way, I'll go this way. Long hair, short?"

"Long, loose, over her shoulders. She had bags. A lot of shopping bags."

"I like her already."

But twenty minutes later, they met up at the same spot.

"I'm sorry, Bo. Really."

Disappointment and frustration fought such a vicious war inside him, he was almost sick from it. "I can't believe I saw her again and couldn't get to her."

"Are you sure it was the same girl? It's been, what, four years."

"Yeah. I'm sure."

"Well, look at it this way. You know she's still around. You're going to see her again." Mandy gave him a little squeeze. "I just know it."

# 9

Sexy red shoes aside, Reena could think of little more entertaining on a Sunday afternoon than a turn in the batting cage. Sunshine, baseball and a really cute guy to share them with.

Who could complain?

She adjusted her helmet, moved into her stance, and took a hard cut at the ball that flew toward her. It sailed up and out.

"I gotta say, Hale. You've got nice form."

She smiled, kicked dirt, prepared to bat again. Maybe she'd prefer the form he was admiring was her body rather than her batting prowess, but her competitive streak wouldn't allow her to bat like a girl.

"Damn right," she agreed and swung away. "Easy right-field shag on that one."

"Depends on the fielder." Hugh took his own swing. Ball cracked against bat. "There's a double."

"Depends on the runner."

"Shit." But he laughed and slammed the next ball.

"Speaking of form, yours isn't half bad either. You ever play?"

"High school." He caught one on a foul tip. "Company's got a softball team. I ride second."

"I usually take left field if I pick up a game."

"You got the legs for it."

"Ran track in high school." She'd been advised to learn how to run, so she had.

She took her turn again, cut too soon and took a strike. "I thought about keeping up with it in college, but my course load was too heavy. So I bookwormed it. Gotta keep your eye on the ball," she said half to herself, and swung away.

"Now that one's out of here. We ought to take in a game sometime, at Camden Yards."

She glanced over, smiled. "Absolutely."

When he mentioned grabbing a beer and some bar food, she nearly suggested they head over to Sirico's. Not yet, she decided. She wasn't quite ready to have him eyeballed by family, or the neighborhood.

They settled on a Ruby Tuesday's, and shared nachos and Coors.

"So, where'd you learn to swing a bat?"

"Mmm." She licked melted cheese off her thumb. "My father, mostly. He loves the game. We always managed to get to a few a year when we were kids."

"Yeah, you got a big family, right?"

"Two older sisters, younger brother. Brother-in-law, niece and nephew courtesy of middle sister. Brother-in-law coming up thanks to oldest sister. She's getting married this fall. Aunts, uncles, cousins too numerous to mention—and that's just first cousins. How about you?"

"Three older sisters."

"Really?" Points on the mutual ground scorecard, she decided. He wouldn't be cowed by a large family. "And you're the prince."

"Bet your ass." He grinned, toasting her. "They're married. Got five kids between them."

"What do your sisters do?"

He looked blank for a moment. "About what?"

"Work."

"They don't. They're, you know, housewives."

She cocked her eyebrows at him as she took another sip of beer. "I hear that's work."

"Couldn't pay me enough to do it, so yeah, guess so. Your family's got that restaurant, Sirico's. Great pizza."

"Best in Baltimore. Starting on the third generation there. My sister Fran's co-manager now. And her Jack—the guy she's marrying's tossing dough. You're second generation on the job, right?"

"Third. My dad's still on. Making noises about retiring, but I don't know. Gets in you."

She thought about the maze, and the fact that she wanted to do it again. Do it faster, do it better. "I know it does."

"He's fifty-five, though. People—civilians—don't really understand the physical stress of it."

"Or the emotional, the psychological."

"Well, yeah, that, too." He sat back, giving her a long study. "You handle yourself, physically. The maze isn't for wimps. And you worked the burn buildings, stuck it out through a couple of tough shifts. You've got a good build, like a—what is it?—greyhound."

She may have hit a dry spell in the dating pool, but she still remembered how to flirt. "Wondered if you'd notice."

She liked his grin, the quickness of it, the cockiness. The grin said he was a man who knew just who he was, what he was and what he was after.

He flashed it now. "I noticed. Especially when you're wearing those little shorts running track at the Academy. Anyway, most women can't manage the physical part of it."

"A lot of men can't either."

"No question. No sexist line." He held up a hand. "What I'm saying is you're one of the few women I've seen who make the cut. You've got the stamina, the instincts, the brains. And you don't lack guts either. So I wonder why you're not signing on."

She picked at another nacho. He wasn't one to heap on praise, she knew. So she took his observations seriously and gave him a serious answer. "I've thought about it, and I get caught up in it sometimes. During training, or when I'm working a shift. But fighting fires isn't what pulls me. It has to pull you. Knowing how they work, why. Figuring how they start, why, who starts them. That's my thing. Running into a burning building takes a singular kind of courage and drive."

"Seen you do it," he pointed out.

"Yeah. Well, yeah, I needed to do it, to see how it's done. But it's not my life's work. It's going into that building after, putting it together and finding the why."

"The department has fire inspectors. Minger's one of the best."

"Yeah. I considered going that direction. John's, well, he's one of my major heroes. But . . . there's something else a lot of people, a lot of civilians, don't understand. Arson. What it does, not just to property. What an incendiary fire can do to people, to a neighborhood, to business, to economy. To a city."

She lifted a dripping nacho, shrugged to lighten things up. "So that's my mission in life. You fight them, Fitzgerald. I'll do the cleanup."

He wasn't a hand holder, she noted, but he walked her to her door. And once he had, backed her right up against it for another of those lush, out-of-nowhere kisses.

"It's early yet," he said when he lifted his head.

"It is." And it annoyed her that a couple of casual dates made it *too* early for her personal gauge. "But . . ."

He winced, but those foggy lake eyes held humor. "I had a feeling you were going to say that. Want to try to catch a game this week?"

"Yeah, I'd like that."

"I'll call you, we'll set it up." He started to walk away, turned back, kissed her again. "You've got great lips."

"I like yours, too."

"Listen, do you have any vacation time coming?"

"I can probably squeeze out a day in addition to my off days. Why?"

"We've got this place down on the Outer Banks. Old beach cottage. It's not bad. We could take a couple days down there next time I'm off if you can work it. Hook Steve and Gina into it."

"A couple days at the beach? When do we leave?"

He flashed that grin again. "We'll juggle the schedules, get it set up."

"I'll start packing."

She let herself in, did a little victory dance around the tiny living room. The beach, hot guy, good friends. Life was currently just excellent.

Too good, in fact, to stay in an empty apartment on a summer evening. She grabbed her keys again and went back out.

She caught the tail of Hugh's car turning left at the corner, and absently noted the car that turned behind him. She kissed her fingers in his direction, then set off the opposite way to walk to Sirico's.

It was good to be back in the neighborhood. She'd enjoyed her time in the group house, and she'd liked the broom closet she'd been able to finesse during her training at the Shady Grove campus west of Baltimore. But this was home.

The row houses with their white steps or little porches, pots of flowers on stoops or Italian flags flying from rooftop poles.

There was always someone around to call out a greeting.

She took her time, admired some of the murals painted on window screens and wondered if she should ask her mother to do one for her and Gina. Probably needed to run that one by the landlord, but since it was Gina's second cousin, she doubted it would be an issue.

She detoured half a block to watch a few minutes of a boccie game between old men in colorful shirts.

Why hadn't she thought to ask Hugh if he wanted to stroll down, check out some of the local color?

What she should do is ask him, casually, if he wanted to take in the open-air movie on Friday night. It was a neighborhood tradition. Movie night meant live music, too—which could lead to dancing. She might put those red shoes to use, after all.

She'd think about that, maybe make it a double with Gina and Steve. But for now, she might as well enjoy the rest of her evening.

She reminded herself that Sunday nights were busy at Sirico's. If she wanted a few minutes with some of the family before the chaos, she shouldn't linger.

Things were already heating up when she walked in the door of the restaurant. Buzzing conversations, the clatter of cutlery, the phone ringing greeted her when she stepped inside.

Pete was at the pizza counter, her mother at the stove. Fran, along with a couple of the waitstaff her father still called his kids, was manning the tables.

Reena saw her immediate future flash in front of her eyes in the form of an apron and an order pad. She started to call out to Fran, then saw Bella sitting at a table nibbling on some antipasto.

"Hey, stranger." Reena plopped on the other chair at the table. "What are you doing around here?"

"Vince is golfing today. Thought I'd bring the kids by for a while."

"Where are they?"

"Dad and Jack took them for a walk, over to the harbor. Mama called to let you know I was here, but you weren't home."

"Just got back, didn't even check the machine." She reached over, nipped one of the olives from Bella's plate. "Boccie contest is winding down. We're going to be swamped in about a half hour."

"Business is good." Bella gave a little shrug.

She looked amazing, Reena thought. The lifestyle she'd aimed for all of her life suited her. She was polished. Her deep blond hair expertly high-lighted and swept silkily around a face of fine, smooth skin. There was gold and glitter at her ears, on her fingers, around her throat. Subtle and expensive to match the pale rose linen shirt.

"How about you?" Reena asked. "Are you as good as you look?"

A smile flickered around Bella's mouth. "How good do I look?"

"Magazine-cover level."

"Thanks. I've been working on it. It takes time to lose the baby weight, get back in shape. I've got a personal trainer who makes Attila the Hun look like a pansy. But it's worth it."

She held out her wrist to show off the sapphire-and-diamond tennis bracelet. "My reward from Vince for getting back to my pre-Vinny weight."

"Nice. Sparkly."

Bella laughed, gave that little shrug again and toyed with some prosciutto. "Anyway, I came by to try to pigeonhole Fran about the wedding."

"What about it?"

"I just don't see why she insists on having the reception in some dinky hall when she can use our club. I've even got a list of menus, and florists, musicians. She doesn't need to settle when I'm willing to help."

"It's sweet of you." And she meant it. "But I think Fran and Jack want something a little simpler and closer to home. They're simpler, Bella. That's not a criticism," she added, reaching out for her sister's hand when Bella's eyes flashed. "Honestly. Your wedding was spectacular, and gorgeous and absolutely reflected you. Fran's should reflect her."

"I just want to share some of what I've got. What's wrong with that?"

"Absolutely nothing. And you know what? I think you ought to help with the flowers."

Bella blinked in surprise. "Really?"

"You're better at that than Fran and Mama. I think they should let you have your head there, especially if you're willing to help pay for it."

"I would be, but they won't—"

"I'll talk them into it."

Bella sat back. "You could, too. You always could work them around."

"One condition. If Fran wants simple flowers, you don't buy truckloads of exotic orchids or whatever."

"If she wants simple, I can work simple. But stupendously simple. And I can turn that dinky hall into a garden. A cottage garden," she added at Reena's narrowed stare. "Sweet, old-fashioned, romantic."

"Perfect. When my turn comes, I'm hooking you."

"Got any potentials?"

"Not looking for potential husbands. But I've got a potential guy. Fire-fighter."

"Oh. Big surprise."

"Studly," Reena said around another olive. "Excellent mattress possi-bilities."

Bella gave a choked laugh. "I miss you, Reena."

"Aw, honey, I miss you, too."

"I didn't think I would."

Now it was time for Reena to laugh.

"Seriously. I didn't think I'd miss you, or this." She gestured to encom-pass the restaurant. "But I do, sometimes."

"Well, we're always here."


She stayed longer than she'd intended, long after Bella took her children home to her sprawling suburban estate. When business was light enough, she maneuvered her mother and Fran to a table.

"Girl powwow."

"Any excuse to get off my feet." Bianca sat, poured sparkling water all around.

"It's about the wedding, and Bella."

"Oh, don't start." Fran clamped her hands on her ears. Her waves of hair tossed as she shook her head. "I don't want a country club wedding. I don't want a bunch of waiters in tuxedos serving champagne or a damn ice swan."

"Don't blame you. But you do want flowers, right?"

"Well, of course I want flowers."

"Let Bella do them."

"I don't want—"

"Wait. You know the sort of thing you want, you know the colors you want. But Bella knows more. The one thing she has in spades is style."

"I'd be drowning in pink roses."

"No, you wouldn't." Or, Reena thought, she'd personally drown Bella in them directly after the ceremony. "You want a simple wedding, old-fashioned and romantic. She gets that. Okay, she doesn't get why you want that, but understands this is your line. And your day. She wants to help. She wants to feel part of it."

"She *is* part of it." Fran pulled at her hair now while Bianca sat silently. "She's matron of honor."

"She wants to give you something. She loves you."

"Oh, Reena, don't." Fran put her head on the table, banged it lightly. "Don't guilt me into this."

"She's a little bored, feeling a little separate."

"Mama. Help me."

"I'm waiting to hear it all first. To see why Reena's taking your sister's part in this."

"For one, because I think— No, I know she can do this. And at her expense." She jabbed a finger at Fran as Fran's head whipped up and protest covered her face. "A gift from your sister isn't an insult, so just choke that back. She wants to give you your wedding flowers, and she'll want you to be pleased with them, so she won't screw it up. Quick, name five flowers that aren't a rose."

"Um . . . lily, geranium . . . damn it, mums, pansies. This is too much pressure."

"You remember how she hounded those landscapers when she was putting in those gardens, the shrubberies? She knows more than any of us about this, and about coordinating something like this. She said she could do a kind of cottage garden theme. I'm not sure what that is, but it sounds nice."

Fran bit her lip. "I'm not sure exactly what it means either. But it sounds right."

"It would mean a lot to her, and I think when it was done, it would mean a lot to you."

"I could talk to her. Maybe we could go to a florist, or I could go over and look at her gardens again, and she could show me what she means."

"Good." Knowing when to desert the field, Reena slid out of the booth. "I've got to head home." She leaned down, kissed Fran, started to kiss her mother, but Bianca got up.

"I'm going to walk out with you, get some air."

As they went through the door, Bianca put an arm around Reena's waist. "That was unexpected. You're not one to take Bella's side."

"I don't usually agree with her. Plus, my gut tells me there's no way she'd screw this up. It's partly for Fran, part for her own ego. It's a no lose."

"Smart. You've always been my smart one. Why don't we all go look at flowers? The women of Sirico's."

"Okay, sure."

"Now, call me when you get home."

"Mama."

"Just call, so I know you got home safe."

Four and a half blocks, Reena thought as she strolled away. Through my own neighborhood. A trained police officer.

But she called when she got home.


Being a rookie cop meant Reena was at the bottom of the department food chain. The fact that she'd graduated in the top five percent of her class didn't hold a lot of water once she was in uniform and on patrol.

That was fine. She'd been taught to earn her way.

And she liked patrolling. She liked being able to talk to people, to try to help solve problems or disputes.

She and her partner, a ten-year man named Samuel Smith, responded to a report of a disturbance on West Pratt in the southwest part of the city the locals called Sowebo.

"Thought we were going to hit Krispy Kreme," Smithy complained as he turned in the direction of the call.

"How do you eat all those doughnuts and not put on weight?"

"Cop blood." He winked at her. He was six-four, and a stone-solid two-twenty. His skin was walnut, his eyes sharp and black. Out of uniform he'd have looked intimidating. In it, he looked ferocious.

It was a comfort to someone in her first year on the force to be part-nered with someone built like a truck. And as a Baltimore native, he knew the city as well as—or better than—she did.

She could see the crowd on the sidewalk as they turned down the block. This area ran more to art galleries and historic homes than the street brawl she realized was in progress.

Indeed most of the people watching the two men roll around on the asphalt were dressed in style—a lot of bold colors and New York black.

She got out with Smithy, moved with him through the crowd.

"Break it up, break it up." Smithy's voice boomed, and people flowed back. But the two men kept pummeling each other. And not very skillfully, Reena noted.

Designer shoes were getting scuffed, and the Italian-cut jackets were going to be trash, but there wasn't much blood.

She reached down, as Smithy did, to pull them apart. "Police. Cut it out."

She had her hands on the smaller of the two, and he rolled when she gripped his arm. His other came up, fist clenched. She saw the swing coming, had a moment to think, Shit, and blocked it with her forearm.

Using his momentum, she shoved him over on his face, then yanked his hands behind his back. "You swing at me? You're going to take a punch at me?" She cuffed him while he rocked his body like an upturned turtle. "That'll get you popped for assaulting an officer."

"He started it."

"What are you, twelve?"

She pulled him upright. His face was a little scraped up, and she judged him to be mid-twenties. His opponent, in basically the same shape, and of approximately the same age, sat on the ground where Smithy put him.

"Did you take a swing at my partner?" Smithy pointed to the second man. "Stay," he ordered and stepped up into the first man's face. It was like a redwood towering over a sapling. "Did your dumb ass swing at my partner?"

"I didn't know she was a cop. I didn't know it was a she. And he started it. You can ask anybody. He started pushing me inside."

"I don't hear an apology." Smithy tapped his ear. "Officer Hale, do you hear an apology out of this dumbass?"

"No, I don't."

"I'm sorry." He didn't look sorry, but he did look mortified, and on the verge of tears. "I didn't mean to hit you."

"You didn't hit me. You punch like a girl. You people go about your business," she ordered the onlookers. "Now, you can tell me your side of it while he tells my partner his. And I don't want to hear you say he started it again."

A woman," Smithy said with a sigh when they drove away. "It's always over a woman."

"Hey, don't blame my breed for the stupidity of yours."

He turned his head, widened his eyes. "You a woman, Hale?"

"Why do I always get the wise guys?"

"You did okay. Handled that fine. You've got good reflexes, and you kept it chilled when he tried to pop you."

"If he'd connected, it might've been a different story." But satisfied with a job well done, she eased back. "You buy the doughnuts."

The apartment was empty when she got home after her shift. A note in Gina's large, flowery hand was stuck to the fridge, along with the snapshot of her extra-large aunt Opal. Gina's deterrent to snacking.

*Out with Steve. We're at the Club Dread if you want to hook*
*up. Hugh may swing by, too.*


*XXXOOO*
*G*


She thought about it, actually stood in the kitchen running through
her head what she could wear. Then she shook her head. She wasn't in the
mood for a noisy club.

She wanted to get out of uniform, stretch out and do some studying.
John passed her old case files, let her go through them and try to determine
accident or incendiary, and the hows and whys.

When she moved to the arson unit, those hours of reconstruction
would come in handy.

Instead, she wandered into the bedroom. The reflection in the mirror
caught her eye, made her stop, study herself.

Maybe she didn't look particularly female in the uniform, but she liked
the image she projected. Authority and confidence. Though there'd been
a moment on the street today when she'd gotten a jolt, actively realized
how easy it could be to be hurt. Even just a fist to the face.

But she'd handled herself. Having Smithy say so meant a great deal.

Even if she considered herself more at home with books and files
and study, she could handle herself on the street. She was learning to,
anyway.

She took off her cap, put it on the dresser. Unclipped her weapon and
laid it down. Unbuttoning her uniform shirt, she frowned at the serviceable
white cotton bra.

She was going on another shopping trip, she decided on the spot. For
sexy underwear. Nothing in the regulations about a female officer's underwear. And knowing she had something pretty and female underneath
would be good for her morale.

With that idea in mind, she ran herself a bubble bath, lit candles, poured
a glass of wine.

And read about fire while lounging in the tub.

When the phone rang, she let the machine pick it up.

She listened with half an ear to Gina's bubbly voice inviting the caller to leave a message, then pushed up, sloshing water, as the next voice came on.

"Hello, bitch. All alone? Maybe I'll come see you. Been a while, bet you missed me."

She was up, water guttering out candles. Dripping and naked, she dashed for her weapon, pulled it out of the holster. Gripping it, she yanked on a robe as she hurried toward the door to check the locks.

"Probably a prank," she said aloud to soothe herself with her own voice. "Probably just some asshole."

But she checked the windows, the street below.

Then she played the message back twice. The voice wasn't familiar to her. And the phone didn't ring again.

They didn't make a ball game, or the Friday movie. Her schedule or Hugh's threw them off. But they managed a quick burger at a place near the fire station.

"Gina's packed and unpacked three times," Reena told him. "It's like she's going on safari instead of taking a couple days at the beach."

"Never knew a woman who didn't pack twice what she needs."

"You're looking at one."

He grinned at her, bit into his burger. "Yeah, we'll see about that when you get there. You sure you got the directions okay? I can put off leaving until tomorrow night if you're worried about getting lost."

"I think we can manage it. Sorry I can't leave sooner, but Gina's stuck until tomorrow afternoon anyway. The three of us will cruise on down. We should be there by midnight."

"I'll keep the light on. This works out. Gives me a chance to open the place up. Hasn't been used much this season. And I can stock in some food. I hear you can cook."

"I was born with a saucepan in one hand and a bulb of garlic in the other." Plus she liked cooking, the act and the art. "Why don't you pick up some shrimp? I'll make us some scampi."

"Sounds great. You should make good time. Middle of the week, that late at night. You won't hit much traffic once you're into North Carolina." He glanced at his watch. "I figure I'll hit Hatteras by two in the morning. If I get going."

He hitched up his hip, took out his wallet and tossed bills on the table. "There's no phone at the cottage, but you can call the market in Frisco and they'll get word to me."

"You already explained, Daddy. Don't worry about us."

"Okay." He rose, came over to bend down and kiss her. "Drive safe."

"You, too. See you tomorrow night."

·  ·  ·

*So easy. Pathetically easy. Nobody up and around in bumfuck.*

*Take me home, country roads.*

*Great night, lots of stars but no moon. Just dark enough, just deserted enough. Passed him five miles back, so he'll come right along. Pick your spot, get started.*

*Pull off the side of the road, open the hood. Could set up a flare, for good measure, but some other stupid son of a bitch might stop.*

*Only time for one tonight.*

*Just one.*

*And he'll stop. Oh, that's a given. Do-gooders always stop, the Good Samaritans. Wouldn't be the first you've taken out this way. Probably won't be the last.*

*Got the old rattletrap. Redneck asshole you stole it from will just have to cry in his beer. Got the flashlight. Got the .38.*

*Lean against the hood, whistle a tune. Might as well have a smoke, pass the time. He'll be coming along in a minute.*

*Lights coming, best look helpless. Step out just a little, hold up a hand. If it's not him, just wave them on by. No thanks, I got it, you say. Just got her going again, thanks for stopping!*

*But it's him, all right. Big man in his big blue Bronco. And, predictable as sunrise, pulling over to stop, lend a poor guy a hand.*

*Walk right on up to the door. It's better if he doesn't get out.*

"Hey!" *Big relieved smile, shine the light in his eyes.* "Boy, am I glad to see you."

Hugh shielded his eyes against the glare of the flashlight. "You got trouble?"

"Not anymore." *And raise the gun, shoot him twice in the face.*

*Body jerks like a puppet. A mother wouldn't recognize that face now. Time for the gloves now so you can unbuckle the cocksucker, give him a shove. Now all you have to do is drive this handy four-wheeler into the woods a ways. Not too far. Want him found easy, after all.*

*Flatten one of the tires. Looks like he ran into trouble, and somebody came along and gave him more.*

*Hike on back, get the gas can.*

*Let's see now, we want the wallet, want the watch.*

*Oh no! Poor bastard was robbed and murdered on his way to play at the beach! What an awful tragedy!*

*Gotta laugh. Make it look sloppy, slosh that gas, gouge that upholstery! Pop the hood, light the engine. Get those tires soaked good and proper. Now step back—safety first!*

*And set that bastard on fire.*

*Look at him burn. Just look at him go. The human torch, blazing like a son of a bitch. The first minute's the best, the whoosh and the flash. Amateurs are the ones who have to hang around and watch. It's only the first minute that flashes in, flashes out.*

*Now we just walk away, and drive this rattletrap back toward Maryland. Maybe get us some bacon and eggs for breakfast.*

* * *

It was Steve who brought Reena the news. He came into the precinct, stopped by the desk where she was typing up an incident report. His eyes burned out of a bone-white face.

"Hey, what's up?" She glanced over, stopped typing. "Oh, don't tell me you've got to pull a double and can't go down. I was about to go off shift, head home and pack."

"I . . . Can I have a minute? Private?"

"Sure." She pushed away from the desk as she took a good look at him. Nerves fluttered in her belly. "Something's wrong. Gina—"

"No. No, not Gina."

"Well, what . . . Hugh? Did he have an accident? How bad?"

"No, no accident. It's bad. It's really bad."

She gripped his arm now, pulled him out in the corridor. "What? Say it quick."

"He's dead. Jesus, Reena. He's dead. I just got a call from his mother."

"His mother? But—"

"He was killed. He was murdered—shot."

"Murdered?" Her hand went limp on his arm.

"She was pretty incoherent at first." Steve's mouth thinned, razored as he stared hard over her head. "But I got what I could out of her. Somebody shot him. He was on his way down, just a couple hours from the island, and somebody must have gotten him to stop his car, or ran him off the road, or he had a flat. I'm not sure. She wasn't sure."

He sucked in a breath. "But they shot him, Reena. Jesus, they shot him, then set the car on fire to try to cover it. They took his wallet, his watch. I don't know what else."

There was sickness backing up in her throat, but she swallowed it down. "Have they identified him, positively identified him?"

"He had, ah, stuff in the car, stuff that didn't burn, with his name on it. The registration in the glove box. His parents called me from down there. It's him, Reena. Hugh's dead."

"I'm going to see what I can find out. I'm going to call the locals and see what I can find out."

"They shot him in the face." Steve's voice broke. "His mother told me. They shot him in the fucking face. For a goddamn watch and what was in his wallet."

"Sit down." She nudged him down on a bench, sat beside him, held his hand.

Whatever she found out, she thought, a man—a good man—one she'd kissed good-bye less than twenty-four hours before, was dead.

And once again fire haunted her life.

# CHAIN REACTION

*A series of events so closely related to one another that each one initiates the next.*

*Can a man take fire in his bosom, and his clothes not be burned?*

—PROVERBS 6:27

# 10

Fire sprang out of an untenanted building in South Baltimore on a bitter night in January. Inside, firefighters worked in a holocaust of raging heat and boiling smoke. Outside, they battled temperatures in the single digits, and a frosty wind that blew water into ice and licked flames into torrents.

It was Reena's first day as a member of the city arson unit's task force.

She knew part of the reason she'd bagged the assignment and was working under Captain Brant was because John had pushed a few buttons on her behalf. But it wasn't all the reason. She'd worked like a dog to earn it, studying, training, putting in countless unpaid hours—and had never taken her eye off the goal.

John's influence aside, she'd earned her shiny new shield.

When she could manage it, she continued to give time to the neighborhood's fire department, in the volunteer capacity. She'd eaten her share of smoke.

But it was the cause and effect that continued to drive her. Who or what started the fire? Who was changed by it, grieved by it or benefited from it?

When she and her partner arrived at the scene at dawn, the building was a pit of blackened brick and rubble made fanciful by waterfalls of ice.

She was teamed with Mick O'Donnell, and he had fifteen years on her. He was, Reena knew, old school, but he had what she thought of as a nose.

He smelled out incendiary fires.

He wore a parka and steel-toed boots, with a hard hat over a wool cap. She'd chosen similar garb, and when they arrived on scene at first light, they stood beside the car, one on each side, studying the building.

"Too bad they let buildings like this go to shit." O'Donnell unwrapped two sticks of gum, rolled both into his mouth. "Yuppies aren't coming in to beautify 'round this part of Baltimore yet."

He pronounced it Balmer.

"Circa 1950. Asbestos, plasterboard, ceiling tiles, cheap veneer paneling. Add in the trash heaped around by indigents and junkies, there's a lot of fuel."

She got her field kit out of the trunk, stuffed a digital camera, spare gloves, an extra flashlight in her pockets. She glanced over, noted the black-and-white and the morgue wagon.

"Looks like they haven't transported the body yet."

O'Donnell chewed contemplatively. "You got trouble looking at a crispy critter?"

"No." She'd seen them before. "I'm hoping they haven't moved it yet. I'd like to get my own pictures."

"Starting a scrapbook, Hale?"

She only smiled as they walked to the building. The cops on duty gave them a nod as they ducked under the crime-scene tape.

The fire and its suppression had turned the first level into a wasteland of charred and soaked wood, scorched ceiling tiles, twisted metal and shattered glass. Her preliminary information included the fact that the old building had been a haven for junkies. She knew they'd find needles under the overburden, and drew on her leather gloves for penetration protection.

"You want me to start a grid down here?"

"I'll do that." O'Donnell scanned the scene, took out a notebook to do some sketches. "You're younger than me. You make the climb."

She looked at the ladder standing in place of the stairs that had collapsed. Getting a firmer grip on her kit, she picked her way across, then started up.

Plasterboard, she thought again, studying burn patterns, stopping to take digital shots of the walls, then a bird's-eye view of the first level for the file.

The pattern showed her the fire had traveled up, as it liked best, and washed over the ceiling. Plenty of fuel to feed it, she thought, and enough oxygen to keep it breathing.

A good portion of the second floor had collapsed, and was now part of the overburden O'Donnell would grid. The fire had run along the ceiling here, too, she noted, eating its way through tile, plywood, plasterboard, fueled by it, and the debris left by unofficial tenants.

She saw what was left of an old, overstuffed chair, a metal table. The smooth level of ceiling had allowed the fire to race along, sending the smoke and gases to spread uniformly, in every direction.

And it had taken out the yet-to-be-identified man whose remains were now on the floor, curled, it seemed, inside what had been a closet. A man crouched by him. As it appeared the man had a good yard of leg, it was a long way to crouch.

He was wearing gloves, work boots, a wool cap with ear flaps and a red-checked scarf wrapped multiple times around his neck and chin.

"Hale. Arson unit." Her breath smoked out as she eased onto the edge of the floor.

"Peterson, ME."

"What can you tell me about him?"

"Flash fried." He gave a ghost of a smile, at least his eyes did. He was early forties, by her gauge, tall and black and appeared to be lean as a snake under the layers of winter gear. "Looks like the idiot son of a bitch thought he could get away from the fire by crawling in the closet. Smoke probably got him first, then he cooked. Tell you more when I get him in."

She moved forward cautiously, testing the floor as she went.

The probable suffocation from smoke would have been a mercy, she knew. The body was burned through, lying with its fists raised as fire victims' usually were. The heat contracted the muscles, left them looking as though their last act was to try to box away the flames.

She held up her camera, got his go-ahead nod and took several more shots.

"How come he was the only one in here?" she wondered out loud. "Temps were down to single digits last night. Street people use places like this for shelter, and it had a rep as one for junkies. Preliminary reports said there were blankets, a couple of old chairs, even a little cookstove on the third floor."

Peterson said nothing when she crouched by the body.

"No visible trauma?"

"Not so far. Could find something when I get him in. You're thinking somebody started the fire to cover up a homicide?"

"Wouldn't be the first. But you gotta rule out accident first. Why's he the only one here?" she repeated. "How long before you get an ID— ballpark?"

"Might get some prints. Dental. Few days."

Like O'Donnell, she dug out a notepad, began to make some quick sketches to go with her photos. "What do you figure? Male, about what, five-ten, -eleven? Nobody's been able to reach the owner. Wouldn't it be interesting?"

She began to set up her grid, sectioning off the room in much the same way archaeologists section a dig. She would layer, and she would sift, document and bag.

On the far wall the burn pattern said accelerant to her, just as it had to the fire department's investigator. She took samples, storing them in containers, labeling.

The lightbulb over her head was partially melted. She took another picture, another of the ceiling, and the track of the burn.

And she followed it out, moving over the soaked debris, through the ash. Four units, she thought, putting the pre-fire picture into her head. Untenanted, disrepair, under code.

She ran her gloved fingers over charred wood, down a wall, selected more samples. Then closed her eyes and sniffed at them.

"O'Donnell! Got what looks like multiple points of origin up here. Evidence of accelerant. Plenty of cracks and gaps in this old flooring for it to pool."

She got down on all fours, eased her head over a ragged hole where the floor had crashed down to the level below. O'Donnell had his grid and was working sections.

"I want to check on the owner again, have somebody in the house get us some background."

"Your call."

"You want to take a look at the pattern up here?"

"You just want me to haul my old ass up that ladder."

She grinned down at him. "Want to hear my initial working theory?"

"Evidence, Hale. Evidence first, then theory." He paused a moment. "Tell me anyway."

"He started the fire at the wrong end. Should've done it at the far side, farthest from the steps, working his way toward them, and his escape route. But he was stupid, and started lighting it nearest the steps, working back. Maybe he was drunk, or on something, or just a dumbass, but he trapped himself. Ends up cooking in the closet."

"You find a container, something that held the accelerant?"

"No. Maybe it's under some of these layers. Or maybe it's down there." She pointed. "He drops it here, in his panic, fire chasing after him. Fire hits container of accelerant. Boom, and you got your hole in the floor, and you've got your first level going up, and the debris from up here raining down."

"You're so smart you come on down and work those grids then."

"On that." But first she crawled back from the hole and dug out her cell phone.

It was tedious, filthy work. She loved it. She knew why O'Donnell was letting her take the point, and was grateful. He wanted to see if she could deal with the muck and the stink, the monotony and the physical demand.

And he wanted to see if she could think.

When she found the ten-gallon can under a mountain of debris and a sea of ash, she felt the click.

"O'Donnell."

He turned from his sieving, pursed his lips. "Score one for the new kid."

"Got punctures on the bottom. He trailed it through, lit it up, trailed, lit. Pattern upstairs indicates trailers. Dead guy can't be a bystander or a victim. Fire doesn't map that way. Whoever torched it had to get trapped. Riot bars on the windows first and second floors, so nobody got out that way. I'm betting the body ID's as the owner."

"Why not a pyro, a junkie, somebody with a hard-on for the owner?"

"Firefighters who responded reported the doors were all locked. Dead bolts. They had to break them in. The riot bars upstairs? Who puts bars on second-floor windows? And they're new. They look pretty new. Owner does that. Owner locks the place up tight to keep the riffraff out. Owner's got the keys."

"Finish up, write it up. You might do, Hale."

"Oh yeah, I'll do. I've been waiting for this since I was eleven."


That night, still revved up, Reena sat across from Fran at Sirico's and shoveled in angel hair marinara.

"So, we can't locate the owner of the building, who's got three separate loans on the place and a boatload of insurance. People we talked to said he's been complaining about how the homeless and the junkies ruined his investment, How he couldn't unload the property. Figure the ME's going to ID our CC as the owner, or the owner's in the wind, gone under after the torch job went wrong. Still got a lot of work to do on-site, but it's piecing together. Textbook."

"Listen to you." Fran laughed, sipped mineral water. "My little sister, the investigator. Wait until Mama and Dad hear you solved your first case."

"Closed—and not yet. Still have some reconstructing to do, some interviews to conduct, some background to check. But I was hoping they'd call while I was in here."

"Reena, it's after one in the morning in Florence."

"Right." Reena shook her head. "Right."

"They called this afternoon. They're having the best time. Dad talked Mom into renting one of those little scooters. Can't you see them, zipping around Florence like a couple of kids?"

"I can." Reena grabbed her wine, lifted the glass in toast, drank. "They wouldn't be able to do this without you."

"Not true."

"Absolutely true. You're the one carrying on. The one taking over so much of the responsibility and work here so they can have a little time to travel. Bella, well, she hasn't picked up so much as a glass in here unless it was to drink out of it on the rare occasions she comes by. I'm not much better."

"You waited tables last Sunday, and pitched in for more than an hour on Tuesday after working a full day."

"I live right upstairs, so it's no big." Still, she smiled, a bit wickedly. "I notice you didn't mention Bella."

"Bella is what Bella is. And she does have three kids to deal with."

"And a nanny, a housekeeper, a gardener—oh, I forgot, a *groundskeeper*." Reena waved at Fran's frown. "Okay, don't put the look on me. I'll ease off. I'm not really mad at her. I guess I feel a little guilty that you take the lion's share. And Xander's right behind you, even with the load he carries in med school."

"Forget the guilt. We're all doing what's most important to us." She glanced over and smiled at the man tossing dough at the work counter.

He had big hands, and a sweet face just this side of homely. His bright red hair fell over his forehead like little licks of flame. And when he looked at his wife, as he did now, his eyes lit with fun.

"Well, who knew you'd fall for an Irishman who likes to cook Italian." Amused, Reena ate more pasta. "You know, you and Jack still have that glow, even though you're working on what, three years now."

"Two last fall. But it might be a little something extra causing the glow." Fran reached out, gripped both of Reena's hands. "I can't wait. I was going to wait until you'd eaten, and Jack and I could tell you together, but I can't stand it another minute."

"Oh my God, you're pregnant!"

"Four weeks." Her cheeks went rosy. "It's early, I should shut up, keep it to myself. But I can't, and—"

She broke off as Reena leaped up, caught her around the neck. "Oh boy, oh boy, oh boy! Wait!" She rushed away, around the worktable and jumped onto Jack's back. "Daddy!"

His face turned the same color as his hair as she pressed a kiss to his cheek. "Champagne for the house! On me."

"We were going to keep it to the family for now." Jack grinned foolishly when she bounced down.

Reena looked over, at the applause, at the people who hurried over to congratulate Fran. "Too late. I'll get the wine."


Fran's news and her own solid first day had Reena drinking a little more than was wise. But she enjoyed the buzz as she walked around to the back stairs leading to her apartment.

Gina and Steve were married now, nearly a year into it. There was no reason to keep up a two-bedroom apartment.

She knew her parents thought it was a little silly for her to live there, when her room was still kept at home. And they'd argued with her about paying rent. She'd had to remind them they'd raised her to be responsible, and make her own way.

She considered the apartment a first step. Eventually, she wanted a house of her own. But that was eventually. And there was something cozy and comforting living above the shop, and a stone's throw from her parents. A block from Fran and Jack.

When she reached the back, she saw the light was on in her living room. Instinctively she opened her coat so her weapon was in easy reach.

In all her years on the force, she'd only had to draw it twice in the line. It always felt slightly foreign in her hand.

She started up the steps, going back over her routine. She'd left before dawn, maybe she forgot to turn off the light. But it was a habit, her mother was a bear about wasting electricity, and it had been drummed into her since birth.

One hand stayed on her weapon as she reached for the doorknob to check the lock. The door swung open, her weapon was half out. Then she shot it back into place with a huff of breath.

"Luke! How long have you been here?"

"Couple hours. I told you I might stop by tonight."

True enough, she thought as her heart rate leveled. She'd forgotten. Pleased to see him, she came in out of the cold, offered her lips.

The kiss was brief, perfunctory and had her raising her brows. Normally he couldn't wait to get his hands on her. She felt the same. There was a sexy elegance about Luke Chambers, a tailored sensuality she found exciting. As she found his avid and romantic pursuit of her from the moment they'd met.

She'd enjoyed being pursued, being courted with flowers and phone calls, romantic dinners, long walks by the water.

She enjoyed, very much, being seen as completely female, and just a little delicate. A nice change of pace, she'd thought, from being considered sturdy and competent.

It was probably why it hadn't taken him long to get her into bed. But it had taken three months before she'd given him a key to her door.

"I stopped in downstairs to get some dinner, caught up with Fran." She unwound her scarf, pulled off her hat, then did a little twirl. "I had the *best* day, Luke, and the best news when I—"

"Glad somebody did." He moved away from her, turned off the TV he'd been watching, then slumped in a chair.

Okay, she thought. He was sexy and interesting and often sweetly romantic. But he was also a lot of work. She didn't mind that. In fact, being in what was largely a man's world most of her day helped her enjoy little bits of being softer, and more consolatory in a relationship.

"Rough one?" She peeled off her coat, her gloves, put everything away in the narrow closet.

"My assistant gave her two weeks' notice."

"Oh?" Reena finger-combed her long curls, thought idly about trying a new style. Then felt guilty for not paying attention. "I'm sorry to hear that." She bent to unlace her boots. "Why is she leaving?"

"Decided she wants to move back to Oregon, for God's sake. Just like that. Now I've got to set up interviews, get somebody in she can train before she leaves. This on top of three out-of-office meetings today. My head's killing me."

"I'll get you some aspirin." She walked over, leaned down to kiss the top of his head. He had such nice, silky hair, mink brown like his eyes.

As she straightened, he took her hand, gave her a tired smile. "Thanks. Last meeting ran late, and I just wanted to see you. Decompress."

"You should've stopped in downstairs. Decompression's always on the menu at Sirico's."

"So's noise," he said as she moved into the bathroom. "I was hoping for a quiet evening."

"It's quiet now." She brought out the bottle, carried it into the little kitchen with its old workhorse of a stove and cheerful yellow counters. "I'll join you in a couple of aspirin. I had a lot of champagne down below. Major celebration."

"Yeah, you looked to be having a hell of a time. I glanced in the window before I came around back."

"Well, you should've at least poked your head in." She handed him the aspirin, the water.

"I had a headache, Cat. And I didn't want to sit around in a noisy restaurant waiting for you to finish partying."

And if you had a headache, she thought, why the hell didn't you get your own aspirin sooner? Men could be such babies. "I might've finished partying earlier if I'd known you were here. Fran's pregnant."

"Hmm?"

"My sister Francesca. She and Jack found out they're going to have a baby. Her face could've lit up Baltimore when she told me."

"Didn't they just get married?"

"It's been a couple years, and they've been trying almost since the get-go. We tend to head straight for the nursery in my family. Bella's already had three, and is making noises about having one more."

"Four kids in this day and age. It's irresponsible."

Easing down on the arm of the chair, she gave his shoulder a rub. "That's what you get with a big Italian Catholic family. And she and Vince can afford it."

"You're not thinking about popping one out every couple years, are you?"

"Me?" She laughed, gulped down water. "Kids are way down the road for me. I'm just really getting started on my career. Speaking of which, I had my first major case today. Did you hear about that building on Broadway, untenanted apartment building, single victim?"

"I didn't have time for the news today. I put in twelve hours. And spent a lot of that tap-dancing for a potential client, a major one."

"That's great, about the major account."

"I don't have it yet, but I'm working on it." His hand, long fingers, narrow palm, ran gently over her leg. "I've set up a dinner with him and his wife, Thursday night. Wear something special, will you?"

"Thursday? Luke, my parents are coming back from Italy on Thursday. We're having dinner at the house. I told you."

"So, you can see them on Friday, or over the weekend. For God's sake you live right down the street. This is a major account, Cat."

"Understood. And I'm sorry you won't be able to make it for the welcome back dinner."

"Are you hearing me?" The hand on her leg clenched into a fist. "I need you with me. This is the kind of socializing I need to do to land this account. It's expected. It's already set up."

"I'm sorry. My evening's already set up, and was before you booked Thursday night. If you want to reschedule, I'll—"

"Why should I reschedule?" He pushed out of the chair, threw out his arms. "This is business. This is a major opportunity for me. It could mean the promotion I've been working toward. You all but live with your family as it is. What's the big freaking deal about eating some damn spaghetti, when you can do the same thing any other time?"

"Actually, we're having manicotti." But she pushed down the spurt of irritation as she got to her feet. "My parents have been gone nearly three weeks. I promised I'd be there unless I got called out on a case. They're going to come home to the news that their oldest daughter is having her first child. This is major in my world, Luke."

"So what I need doesn't register?"

"Of course it does. And if you'd asked me before making these plans, I'd have reminded you that I was already committed, and you could have suggested another night."

"The client wants Thursday, the client gets Thursday." He snapped it out as temper ruddied his cheeks. "That's how it works in *my* world. Do you have any idea, any conception, how competitive financial planning is? How much time and effort it takes to swing a multimillion-dollar account?"

"Not really." And it was probably her lack that she couldn't care less. "But I know you work hard, and I know it's important to you."

"Yeah, that shows."

When he turned away, she rolled her eyes behind his back. But she stepped forward, prepared to soothe. "Look, I'm really sorry. If there's any way you can move it to another night, I'll—"

"I just told you." He threw out his arms again as he spun around. And the back of his hand caught her sharply on the cheek.

She jerked back, her eyes going huge as she pressed her fingers to the sting.

"Oh God, oh my God, Cat. I'm sorry. I didn't mean— Did I hurt you? Oh Jesus." He took her arms, and his face was as stunned as she imagined hers was. "It was an accident. I swear."

"It's all right."

"You just walked right into it. I didn't expect . . . I'm so fucking clumsy. God, let me see. Is there a bruise?"

"It was barely a tap." True enough, she thought. More a shock than an actual hit.

"It's red," he murmured and touched his fingers gently to her cheek. "I feel terrible. I feel like a monster. Your beautiful face."

"It's nothing." She found herself soothing him after all. "You didn't mean it, and I'm not fragile."

"You are to me." He drew her into his arms. "I'm so sorry. I shouldn't have come by in such a lousy mood in the first place. I just wanted to see you. Then you were partying downstairs. I just wanted to be with you."

He brushed his lips over her cheek. "Just needed to be with you."

"I'm here now." She touched his hair. "And I'm sorry I can't help you out on Thursday. Really."

He eased back, smiled. "Maybe you can make it up to me."

The sex was good. It was always good with Luke. And because of the spat, and the slap, he was particularly tender. Her body warmed under his, the muscles taxed by her own long day loosened. And while her system climbed to peak, her mind emptied.

Satisfied and sleepy, she curled against him.

"You ever going to get a bigger bed?" he asked.

She smiled in the dark. "One of these days."

"Why don't you come to my place for the weekend? We can hit a couple of clubs Saturday night, do a late brunch Sunday morning."

"Mmmm. Maybe. I may have to help out with the lunch shift downstairs on Saturday, but after. Maybe after."

He was silent a moment, and she thought he'd drifted off to sleep. "You could deal with your parents earlier on Thursday, skip out of the dinner part and meet me at the restaurant at seven."

"Luke, that's just not going to work for me."

"Fine." There was a sulk in his voice as he rolled away, got out of bed. "We'll just leave it all your way, as usual."

"That's not fair, and you know it."

"What's not fair," he snapped back as he began to dress, "is your unwillingness to compromise on anything. The way you put everything ahead of me."

The postcoital glow evaporated. "If you really feel that way, I don't know what you're doing with me."

"At the moment, neither do I. You take more than you give, Cat." He buttoned his shirt with short, sharp movements. "Before much longer, I'm going to be tapped out."

"I'm giving you the best I've got."

He shoved his feet into his shoes. "That's really sad for you."

When he stalked out, she lay back.

Was she that selfish? she wondered. That emotionally stingy? She cared about Luke, but did she take a real interest in his work? Not so much, she admitted, not when she was so wrapped up in her own.

Maybe her best was sad.

She rolled over in the dark and searched a long time for sleep.


When Reena walked into the squad room with O'Donnell after spending most of her shift knocking on doors and interviewing witnesses, getting statements from the owner of the building's ex-wife, former business partner, current girlfriend, there were three dozen long-stemmed white roses spread over the majority of her desk.

The flowers caused a lot of comments from other members of the unit, but the card made her smile.

> *Cat,*
> *I'm sorry.*
> *The Idiot.*

Still, she didn't indulge in sniffing at them until she'd carried them into the break room to give her enough room on her desk to work.

She had reports to write. Though the identity of the body had yet to be confirmed, the owner was still among the missing.

With O'Donnell, she walked into their CO's office to update him.

"Waiting for the lab reports," O'Donnell began. "Owner—James R. Harrison—was last seen knocking a few back in a place called Fan Dance, a strip club a few blocks from the scene. We got a credit card receipt cashing him out at twelve-forty. Ford truck registered to him's parked back of the building."

He glanced at Reena, signaling her to take over.

"We found a toolbox under the debris on the first level, and a screwdriver with a blade that appears to match the punctures on the bottom of the gas can recovered from the scene. Harrison did a turn for fraud five years ago, so his prints are on file. They match ones we lifted from the toolbox, the screwdriver and the gas can. ME wasn't able to get prints off the body, so they're working on dental."

"We should have that tomorrow," O'Donnell added. "Talked to some of his associates. He had serious money problems. Liked the horses, and they didn't like him."

Captain Brant nodded, sat back. His hair was ice white, his eyes a cold blue. There were pictures of his grandchildren on a desk he kept as tidy as her aunt Carmela's company parlor.

"So, it's looking like he lit the place up, trying to cash in on the insurance, got trapped inside."

"Looking that way, Captain. The ME didn't find any signs of foul play, no wounds or injuries. We're still waiting for tox," Reena added, "but nothing's popping that indicates somebody wanted him dead. He has a small life insurance policy. Five thousand, and it goes to the ex-wife. He never changed the beneficiary. She's remarried, got full-time employment, so does her husband. She doesn't look good for it."

"Wrap it up. Quick work," he added.

"I'll write the report," she offered when she and O'Donnell walked into the squad room.

"Have at it. I've got some other paperwork to catch up on."

He sat. His desk faced hers. "It your birthday or something?"

"No. Why? Oh, the flowers." She settled in front of her keyboard with her notes. "Guy I'm seeing was a bit of a jerk last night. I get the bennies."

"Classy."

"Yeah, he's got that going for him."

"This a serious deal?"

"Haven't decided. Why, you hitting on me?"

He grinned, and the tips of his ears reddened. "My sister's got this kid who's done some work for her. Carpenter. Does good work. Nice kid, she tells me. She's trying to fix him up."

"And what, you think I'll go on a blind date with your sister's carpenter?"

"Said I'd ask." He lifted his hands. "Nice-looking boy, she says."

"Then let him find his own girl," Reena suggested, and began to write her report.

# 11

Bo scarfed down the last peanut butter cookie, washed it down with cold milk. Then, sitting at the breakfast counter he'd built himself, gave an exaggerated sigh.

"If you'd ditch that husband of yours, Mrs. M., I'd build you the home of your dreams. All I'd ask in return would be your peanut butter cookies."

She grinned, and flicked her dish towel at him. "Last time it was my apple pie. What you need's a nice young girl to take care of you."

"I've got one. I've got you."

She laughed. He really liked the way she laughed, with her head thrown back so the big boom of it hit the ceiling. She had a round, comfortable body and so would he if she kept feeding him cookies. Her hair was red as a stoplight and all fuzzy curls.

She was old enough to be his mother, and a hell of a lot more fun than the one nature had given him.

"Need a girl your own age." She poked a finger at him. "Handsome boy like you."

"It's just that there are so many to choose from. And none of them hold my heart like you, Mrs. M."

"Go on. You've got more blarney than my old grandda did. And he was Irish as Paddy's pig."

"There was a girl once, but I lost her. Twice."

"How?"

"Just a vision across a crowded room." He lifted his hands, flicked his fingers. "Evaporated. You into love at first sight?"

"Of course I am."

"Maybe this was, and I'm just wandering aimlessly until I find her again. Thought I did once, but she poofed on me that time, too. Now, I've got to get going."

He unfolded himself from the stool, six feet two inches of lean muscle. The years of physical labor had built him up, toughened him.

She might have been twice his age, but she was still female, and Bridgett Malloy appreciated the view.

She had a soft spot for this handsome boy, that was the truth. But she was too practical to have continued to throw work his way over the past six months if he wasn't skilled and honest.

"I'm going to find you a girl yet. Mark my words."

"Make sure she knows how to bake." He bent down, kissed her cheek. "Say hi to Mr. M. for me," he added as he pulled on his coat. "And just give me a call if you need anything."

She handed him a bag of cookies. "I've got your number, Bowen, in more ways than one."

He headed out to his truck. Could it get any colder? he wondered, and stuck to the path he'd dug out for her from steps to driveway. The ground was white with snow that had melted to ice, refrozen. And the sky above was a heavy gray that promised more of the white stuff.

He decided he'd stop at the market on his way home. Man didn't live by peanut butter cookies alone. Maybe he wouldn't have minded finding a woman who knew her way around the kitchen, but he'd gotten to be a good hand in there himself.

He had his own business now. He patted the wheel of the truck as he got in. Goodnight's Custom Carpentry. And together, he and Brad had bought, rehabbed and turned over a couple of small houses.

He could still remember talking Brad into that first investment, pitching the sagging wreck of a house as a diamond in the rough. He had to give Brad credit for vision—or utter faith.

He had to give his grandmother credit for trusting him enough to front some of the money. Which reminded him to call her when he got home, see if she needed him to fix anything around her house.

He and Brad had worked like dogs, rehabbing that first house. They'd turned a good profit, repaid his grandmother plus interest. And reinvested the rest.

When he took the time to think about it, to really think back, he had a dead boy to thank for where he was today. Why that event, the death of a virtual stranger, had changed his life he couldn't be sure. But it had motivated him to stop drifting, to get moving.

Josh, he thought now as he drove away from the Malloy house in Owen's Mill. Mandy had been really broken up about it. And oddly enough, the fire and the kid's death had been some of the elements that had cemented their friendship.

Brad and . . . what the hell was her name? The little blonde who'd been the object of his friend's intense desire back in those days. Carrie? Cathie? Shit, it didn't matter. That hadn't gone anywhere.

Right now, Brad's object was a spicy brunette who liked to salsa dance.

But his own blonde—the one glimpsed at a party a lifetime ago—still cropped up in his mind now and then. He could still see that face, the tumble of curls, the little mole near her mouth.

Gone, long gone, he reminded himself. He'd never known her name, the sound of her voice, her scent. Which was probably what made that memory, that *feeling* all the sweeter. She was whatever he wanted her to be.

He streamed into traffic, decided everybody in Baltimore had opted to go to the grocery store after work. All it took was dire whispers of snow, and every mother's son and daughter jammed the aisles. Maybe he could skip it, make due with what he had.

Or just order in a pizza.

He had to go over his drawings for another job, and the supply list for the house he and Brad had just settled on.

His time was better spent . . .

He glanced idly to his left as the traffic in his lane stopped.

At first all he saw was a woman, a really pretty woman driving a dark blue Chevy Blazer. Lots of hair, curling hair the color of light caramel, springing out from under a black watch cap. She was tapping her fingers on the steering wheel in a way that told him she was keeping time to something on the radio. His was rocking with Springsteen's "Growin' Up." And from the rhythm of her fingers, he thought she had the same station going.

Funny.

Entertained at the thought, he angled so he could get a better look at her face.

And there she was. Dream Girl. The cheekbones, the curve of lips, the little mole.

His mouth dropped open, and shock had him jerking, stalling his truck. She flicked a glance in his direction, and for a moment—a kind of breathless moment—those long, tawny eyes met his.

And once again, the music stopped.

He thought, Holy shit!, then she frowned, turned her head away. Drove off.

"But, but, but—" His own stutter brought him back. He cursed himself, turned on the engine. But his lane was stuck, and hers was moving right along. Horns blasted irritably as he dragged off his seat belt, shoved open his door.

He actually had the wild idea of running after her car. Just running down the street like a mental patient. But she was too far ahead. Too far, he thought, furious with himself, for him to even read her plate.

"There you go again," he murmured, and simply stood, horns blaring around him, as the first flakes of snow fell.

A nyway, it was weird." Reena leaned on the counter in the kitchen at Sirico's, where her mother was back, manning the stove. "I mean he was really good-looking, if you discount the fact that his mouth was hanging open wide enough to catch a swarm of flies, and his eyes were bugged out like somebody'd just rammed a stick up his butt. I mean I could *feel* him staring at me, you know? And when I looked over, he's like this."

Reena mimed the look.

"Maybe he was having a heart attack."

"Mama." With a laugh, Reena leaned over to kiss her cheek. "He was just weird."

"You keep your doors locked?"

"Mama, I'm a cop. Speaking of which, I caught another case today. Couple of kids broke into their school, set fires in a couple of classrooms. Didn't do a good job of it, lucky for them."

"Where are the parents?"

"They're not all you. Fire-setting like this is a big problem with kids. Nobody was hurt, which was a godsend, and the property damage was minimal. O'Donnell and I rounded them up, but one of them—I've got a bad feeling about him. I think the psych eval's going to back me up. Ten years old, and he's got that look in his eyes. Remember Joey Pastorelli? That look."

"Then it's good you caught him."

"This time. Well, I've got to go spruce myself up for my date."

"Where are you going tonight?"

"I don't know. Luke's being very mysterious about it. I'm ordered to wear something fantastic, which is why I was hitting the mall for a new dress and had my weird-guy sighting."

"Luke. Is he the one?"

"He's the one right now." She rubbed a hand down her mother's back. He wasn't the long-haul guy, she knew that already. "You've got Bella and Fran tucked in and giving you grandbabies."

"I don't say you have to be married and having babies. I just want you happy."

"Me, too. I am."

He'd chosen upscale and French, so Reena was glad she'd sprung for the deep blue velvet. And the way his eyes had warmed when he saw her in it took the sting out of the price tag.

But when he ordered a bottle of Dom Pérignon and caviar, she stared. "What *is* going on. What's the occasion?"

"I'm having dinner with a beautiful woman. My beautiful woman," he added, taking her hand, kissing her fingers in a way that softened every muscle in her body. "You look amazing tonight, Cat."

"Thanks." She'd certainly worked at it. "But there's something going on. I can see it."

"You know me too well. Let's wait for the champagne. If they ever get it to the table."

"No hurry. You can pass the time by telling me again how amazing I look."

"Every inch. I love when you wear your hair that way. All straight and sleek."

Which took endless time, made her arms ache from fighting the curls away with the round brush and the hair dryer. But since it was the look he favored, she didn't mind indulging him now and then. He nodded to the waiter who brought the bottle to the table, revealed the label. And tapped his own glass to indicate he'd do the tasting.

When it was approved, poured, Luke lifted his glass. "To my delicious, delectable Cat."

"I'm willing to be on the menu, when I'm served with this." She tapped her glass to his, sipped. "Mmmm. Sure beats the hell out of the house sparkling at Sirico's."

"The wine cellar there doesn't exactly run deep. The one here's extraordinary. An exceptional French like this doesn't go with pepperoni pizza."

"I don't know." She chose to be amused. "I think it'd be a nice complement to both. Now, we've got our wine, had our toast. What's going on?"

"Nosy, aren't you?" He tapped his finger to his nose. "I got a promotion. A big one."

"Luke! That's great, that's wonderful! Congratulations. Wow, here's to you." She lifted her glass again and drank.

"Thanks." He beamed at her. "I don't mind saying I worked for it. The Laurder account was the last card in the deck. When I sewed that up, I had it. Would have been smoother if you'd helped me schmooze them, but . . ."

"You managed it yourself. I'm really proud of you." She reached over to lay her hand on his. "So, do you get a new title, another office? Let me have all the details."

"Fat raise in salary."

"Goes without saying." She set her glass down, and the waiter appeared like magic to top it off.

"If you're ready to order—"

Reena's hand squeezed Luke's as his tensed. "Why don't we? I'm starved, and then you can tell me every tiny detail while we eat."

"If that's the way you want it."

She waited until they'd given their choices—and maybe it was a little pretentious for Luke to order in French. But it was cute, and he was entitled to a little leeway tonight.

"When did it happen anyway?" she asked him.

"Day before yesterday. I wanted to set tonight up before I told you. Reservations here can be hard to come by."

"And what do we call you now? The king of financial planning?"

The pleased grin spread over his face. "That's next. For now, I've settled for a VP slot."

"Vice president. Wow. We should have a party."

"Oh, I've got some plans. You know, Cat, you might put a bug in your sister's ear again. Now that I'm in this position, maybe she can convince her husband to throw his account my way."

"Vince seems satisfied where he is," she began, and saw his eyes cloud. "But I'll mention it. I'll see her on Sunday, for Sophia's birthday party. You never told me if you were going to be able to make that."

"Cat, you know how I feel about those big family things, and a kid's birthday on top of it." His eyes aimed toward the ceiling. "Spare me."

"I know, it can be overwhelming. That's fine. I just wanted you to know you're welcome."

"If you think it would help sway your brother-in-law . . ."

This time she tensed, then deliberately relaxed again. "Let's keep family and business separate, okay? I'll see if I can talk to Vince about meeting with you, but it's, well, it's tacky to try to scoop his account at his daughter's party."

"Tacky? Now I'm tacky for trying to do my job and give your brother-in-law good financial advice?"

She let him stew while their first course was served. "No. But I can tell you Vince wouldn't appreciate you talking business at a family event."

"I've been to some of your family events," he reminded her. "There's plenty of business discussion. Pizza business."

"Sirico's *is* family. I'll do what I can."

"I'm sorry." He waved a hand, then patted it on hers. "You know I get wound up when it comes to my work. We're here to celebrate, not to argue. I know you'll try a little harder to bring your brother-in-law around."

Had she said that? she wondered. She didn't think so, but it was smarter to let it go. Otherwise they'd just go in circles, and she'd lose her appetite.

"So, tell me more, Mr. Vice President. Will you be heading a department?"

He told her more, and while she listened she enjoyed watching the animation on his face. She knew what it was to work toward a goal, then reach it. Exhilarating. The little ripples of tension smoothed away as they ate.

"This fish is fabulous. Want a bite?" As soon as she said it, saw his expression, she laughed. "Sorry, I always forget you don't like eating off each other's plates. But you're missing out, let me tell you. Oh, I didn't tell you I caught another case today. There—"

"I wasn't finished. I haven't gotten to the most important part."

"Oh. Sorry. There's more?"

"The big bang. You asked if I'll be getting a new office. I will be."

"Big and splashy?" she said, playing in.

"That's right. Big and splashy. And on Wall Street."

"Wall Street?" Stunned, she set down her fork. "New York? They're promoting you to New York?"

"I've been busting my ass for this, and now I've got it. The Baltimore office is chump change compared to the setup I'll have in New York." His face was grim as he drank more champagne. "I earned this."

"Absolutely. I'm just surprised. I didn't know you'd hoped to relocate."

"No point in talking about it until it's done. And it's not just relocating, Cat. It's a major leap for me."

"Congratulations all around." She smiled as she tapped her glass to his. "I'm going to miss you. When do you leave?"

"Two weeks." His eyes warmed, and his lips curved in the smile that had first caught her eye months before. "I'm taking the train up tomorrow to check out some apartments."

"Fast work."

"Why waste time? Which brings me to the second part of all this. Cat, I want you to go with me."

"Oh, Luke, that would be great. I'd love a quick trip to New York, but I can't take off tomorrow. With a little more notice, I could—"

"I don't mean tomorrow. I've got a realtor working with me, and I know what I'm looking for in an apartment. I mean I want you in New York with me, Cat." Even as she opened her mouth to speak, he took her hand. "You're exactly what I want. You're the icing on this cake. Come with me to New York."

Her heart tripped as he took a small box out of his pocket, thumbed it open. "Marry me."

"Luke." It was a staggering solitaire. She didn't know anything about diamonds, but she knew staggering when it was blinding her. "It's gorgeous. It's . . . Well, wow, but—"

"Classic, like you. We'll have an amazing life together, Cat. Exciting. Rich." He glanced away from her for an instant, gave a little nod. Then his eyes were back on hers as he slid the ring on her finger.

"Wait—"

But the waiter was there with a fresh bottle of champagne and beaming smiles. "Congratulations! We wish you every happiness."

Even as he poured there was applause from neighboring tables, and Luke was up and coming around to her to stop any words she might have said with a long, warm kiss.

"To us," he said as he sat back down. "To the beginning of the rest."

And when he tapped his glass to hers, she said nothing.

There was a knot of distress in the pit of her stomach. Trapped, she thought. That was how she felt. Trapped into accepting the congratulations and good wishes from the restaurant staff, other diners as Luke led her outside. The ring on her finger sparkled like a mad thing in the streetlights, and weighed like lead on her finger.

"We'll go to my place." He caught her in his arms beside his car, bent his head to nuzzle her neck. "And really celebrate."

"No, I need to go home. I need to be at work early, and . . . Luke, we need to talk."

"Have it your way." He kissed her again. "It's your night."

Far from it, was all she could think. The knot in her belly was beginning to make her queasy, and the leading edge of a tension headache cut at the base of her neck.

"I'll take some digitals of the apartments so you'll have an idea." He drove with a smile on his face. "Unless you want to ditch work now and run up there with me. Be more fun." He turned his head, winked at her.

"We could go shopping. I can get my assistant to book us a suite at the Plaza, get us some tickets to a show."

"I can't. It's just too—"

"All right, all right." He shrugged a dismissive shoulder. "But don't complain when I sign a lease on a place you haven't seen. I've got three places earmarked in Lower Manhattan. The one I'm leaning toward is a three-bedroom loft. Realtor claims it's a great space for entertaining. Just came on the market, so my timing's good. Close enough to the office I should be able to walk to work in good weather. Price is stiff, but with my new position, I can afford it. And I'll be expected to do some entertaining. Traveling, too. Going places, Cat."

"Sounds like you've got it all planned out."

"What I'm best at. Oh, I want to throw a little party before we go. We can make it a combination farewell and engagement deal. If we want to have it at my place, we'll have to put it together fast. Have to start packing up."

Again, she said nothing, just let him ramble as they drove to her apartment over Sirico's.

"Let's hold off making the big announcement." He nodded toward the restaurant. "I want you all to myself for tonight. You can show off your ring tomorrow."

He came around to open her door. It was one of the gestures he always made, gestures she'd always considered sweet and old-fashioned.

When they were inside, he helped her off with her coat. Nuzzled her neck again. She stepped away, taking a breath before she turned to face him. "Let's sit down."

"Wedding plans." He laughed as he spread his arms. "I know women like to dive right in, but let's just concentrate on being engaged tonight." He stepped forward to trail his fingers down her cheek. "Let me concentrate on you."

"Luke, I need you to listen to me. You didn't give me a chance in the restaurant. One minute you're showing me a ring, the next the waiter's pouring champagne and people are clapping. You put me in an impossible position."

"What are you talking about? You don't like the ring?"

"Of course I like the ring, but I didn't accept it. You didn't let me. You just assumed. And I'm sorry, I'm really sorry, Luke, but you assumed too much."

"What are you talking about?"

"Luke, we never even mentioned marriage before tonight, now suddenly you have us engaged and moving to New York. I don't want to move to New York, for starters. My family is here. My work is here."

"For Christ's sake, it's a couple hours on the train. You can see your family every few weeks if you want to. Though it's past time you cut the cord there, if you ask me."

"I haven't asked you," she said quietly. "Any more than you've asked me. I've recently gotten promoted myself, which it occurs to me we never bothered to celebrate."

"Oh, for God's sake. You can't really compare—"

"I'm not. I'm just taking stock." Long past time to take it, she admitted. Her fault. "You couldn't have been less interested in my work, but you assume I'll resign from the unit here and happily move off with you to New York."

"You want to keep playing with fire? I hear they have them in New York, too."

"Don't belittle what I do."

"What do you expect?" He shouted now. "You're putting your job ahead of me, ahead of us. You think I can afford to turn down this promotion so you can stay here in Baltimore and cook up spaghetti on Sundays? If you can't see why my career's more important, then I've seriously misjudged you."

"I can't, so you have. But even that's beside the point. I never said I wanted to get married—and I don't. Not now. I never said I would marry you. You didn't bother to let me answer."

"Don't be ridiculous." His face was ruddy, as it became with temper.

And was moving toward red. "You sat right there and accepted. You've got the ring on your finger."

"I didn't want to make a scene. I didn't want to embarrass you."

"*Embarrass* me?"

"Luke, the waiter was right there." She lifted her hands to scrub them over her face. "And those people at the next table. I didn't know what else to do."

"So, what, you just strung me along?"

"That wasn't my intention. It's not my intention to hurt you now. But you've made all these plans without consulting me first. Marriage is . . . I'm just not ready for it. I'm sorry." She pulled the ring off her finger, held it out to him. "I can't marry you."

"What the hell is this?" He gripped her shoulders, gave her a quick shake. "You've got some sort of hang-up about leaving Baltimore? For God's sake, grow up."

"I'm happy here, and I don't consider that a hang-up." She pulled away. "My home is here, my family is here, my work's here. But Luke, if I were ready to get married, if I wanted to get married, and leaving here was part of it, I would. Marriage isn't on the table for me right now."

"What about what I need? Why don't you think about someone else for a change? What the hell do you think I've been doing with you these past months?"

"I thought we were enjoying each other. If you were thinking along these lines, I didn't pick up on it. I'm sorry."

"You're sorry. You've humiliated me, and you're sorry. That makes it all fine, doesn't it?"

"I went out of my way not to humiliate you. Don't make this harder than it is."

"Harder than it is." He whirled away. "Do you know how much trouble I went to, with everything else I have to deal with, to give you the perfect night? To find the perfect ring? And you're throwing it back in my face."

"I'm saying no, Luke. You and I don't want the same things. There's nothing else I can do but say no, and I'm sorry."

"Oh yeah, you're sorry." He spun back, and something in his face made her palms go clammy. "You're sorry you're putting your stupid job before me, your smothering, middle-class family before me, your fucking blue-collar lifestyle before me. After everything I've invested in you—"

"Whoa." Her temper began to stir, to mix with his. "Invested? I'm not a stock, Luke. I'm not a client. And you're going to be careful what you say about my family."

"I'm sick to death of your fucking family."

"You need to go now." The stirring was moving toward rapid boil. "You're angry with me, we've both been drinking—"

"Sure. You didn't have any problem sucking down champagne at two-fifty a bottle while you were planning on kicking me in the face."

"Okay. Okay." She stalked into the bedroom, yanked open her desk drawer to pull out her checkbook. "I'll write you a check—I'll write you one for both bottles and we'll call it a day. We'll just consider we both made a mistake and—"

He jerked her arm, throwing her off balance. Before she could blink, he'd backhanded her. The checkbook flew out of her hand, and her shoulder rammed against the wall as she fell in the same direction.

"You bitch. Write me a *check*? You fucking ball-busting bitch."

She saw stars, little red stars that danced in front of her eyes. More than pain, shock had her freezing for a moment when he reached down and dragged her to her feet.

"Take your hands off me." She heard the tremor in her voice, fought to calm it. Learn to run, her grandfather had told her once. And she had. But there was nowhere to run. "Take them off me, Luke. Right now."

"I'm done letting you tell me what to do. You're done running this show. It's about time you learn what happens when somebody tries to play me."

She didn't think. Didn't think that he was about to hit her again, or how to stop it. She simply reacted, as she'd been trained to react.

She plowed the heel of her hand up, connecting hard with his chin, and rammed her knee viciously between his legs.

The stars were still dancing when he crumbled, and her breath was coming fast and short. But by God, there was no tremor in her voice.

"Now you can call me a ball-busting bitch. Too bad for you that you forgot cop's part of that, too. Get your sorry ass up and out of my house." She grabbed a lamp, yanked the cord to pull it out of the wall. And reared it back on her shoulder like a bat. "Or we can go another round, you bastard. Get out, and consider yourself lucky you're not spending the night in a cell, or the goddamn hospital."

"I'm not going to forget this." His face was pale as wax, and he had to crawl before he gained his feet. His eyes were molten as he stared at her. "I'm not going to forget this."

"Good. Neither am I. Get the hell out. Don't come near me again."

She didn't shake, not when she followed him out into the living room. She didn't shake while she waited for him to grab his coat, limp to the door. She stayed calm as she bolted the door behind him, and even when she stepped up to the mirror to examine her face.

She got her digital camera, set the timer, took shots full face and profile, then sent them with a brief e-mail explanation to her partner.

Cover your ass, she told herself. Then she got a bag of frozen peas out of her freezer, sat down with them pressed to her bruised cheek.

And shook like a leaf.

# 12

*Sitting in the car, smoking a Camel. Little slut's come up in the world. Riding around with Fancy Suit in the shiny Mercedes. Ride like that went for thirty grand easy. Ought to have one like it. Maybe just boost that one. Wouldn't that be a kick in the ass? Fancy Suit comes back out, swishing in his cashmere coat, and he's got no car.*

*Be worth a few laughs.*

*But first watching was the name of the game.*

*Get the binoculars. Slut left her shades up most times. Probably liked having guys jack off watching her up there.*

*No whore like a Catholic whore.*

*Standing in the living room. Looks intense. Love birds having a love spat maybe. Should've gotten a beer. Better watching with a cold one.*

*Look at her face. Sexy face, little mole, curvy lips. Get a boner instead of a beer.*

*Into the bedroom. Now we're talking! Peel it off, baby. Take it off for Daddy.*

*Whoops! Solid backhand! Somebody's feeling a little out of sorts. Hope he hits her again. Come on, Fancy Suit, hit the bitch again. Fans in the front row want to see the smackdown.*

*Jesus, what a pussy. Let some skinny woman take you down?*

*Get another smoke. Something to think about. Maybe kick his ass when he comes out. Maybe beat him to fucking death. Use a pipe, a bat. Blood all over Fancy Suit. Fingers point to her. Could point right at her.*

*See how long she stays a frigging cop when she's a murder suspect.*

*Could be fun. And she'd always wonder, wouldn't she?*

*Fancy Suit comes out, limping like his balls are the size of cantaloupes. Have to laugh. It's a real knee-slapper.*

*Still laughing as you pull out to follow the shiny blue Mercedes. Hell of a car.*

*And smiling, big, shit-eating grin because there's a better idea in there. Better, and big-time fun with it.*

*Takes a little time, but good things come. Have to make a detour, get some supplies. Keep it simple. Simple's always better. Simple is your stock-in-trade.*

*Get that beer now while you work. Explosives 101. She'd know enough for that. Sure, she would. Arson unit's kissing cousins to the bomb squad. Nice little device. Simple. Boys and girls, don't try this trick at home.*

*Late enough now, plenty late enough now. Little bitch is sleeping by now, all by her lonesome. Not much traffic. Town's dead at four A.M. Shit-hole of a town. Fucking Charm City never gave him anything but grief.*

*Fancy Suit's up in his Fancy Suit apartment, sleeping with his cantaloupe balls. Be fun to take him out. So easy, so juicy. But this is better. Few minutes with the thirty grand and we're all set. Locked and loaded.*

*Just stroll away, drive off a little ways. Might as well see some of the show.*

*Light another smoke and wait for the fireworks.*

*And five, four, three, two, one.*

*Ka-boom!*

*Look at that sucker fly. Look at her burn!*

*Oh yeah, baby, good job. Ace of a job. Fingers going to point now, because Fancy Suit's going to point them. Going to hold his bruised balls and point his finger right at her.*

*Good night's work.*

*Too bad about the car, though.*

. . .

At six A.M., a full thirty minutes before her alarm was set to go off, Reena was wakened by banging on her front door. She dragged herself out of bed, instinctively pressing her fingers to her cheekbone when it began to throb.

Throbbed all the way into her ear, she thought in disgust. Men like Luke knew just where to aim.

She pulled on a robe, avoiding the mirror over her dresser, and walked quietly out of the bedroom.

A peek out the window left her puzzled. Shoving at her hair, she unlocked the door, drew it open. "O'Donnell? Captain? Is there a problem?"

"All right if we come in a minute?" There were storm clouds in O'Donnell's eyes, only adding to her confusion as she stepped back. "I'm not on till eight."

"Got a good bruise going there." O'Donnell nodded at her face. "Working up to a shiner."

"Walked into something nasty. Is this about the e-mail I sent you last night? There was no need to make a big deal out of it."

"I haven't checked my e-mail. We're here about an incident involving Luke Chambers."

"Well, God, did he file a complaint because I kicked him out of here?" Reena pushed at her hair, and the flush that worked its way under the bruising was as much from temper now as embarrassment. "I wanted to keep this personal, send you an e-mail on the matter, with a couple of photos as backup in case he pushed it. Guess he did."

"Detective Hale, we're going to need to ask you where you were this morning between three-thirty and four A.M."

"I was here." She shifted her gaze to Captain Brant. "I was here all night. What happened?"

"Somebody torched Chambers's car. He insists it was you."

"Torched his car? Was he hurt? Oh good God." She let herself drift down into a chair. "How bad is he hurt?"

"He wasn't in the vehicle at the time it was lit up."

"Okay." She closed her eyes. "Okay. I don't understand."

"You and Mr. Chambers had an altercation last evening."

She looked at her captain, felt the weight and a fresh flutter of nerves. "Yes. During which he struck me in the face, knocked me down. He then proceeded to drag me to my feet and threatened me with additional bodily harm. I protected myself, applying the heel of my hand in a firm manner to his jaw, and my knee in an equally firm manner to his groin. I then ordered him to leave."

"Did you at any time threaten Mr. Chambers with a weapon?"

"A lamp." Reena clutched her hands together in her lap. "My bedroom lamp. I picked it up and informed him if he didn't get out I'd be going another round with him. I was pissed. He'd just finished clocking me, for God's sake. He outweighs me by a good fifty pounds."

Remembering it, that shock, that moment when she knew he'd hurt her, had her muscles quivering under her skin. She had to swallow, carefully, as her throat was already starting to burn. "If he'd come at me again, I'd have used any and all measures to protect myself. But it wasn't necessary, as he left. I locked up behind him, took the digitals, e-mailed my partner in case Luke decided to change the story around and file any charges."

"A man assaulted you, in your home, but you failed to report it?"

"That's right. I handled it, and I hoped that would be the end of it. I don't know anything about his car or a fire."

The captain sat back. "He's made several allegations. His story is that you assaulted him, being intoxicated and upset by the fact that he is relocating to New York. That in attempting to hold you off, reason with you, he may have inadvertently struck you."

Nerves turned to insult, with a good dose of self-disgust. She turned her injured cheek. "Take a good look. Does that look inadvertent to you? It happened the way I said it happened. Yes, we had both been drinking. I was not intoxicated. He was angry because I'd refused to relocate with him. I broke up with the son of a bitch, I didn't torch his car. I haven't left this apartment since I got in at approximately ten last night."

"Let's see if we can verify that," O'Donnell began.

"I can verify it." Her hands were no longer clutched in her lap, but gripped the arms of her chair. The only way she could stop them from balling into fists of rage. "I called a friend at about eleven. Because I was feeling sorry for myself and my face hurt and I was supremely pissed off. Just a minute."

She rose, strode to the bedroom. "Gina, put on a robe and come out here, will you? No, it's important."

Reena closed the door, stepped back out. "Gina Rivero—Rossi," Reena corrected. "Steve Rossi's wife. She came over. I told her not to because she's a newlywed, but she came over, with a half gallon of Baskin-Robbins, and we sat around until, I don't know, after midnight. Eating ice cream, bitching about men. She insisted on staying in case he came back and tried to get in."

The bedroom door opened and a tousled and irritated Gina came out. "What's going on? Do you *know* what time it is?" She focused long enough to stare at the men. "What? Reena?"

"Gina, you know my partner, Detective O'Donnell, and Captain Brant. They just need to ask you a couple questions. I'll make coffee."

She walked into the kitchen, then braced her hands on the counter and just breathed. She had to think, and she had to think like a cop whose ass is on the line. But she was struggling to get past the idea of someone setting Luke's car on fire. How was it done? Why? Who would target Luke? Or was it random?

She pulled back, forced herself to go through the routine of coffee preparation. Beans out of the refrigerator, into the grinder. An extra measure for the pot, a dash of salt.

She didn't drink the stuff, but she kept it on hand for Luke. Thinking of that brought on another wave of disgust. She'd pandered and pampered the bastard, and what had she gotten for the trouble? A black eye and the strong possibility of an internal investigation.

She stared at the glass carafe as it began to brew and heard Gina's voice spike up in the other room. Heard the insult and the outrage.

"That bastard probably set it himself. Just to take another shot at her. Did you *see* her face?"

Reena got down cups, poured half-and-half into a little white pitcher. Crisis didn't mean a lack of hospitality, she reminded herself. Her mother had drummed such things into her from birth.

O'Donnell came to the doorway. "Hale? You want to come back in?"

She nodded, hefted the tray. Gina's cheeks were still pink with temper as Reena set the tray on the coffee table. "It's routine," Reena said, and touched a hand to Gina's before she poured coffee. "It's procedure. They have to ask."

"Well, I think it's bullshit. He *hit* you, Reena. And it's not the first time."

"This individual's assaulted her before last night?"

Reena shoved down the embarrassment. "Slapped. Once before, and I thought it was an accident, as he claimed. I don't now. It was during an argument—a fairly minor one. It was quick, and there wasn't much behind it. Last night was different."

"Ms. Rossi's verified your statement. If Chambers pushes, it may be necessary to inform IAB." Brant shook his head before Reena could speak. "I'm going to discourage him from pushing." Brant took the coffee, added cream. "Do you have any idea who else might want to cause this guy trouble?"

"No." Her voice wanted to break. Internal Affairs. She'd just gotten her detective's shield, was just beginning to do the work she'd trained to do, dreamed of doing more than half of her life.

"No," she said again, struggling to stay calm. "He just got a promotion. I imagine he beat out several other candidates for it. But it's hard to imagine one of the brokers figuring out how to torch a Mercedes."

"You can read just how to do the job on the Internet," O'Donnell reminded her. "What about clients? He ever talk to you about a client who was upset with how he handled business?"

"No. He'd complain about work—being overworked, not being appreciated enough. But mostly he liked to brag."

"Another woman?"

She sighed now, wished she drank coffee. Holding a cup would give her something to do with her hands. "We've been seeing each other about four months. Exclusively, as far as I know. He was involved with someone before me. Ah . . . Jennifer. I don't know the last name. She was a bitch, of course, according to him. Selfish, demanding, nagging. All the things I'm sure he'd say about me now. I think she was in banking. I'm sorry, I don't know more."

Steadier, she straightened her shoulders. "I think you should look around. I think you should search the apartment, and my car. The sooner this is cleared up, the better."

"You're entitled to department representation."

"I'm not requesting any, at this time. He hit me, I hit him back. For me that was the end of it."

She would make it the end, Reena promised herself. She wouldn't let this stupidity smear her reputation or slice up her career. She wouldn't *have* it. "This other business isn't connected to me. The sooner we establish that, the sooner I can get back to the job, and the sooner the investigators on this can move in other directions."

"I'm sorry about this, Hale."

She shook her head at her partner. "It's not your fault. It's not the department's fault. And it's not mine."

She refused to be embarrassed or insulted at having her own colleagues go through her home, her things. The more thorough this unofficial inquiry, the sooner the door on it closed for good.

When they were finished in the bedroom, she went in with Gina to dress. "This is outrageous, Reena. I don't know why you take it."

"I want my record clear. There's nothing to find, so they find nothing. And it moves on." Because it was Gina, she closed her eyes, pressed a hand to her belly. "I feel a little sick."

"Oh, hon." Gina gathered Reena into a strong hug. "This sucks so wide. But you know it's going to be cleared up. It's going to be cleared up in, like, five minutes."

"That's what I'm telling myself." But even five minutes of being under suspicion was five minutes too long. "The only thing pointing at me is the fact that Luke and I had a fight last night." She eased away, pulled on a sweater. "Something like this, you've got to look at the ex—especially when she happens to be a cop in the arson unit. Sometimes it's the ones who fight or investigate fires who set them. You've heard the stories."

Her voice shook a little. "Set a fire so you can play the hero and suppress it, or just to get back at someone."

"That's not you. That's not anyone I know."

"But it happens, Gina." She covered her eyes, winced as she set her cheek throbbing once more. "If this were my case, I'd take a good, hard look at the angry ex-girlfriend who knows just how to set a vehicular fire."

"Okay. And once you took that good, hard look, you'd eliminate her. Not only because she'd never hurt anyone, and never use fire to strike back even at the most deserving asshole. But you'd have to eliminate her when she spent the night in her own apartment, eating ice cream with her best friend."

"I'd have to ask myself if that best friend would cover for her. Fortunately, she also has a veteran firefighter who knows his wife answered an SOS and went to stay with her friend. That adds to my side. And the fact that Luke lied about this." She tapped a finger gently to her cheek. "That smears it on his side. Nobody looks at this and thinks it's accidental. I documented it, and thank God I called you and you didn't listen to me and came over."

"Steve insisted as much as me. He'd have come himself, but I didn't think you wanted a guy around."

"No, I wouldn't have." The roiling in her stomach eased as she thought it through, studied the facts as she would any case. "My record's clean, Gina, and it's going to stay that way."

She started to reach for her makeup, to disguise the bruise. Then thought, Hell with it.

"I've got to go down, tell my parents. They're going to hear about this on the news. I'd rather they hear it all from me first."

"I'll go down with you."

"You've got to get home, get yourself ready for work."

"I'll call in sick."

"You will not." She stepped over, kissed Gina's cheek. "Thanks, pal."

"I never liked his sorry ass. And I know how that sounds now." Gina lifted her chin, and her eyes continued to spark with anger. "But I didn't, despite the fact that he was great to look at. Every time he opened his mouth it was all about me, me, me. Plus he was patronizing."

"What can I say? When you're right, you're right. I liked him because he was great to look at, good in bed, and he was needy. Let me be girly." She shrugged. "Shallow—just like him."

"You're not shallow. What, he do a mind fuck on you?"

"Maybe. I'll get over it." She blew out a breath, studied herself in the mirror. The shiner was coming on strong. "Now I've got to go deal with my parents. And won't that be fun?"

Bianca beat eggs in a bowl with the focused violence of a middleweight champ doing the rope-a-dope on a contender. "Why isn't he in jail?" she demanded. "No, no, first why isn't he in the hospital, then in jail? And you!" A string of egg flew as she swung the fork to point at Reena. "You didn't come to tell your father so he could put this miserable bastard in the hospital before you arrested him?"

"Mama. I took care of it."

"You took care of it." Bianca went back to beating eggs that were already down for the count. "*You* took care of it. Well, let me tell you something, Catarina, there are some things, no matter how old you are, your father takes care of."

"Dad would hardly have gone tearing after Luke and pounding him into dust. He—"

"You're wrong." Gib spoke quietly. He stood with his back to the room, staring out the window. "You're wrong about that."

"Dad." She couldn't imagine her even-tempered father hunting down Luke, getting into a fistfight. Then she remembered the way he'd faced down Mr. Pastorelli years before.

"Okay." Reena put her hands to her temples, pushed back her hair. "Okay. But, family honor aside, I wouldn't want to see Dad arrested for assault."

"You don't want to see this bastard arrested for assault either," Bianca snapped. "You're very softhearted for a cop."

"I wasn't being softhearted. Mama, please."

"Bianca." Again Gib's quiet voice silenced the room. But this time he turned, studied his daughter. "What were you being?"

"Practical, I thought. Private, I hoped. The fact is, I was stunned. I've been going out with Luke for months, and I missed all the signs. I can see them now, hindsight. But when he hit me, I was so surprised. If it makes you guys feel any better, I can promise I hurt him more than he hurt me. He'll be limping for days."

"Some consolation." Bianca poured the eggs into a cast-iron pan. "But now he's making trouble for you."

"Well, someone did torch his car."

"I'd like to make them a cake."

"Mama," Reena scolded on a half laugh. "This is serious. Someone could have been hurt. I'm not worried, too much, about the investigation. As luck would have it, I have Gina to back me up that I was home all night. And there's nothing to tie me to something like this except a fight with Luke. I'll feel better when they find out who did it, but I'm not worried. I'm upset," she admitted. "And I'm upset that I had to upset both of you like this."

"We're your parents," Bianca pointed out. "You're supposed to upset us."

"Did he hit you before last night?"

She started to say no to Gib's question, then settled for the complicated truth. "Once, but I thought it was an accident," she said quickly when Bianca cursed. "Honest to God, I thought it was an accident. He was gesturing, I stepped forward, and his hand slapped across my cheek. He acted so shocked and appalled. Hindsight," she repeated, rising to take her father's hand because it had balled into a fist. "Believe me. Look at me, and believe me, I'd never stand for anyone abusing me. You raised me to be strong and smart. You did a good job.

"He's out of my life." She moved in, wrapped her arms around Gib. "He's done, he's over. And it taught me an important lesson. I'll never try to be something I'm not, even on the little things, to placate someone else. Plus, I know I can stand up and take care of myself."

Gib rubbed her back, brushed a light kiss on her bruised cheek. "Took him down, did you?"

"Two shots." She stepped back, demonstrated. "Pow, pow, and he was on the floor, curled up like a steamed shrimp. I don't want you to worry about this, about me."

"We decide what to worry about." Bianca set the pile of eggs on the table. "Eat."

S he ate, and she went in to work. The blue line formed. Every cop in her unit stepped up—with a brisk nod, a pithy comment, a lame joke. Their support followed her into the captain's office.

"Guy's sticking that you hit him first. Pushed on the ex-girlfriend angle. He got a little sweaty there, claimed she's wacked, and how *she* assaulted him prior to their breakup."

"Can I pick 'em or can I pick 'em?"

"We're going to talk to her. We got a few names out of him—people he claims might have a grudge, seeing as he's so successful and handsome. Few clients, few coworkers. His former assistant. Takes the heat off you, Hale. Added to which, you've got a solid alibi, and cooperated with a search that turned up nothing to tie you. Unless he presses formal charges, which he's rethinking at this point, you're cleared for full duty."

"Thanks. Sincerely."

"Got a call from John Minger. He got wind of this."

"Yeah." She thought of her parents. "I think I know where the wind blew in from. I'm sorry if that complicates matters."

"I don't see how it does." But he sat back and she knew he was measuring her. "John's a good man, he's a solid investigator. He wants to poke around on his own time. I've got no problem with that. Do you?"

"None. Can you give me any more details?"

"Younger and Trippley are working it. They want to share, it's up to them."

"Thanks."

She stepped out, thought about the best way to approach the men assigned. Before she could decide, Trippley shot a finger toward her desk.

"File on your desk," he said, then went back to his phone.

She crossed to it, flipped open the file. Inside were photos of Luke's car, exterior and interior shots, the preliminary reports and statements. She glanced back at Trippley. "Appreciate it."

He shrugged a shoulder, cupped a hand over the phone. "Guy's an asshole. You like assholes, you ought to go out with Younger."

With barely a pause from typing on his keyboard, Younger shot his partner the finger, and sent Reena a sunny smile.

I t was hard to stay away from the scene, to restrain herself from taking a direct look at the collected evidence. But there was no point in muddying the waters. Instead, she treated the case like an exercise, studied the file, the updates the investigators passed her way.

It was straightforward, almost simplistically so, in her opinion. Someone had done a quick and nasty job—and had probably done others before targeting Luke.

She mulled it over, sipping a glass of Chianti as she reread the file and ignored the noise of Sirico's.

She'd taken a table facing the door so she spotted John as soon as he came in. She sent a wave, patted the tabletop, then rose to get him a Peroni herself.

"Thanks for coming by," she said when she came back to the table.

"Never a hardship. Split a pizza?"

"Sure." She called out the order to Fran. It wasn't food she wanted but conversation. "I know you've been looking into this mess on your off time. Can you tell me what you think?"

He picked up his beer, sipped at it. "You tell me first." He nodded toward the file.

"Down and dirty job. Somebody who knows vehicles. Pops the lock, disengages the alarm. If it went off, nobody's coming forward to say they heard it. But nobody pays much attention to a car alarm—especially if it stops within a couple minutes. Gas as accelerant, poured over interior, on the hood, inside the hood. Used the flares in the trunk as an ignition device there."

She paused, gathered her thoughts while John remained silent. "That would've been enough to do a decent job. The synthetics in the interior are susceptible to flame ignition. Thermoplastics melt as they burn and ignite other surfaces, as they likely did here. Fast fire. The gas was insurance. He didn't need it. He had ventilation, and could've accomplished a pretty damn destructive fire with enough crumpled newspaper lit under the seat or dash."

"Thorough or sloppy?"

She shook her head. "You almost want to say both. He took the stereo out—most arsonists can't resist taking valuables they can sell or use, but it doesn't feel like a random vehicular stripping."

"Because?"

"Too violent, too thorough. Plus, you've got high-end tires, and he didn't take them. And he knew what he was doing, John. We've got soot and pyrolysis product on what's left of the window glass, which indicate ventilation. Without it, most vehicular fires fizzle out. Cars are fairly airtight when the doors and windows are shut. He wanted a fast fire, and added the accelerant to the already rich fuel load of the vehicle. He probably had flashover in under two minutes."

"Working theory?"

"Vengeance fire. The guy wanted that car toasted. He puts a soaked rag trailer in the gas tank. What it's looking like is he floated a plastic cup with a firecracker in it. Simple, efficient. And again thorough. Multiple points of origin—under the driver's seat, in the trunk. Couple of what the lab's identified as potato chip bags, probably used as trailers in the interior.

They're a good one. Give off plenty of heat, burn away to nearly unrecognizable carbonaceous ash, and the oils give you a nice, prolonged fire—enough to engage the upholstery, so if something goes wrong with the device in the tank, the vehicle's still toast. Torch used basic household items to do the job, and knew what he was doing."

"High-end car, all the trimmings. But you don't figure somebody wanted a pricey car stereo and a little fire fun?"

"No, I figure it was personal, and the stereo was just a little cake. It was a straight job, not just a little extra fun. The arson was the point."

With a nod, John sat back, picked up his beer. "Not much left for me to tell you, then. Got your prints, the owner's. Valet's at the restaurant where you ate prior to the incident. The mechanic's from the owner's garage." He eyed her as he sipped his beer. "How's the face?"

A couple of days—and a lot of ice—had dulled the ache. But she knew her face sported several unattractive colors as it healed. "Looks worse than it is."

He leaned forward, lowered his voice. "Tell me this. Did you call anybody but Gina after he slugged you?"

"No. I gave assent to having my phone records checked."

"Did she call anyone? Tell anybody?"

"No. Well, Steve. But nobody's looking at him, John. The guys who caught the case talked to all three of us. We're keeping this up front all the way. I called Gina because I was pissed off, and because I wanted some sympathy. She came over because she was pissed off, and wanted to give some sympathy."

She glanced over to make sure none of her family or any neighbors were within earshot. "The fact is, John, getting popped by a guy you're sleeping with isn't something a woman likes to spread around. I'd hoped to keep this under the radar, more or less. I don't know anybody who'd do something like this on my behalf."

"You weren't seeing anybody besides this character?"

"No. John, I know the timing points to it being connected to me, or at least to the dustup I had with Luke, but I've thought about it, I've gone over and over it. I can't see it's anything but coincidence. You look at the statements." She tapped the file. "Luke wasn't Mr. Popularity among his coworkers, his former relationships. Still, none of them look any better for it than I do, at this point. What it looks like is somebody hired a torch. Hell, I'd say the son of a bitch hired one himself to slap back at me, but the timing's too tight for that to fly."

"Pretty tight," John agreed. "But it's an angle—the hiring a torch to slap at you. Maybe you ought to think of somebody you might've ticked off lately."

"Cops are always ticking somebody off," she muttered.

"Ain't that the truth?" He eased back, smiled when Fran brought their pizza to the table. "How's it going, sweetie?"

"It's going good." But her hand moved over to rub at Reena's shoulder. "Now, make my baby sister put that work away and eat something."

"See what I can do. Put it away," John advised when Fran walked off. "You'll handle any heat that comes your way on this. Unofficially, nobody's looking at you. You've got a solid record because you earned it, and your alibi holds. Set it aside, let the system work."

"Yeah. You know, John, I don't know if I chose my career or it chose me. Fire seems to follow me around. Sirico's, the first boy I really cared about, Hugh. Now this."

He slid a slice of pizza onto his plate. "Fate's a mean bastard."

# 13

For better or worse, it was done. Reena's heart was pounding, her throat bone-dry, and at the base of her belly was a little tickle that could have been panic or excitement.

She'd bought herself a house.

She stood on the white marble steps, the keys in her clammy hand. Settlement was over, the papers were signed. She had a mortgage.

And a bank loan, she thought, that stretched out so long she'd be ready for retirement when it was paid off.

Did the math, didn't you? she reminded herself. You can make this work. It was time she owned property. Oh God, she was a property owner.

And hadn't she fallen in love with this house? It was so like home. What that said about her, she wasn't entirely sure, but it had been love at first sight. Everything about it had called to her.

The location, the familiarity, even the slightly tired interior that just begged her to liven it up, her way. It even had a backyard—maybe it was narrow enough to spit from line to line, but it was an actual yard with actual grass. It even had a tree.

Which meant she'd have to mow grass and rake leaves, which meant

buying a lawn mower. And a rake. But for a woman who'd lived in apartments for the last ten years, it was heady stuff.

So, here she was, moving into a three-story row, three short blocks
from the house where her parents still lived.

Still in the neighborhood, she thought. And as distant as the moon.

But it was good. It was all good. Hadn't the uncles, along with her father,
inspected the place top to bottom? There'd been no stopping them. Needed
a little fixing up, sure. And more furniture than she could currently claim.

But that would all come.

All she had to do was put the key in the lock and walk through the
door, and she'd be standing in her own house.

Instead, she turned around, sat on the steps and waited to get her breath
back.

She'd taken a big bite of her savings, plus the generous lump of dough
her grandparents had given her—and the rest of the grands.

Now look what I've done. Gone into debt. And didn't a house keep
siphoning away money? Insurance, taxes, repairs, upkeep. She'd managed
to avoid all that up till now. Those pesky details had gone from being her
parents' problem to her landlords' problem.

Never hers.

Managed to avoid all that, she thought, and most every other kind of
commitment. She had the job and her family, friends she'd kept from
childhood.

But she was the only unmarried Hale. The only child of Gibson and
Bianca Hale yet to go forth and multiply. Not enough time, that's what
she told her family if they teased or pressed the matter. Haven't found the
right man.

True, all true. But how many times had she retreated from—or just
sidestepped—a potential relationship in the last few years?

Dating was fine, sex was good, but don't ask me to form an attachment.
Xander said she thought like a man. Maybe it was true.

And maybe she'd bought this house as a kind of compensation, the
way some singles or no-children couples bought a puppy.

See! I can make a commitment when I want to. I bought a house.

A house, she admitted, she couldn't seem to make herself enter now that everything was signed and sealed.

Maybe she could just turn it over. Give it a slap of paint, fix it up here and there, then resell it. There was no law that said she had to keep it for thirty years.

Thirty years. She pressed a hand to her belly. What had she done?

She was thirty-one years old, damn it. She was a cop with a decade on the job. She could walk into a stupid house without having a crisis. Besides, some portion of her family was bound to descend before much longer, and she didn't want to be caught sitting on the stairs having a neurotic attack.

She stood up, unlocked the door and walked deliberately inside.

Instantly, as if she'd popped a cork on a bottle labeled Stress, the tension drained out.

The hell with mortgages and loans and the terror of picking out paint colors. This is what she'd wanted. This big, old, high-ceilinged place with its carved trim, its hardwood floors.

Of course it was too much room for one person. She didn't care. She'd use one of the bedrooms for storage, once she had enough to store. She'd make another into an office space, another into a home gym, and keep the last spare for a guest room.

Ignoring the echoes, the emptiness, she strolled into the living room. Maybe she'd take the various offers from various relatives on hand-me-down furniture. At least for now. Put some of Mama's drawings on the walls. Make this a cozy, comfortable space.

And the smaller parlor, that was going to be her library. Then she'd need a big table for the dining room. Lots of chairs for when she had family over.

The kitchen was good, she thought as she took a tour of the first floor. It was one of the points that had cemented her decision. The previous owners had outfitted it well with glossy black appliances that had a lot of years left in them. Lots of smooth, sand-colored counters and honey-toned cabinets. She might get around to having a few of the doors replaced with glass. Stained glass maybe, or some fancy ripply glass.

She'd enjoy cooking here. Bella was the only one of the lot who'd apparently escaped the love of making food. There were nice, generous windows over the sink and they opened up to a view of the skinny backyard.

The lilacs were blooming. *Her* lilacs were blooming. She could talk to Uncle Sal about putting in a little postage stamp patio, and pick Bella's brain about designing a small garden.

Of course it had been years since she'd planted anything other than a geranium in a windowsill pot. Years, she recalled, since she and Gina had planted tomatoes and peppers and cosmos in the yard of the group house they'd shared in college.

But it seemed to her—at least with the sweetened distance of memory—that she'd enjoyed the digging and weeding.

Probably stick with flowers this time, she decided, and keep it low-maintenance. Yes, Bella would be the one to ask what would work best.

For flowers, fashion and the right place to be seen, Bella was your girl.

She thought about heading upstairs, to tour the second floor, to mentally arrange furniture. But decided to finish off the first-level walk-through by stepping out in her backyard.

She wanted to walk on her own grass.

The yard was bordered on both sides by a chain-link fence. Her neighbor to the right had some sort of spreading bushes planted along the line. Nice touch, she mused. She'd think about something like that. It wasn't just pretty, but added an illusion of privacy.

And to the left . . .

Well, well, well, she thought. She couldn't say much about the yard, but its occupant was worth the price of a ticket.

Fortunately for her, there were no bushes to obstruct the view.

The man had his back to her, and the rear view was very promising. Mid-May temperatures hadn't dissuaded him from taking off his shirt. But maybe whatever he was doing with the lumber and the power tools heated him up.

His jeans ran low on the hips, and the tool belt lower yet. But he man-

aged to avoid the butt crack reveal, which racked up points. He wore a
ball cap backward, which may or may not deduct points from the total
score, and there seemed to be a lot of wavy black hair under the cap.

She might make a pass at him right there as he was working. She caught
music from the boom box beside his sawhorses and gave him additional points
for keeping it at a reasonable volume. She could barely catch Sugar Ray.

Six-two, she judged. About one-eighty of good, toned muscle. She didn't
want to guess his age until she saw his face. But so far, as next-door neighbors went, he looked like a nice perk.

The realtor had mentioned the carpenter next door, in case she wanted
to get any bids on work. But the realtor had failed to mention the carpenter next door had an excellent ass.

His grass was mowed, and he appeared to know what he was doing
with the big, sexy tool. No rings on good, strong-looking hands. No visible tattoos or piercings.

Possibilities went up.

His house was similar to hers, though he already had that postage-stamp
patio in some sort of stone. No flowers—too bad on that as she considered
it showed flair and responsibility to pot and tend flowers. Still, the patio
looked clean and boasted a muscular barbecue grill.

If the rest of him lived up to the rear view, she might wangle her way
to an invite for grilled steak.

He paused, set aside what she was pretty sure was a nail gun. The noise
from the compressor shut down, and she heard Sugar Ray more clearly as
Carpenter Guy reached for a big bottle of water and aimed it toward his
mouth.

He stepped back from his work as he did, and she made out his profile.
Good nose, strong mouth—smart enough to wear safety glasses, and cool
enough to make them sexy. It looked like the face was going to live up to
the rest of the package.

Early thirties, she decided. And wasn't that handy?

When he turned his head and glanced her way, she lifted a hand in
what she considered a friendly, hi-new-neighbor salute.

He seemed to freeze, more like she'd aimed her weapon at him rather than a casual wave. He reached up, slowly, drew off his glasses. She couldn't make out the color of his eyes, but she felt the intensity of the stare.

The grin seemed to explode on his face. He tossed the glasses on the ground, strode straight to the fence and vaulted over.

Moved well—quick and agile. Green, she noted. His eyes were a misty green—and lit up a little too manically at the moment for comfort.

"There you are," he said. "Son of a bitch. There you are."

"Yeah, here I am." She gave him a cautious smile. He smelled of saw-dust and sweat—which would have been appealing if he wasn't looking at her like he was prepared to gobble her up in one bite. "Catarina Hale." She offered her hand. "I just bought the house."

"Catarina Hale." He took her hand and held it, just held it with his calloused one. "Dream Girl."

"Uh-huh." His score plummeted. "Well, it's nice to meet you. I've got to get back inside."

"All this time." He continued to stare at her. "All these years. You're better than I remembered. How about that?"

"How about that?" She tugged her hand free, backed up.

"I can't believe it. You're just here. Boom. Or maybe I'm having a hal-lucination."

He grabbed for her hand again, and she slapped hers on his chest. "Maybe you are. Maybe you've had a little too much sun. Better go back to your corner now, Carpenter Boy."

"No, wait. You don't get it. You were there, then you weren't. Then the other time, and then again. And you keep getting away before I can catch up. And now you're right here, talking to me. I'm talking to you."

"Not anymore." Nobody had mentioned the carpenter next door was a lunatic. Shouldn't there have been full disclosure? "Go home. Lie down. Seek help."

She turned, started back to the door.

"Wait, wait, wait." He lunged after her.

In response, she spun around, caught his arm, tipped him off balance and jerked his arm behind his back. "Don't make me arrest you, for God's sake. I haven't even moved in yet."

"The cop. The cop." He laughed, twisted his head around to grin at her. "I forgot they said a cop was moving in. You're a cop. That's so cool."

"You're one second away from serious trouble."

"And you smell really good."

"That's it." She pushed him up against the back wall of her house. "Spread 'em."

"Okay, okay, hold on." He was laughing and tapping his forehead against the wall. "If I sound like a crazy person, it's just the shock. Um, oh, shit. Don't cuff me—at least until we know each other better. College Park, May 1992. A party—crap, I don't know whose house it was. Group house, off campus. Jill, Jessie—no Jan. I think Jan somebody lived in the house."

Reena hesitated, the cuffs still in her hand. "Keep going."

"I saw you. I didn't know anybody. Came with a friend, and I saw you across the room. You were wearing this little pink top—your hair was longer, just past your shoulders. I like the way you're wearing it now. Sort of exploding to the jaw."

"I'll tell my hairdresser you approve. I met you at a party in College Park?"

"No. I never got to you. The music stopped. It was a moment for me. Can I turn around?"

He didn't sound crazy—exactly. And she was intrigued. She stepped back. "Hands to yourself."

"No problem." He held them up, palms out, then lowered them to hook his thumbs on his tool belt. "I saw you, and I was . . . Pow." He punched a fist to his heart. "But by the time I got across the room—place was packed—you were gone. I looked everywhere. Upstairs, outside, everywhere."

"You saw me over ten years ago, across the room at a college party, and you remember what I was wearing?"

"It was like . . . for a minute, it was just you. Sounds weird, but there it is. Then this other time? A pal dragged me to the stupid mall on a Saturday, and I saw you up a level. Just there, and I went running around looking for the damn stairs. But by the time I got up, you'd Houdini'd again. Wow. Wow."

He grinned like a mental patient, shoved his hat farther back on his head. "Then winter of '99? I'm stuck in traffic coming from a client's place. Got the Boss on the radio. 'Growin' Up.' And I look over, and I see you in the car beside me. You're tapping out the beat on the wheel. You're just there. And I—"

"Oh my God. Weird Guy."

"Sorry."

"The weird guy who goggle-eyed me on my way to the mall."

His grin spread again, but this time seemed more amused than manic. "That would be me. Half the time I thought I made you up. But I didn't. You're right here."

"Doesn't mean you're not still Weird Guy."

"Not criminally. We could talk. You could ask me in for coffee."

"I don't have any coffee. I don't have anything yet."

"You could come to my place for coffee—except I don't have any either. See, it's right next door. You could come over for a beer, or a Coke. Or the rest of your life."

"I think I'll pass."

"Why don't I make you dinner? Take you to dinner. Take you to Aruba."

Laughter trembled up her throat but she swallowed it back down. "I'll take Aruba under advisement. As for dinner, it's one in the afternoon."

"Lunch." He laughed, pulled off the ball cap and stuffed it in his back pocket, raked long fingers through his dense black hair. "I can't believe how completely I'm screwing this up. I didn't expect to see Dream Girl next door. Let me start over, sort of. Bo. Bowen Goodnight."

She accepted the hand. She liked the strength of it; she liked the calloused roughness of the palm. "Bo."

"I'm thirty-three, single, no criminal record. Got thumbs-up my last physical. I run my own business. Goodnight's Custom Carpentry. And

I've got this real estate thing with a partner. The pal I came to that party with. I can get you references, medical reports, financial statements. Please don't disappear again."

"How do you know I'm not married with three kids?"

His face went blank. It actually paled. "You can't be. There is no God so cruel."

Enjoying him now, she angled her head. "I could be a lesbian."

"I've done nothing in my life to earn such a vicious slap by Fate. Catarina, it's been thirteen years. Give me a break."

"I'll think about it. It's Reena," she added. "Friends generally call me Reena. I've got to go. I've got people coming over."

"Don't disappear."

"Not until my mortgage is paid off. It's been interesting meeting you, Bo."

She slipped back inside, left him standing there.

They brought food, of course. And wine. And flowers.

And most of her furniture.

Since they were moving her in, Reena decided she'd better get in the spirit. She made trips back to the apartment over Sirico's for boxes, for suitcases packed with clothes. For a last good-bye.

She'd been comfortable here, she thought. Maybe too comfortable. Comfort could become a rut if you didn't keep an eye out. But she'd miss being able to dash downstairs for a meal, or just to chat. She'd miss the easy routine of strolling up the block and stepping into her parents' home.

"You'd think I was moving to Montana instead of a few blocks away." She turned to her mother, saw the tears swimming. "Oh, Mama."

"It's silly. I'm so lucky to have all my children close. But I liked having you right here. I'm proud that you bought a house. It's a good, smart thing to do. But I'll miss knowing you're right here."

"I'm still right here." She lifted the last box. "Part of me worries that I've taken on more than I can handle."

"There's nothing my girl can't handle."

"Hope you're right. And remind me of that the first time I have to call the plumber."

"You call your cousin Frank. And you should talk to your cousin Matthew about the painting."

"Bases covered." Reena walked to the door, waited for her mother to open it. "And I've got a handyman right next door."

"You don't hire somebody to work in your house if you don't know him."

"Turns out I do—or he knows me."

She told Bianca the story as they finished loading the car and started the short drive to the new house.

"He sees you once at a party when you're in college? And he's smitten."

"I don't know about smitten. He remembered me. And he's very cute."

"Hmmm."

"He took it well when I threatened to cuff him."

"So, maybe he's used to it. Maybe he's a criminal. Or he enjoys bondage."

"Mama! Maybe he's just a cute, slightly strange guy with a great butt and power tools. Mama, I'm a big girl. And I carry a gun."

"Don't remind me." Bianca waved it away. "What kind of name is Goodnight?"

"It's not Italian," Reena murmured. She pulled up, then watched the door of the house next door open. "Well, it looks like you're going to get the chance to judge for yourself."

"That's him?"

"Um-hmm."

"Good-looking," Bianca commented, then stepped out of the car.

He'd cleaned up, Reena noted. His hair was still a bit damp, and he'd put on a fresh shirt—ditched the tool belt.

"Saw you hauling stuff in. Thought maybe you could use a hand. Can I get this out of the way?" he said to Bianca. "Wow, beautiful women run in the family. I'm Bo, from next door."

"Yes, my daughter told me about you."

"She thinks I'm crazy—because I gave her pretty good reason. I'm generally less bizarre."

"So, you're harmless."

"God, I hope not."

It made her smile. "Bianca Hale, Catarina's mother."

"It's nice to meet you."

"You've lived here long?"

"No, actually, only about five months."

"Five months. I don't remember seeing you in Sirico's."

"Sirico's? Best pizza in Baltimore. I get delivery all the time. The spaghetti and meatballs is incredible."

"My parents own Sirico's," Reena said as she popped the trunk.

"Get out. Seriously?"

"Why don't you come in," Bianca said, "have a meal?"

"I will. It's just I've been working pretty much round the clock the past couple months, and— Here let me get those." He nudged Reena aside to pull out boxes while he addressed her mother. "I haven't been seeing anyone— dating—just recently. I don't like eating alone in a restaurant."

"What's wrong with you?" Bianca asked. "Young, good-looking. Why don't you date?"

"I do—I mean, did. Will. But I've had a lot of work, and I'm working on this place in my spare."

"Have you been married before?"

"Mama."

"We're having a conversation."

"It's not a conversation. It's an inquisition."

"I don't mind. No, ma'am, no marriages, no engagements. I've been waiting for Reena."

"Stop it," Reena ordered.

"We're having a conversation," he reminded her. "Do you believe in love at first sight, Mrs. Hale?"

"I'm Italian. Of course I do. And call me Bianca. Come in, meet the family."

"I'd love to."

"Slick," Reena muttered as he stepped aside for Bianca to enter.

"Desperate," he corrected.

"Just put that down there."

"I can take it where it goes."

"For now, it goes there." She pointed to the base of the steps, closed the door.

"Okay. I like your mother."

"Why shouldn't you?" She took off her sunglasses, tapped them against her palm as she studied him. "You might as well come on back—and remember, you asked for it."

She walked back toward the kitchen, avoiding a couple of her nephews who raced in the opposite direction. In the kitchen, sauce was simmering on the stove, wine was being poured, and several arguments were taking place at once.

"This is Bo," Bianca announced, and silence fell. "He lives next door. He's a carpenter and has a crush on Reena."

"Actually, I'm pretty sure she's the love of my life."

"Will you stop." But Reena laughed as she shook her head. "This is my father, Gib, my sister Fran, her husband, Jack, one of the kids running out of here was their son, Anthony. This is my sister Bella—the other one streaking by was her son Dom; her other kids, Vinny, Sophia and Louisa, are around somewhere. My brother, Xander, and his wife, An; their baby is Dillon."

"It's nice to meet you." Fran offered him a smile. "Can I get you a glass of wine?"

"Sure, thanks."

"Fran and Jack manage the restaurant for my parents. Bella's husband couldn't make it by today. Xander and An are doctors, and work at the neighborhood clinic."

"It's nice to meet everyone."

She knew what he saw. The tall, handsome man at the stove giving him a careful measure. Lovely, pregnant Fran pouring wine, while redheaded Jack gave their redheaded daughter a piggyback ride. Bella leaning against the counter in her designer shoes and country club hair. Xander sipping wine and standing beside his gorgeous golden-skinned wife as she burped their six-week-old infant.

Of course the questions came popping out from all directions, but he fielded them easily enough. And didn't seem surprised to see the Italian, Irish, Chinese mix in the kitchen of a nearly empty row house.

He slid into the flow so easily, she was surprised to hear him say he was an only child when asked about his family.

"My parents split when I was a kid. I grew up in PG County. My mother lives in North Carolina now. My father's out in Arizona. I guess my partner's like my brother. We've known each other forever. Maybe you remember him," he said to Reena. "He dated a girl who knew Jan, went to Maryland. I think her name was Cammie."

"No, sorry. I didn't socialize all that much in college."

"She spent most of her time studying," Bella put in, with the slightest smirk. "Then she had her heart broken by tragedy."

"Bella." Bianca's voice was sharp as a whip.

"Oh, for God's sake, it was years ago. If she's not over it, she ought to be."

"When someone dies, they stay dead no matter how many years pass."

"I'm sorry." Bo turned to Reena.

"You don't have anything to apologize for," she said with a long look at her sister. "Here, have some antipasto." She picked up a platter. "Until I get a dining room table, we'll be eating standing up or sitting on the floor."

"I could make you one."

"One what? A table?"

"Yeah. It's one of the things I do. Actually, my favorite thing. Building furniture. Give me an idea what you want, and I'll make you a table. Ah, like a housewarming deal."

"You can't just make me a table."

"Hush." Bianca moved in. "You do good work?"

"I do exceptional work. I offered her references before. Maybe you know Mr. and Mrs. Baccho, over on Fawn Street?"

Bianca's eyes narrowed. "I know them. Dave and Mary Teresa. You're the boy who did their china cabinets."

"The oak and glass built-ins. Yeah, that's my work."

"It's good work." Her gaze slid toward her husband. "I'd like something like those. Come in here, look at the dining room."

"Mama."

"It doesn't hurt to have him look," Bianca called back, and drew Bo away.

An passed the baby to Xander. She was a tiny thing, barely five feet with a glossy wedge of coal black hair and deep black eyes. She plucked a stuffed mushroom from the platter Reena held. "He's hot," she murmured. "Serious hotness factor."

"I haven't moved in yet, and she's got me dating the boy next door."

"Hey, worst you can do is get a free table out of it." She grinned around the mushroom. "And the guy looks like he can swing a hammer to me."

"I heard that innuendo," Xander called out.

"I'm going to go separate them." Reena handed the platter to An and walked quickly to the dining room.

Her mother was gesturing, holding her hands apart, talking about necessary seating.

Bo looked over, patted a hand on his heart. "She just walks into the room and my head spins."

Reena arched her eyebrows. "You're going to want to take that down a few levels."

"It's my first day, so you need to cut me some slack. We're thinking drop leaf. That way, you'd have the smaller size, and the extension for dinner parties and family meals without the bother of the leaves."

"I don't know what I want yet." About tables, she thought, about you. About anything but the job. "I just can't say."

"I'll make you up a few designs. Get the ball rolling. It's the same setup I've got next door, so I can use my space for measurements. Lots of potential here." He smiled at her. "Unlimited potential. I'd better go."

"You should stay," Bianca objected. "Eat."

"Thanks, I'll take a rain check. You need anything," he said to Reena, "I'm right next door. I wrote down my number." He pulled a card out of his pocket. "Cell's printed on there, home number's on the back. You need anything, just call."

"All right. I'll walk you out."

He handed her his wineglass. "That's okay. I know the way. You stay with your family. I'll be in for that meal, Bianca."

"See that you are."

Bianca waited until she was sure he was out of earshot. "He has good manners. He has good eyes. You should give him a chance."

"I've got his number." Reena stuffed it in her pocket. "I'll think about it."

# 14

The fire started in the attic of a lovely old brownstone on Bolton Hill. The upscale neighborhood had pretty little parks, and leafy trees lining the streets.

The occupants had lost the entire third story, most of the roof and portions of the second floor. As the fire had started mid-morning on a weekday, no one was home.

An alert—or nosy—neighbor had spotted the smoke and flames and called the fire department.

Reena read through the reports as they headed to the scene.

"No signs of forced entry. Owners have a security system. Weekly housekeeper has the code. Fire inspector has the point of origin in the attic. Newspapers, the remains of a matchbook."

"Nice neighborhood," O'Donnell commented.

"Yeah. I poked around here a little when I was shopping for a house. Just kept winding back to the old neighborhood."

"Nothing wrong with that. Heard you've got an interesting neighbor."

Her eyes narrowed on his face. "How'd you hear about that?"

"Maybe your father mentioned it to John, maybe John mentioned it to me."

"Maybe you all should find more interesting things to talk about than my boy next door."

"Got no criminal."

"You did a run on him? For God's sake."

"Safety first." O'Donnell winked at her, then slid into a parking spot at the curb. "Speeding ticket about six months ago."

"I don't want to know." She got out of the car, rounded to the back for her field kit.

"Single, no marriage on record."

"Shut up, O'Donnell."

He got his own kit. "Got his business licenses for Baltimore and Prince George's counties. Lists a PG County address for business. That's his partner's place. Your guy moves around a lot. Relocates about every six, eight months."

"This is so intrusive."

"Yeah." O'Donnell had a spring to his step as he walked toward the house. "That's what makes it fun. See, what he does is he and his partner buy buildings—houses mostly—then do the fixer-upper deal, turn them. Your boy—"

"Not my boy."

"Your boy moves in, works from inside, gets the place tuned up, sells it, buys another, moves on. Been doing it the last ten or twelve years, looks like."

"Good for him. Now maybe we could focus on the job instead of my life."

She studied the building first, the scorching on the brown brick, the angles of the roof collapse. She took pictures for the file. "Report says the attic door and window were open."

"Get some nice cross-ventilation going that way," O'Donnell commented. "Stored stuff up there, like you do. Off-season clothes, holiday decorations. Good fuel."

"Neighbor's coming out," Reena said quietly as she lowered the camera. "I'll take her."

"Get started, then." O'Donnell hefted his kit and started for the door.

"Ma'am." Reena drew her badge from her waistband. "I'm Detective Hale from the Baltimore City Police, Arson Unit."

"Arson. Well, well." The woman was tiny, dark-skinned and neat as pressed linen.

"My partner and I are doing a follow-up on the incident. Are you Mrs. Nichols? Shari Nichols?"

"That's right."

"You reported the fire."

"That I did. I was out in the back. I've got a little container garden out there. Smelled it first. The smoke."

"That was about eleven A.M.?"

"About eleven-fifteen. I know because I was thinking my youngest would be home from kindergarten in about an hour, and that would be the end of the quiet." She smiled a little. "She's a hellion."

"How long had you been outside before you smelled smoke?"

"Oh, an hour maybe, if that. And I went back in about quarter of for a few minutes because I'd forgotten to bring out the phone. The fire inspector, he already asked me if I saw anyone around. I didn't."

She looked up at her neighbor's house. "Damn shame. But thank God nobody was home, nobody was hurt. I can tell you it scared me, scared me good. The idea it could spread to my house."

She rubbed a hand over her throat as she looked up at the blistered trim, the soot-blackened bricks. "The fire department came quick. Gives you some peace of mind."

"Yes, ma'am. If you didn't see anything, maybe you heard something."

"I heard the smoke alarms from inside the house. Didn't notice them at first. I had music on. But once I smelled the smoke, looked around and saw it coming out of the window up in the attic, I heard their smoke alarms ringing. I guess it's an awful mess inside. She won't care for that."

"Sorry?"

"I only meant Ella Parker—the woman who lives there—she likes things just so. We have the same housekeeper, though I only use Annie once a month, since I'm not working outside the home right now. Ella's fussy. She'd be as upset about the mess as she would the fire. That doesn't sound kind," Shari added after a moment. "I don't mean to sound callous."

"Do you and Mrs. Parker get along?"

"Well enough." Reena heard the reservation in her voice, stayed quiet. "We're friendly without being friends," she added after that long silence. "My middle boy plays with her oldest now and then."

She shifted her feet, looked uncomfortable when Reena only nodded. "Do you really think this was arson, not just an accident?"

"We haven't made that determination."

"Oh lord, oh hell. I guess I'd better say Ella and I had some words a few weeks ago. God." She rubbed a hand at her neck. "I don't want the police thinking I had anything to do with this."

"Why would we?"

"Well, we had some strong words, and we have the same housekeeper, and our kids played together. I'm the one who called nine-one-one. I was talking to my husband about this last night, and he says I'm looking for trouble. But I can't get it off my mind."

"Why don't you tell me what you had words about."

"The boys. Her Trevor and my Malcomb." She blew out a breath. "I caught them hooking school three weeks back. Idiots. It was a pretty day, so I decided to walk to school and pick my youngest up, thought I'd take her to the park, let her run off some of that steam she's always full of. And there they were, the two of them, running across the street to the park. Well, I can tell you I hauled off after them, put a bug in their ear and marched them both right to school."

Reena allowed herself a smile. An adult female to adult female expression. "Bet they were surprised to see you."

"Didn't have enough sense to keep out of sight. You're going to play hooky, at least do a good job of it." She shook her head. "When Ella got home from work, I went over—with my boy—to fill her in. Before I know it, she's saying it's my kid's fault, and how I didn't have any right to put hands on her boy."

She spread those hands now. "All I did was take his hand and march him to school, where he belonged. I'd appreciate someone who looked after my kid that way, wouldn't you?"

"Yes. Yes, I would. But Mrs. Parker was upset."

"Pissed off is what she was. So I had words right back at her, saying next time I saw him on the street during school hours, I'd just walk right by. We said more, but you get the idea."

"Can't blame you for being upset," Reena prompted. "You were only trying to do the right thing."

"And got told to mind my own business. Which if I had, her damn house would've burned down. Boys haven't played with each other since, and I'm sorry about it. But I can't have Malc running around as he pleases. According to him, it wasn't the first time Trevor had taken a school holiday, and he was scared enough to tell me the truth."

"He claims Trevor skips school routinely?"

"Oh, *hell*. I don't want to get that child in any more trouble."

"It'd be better for him, for everyone, if we had the facts, Mrs. Nichols. The more you can tell me, the quicker we can get all this put to rest."

"Well. Oh well. I don't know about routine, but my boy says Trevor takes off occasionally, and talked him into joining the party this time. Doesn't excuse what Malc did, and he's been righteously punished for it. For the last three weeks I've been walking him to school every morning, picking him up every afternoon. Not much else humiliates a nine-year-old boy more than having his mama walk him to and from school."

"My mother did the same with my brother once. He was twelve. I don't think he's lived it down yet."

"Parents ought to be more worried about doing their job instead of being best pals with their kids, you ask me."

"Is that the way it is next door?"

"Now I'm just gossiping," Shari replied. "Not that I have anything against gossip. I'll say I don't see much discipline. But that's just my opinion, which my husband tells me I express much too often. Trevor runs a little wild, but he's a nice enough boy. I just want to say, I might not be on the best terms with Ella right at the moment, but I wouldn't wish this sort of thing on anybody. I think it must've been some freak accident. Spontaneous combustion or something."

"We'll be looking into it. I appreciate the time."

Reena went inside. She stood in the front hall, absorbing the tone and feel of the house. The fire hadn't come this far, but she could smell the smoke. Fire suppression had caused some minor damage. Soot and dirt on the floor, the stairs.

But she could see what the neighbor meant. Looking beyond the mess of emergency, everything was scrupulous. A gleam under the debris dust, flowers arranged just so in vases, color-coordinating cushions and drapes, all chosen to accent the tones of the walls, the tones in the art.

Upstairs, she found the same. The master bedroom had taken the worst. Blistered paint, scorched ceilings, water and smoke damage.

The duvet on the king-sized bed had caught, as had the coordinating curtains. The natural wood blinds were scorched.

She could see the path the fire had taken, down the attic steps, eating its way across the polished wood floor, gnawing on the antique rug.

She moved down the hall, found two home offices. More antiques, she noted, more careful decorating.

The boy's room was at the other end of the hall. It was big and airy, done in a soccer theme. Framed posters, lots of black and white with red splashes. Rigorously organized bookshelves. No scatter of toys, no piles of discarded clothes.

She took out the file, checked information. Then took out her phone and made a call.

O'Donnell was working through layers of debris when she picked her way carefully up the damaged steps.

"Nice of you to join me."

"Had some background to check." She glanced up, studied the sky. "Most of the fire headed up. They're lucky. Damage to the second floor's not that bad. Just smoke and water damage on the main floor."

"No evidence of an accelerant so far. Point of origin, southeast corner."

He gestured as she took more photos. "Got the plywood, flashed the in-sulation behind it, traveled up, took the roof."

She crouched, picked through debris with her gloved hands and pulled out the scorched remains of a snapshot. "Photographs. Pile of photos, probably the starter."

"Yeah. Little bonfire of photos. Fire travels up, travels out. Storage bags, clothes inside, storage boxes, decorations inside, fueled it, carrying it down the stairs. Ventilated by the open window and the open door."

"Have you checked for prints? Door handle, around the window frame?"

"Waiting for you."

"Had a nice chat with the neighbor. Guess who likes to hook school?"

O'Donnell leaned back on his haunches. "Is that so?"

"Young Trevor Parker's been truant six times in the last three months. On the day of the fire, he was tardy, came in between eleven and eleven-thirty. Had a note," she added, "claiming he'd had a doctor's appointment."

She began to check for prints on the burned wood of the window frame. "The school has the students' medical information on record and was persuaded to give me the name of Trevor's pediatrician. He didn't have an appointment on the day in question."

"Nothing in the report about that either," O'Donnell pointed out. "Both adults were at work, until they were notified of the fire."

"Got a thumbprint here. Small. Looks like a kid's to me."

"I guess we'd better go have a talk with the Parkers."

E lla Parker was a buff and stylish thirty-eight. She was a senior vice president in marketing for a local firm, and came in to the station house carrying a Gucci briefcase. Her husband was her counterpart, heading the procurement department for a research and development organization.

He wore a Rolex and Italian loafers.

They'd brought Trevor with them, as requested. He was a small and wiry nine wearing two-hundred-dollar high-tops and a sullen expression.

"We appreciate you coming in," O'Donnell began.

"If you have a progress report, we want to hear it." Ella set her briefcase on the conference table in front of her. "We're dealing with insurance and estimates. We need to get back in the house as soon as possible so we can start repairs."

"Understood. While we've determined the cause of the fire, there are still questions to be addressed."

"I assume you've spoken with our former housekeeper."

"Former?" Reena prompted.

"I fired her yesterday. There's no question she's responsible. No one else had our security code. I told you that was a mistake," she said to her husband.

"She came highly recommended," he reminded her. "And she's worked for us for six years. What possible reason would Annie have to start a fire in our house?"

"People don't need a reason to do destructive things. They just do them. Have you spoken with her?" Ella demanded.

"We will be."

"I don't understand why she wasn't first on your list. Why you've dragged us down here at a time like this. Do you have any idea how much time and stress and energy are involved after you've had a fire in your home?"

"Actually, I do," Reena said. "I'm sorry you have to deal with it."

"I had several thousand dollars' worth of personal items destroyed, not to mention the damage to my home. I've had to cancel appointments, completely rearrange my schedule—"

"Ella." There was a weariness in William Parker's voice, and it sounded habitual to Reena.

"Don't Ella me," she snapped. "I'm the one dealing with all the details. Not that you ever—" She cut herself off, lifted a hand. "I'm sorry. I'm very upset."

"Understandable. Can you tell us how often you go up to the attic?" O'Donnell asked.

"At least once a month. And I have—had—the housekeeper clean up there regularly."

"Mr. Parker?"

"Two, three times a year, I guess. Hauling stuff up or down. Christmas decorations, that sort of thing."

"Trevor?"

"Trevor's not allowed in the attic," Ella cut in.

Reena caught the quick glance he shot his mother before he went back to staring at the table.

"I used to like to play in the attic when I was a kid." Reena spoke casually. "All kinds of interesting stuff up there."

"I said he isn't allowed."

"What a boy isn't allowed and what he does are often the same things. According to our information, Trevor occasionally hooks school."

"Once—and he's not allowed to play with the boy responsible. I don't see what business that is of yours."

"Trevor wasn't in school on the morning of the fire. Were you, Trevor?"

"Of course he was." Anger and impatience sharpened Ella's voice to a pinpoint. "My husband picked him up after we learned about the fire."

"But you weren't in school until nearly noon, isn't that right, Trevor? You came in late. With a note that said you had a doctor's appointment."

"That's ridiculous."

"Mrs. Parker." O'Donnell spoke in his slow, patient drawl. "Any reason you can't let your boy answer for himself?"

"I'm his mother, and I'm not going to allow him to be interrogated or browbeaten by the police. We've been victimized, and now you're making some sort of veiled accusation involving a nine-year-old boy." She pushed to her feet. "I've had enough. Come on, Trevor."

"Ella, shut up. Just shut the hell up for five damn minutes." William dismissed her, focused on the boy. "Trevor, did you skip school again?"

The boy jerked a shoulder, stared at the table. But Reena saw the gleam of tears in his eyes.

"Did you go up into the attic that morning, Trevor?" she asked quietly. "Maybe just to play, just to hang out?"

"I don't want you questioning him," Ella said.

"I do." Her husband rose. "If you can't handle it, step out of the room. But I'm going to hear what Trevor has to say."

"Like you care. Like you care about either of us. You're so busy screwing your big-breasted blonde you don't have time to care."

"I'm so busy trying to tolerate living in the same house with you, I haven't cared enough. About Trevor."

"I didn't hear you deny cheating on me, you son of a bitch."

"Stop it! Stop it!" Trevor clamped his hands over his ears. "Stop yelling all the time! I didn't mean to do it. I didn't *mean* it. I just wanted to see what would happen."

"Oh my God. Oh my God, Trevor. What have you done? Don't say another word. I'm not letting him say another word," Ella said to Reena. "I'm calling my lawyer."

"Back off, Ella." William laid his hand on his son's shoulder. Then he lowered his head, rested it against the top of his son's. "I'm sorry, kiddo. Your mom and I have messed things up good. We're going to stand up to it. You need to stand up, too. Tell what happened."

"I was mad. I was mad because you were fighting again, and I didn't want to go to school. So I didn't."

Reena handed Trevor a tissue. "You came back home instead?"

"I was just going to play in my room, and watch TV. But . . ."

"You were feeling mad."

"They're going to get a divorce."

"Oh, Trev." William sat again. "It's not because of you."

"You wrecked the house. That's what Mom said. You're wrecking it, so I thought if there was a fire, you'd stay home to fix it. But I didn't mean it. I got matches and lit the pictures and the papers, then I couldn't put it out. I got scared and I ran away. I had the note 'cause I wrote it on the computer before. And I went to school."

"This is all your fault," Ella spat out.

William took Trevor's hand. "Sure, why not? Enough of it is. We'll work through this, kiddo. It's good you told the truth, and we'll work through it."

"If the house got burned down, you won't get divorced." Trevor buried his face against his father's chest. "Don't go away."

She got home late, and she got home depressed. There wasn't going to be any perfect, or even easy, ending for Trevor Parker. Counseling would help, but it wouldn't put his family back together. That, in Reena's opinion, was doomed.

Too many were as far as she could see.

For every Fran and Jack, every Gib and Bianca, there were failed couples on the other part of the scale. And the failures generally outweighed the successes.

The kid's home might not have burned down, but it was sure as hell broken.

She pulled up in front of her house, got out of the car, locked it. And saw Bo sitting on his front steps, nursing a bottle of beer.

She nearly ignored him—everything about him said complicated and time-consuming. Simpler, she thought, just to go into her own house, close the door. And close out the hardship of the day.

But she crossed over instead, sat down on the step beside him. She took his beer and had a good long drink.

"If you're going to tell me you've been sitting out here waiting for me, I'm going to get weirded out."

"Then I won't tell you. But I can say that I've been known to take in a nice evening with a cold one on the front steps. Rough one?"

"Sad one."

"Somebody die?"

"No." She passed the beer back to him. "Which is a question that forces me to put today in some perspective. A lot of times someone has. One thing you can't come back from is death."

"What, no reincarnation in your world? Where's the karma?"

She smiled, which surprised her. "I didn't deal with someone who may come back as a beagle today. Just some little kid who nearly burned his house down trying to keep his parents together."

"He hurt?"

"Not physically, no."

"That's something."

"Something. You said your parents split when you were a kid."

"Yeah." He took a drink from the beer she passed back to him. "It was . . . unpleasant. Okay," he corrected when she merely looked at him. "It was a nightmare. You don't want to add to the weight of the day hearing about my childhood traumas."

"My parents have been married thirty-seven years. Sometimes they're like one body with two heads. They fight, but it's never ugly, if you get me."

"Oh boy, do I."

"I'd say they're glued together, but you know what? They are the glue. Somehow the solidity of them is intimidating. Because you never want to settle for less than that."

"We could start out having dinner. See where it went from there."

"We could." She took the bottle again, drank contemplatively. She could smell his soap, and a trace of something else. Maybe linseed oil, she thought. Something he might rub into wood.

"Or we could just go inside and have some wild sex. That's what you want."

"Well, rock and a hard place." He gave a nervous little *heh-heh*, stretched out his legs. "I can't say no, because—hey, guy here. So yeah, having wild sex with you would suit me fine. I thought about making love with you for seven-seventeenths of my life."

A quick, unladylike snort escaped her. "Seven-seventeenths?"

"That's rounded a little, but I figured it out. So getting to that in reality would be a big moment for me. On the other hand, I've thought about making love with you for seven-seventeenths of my life, so waiting a little longer won't hurt me."

"You're a funny guy, Bowen."

"Yep. I can be a funny guy. I can be a serious guy, or an astute guy, or a casual guy. I am a guy of many facets. We could have dinner, and I could treat you to a few of them."

"Maybe. My partner ran you."

"Ran me where?"

This time she laughed, stretched out her legs companionably. "Did a background check on you."

"No shit?" He looked fascinated rather than insulted. "Wow. Did I pass?"

"Apparently." Her forehead creased as she studied him. "Why aren't you annoyed? I was annoyed."

"I don't know. I guess it's sort of interesting. I don't think I've ever been run before."

"I have a big, noisy, irritating, often interfering, overprotective family. They're the center of my life, even when I don't want them to be."

"I'm the only child of a broken home. Feel my pain."

"You're not in pain."

"Nope. Doesn't mean I'm scared of your family either. I just want to touch you." He ran a hand up her arm, over her shoulder, then brought her face around so their eyes met. "You may not be what I've got in my head, but it's been there so long. I just want to find out."

"Relationships don't stick to me. Maybe more accurately, I don't stick to them. Have you considered how irritating it would be to end up living next door to each other if we end up hating each other?"

"One of us would have to move. But in the meantime." He reached behind him to open the front door, set the empty beer bottle inside. "Want to take a walk? I hear there's a really good Italian place a few blocks away. We could grab a meal."

"All right." She braced her hands on her knees and hoped she wasn't making a mistake. "All right, let's take a walk."

# 15

Reena walked the baby around Xander and An's living room in their doll-sized apartment. Their packing-up process had already begun.

She'd moved out of the apartment over Sirico's, and now her brother and his little family would move in.

The windows—both of them—were wide open so she could hear the traffic, and the shouts of kids playing in a nearby park.

The baby had already burped, but Reena wasn't ready to put him down yet. "So we've had dinner at Sirico's. Twice. Sat out on his steps a couple of times. He drew up a design for a dining room table for me. It's great. In fact, it's perfect. I don't know what to make of him."

"More to the point." An continued to fold baby clothes. "Why haven't you made him?"

"Nice talk, Mommy."

"At the moment, due to childbirth, child rearing, work and preparing to move, my sex life is at a low ebb. I've got to get my thrills somewhere. How's he in the kissing department?"

"I don't know."

"You haven't kissed him?" An tossed down a onesie and clutched at her chest. "You moved in, what, three weeks ago? You're breaking my heart."

"He works, I work." Reena shrugged. "Even though we live next door, we don't see each other every day. Maybe we're making a point not to see each other every day. He hasn't made a move. Neither have I. We're sort of . . ." She twirled a finger in the air. "Circling it. I keep expecting him to. And I think he expects I'm expecting so he lays back, which keeps me just a little off balance. I have to admire that."

"Okay, you admire him, you've spent time with him, so you must enjoy him. You still have a pulse so you find him attractive. But you're not jumping him."

"No." Reena eased Dillon back so she could look into his face. "What's wrong with me?"

"Scares you a little, doesn't he?"

"I fear no man." Could, would, not allow herself to. "Not even this one, who I believe has just filled his diaper admirably. Go to Mama, sweetie pie."

An took the baby, carried him to the bedroom the three of them currently shared. She laid him on the changing table. "I think he scares you a little," she continued. "Xander scared me a little at first. He was so cute and funny, and he's such a damn good doctor. I wanted to bite him in the throat. Then after we started seeing each other, I was really scared to meet your family. I had this image in my head. Sort of Sopranos—without the blood and murder and crime."

"Good to know."

"But the big family, the *Italian* family. How would a nice Chinese girl like me fit in with his family?"

"Like a lotus blossom, elegantly twined in a grapevine."

"Hey, nice image. I love them, you know. I loved your family even before I loved Xander. I lusted for him, admired him, but boy, was I dazzled by them. Now look what I've got to show for it."

She kissed Dillon on the belly, wrapped an arm around Reena's waist. "Isn't he the most beautiful thing you've ever seen?"

"Takes the prize."

"I said no the first time Xander asked me to marry him."

"What?" Surprised, Reena looked down at her sister-in-law's gleaming hair. "You said no to Xander?"

"Complete panic. No, no, are you crazy? Let's just keep everything the way it is. We don't have to get married. We're fine, let it alone. Which he did, for nearly an hour. He came back at me and told me to stop being stupid."

"Romantic devil."

"Actually he was. He was so revved up and sexy. I love you, you love me, so let's start building a life together. I said yes, and we did." She picked up the baby, pressed her cheek to his. "Thank God. And the reason I'm telling you," she added, "is just to illustrate it's okay to be a little scared. But it's better to make a move."

Maybe she would, she mused on the drive home. What was stopping her? An had a point—as An invariably did. It was better to make a move. And the person who made the move, Reena reminded herself, generally had the upper hand.

She didn't *have* to have the upper hand in a relationship, but she didn't object to having it. And it made sense when she really thought it through. He'd been carrying a fantasy torch for her for . . . what had he said? Seven-seventeenths of his life. And how cute was that? So that meant, logically, he had all manner of ideas and images of her built up. Most of them, undoubtedly, exaggerated and inaccurate.

But if she made the move, they'd have a fresh playing field.

And she did like to play.

Sometimes you just went with the urge, she decided as she parked her car and grabbed her bag. No point in making a big fuss or overanalyzing.

So she walked straight to Bo's door and knocked. He took so long to answer she wondered if he was out in the back working, as he did some evenings. But when he opened the door, she had a flirtatious smile in place.

"Hi. I was in the neighborhood, so I thought . . ." He looked shocky, she realized. Pale and punched. "What's wrong?"

"I . . . I have to go. Sorry. I need to—" He broke off, looked blankly behind him as if he'd forgotten what he was doing.

"Bo, what happened?"

"What? I have to . . . my grandmother."

She took his arm, spoke carefully. She knew a victim when she saw one. "What happened to your grandmother?"

"She died."

"Oh, I'm sorry. I'm so sorry. When?"

"They . . . they just called. Just now called. I have to go to her house. She's in her house. I have to go take care of things. Something."

"Okay. I'll take you."

"What? Wait, give me a second." He pressed his fingers to his eyes. "I'm messed up."

"Of course you are. So I'll drive you."

"No. No, that's okay." He dropped his hands, shook his head. "It's way out in Glendale."

"Come on, we'll take my car. Got your house keys?"

"My . . ." He stuck a hand in his pocket, pulled them out. "Yeah. Yeah. Listen, Reena, you don't have to do this. I just need a minute to get my head around it."

"You shouldn't drive, trust me. And you shouldn't go alone. Lock your door," she told him, then led him to her car. "Where in Glendale?"

He rubbed his face like a man trying to scrub off sleep, then gave her an address and vague directions. She knew the area well enough from her college days.

"Had your grandmother been ill?"

"No. At least nothing major. Nothing I knew about. A lot of little stuff, I guess, that you deal with when you're eighty-seven. Or -eight. Shit. I can't remember."

"Women don't mind you not remembering their age." She brushed a hand over the back of his as she drove. "Do you want to tell me what happened? Or would you rather just be quiet?"

"I don't know. I don't know exactly. Her neighbor found her. Got worried because she didn't answer the phone. And she hadn't been out to get her mail this morning. She's—my grandmother, she's habitual, you know?"

"Yes."

"She has keys. The neighbor. Went over to check on her. She was still in bed. She must've died in her sleep. I guess. I don't know. She was there all day, by herself all day."

"Bowen, it's hard to lose someone. But let me ask you, when your time comes, can you think of a better way to leave than to slip away in your own bed, in your own home, while you sleep?"

"Probably not." He took a long breath. "Probably not. I just talked to her yesterday. Call every couple days. Just hey, how's it going? She said her kitchen faucet was leaking again, so I was going to go by today or tomorrow, take care of it. I got hung up today and didn't get over. Oh, shit."

"You took care of her."

"No, I just fixed stuff around the house. I went by every couple weeks, maybe. Not enough. I should've gone by more. Why do you always think of that after?"

"Because being human we tend to beat ourselves up. Is there any other family around?"

"Not really. My father's in Arizona. Hell, I didn't even call him. Uncle in Florida. A cousin in Pennsylvania." He leaned his head back. "I have to find the numbers."

The picture was coming clear, and the picture told her he was on his own in this. "Do you know what she wanted? Did she ever talk to you about arrangements?"

"Not really. A Mass, I guess. She'd want a Mass."

"You're Catholic?"

"She is—was. I mostly got over it. Last rites. Damn it. It's too late for that. I feel stupid," he said with a sigh. "I've never done anything like this before. My grandfather died almost twenty years ago. Car accident. My mother's parents are out in Vegas."

"Your grandparents live in Vegas?"

"Yeah. They love it. The last time I saw her, a couple weeks ago? We had really lousy iced tea—you know the kind you get out of a jar that's got fake sugar and lemon flavoring in it."

"Should be illegal."

"Right." He laughed a little. "We had lousy iced tea and Chips Ahoy! cookies out on her patio. She wasn't the kind who baked and stuff. She liked to play pinochle and watch those *World's Worst* whatever on TV. Like *World's Worst Pet Attacks. World's Worst Vacation Disasters*. She really dug on that crap. She smoked three cigarettes a day. Virginia Slims. Three. Not one less, not one more."

"And you loved her."

"I did. I never thought much about it, but I really did. Thanks. Thanks for talking me through this."

"It's okay."

Steadier, he guided her in the rest of the way, to a pretty brick house with a meticulous yard.

There were white shutters and a short white porch. She imagined Bo had painted them for her—had probably built the little porch as well.

A woman in her mid-forties stepped out. Her eyes were red from weeping. She wore a powder blue tracksuit and had her light brown hair pulled back in a short tail.

"Bo. Bo. I'm so sorry." She wrapped her arms around him, and her body shook as she hugged him. "I'm so glad you're here." She sniffled, drew back. "Sorry," she said to Reena. "I'm Judy Dauber, from next door."

"This is Reena. Catarina Hale. Thanks, Judy, for . . . waiting with her."

"Of course, sweetie. Of course."

"I should go in."

"Go ahead." Reena took his hand, gave it a squeeze. "I'll come in a minute."

Reena waited on the lawn, watched him go to the door, go inside.

"I thought she was sleeping," Judy began. "For just a second. I thought, well, for heaven's sake, Marge, what are you doing in bed this time of day?

She stayed active. Then I realized, almost immediately, I realized. I talked to her just yesterday. She said Bo was coming by in a day or two, fix her faucet. And she'd have a list of little chores for him to do when he got here. She was awfully proud of him. Didn't have two good words to say at once about his father, but she prized Bo."

She fumbled out a tissue, wiped at her eyes. "She really prized Bo. He was the only one who took care, if you understand me. The only one who paid attention."

"You did."

Judy glanced over, and the tears rolled again.

"Judy." Reena draped an arm over the woman's shoulders as they walked toward the house. "Bo said his grandmother was Catholic. Do you know the name of her church, her pastor?"

"Oh, yes, yes, of course. I should've thought of that."

"We can call. And maybe we can find numbers for her sons."

D eath might come simply, but its aftermath was invariably complicated. Reena did what she could, contacting the priest while Bo called his father. In a little desk in the spare room, papers were competently organized in a file drawer. Insurance, burial plot, a copy of the will, the deed to the house, the title to the aging Chevy Reena learned Marge Goodnight had driven to church and the grocery store.

The priest arrived so quickly, with a face so solemn Reena deduced Marge had been a prominent member of the parish.

She began to see more of Bo here. The tidiness of the house was certainly Marge. But its upkeep was undoubtedly his doing. There was none of the slapdash repairs, the jury-rigged details she often saw in the homes and apartments of seniors.

As Judy had said, he paid attention. He took care.

He handled the details, made the calls, spoke with the priest, made the decisions. Once, she saw him falter and moved over to take his hand.

"What can I do?"

"They, ah . . . They need to know what she should wear. For the funeral. I have to pick something."

"Why don't I do that? Men never know what we want to wear."

"I'd appreciate it. Her stuff's in there, in the closet. You could wait on it. They haven't . . . I mean, she's still in there."

"It's okay. I'll take care of this."

Maybe it was surreal, to go into the bedroom of a woman she'd never met, to go through the closet while a body lay in the bed. Out of respect, Reena stepped to the bed first, looked down.

Marge Goodnight had let her hair go slate gray, and had kept it short and straight. No-nonsense then, Reena decided. Her left hand, with its wedding ring set, lay outside the covers.

She imagined Bo had sat there, held her hand while he said his good-byes.

"It's too much for him," she said quietly. "Picking a dress for you is just a little out of his scope. I hope you don't mind if I handle this part."

She opened the closet, smiled when she saw built-in shelves and cubbies. "He built these, didn't he?" She glanced over her shoulder at Marge. "You like things organized, and he did the work. It's a good design. I may have to hire him to do something similar for me. What about this blue suit, Marge? Dignified, but not stuffy. And this blouse, with just a little bit of lace down the placket. Pretty, but not too frilly. I think I'd have liked you."

She found a garment bag, hung the outfit inside, and though she realized it was unnecessary, selected shoes, then underwear from the bureau.

Before she left the room, she turned to the bed again. "I'll light a candle for you, and have my mother say a rosary. Nobody says a rosary like my mama. Safe passage, Marge."

Reena took two hours' personal time to attend the funeral. He hadn't asked her to come. In fact, she thought he'd deliberately avoided asking her. She sat in the back, not surprised the Mass was so well attended.

Her brief conversation with the pastor had cemented her conclusion that Margaret Goodnight had been a fixture of the church.

They'd brought flowers, as friends and neighbors do, so the church smelled of lilies and incense and candle wax. She stood and knelt, sat and spoke, the rhythm of the Mass as familiar to her as her own heartbeat. When the priest spoke of the dead, he spoke of her in personal and affectionate terms.

She'd mattered, Reena thought. She'd left her mark. And wasn't that the point?

When Bo walked up to the pulpit to speak, she didn't think Marge would mind if she admired the way he looked in a dark suit.

"My grandmother," he began, "was tough. She didn't suffer fools. She figured you should use the brains God gave you, otherwise you were just taking up space. She did a lot more than take up space. She told me that during the Depression she worked in a dime store, made a dollar a day. Had to walk two miles each way—fair weather or foul. She didn't think it was that big a deal, she just did what she had to do.

"She told me once she thought she'd become a nun, then decided she'd rather have sex. I hope it's okay to say that in here," he added after a ripple of laughter. "She married my grandfather in 1939. They had what she called a two-hour honeymoon before they both had to go back to work. Apparently, they managed to make my uncle Tom in that short window. She lost a daughter at six months, and a son in Vietnam who never saw his twentieth birthday. She lost her husband, but she never lost, well, her faith. Or her independence, which was just as important to her. She taught me how to ride a two-wheeler, and to finish what I start."

He cleared his throat. "She's survived by her two sons, my cousin Jim and me. I'm going to miss her."

Reena waited outside the church while people spoke to Bo before walking to their cars. It was a pretty morning, with strong sun and the smell of freshly mown grass.

She noted the two people who stayed closest to him. A man of about his age, about five-ten, trendy wire-framed glasses, good, dark suit and shoes. And a woman around thirty with short, bright red hair wearing sunglasses and a sleeveless black dress.

From what he'd told her, they couldn't be blood kin. But she recognized family when she saw it.

He broke away, walked to Reena. "Thanks for coming. I haven't had much chance to talk to you, to thank you for everything."

"It's all right. I'm sorry I can't go to the cemetery. I have to get back. It was a lovely service, Bo. You did just right."

"Scary." He put sunglasses over his tired eyes. "I haven't had to talk in front of so many people since the nightmare of public speaking in high school."

"Well, you aced it."

"Glad it's done." He looked over, and his jaw tightened. "I've got to ride out with my father." He nodded toward a man in a black suit. His black hair had just a touch of silver at the temples, like gleaming wings. Tanned and fit, she thought. And impatient.

"We don't seem to have anything to say to each other. How does that happen?"

"I don't know, but it does." She touched her lips to each of his cheeks in turn. "Take care."

At ten on a rainy morning in June that turned the air to steam, Reena stood over the partially destroyed body of a twenty-three-year-old woman. What was left of her was on the nasty carpet in a nasty room in a hotel where "fleabag" would have been a generous adjective.

Her name was DeWanna Johnson, according to the driver's license in the vinyl purse found under the bed—and the desk clerk's statement.

As her face and upper torso were all but gone, official identification would come later. She'd been wrapped in a blanket, with stuffing from the mattress strewn over and around her to act as trailers.

Reena took pictures while O'Donnell started the grid.

"So, DeWanna checks in three days ago with some guy. She pays cash for two nights. While it is possible DeWanna decided to sleep on the floor, and set her own face on fire, I scent a whiff of foul play."

O'Donnell chewed contemplatively on his gum. "Maybe the frying pan over there covered with blood and gray matter gave you the first clue."

"It didn't hurt. Jesus, DeWanna, bet he did a number on you first. He had a good combustible source of fuel with the blanket and mattress stuffing, then you've got her body fat for the candle effect. But he screwed up. Should've opened a window, should have coated this carpet with flammable liquid. Not enough oxygen, not enough flame to finish the job. Hope she was dead before he lit her. Hope the ME and radiologists confirm that."

She stepped out to go through the rest of the room, the excuse for a kitchenette. Broken dishes on the floor, what she identified as ground beef mixed with Hamburger Helper sloshed over the graying linoleum.

"Looks like she was fixing dinner when they got into it. Remains of that in the skillet along with pieces of her. He probably grabbed the pan right off the stove."

She turned from it, gripped her hands as if gripping the handle, swung out. "Knocked her back. Blood spatter here looks consistent with that. Comes right back with a backhanded follow-through. Knocks her back again, and down. Maybe pounds on her some more before he thinks, Whoa, shit, look what I did."

She stepped around the body. "Figures to light her up, cover up the murder. But animal fat doesn't burn cleanly. Modest flame destroys tissues, takes her face and more, but it doesn't bring the room temp, not a closed room, up enough to ignite the stuffing, even the bulk of the blanket he wrapped around her."

"So we're probably not going to be looking for a chemist."

"Or somebody who planned ahead. Frenzy of the moment, not premeditated, from the looks of the scene."

She moved into the bathroom. The back of the toilet was crammed with cosmetics. Hair spray, hair gel, mascara, lipsticks, blusher, eyeshadows.

Crouching down, she began to pick through the trash with her gloved hands. Moments later, she came back in holding a box.

"I think we've got a motive." She held up the home pregnancy test.

The desk clerk's vague description of the man who'd checked in with the victim was given a boost by the prints Reena lifted from the frying pan.

"Got him," she told O'Donnell, and swiveled around in her chair to face his desk. "Jamal Earl Gregg, twenty-five. Got a sheet. Assault, possession with intent, malicious wounding. Did a stint in Red Onion in Virginia. Released three months ago. Got a Richmond address listed. DeWanna Johnson's driver's license had a Richmond address."

"So maybe we'll take a field trip."

"I've got a current MasterCard in her name. It wasn't in her purse, or on the scene."

"If he took it, he'll use it. Asshole. Let's put out the alert. Maybe we'll save ourselves a trip down Ninety-five."

Reena wrote the report, did a search for known associates.

"The only tie I can find to Baltimore is an inmate on his block at Red Onion. Guy's still inside, doing a nickel for dealing."

"Jamal got busted for possession with intent. Maybe he came up this way looking to move in with his pal's connections."

"There's no record on DeWanna Johnson. No criminal, no juvie, no arrests. But she and Gregg went to the same high school."

O'Donnell tipped down the reading glasses he'd been forced to use. "High school sweethearts?"

"Stranger things. He gets out, scoops her up, and they're off to Baltimore— on her dime, in her car. Must be love. I'm going to call the address listed on her license, see what I can dig out."

"Let me update the captain," O'Donnell said. "See if he wants us to go to Richmond on this."

When O'Donnell came back, Reena held up a finger. "I appreciate that, Mrs. Johnson. If you hear from your daughter, or hear anything about Jamal Gregg's whereabouts, please contact me. You have my number. Yes. Thank you."

Reena pushed back in her chair. "High school sweethearts. In fact, so sweet, DeWanna has a five-year-old daughter. Her mother's got the kid. Jamal and DeWanna left three days ago—over the mother's objections. Job opportunity. She said her girl didn't have a brain cell working when it came to that no-account, and she hopes we lock the thieving bastard up good this time, so her girl has a chance to make a decent life. I didn't tell her the probability is high DeWanna's already lost her chance."

"Got one kid by her. He just gets out of prison, ready to get something going, and she tells him she's got another cooking. He loses it, does her, lights her, takes her credit card, cash, car."

"Works for me."

"We're getting cleared to drive down to Richmond. Hold on." He picked up his ringing phone. "Arson Unit. O'Donnell. Yeah. Yeah." He scribbled as he spoke. "Stall the authorization. We're on our way."

Reena was already up, grabbing her jacket. "Where?"

"Liquor store on Central."

Reena grabbed a radio on the run, requested backup.

He was gone when they got there, and frustration had Reena standing in the rain, kicking the rear tire of the car Jamal had left sitting at the curb. She pulled out her cell phone when it sang. "Hale. Okay. Got it." She clicked off. "Victim was six weeks pregnant. Cause of death, bludgeoning."

"That's fast work for the ME."

"I sweet-talked him. He couldn't have gone far. Even if he decided to ditch the car, he couldn't have gone far."

"So we look for him. Get in out of the rain." O'Donnell slid behind the wheel again. "Got the APB out. He's on foot. He's pissed off he didn't get his booze."

"Bar. Where's the closest bar?"

O'Donnell looked at her and grinned. "Now that's thinking." He turned the corner, nodded. "Let's have a look."

It was called Hideout. A number of patrons seemed to be doing just that, holed up with a bottle on a rainy afternoon.

Jamal was at the end of the bar, drinking boilermakers.

He was off the stool like lightning, and sprinting toward the back.

Good eye for cops, was Reena's only thought as she ran after him. She hit the alley door three steps ahead of O'Donnell. She evaded the metal trash can Jamal heaved. O'Donnell didn't.

"You hurt?" she called back.

"Get him. I'm right behind you."

Jamal was fast, but so was she. When he scurried up and over the fence backing the alley, she was right behind him. "Police! Freeze!"

He was fast, she thought again, but he didn't know Baltimore. She was faster—and she did.

The rain-drenched alley he'd run into this time dead-ended. He whirled, eyes wild, and flipped out a knife.

"Come on, bitch."

Keeping her eyes locked on his, Reena drew her weapon. "What, are you just really stupid? Toss down the knife, Jamal, before I shoot you."

"Ain't got the balls."

Now she grinned, though her palms had gone clammy and her knees wanted badly to shake. "Bet me."

From behind her, she heard O'Donnell swear and puff, and had never heard sweeter music. "And me," he said, bracing his weapon on the top of the fence.

"I didn't do nothing." Jamal dropped the knife. "I'm just having a drink."

"Yeah, tell that to DeWanna, and the baby she was carrying." Her heart pistoned painfully against her ribs as she moved forward. "On the ground, you bastard. Hands behind your head."

"I don't know what you're talking about." He got down, laced his hands behind his head. "You got the wrong person."

"This next stint you do in a cage, maybe you can study up on the properties of fire. Meanwhile, Jamal Earl Gregg, you're under arrest for suspicion of murder." She kicked the knife away, cuffed him.

They were soaked to the skin and dripping when they heard the sirens. O'Donnell shot her a fierce grin. "Fast on your feet, Hale."

"Yeah."

And since it was over, she sat on the wet pavement until she got her breath back.

# 16

Well, it was done, Bo thought as he let himself into his house. At least he hoped to God it was done. Mostly. Lawyers, insurance, accountants, realtors. All those meetings, all that paperwork made his ears ring. Not to mention, he thought, a couple of go-rounds with his father.

Over and done, he decided, and couldn't figure out if he was relieved or depressed.

He set a packing box beside the one he'd already brought in and dumped at the foot of the stairs. One more in the car, he mused. He could just leave it there, deal with it all later.

And he could've sworn he heard his grandmother's voice, telling him to finish what he started.

"Okay, okay." He pushed at his already dripping hair and headed back out.

A beer would be good. A beer, a hot shower, maybe some ESPN. Chill out. Decompress. Then, as he pulled the tarp up to get to the last of the boxes, Reena pulled in. He forgot all about an evening in his underwear watching the game.

"Hi." He thought she looked a little pale and tired, but it might've been the rain.

"Hi back."

She wasn't wearing a hat either, and her hair was a riot of tawny corkscrews. "Got a minute?" he asked her. "Want to come in?"

She hesitated, then gave a little shrug. "Sure. Need a hand?"

"No, I've got it."

"Haven't seen you around much this week," she commented.

"Work squeezed between meetings. Turns out I'm executor of my grandmother's estate. That sounds like it's really big and shiny. It's not like she was rolling in it or anything. Mostly it's just lawyers and paperwork. Thanks," he added when she opened the door for him. "Want some wine?"

"About as much as I want to keep breathing."

"Let me get you a towel." He dumped the box with the others, walked down the hall and into what she knew was the half bath.

The house was nearly a twin of hers in its setup. But what he'd done set it apart. The trim and floors had been taken down to their natural color and varnished, and the walls were a deep, warm green that set off the honey oak. He'd suspended a mission-style light from the lofty ceiling.

The hall could have used a runner, she thought. Something old and a little threadbare and full of character. And he probably planned to refinish the table near the door where he threw his keys.

He came back with a couple of navy blue towels. "You've done some beautiful work in here."

"Yeah?" He glanced around as he scrubbed his hair with a towel. "Good start anyway."

"Really good start," she said as she wandered into the living room. His furniture needed help. Slipcovers, or better yet replacement. And he had perhaps the biggest television she'd ever seen dominating one wall. But the walls were a slightly deeper shade of that green, the woodwork gorgeous. And the little fireplace had been fronted in creamy granite, framed in more of that honey oak with a wide, chunky mantel topping it.

"God, that's gorgeous, Bo. Seriously." She crossed to the fireplace, ran her fingers over the mantel. There was dust, but beneath it was silky wood. "Oh, look what you've done around the window!"

It was flanked with shelves, mirroring the wood and beaded accents on the trim. "It's just the sort of detail a room this size needs. Brings it in without losing the sense of space. Makes it cozy."

"Thanks. I'm thinking about fronting them with glass—pebbled maybe. Haven't decided. But I'm doing that with the built-ins I'm making for the dining room, so I may just leave these open."

He was proud of his work, but her enthusiastic response gave him an extra boost. "Kitchen's done, if you want to see."

"I do." She glanced back at the fireplace as she walked out. "Can you do something like that in my place?"

"I can do anything you want."

She passed him back the towel. "We'll have to talk about your rates."

"I'll give you an infatuation discount."

"I'd be a fool to say no." She poked her head in other rooms on the way. "I'm nosy. What's this going to be? Like a TV room?"

"That's the plan. Room enough for a good-sized entertainment unit. I'm working on a design."

"Using the monster in your living room as a measuring tool."

He smiled easily. "You're going to watch, why not *watch*?"

"I'm thinking of using this space in my house for a library. Lots of shelves, warm colors, maybe putting in one of those little gas fireplaces. Big cushy chairs."

"That wall'd be best for the fireplace." He gestured with a lift of his chin. "Could do a nice window seat over there."

"A window seat." She considered him. "Just how infatuated are you?"

"I was going to have a beer and the ball game. Then I saw you."

"Pretty infatuated." She strolled out, glanced into the half bath. New tiles, she noted, new fixtures. Then the dining room, where she found major construction in progress. "It's a lot of work."

"I like the work. Even when I have to shoehorn it in between active clients. Business is good, so this place is taking me longer than the last one. But I like it here, so that's a point. Then there's you."

"Hmmm." She left that without comment and wandered into the kitchen. "Holy crap, Bo. This is amazing. It's like a magazine."

"Kitchens are the hub." He opened the laundry room door, tossed the towels inside. "Major selling point. It's generally where I start the rehab."

He'd done the floors in big slate-colored tiles, echoed that on the counters and used white-washed cabinets. Some were fronted with leaded glass. He'd put in a bar for casual seating, added in a box window to bring in the backyard. Wide windowsills were stone and called out for pretty pots of plants or herbs.

"You went high-end on the appliances. I know my appliances. I'd love to have one of these built-in grills."

"I can get you a good price. Contractor's rate."

"I love the lighting. This mission style is perfect."

He flipped on a switch and made her eyes gleam. Light beamed down from under the top cabinets.

"Nice touch. Now I have kitchen envy. This display cabinet's great. Why don't you have anything in it?"

"Didn't have anything. Guess I do now. Some of my grandmother's stuff." He opened the refrigerator, took out a bottle of white wine. "She left me everything. Well, she made a bequest to the church, but the rest she left to me. The house. Everything."

"It makes you sad," she stated softly.

"Some, I guess. Grateful." For a moment, he just held the wine bottle, leaned back against the refrigerator. "The house is free and clear, and once I get over the guilt, I'll sell it."

"She wouldn't want you to feel guilty. She didn't expect you to move in. It's just a house."

He got glasses, poured the wine. "I'm coming around to that. Doesn't need much work. I've kept it up for her. I've started clearing stuff out. The boxes in the other room." He handed her a glass. "Mostly photographs, some of her jewelry and . . ."

"Things that matter."

"Yeah, things that matter. She had a couple of pictures I drew her when I was a kid. You know, box houses with triangle roofs. Big round yellow sun. W birds flying around."

"She loved you."

"I know. My father's decided to be hurt and insulted because she didn't leave him anything. He's seen her maybe twice in the last five, six years, and he's playing the grieving son." He stopped himself, shook his head. "Sorry."

"Families are complicated. I should know. She made her choices, Bo. It was her right."

"I get that." But he rubbed his fingers hard over the middle of his forehead. "I could give him a cut when I sell the house, but she wouldn't like it. So I won't. She did leave my uncle and my cousin a few odds and ends. I guess she made her statement. Anyway." He shook it off. "Hungry? Why don't I fix you dinner?"

"You cook?"

"A little turn of the leaf I made a long time ago—and by happy coincidence, I learned that having a guy cook is like foreplay to a woman."

"You're not wrong. What's on the menu?"

He smiled. "I'll figure that out. While I am, why don't you tell me why you look tired?"

"Do I?" She sipped while he opened the freezer. "I guess I am. Or was. Hard day. Want me to bore you with it?"

"I do." He found a couple of chicken breasts, put them in the microwave to defrost, then opened a vegetable drawer.

"My partner and I worked this case. Flop hotel in south Baltimore. Single victim, female. Her head and most of her torso were . . . and I've just realized this is not really pre-dinner conversation."

"It's okay. I've got a strong stomach."

"Let's say she was badly burned, in an attempt to hide the fact that she'd been beaten to death. He didn't do a good job of it, either. It's all right there, like flashing lights."

She ran him through it, watching as he whipped something up in a small stainless steel bowl, dumped it over the chicken.

"It's hard, what you do. Seeing what you see."

"You have to walk a line between objectivity and compassion. It gets shaky. I guess it shook a little for me with DeWanna. All her cosmetics piled on the back of the toilet, the meal she was trying to put together. She loved the son of a bitch, and he's so annoyed she's pregnant again—like it was all her fault—he smashes her face with a frying pan, then beats her to death with it, panics, sets her on fire. Sets her hair on fire. It takes a special kind of callousness to do that."

Bo poured her more wine. "But you got him?"

"Wasn't hard. He's dumb as a brick. Used her credit card—or tried to. Made us, though. Smelled cop the minute we walked into this sluggy little bar. Ran out the back, tipped my partner over with a garbage can. I'm in pursuit, catching up with him, climbing over a fence, rain's pouring. I'm not even thinking then, just doing. He doesn't know the city, traps himself in a blind alley. Turns around and pulls a knife."

"Jesus, Reena."

She shook her head. "I've got a gun. A gun, for God's sake. What does he think, I'll go *eek* and run away?" But a part of her had wanted to. "I've had to draw my weapon before, a few times before, but it was almost an afterthought. This . . . my hands were shaking, and I was so cold. Inside, not from the rain. Because I knew I might have to use it. I've never had to fire my weapon. I was cold because I might have to fire. I was cold because I knew I could. Maybe wanted to, because . . . I still had the picture of what he'd done to her in my head. I was scared. It's the first time I've really been scared on the job. I guess it caught me by surprise. So . . ."

She took a breath, and a drink. "Your offer of wine and dinner was well timed. I'm better off with company than alone. And it's not the sort of thing I like to talk about with my family. It worries them."

It worried him, too, but that didn't seem like the right response. Instead he gave her another that came to his mind. "Regular people don't—can't—understand what you deal with. Not just the stress, which must be through the roof, not even the personal danger. But the emotion of it, I guess. What you see, what you have to do about it, and how that sits inside you."

"There are reasons I got into this type of work. What happened to DeWanna Johnson's one of them. And I feel better, so thanks for letting me go on about it. Writing a report doesn't have the same cathartic benefit. Want a hand with dinner?"

"No, I got it. It loses the seductive value if I ask you to peel potatoes."

"You seducing me, Bo?"

"Working up to it."

"How long does it generally take for you to get through the working-up-to-it stage?"

"Not usually this long. Especially if you count back the full thirteen years."

"Then I'd say it's been long enough." She set her glass down, rose. "You're going to want that chicken to marinate awhile anyway," she added as she crossed to him.

"I feel like I should say something clever right now. But my mind's blank." He put his hands on her hips, sliding them slowly up her body as he drew her in.

His head dipped, then paused with his lips a whisper from hers, just to catch her quick breath of anticipation. His eyes stayed open, watching hers, as he changed the angle, grazed his teeth over her bottom lip.

Then slowly sank in.

She smelled of the rain, tasted of wine. Her hands gripped his shoulders, then combed up through his hair and fisted there as that tight, angular body fit to his. He moved without thinking, half turning so her back was braced against the counter, locking her there while his mouth did a long, thorough exploration of hers.

Her teeth clamped lightly over his tongue, shooting his blood from hot to fevered. And the sound she made was something between a laugh and a moan.

His vision blurred.

Her hands weren't quite steady when she tugged his shirt out of his waistband. "You're good at this," she managed.

"Right back at you, Reena." His mouth raced to her throat, branded its way up to her lips again. "I want to . . . let's go upstairs."

Everything inside her was open and aching and ready. With her hands under his shirt, she dug her fingers into hard muscle. She wanted that body on hers, the brawn of it, the heat of it, the need of it. "I like your floor. Let's see how it holds up."

He thought he heard his heart knocking, hard, insistent bangs. When he pulled back far enough to yank her jacket down her arms, he recognized the knocking on his front door. "Oh, for the sake of the tiny baby Jesus."

She closed her teeth over his jaw. "Expecting someone?"

"No. Maybe they'll . . ." But the knocking only increased. "Damn it. Listen, don't move. Breathe only if you have to, but don't move." He gripped her shoulders. "Oh God, look at you. I could just . . . Just wait here, right here because I can just slip right back into position after I go kill whoever's at the door. It'll only take a minute for me to murder them."

"I have a gun," she offered.

His laugh was a little pained. "Thanks, but I can do it with my bare hands. Don't disappear, don't change your mind. Don't do anything."

She grinned after him, then patted a hand on her heart. He *was* good at it, she mused. In fact, he was exceptional. A man who could kiss like that . . . and she already knew he was good with his hands . . . had the potential to be an amazing lover. Still, now that she'd had a minute to clear the fire out of her brain, maybe going upstairs was a better idea.

She shook back her hair, then wandered out of the kitchen to see if he'd sent the interruption on its way.

And found him in the doorway, holding a pretty little redhead. The woman—the redhead Reena had seen at the funeral—had her head on his shoulder, and her own body shook with sobs.

"I feel so bad, Bo. I didn't think I'd feel this bad. I don't know what to do."

"It's okay. Come on. Let me close the door."

"It's stupid. I'm stupid, but I can't help it."

"You're not stupid. Come on, Mandy, just . . ." He trailed off when he spotted Reena, and she watched his face go through several emotions. Surprise, embarrassment, apology, denial. "Ah . . . ah . . . Well."

Tears continued to stream down Mandy's face as she stared at Reena, then pulled back from Bo. Flushed as red as her hair. "Oh Jesus, I'm sorry. I'm so sorry. I didn't realize anyone was here. God, what an *idiot*. I'm sorry. I'm going."

"It's all right. I was just leaving."

"No. God. I am." Mandy rubbed both hands over her wet cheeks. "Pretend I wasn't here. The dignified part of me wasn't."

"Don't worry about it. Really. I was just looking at the house. I live next door. Reena Hale."

"Mandy— Reena?" she repeated. "I know you." She sniffled, brushed at more tears. "I mean, not really. I went to Maryland the same time you did. I was Josh Bolton's downstairs neighbor. I met you once for a minute before he . . ." Her voice cracked, her face melted in misery. "Oh God, I'm a mess."

"You knew Josh?"

"Yeah. Yeah." She pressed her hand over her mouth and rocked herself. "Small, horrible world, isn't it?"

"Sometimes. I really have to go."

"Mandy, give me a minute," Bo began, but Reena was already shaking her head and walking out the door.

"No, that's fine. We'll catch up later." She made the quick dash through the incessant drizzle.

"Bo, I'm so sorry. I should've called. I should've drunk myself into a stupor. Go after her."

But he knew the mood was shattered. And he'd seen Reena's face when Josh Bolton's name was mentioned. More than surprise, he thought, there'd been grief. "It's okay. Let's sit down."

M aybe it was the day or the wine or the rain, but Reena filled the tub, poured yet another glass of wine, then slid into the water. And wept. Her heart, her head, her gut ached with the tears, and when they were done, finally done, she was numb and light-headed.

She dried off, pulled on thin flannel pants and a T-shirt before going downstairs to fix herself a solitary meal.

Her kitchen seemed dull and lifeless. Lonely, she thought—she felt squeezed empty with loneliness.

The wine and the rain, and probably the crying jag, had a headache simmering. Rather than face actual cooking, she pulled out one of her mother's care packages and heated up some minestrone.

But she left it warming on the stove, and poured more wine.

Funny how pain could reach across the years and still claw right through you. She rarely thought of Josh, and when she did, it was usually with more of a pang than this stabbing shock. Sorrow for the boy who'd never become fully a man, and a kind of bittersweet regret.

Defenses were down, that's what she told herself as she stared down into the pot of soup. Hard day, and now the loneliness was so acute it was just another knife in the heart.

She glanced over at the knock on her back door and let out a sigh. She knew it would be Bo before she opened the door.

His hair was wet again.

"Listen, can I come in a minute? I just want to explain—"

She turned away, leaving the door open. "You don't need to explain."

"Well, yeah, because it looked like . . . And it wasn't. It's not. Mandy and I are friends, and we don't— Well, we used to, but that was a long time ago. Reena . . . could you just look at me?"

She knew he'd see the damage the weeping had left on her face. Tears weren't something she was ashamed of, but at the moment she was impatient with them, with herself. With him.

"I've had a bad day." But she turned to face him. "Just a lot of things piling up. I can deal. Seems to me your friend's having a worse day."

"She is. We are—friends."

Reena watched him slide his hands into his pockets, the way a man did when he was miserably uncomfortable and didn't know what else to do with them.

"And she—Mandy—was twisted up because she just found out her ex-husband's getting married. Fucking jerk. Sorry. The divorce was tough on her, and it was only final, like, two weeks ago. This hit her hard."

Reena leaned back against the counter, sipped her wine and let him rush through his explanation. And thought, Poor guy, caught between two emotional women on a hot rainy night. "I'm getting a little drunk. Do you want?"

"No, but thanks. Reena—"

"First, I'm a trained observer. I didn't mistake the scene in your doorway as a lovers' embrace. I saw her with you at your grandmother's funeral and recognized what she is to you."

"We're just—"

"Family," she interrupted. "She's your family. She's your family, Bo."

Some of the tension in his face dissolved. "Yeah. Yeah, she is."

"And what I saw tonight was a woman in serious distress, and imagined she didn't need, or want, a stranger being part of all that. I wouldn't have. Second, if we're keeping score, you get points for not being so self-involved you'd brush off a friend in serious distress so you could roll between the sheets with me. Where is she?"

"Asleep. Cried herself out, and I put her to bed. I saw your light come on out here, so I wanted to . . . I wanted to explain."

"And you did. I'm not mad." Not only not mad, she realized, but not lonely any longer either. "I'm not the jealous type, and we haven't established any ground rules. Or even if we're going to require them. We were going to have sex, we didn't." She lifted her glass. "There's always another time."

"You're not mad," he said with a nod. "But you're upset."

"It's not you." To give herself something to do, she picked up a spoon to stir the soup. "Not just you," she corrected. "It's the past. It's a sweet lost boy."

"Josh. You were involved with him?"

"He was my first in this small, horrible world." But there weren't any tears left inside her, not now, to shed for him. "Oddly enough, I was with him the night you saw me at that party. I left with him, went with him. It was my first time."

"I met him."

Her spoon clanged against the pot as her head whipped around. "You knew Josh?"

"No. I met him. I met him the day he died. Same day I met Mandy. Blind date—double date with my friend Brad and that girl he was seeing. When we picked her up, Josh was coming down the stairs. Going to a wedding."

"Oh God, Bella's wedding." Maybe she had a few tears left after all. They were pressing hot on the back of her eyes. "My sister's wedding."

"Yeah. He couldn't get his tie right. Mandy fixed it."

A tear slipped out, plopped in the soup. "He was a sweet boy."

"He changed my life."

Reena wiped at the tears, faced Bo again. His eyes weren't dreamy green now but very intense. "I don't understand."

"I partied a lot back then. Well, who didn't? I was drifting. Making plans for someday. Yeah, I'll get around to doing that someday. Clean myself up, get my shit together. I woke up that morning, after going out with Mandy—and hitting a party after I dropped her off—with a hangover of biblical proportions. Woke up in the dump of my apartment. I decided to clean it up. I'd do that about every six months when I couldn't stand myself anymore. Told myself I'd straighten up, but I told myself that every six months or so, too. Then Brad came by, told me about the kid we'd seen in Mandy's apartment building. What happened to him."

"But you didn't know him."

"No, I didn't know him. But . . ." He trailed off, then shook his head, obviously struggling to find the right way to make her understand. "But he was my age, and he was dead. I'd just met him—watched Mandy fix his tie, and now he was dead. He'd never have the chance to get his act together, if he needed to. One minute he's heading out to a wedding in his best suit, and the next . . ."

"He's gone," Reena whispered.

"His life was over, out of the blue, and what was I doing with mine? Pissing it away, like my father did his."

He stopped, blew out a breath. "So, it was epiphany time for me. Instead of thinking about someday, I got my contractor's license. I talked Brad into buying a house with me. A dump. My grandmother fronted us some of the money. I never worked harder in my life than I did on that place. When I— Damn, this sounds stupid and self-involved."

"No, it doesn't. Keep going."

"Well, whenever I got to the point where I was disgusted or discouraged or wondered why the hell I'd gotten into that mess, working ten, twelve hours a day, I'd think of Josh, how he never got the chance. And I found out what I could do, if I stuck. Maybe I'd have done it anyway, I don't know. But I've never forgotten him, or that his dying turned my life around."

Reena put the wine down, stirred the soup. "Fate's a kick in the ass, isn't it?"

"I don't want to lose the chance I have with you, Reena."

"You haven't lost anything." After turning the burner off, she faced him. "It's no prize standing here in front of you, let me tell you. I have a long line of short-term or messed-up relationships leading from Josh to you. Bad judgment, bad timing or just bad luck."

"I'll risk it." He stepped to her, lowered his head to press his lips to hers. "I can't leave her over there alone tonight."

"No, you can't. That's one of the reasons you haven't lost anything. Here, take some soup. If she wakes up, there's nothing like my mother's minestrone to chase away the blues."

"Thanks. Seriously." Thoughtfully, he brushed his thumb over the little mole above her lip. "Why don't I fix you dinner tomorrow?"

She got out a container for the soup, and her lips curved. "Why don't you?"

His living room light was still on when she prepared for bed. Watching his mammoth TV? she wondered. Letting his friend have his bed in her hour of need.

She hoped they'd shared a little minestrone, a little TLC.

She'd never had a male friend, a contemporary, who would have done that for her, she realized. The men in her life who weren't family were teachers like John, partners and associates. Or lovers.

It was interesting, and different, she decided, to feel like friends with a man before you took him to bed, or allowed yourself to be taken.

She turned off her light, closed her eyes and hoped sleep would smooth out the rougher edges of her day.

It was just before three A.M. when her phone rang. She came alert quickly, switching on the light before grabbing the phone. Even with her job, middle-of-the-night phone calls always rammed her heart in her throat. Thoughts of family, accidents and death to loved ones came first.

"Yes, hello."

"I got a surprise for you."

Part of her mind registered the number on the Caller ID as unfamiliar, another focused on the voice. Low, a little harsh, male. "What? What number are you calling?"

"Big surprise for you. Coming soon. When you get it, I'll be jerking off—and imagining your mouth on my cock."

"Oh, for God's sake. If you're going to wake somebody up with a lame obscene call, don't call a cop."

She hung up, took the time to write down the number, the time of the call.

And switching off the light again, went back to sleep and forgot about it.

# 17

It had been a long time since Reena had reviewed Joshua Bolton's case file. She didn't know why she did so now. There was nothing new to see there. The matter had been closed for years, with the investigators, the ME, the lab all signing off on accidental death.

There was no reason to see anything else. No forced entry, head trauma consistent with a fall, no burglary, no vandalism, no motive. Just a young man falling asleep while smoking in bed.

Except she'd never known him to smoke.

Still, the team had recovered a pack of cigarettes, a book of matches—both with his fingerprints. That had weighed against the fact that the girl he'd been sleeping with had insisted the victim didn't smoke.

She'd have weighed it the same, Reena admitted, as she read over the reports. She probably would have weighed it the same, come to the same conclusions. Closed the file.

But she'd never completely accepted it, and couldn't now.

She was still reading the reports, with the crime-scene photos spread over her desk, when her phone rang.

"Arson Unit, Detective Hale."

"Reena? This is Amanda Greenburg. Mandy? We met—in a moment of humiliation last night at Bo's."

"Sure. I remember." She stared at what the fire had done to the boy she'd known.

"How could you forget? Listen, I just wanted to apologize."

"No need. Really." She touched her fingers to the photo of Josh. "But I wonder if you've got time to meet me. I'd like to talk to you, if you can manage it."

"Sure. When?"

"How about now?"

Since the day was fine, Reena snagged an outdoor table at a little coffeehouse a five-minute walk from the station house. She'd barely settled in when she saw Mandy jogging up the sidewalk, a large square shoulder bag bumping against her hip.

Her hair was an explosion of screaming red, her face as foxy as a terrier's. She wore Jackie O–style sunglasses that, inexplicably, suited her.

"Hi." Mandy dropped into a chair.

"Thanks for meeting me."

"No problem. Coffee," she said when the waiter came out. "And keep it coming."

"Diet Pepsi."

"Okay, I just want to get this off my chest. I was really messed up last night, and Bo's not just my best friend, he handles hysterical females pretty well for a guy. We don't sleep together."

"Anymore," Reena finished.

"Anymore. Haven't been down that road for years. We're like, you know, Jerry and Elaine. *Seinfeld*? Except Bo's not as cynical. My ex . . ."

Mandy paused, waited until their drinks were served. "We lived together for over a year, Mark and me. Eloped to Vegas on a whim. Things got shaky almost from the minute we got back, I don't know why. It's easier if you know, don't you think?"

"Yes. It's always best to know."

"I didn't. Then he comes to me one night, tells me he's sorry—and he was—he's sorry but this isn't working for him, and he's met somebody. He thinks he's in love. He's standing there, looking pitiful and telling me—his wife—that he's sorry, but he thinks he's in love with somebody else. Didn't want to cheat on me, so he figures we need to get a divorce."

"Hard hit."

"Yeah, it was." She picked up her coffee, and the wide silver band she wore on her left thumb winked in the sunlight. "Naturally, I got pissed off. Big scene, big fight. I ended up crying all over Bo then, too. But what am I going to do? Jerk doesn't want me anymore. Then yesterday I find out he's marrying her, and it hits all over again."

"I'm sorry."

"Yeah, well, screw it. And them. But the thing is, I don't want to mess things up for Bo because I needed a shoulder. I'm an old pal. But you're Dream Girl."

Reena winced. "Do you know how hard it is to live up to that title?"

Mandy grinned. "Never been anybody's Dream Girl, but I can imagine. Still, you're stuck with it. Brad and I would rag on him about you sometimes."

"What are friends for?"

"You got it. But it's wild, isn't it? You moving in right next door. Now he's got little hearts in his eyes . . . and I'm making it worse."

"Just a little."

"Let me change the subject real quick." Mandy motioned the waiter for a top off on her cup. "DeWanna Johnson."

"How do you know about her?"

"I work for *The Sun*."

"You're a reporter?"

"Photographer. You gave a statement on the case yesterday, and I know they'll want a follow-up. I thought if I could get a photo—"

"Jamal Earl Gregg has been charged with murder in the second in the matter of the death of DeWanna Johnson. If you want a follow-up, you'll need to talk to the DA's office."

"You're a local girl, strong local ties. And being a girl, whether we like it or not, gives the story a meaty angle."

"My partner's not a girl, and we apprehended the suspect together. You're going to want to go through the press rep, Mandy. It's cleared, I've got no problem with a photo. And actually, I asked you to meet me because I wanted to talk to you about another fire. Josh."

"Okay." Mandy looked down at her coffee, which Reena noted she drank black—and like water. "I was pretty wrecked over that. We all were. Reporter came to talk to me after. I was interning for *The Sun* back then. Went to New York for about six months after I graduated and found out I'm a small-town girl. Came back to Baltimore. I talked to his mother once after he died, when they came to get his stuff. It was dark."

"The investigators talked to you? The fire investigator, the police?"

"Sure. They talked to everyone in the building as far as I know, some of the kids he had classes with, his friends. They must've talked to you, too."

"Yes, they talked to me. I was probably the last to see him alive. I was with him that evening."

"Oh." Sympathy raced over her face as she shoved the sunglasses on top of her head. "God, I'm sorry. I didn't know. I'd been out, blind date with Bo—our first. Doubled with Brad and this friend of mine he was stuck on back then."

"You got home between ten-thirty and eleven."

Mandy lifted her eyebrows as she drank more coffee. "Did I?"

"That's what you said in your statement."

"That's about right, best I can remember. Bo dropped me off at the door. I thought about asking him in, figured I'd play it cool, see what happened. My roommate was gone for the weekend, so I had the place to myself. I turned on some music, and I had a joint. Something I left out of my statement, and indulged in, occasionally, during my college days. I watched *SNL* until about midnight, went to bed. Next thing I knew, alarms are going off, people are running in the hall, shouting."

"You knew most of the kids in the building."

"Sure. By face if not name."

"Did Josh have a problem with any of them?"

"No. You know how he was, Reena. Sweet guy."

"Yeah, but even sweet guys have problems with some people. Maybe a girl." Bedroom fires, she thought. A more typical female method. More personal, more emotional. I'll get you where you sleep, you bastard.

As she thought back, Mandy twiddled with one of several silver necklaces she wore. "He dated, he hung out. Off-campus buildings like that were little hives of drama and sex and excessive partying. And abject fear around finals. But there was the changeover. Semester ending in May, a lot of the kids went home for the summer, or graduated. New ones coming in. We weren't full up yet, that early in June. And Josh was pretty focused on you once you started dating. I honestly don't remember him having any dramatic breakups, no serious issues with anybody. In the building or on campus. People liked Josh. He was easy to like."

"Yes, he was. Did you ever see him smoke?"

"He must've. I remember drawing blank on that back then. A lot of us smoked socially—or toked recreationally. You had a few smoke nazis—and those I remember. He wasn't one of them. He got along."

"And you didn't hear or see anything off the night of the fire?"

"Nothing. Is the case being reopened?"

"No. No," Reena repeated with a shake of her head. "It's personal. Just something that keeps coming back around on me."

"I know." In an absent gesture, Mandy pulled her sunglasses back in place. "Still does on me, too. It's harder when you're young like we were, and it's one of us. You're not supposed to die at twenty. At least that's what you think when you're twenty. Life's forever. Plenty of time out there."

"DeWanna Johnson was twenty-three. There's always less time than you think."

———

But she put it away, put the file away as she'd done before and concentrated on now.

When DeWanna Johnson's mother walked into the squad room, Reena rose. "I'll take her," she told O'Donnell, and stepped over.

"Mrs. Johnson? I'm Detective Hale. We spoke on the phone."

"They said I should come up here. They said I couldn't take DeWanna yet."

"Why don't we go back here?" Reena laid a hand on the woman's arm to lead her into the break room. There was a short counter crammed with a coffeemaker, an ancient microwave, foam cups.

Reena gestured Mrs. Johnson to a chair at the table. "Why don't you sit down. Can I get you some coffee, some tea?"

"No, nothing. Nothing." She sat. Her eyes were dark and tired.

She couldn't have been much past forty, Reena judged, and would soon bury her daughter.

"I'm sorry for your loss, Mrs. Johnson."

"Lost her the minute he got out of prison. Should've kept him in there. Should've kept him locked away. Now he's killed my girl, and left her baby an orphan."

"I'm sorry for what happened to DeWanna." Reena sat across from her. "Jamal's going to pay for it."

Grief and rage warred with fatigue in those dark eyes. "How do I tell that baby her daddy killed her mama? How do I do that?"

"I don't know."

"Did she . . . the fire. Did she feel it?"

"No." Reena reached out, closed her hand over Mrs. Johnson's. "She didn't feel it. She didn't suffer."

"I raised her on my own, and I did my best." She drew a deep breath. "She was a good girl. Blind when it came to that murdering bastard, but she was a good girl. When can I take her home?"

"I'll find out for you."

"You have children, Detective Hale?"

"No, ma'am, I don't."

"Sometimes I think we have them just so they can break our hearts."

Because those words played over and over in her head, Reena stopped by Sirico's on the way home. She found her mother at the big stove, her father at the work counter.

She was surprised to see her uncle Larry and aunt Carmela sitting in a booth nibbling on stuffed mushrooms.

"Sit, sit," Larry insisted after she bent to kiss him. "Tell us all about your life."

"Right now that would take about two minutes, and I don't even have that. I'm already going to be late."

"Hot date," her aunt said with a wink.

"As a matter of fact."

"What's his name? What does he do? When are you going to get married and give your mama pretty grandbabies?"

"His name is Bowen, he's a carpenter. And between Fran, Bella and Xander, my mama has about all the pretty grandbabies she can handle."

"There's never too many. Is this the one who lives next door? What's his last name?"

"It's not Italian," Reena said, and with a laugh kissed her aunt again. *"Buon appetito."*

She wound her way back, pulled herself a soft drink from the dispenser. Her father's hands were in dough, so she rose on her toes and kissed his chin. "Hello, handsome."

"Who is this?" He glanced around to his wife. "Who is this strange girl giving out kisses? She looks a little familiar."

"It hasn't been a week," Reena complained. "And I called two days ago."

"Oh, now I recognize you." He lifted his hands, pinched her cheeks with doughy fingers. "It's our long-lost daughter. What's your name again?"

"Wisecracks, all I get are wisecracks." She turned to buss her mother's cheek. "Something smells good. New perfume, and Bolognese."

"Sit. I'll fix you a plate."

"I can't. I've got a good-looking man cooking me dinner."

"The carpenter cooks?"

"I didn't say it was the carpenter. But yes, it is and he does. Apparently. Mama, have your children broken your heart?"

"Countless times. Here, have some mushrooms. What if he burns the dinner?"

"Just one. If we broke your heart, why did you have four of us?"

"Because your father wouldn't leave me alone and let me sleep."

He turned his head at that, chuckled.

"Seriously."

"I am serious. Every time I turn around, the man's hands get busy." Bianca tapped her spoon on the edge of the pot, set it down. "I had four because as often as you broke my heart, you filled it. You're the treasures of my life, and the biggest pains in my ass." She tugged Reena toward the prep room, lowered her voice. "You're not pregnant."

"No, Mama."

"Just checking."

"A lot of strange things on my mind the last couple of days, that's all. Good mushrooms," she added. "I've got to go."

"Come to dinner Sunday," Bianca called out. "Bring your carpenter. I'll show him how to cook."

"I'll see how it goes tonight, then maybe I'll ask him."

He stuck with chicken because he felt he had a pretty good hand with poultry. He had stopped off for fresh produce, and had intended to swing by the bakery. But he'd built an arbor for Mrs. Mallory that afternoon, and when she learned of his plans for the evening, she'd given him a freshly made lemon meringue pie.

He was still debating the ethics of passing it off as his own when Reena knocked.

He had music on—some jazzy Norah Jones—and had taken a swipe at the dust. His intentions to do a more thorough sprucing job had been waylaid by his time at Mrs. M.'s. And his weakness for her cookies.

But the place looked good, he decided. And he had changed the sheets on his bed. In case.

When he opened the door and looked at her, he was really hoping they'd get to use the fresh sheets.

"Hello, neighbor." He moved straight in—why waste time?—cupped his hands on her torso and caught her mouth with his.

She softened against him, just a little. Just a tantalizing bit. Then eased back. "Not bad as appetizers go. What's the main course?" She handed him a bottle cheerfully bagged in a silver sack. "And I hope it goes with Pinot Grigio."

"We're still on for chicken, so this is great." He took her hand to walk her back to the kitchen.

"Flowers." She turned at the table to admire the Shasta daisies he'd stuck in a blue bottle. "And candles. Aren't you clever?"

"I have moments. It's my grandmother's stuff. I spent some time going through the boxes last night."

She followed the direction of his gaze, studied the display cabinet. There were more old bottles, interesting shapes, and some dark blue dishes, some wineglasses with etched cups.

"That's nice. She'd like you putting her things out."

"I never got much of that sort of thing on my own. Just more to pack up when you move."

"Which you do, regularly."

He opened the wine, got two of the etched glasses from the cabinet. "Can't turn a place if you're still living in it."

"Don't you get attached?"

"A couple of times. But then I'd see this other place and think, Wow, think what we could do with that. Potential and profit versus comfort and familiarity."

"You're a house slut."

"I am." Laughter warmed his eyes as he tapped his glass to hers. "Have a seat. I'll get things moving here."

She slid onto a counter stool. "How about starting from scratch? Have you ever bought a lot and done the whole works?"

"Thought about it. Maybe one day. Dream house deal. But mostly I like seeing what there is, how to make it better or bring it back from the dead."

When he checked something in the oven, she caught the scent of rosemary. And made a note to pick him up a couple of pots of herbs for his windowsill—if things progressed.

"You said you could do anything with my house I wanted. Was that lust talking, or is that straight scoop?"

"Lust is a factor, but within reason, sure. You can have pretty much what you want." He dribbled oil in a sauté pan.

"Can I have a fireplace in my bedroom?"

"Wood-burning?"

"Not necessarily. Gas or electric would do. Probably better, actually. I don't think I want to haul wood up the stairs."

"We could do that."

"Really? I always wanted that—like in the movies. A fireplace in the bedroom. One in the library. And what I'd really like is to turn the bedroom into more of a master suite. Incorporating the bath, maybe enlarging it some. And I want a skylight over the tub."

He glanced back again, considered her. "You want a skylight over the tub."

"I think that falls into the within-reason category. Of course, all this has to be done in small stages. I've got a budget."

He added minced garlic to the oil. "I'll take a look, play with some designs, work you up a bid. How's that?"

She smiled, resting her elbow on the table, sipping wine. "Handy. You may turn out to be too good to be true."

"That's what I thought about you."

"I don't know what I want, Bo. For this, for myself. Hell, I don't know what I want tomorrow, much less a year from tomorrow."

"Me, either."

"I think you do, or you have a rough design. I think when you do what you do, when you build and project, you're able to visualize next year."

"I know I want you tonight. I know I've wanted you—or the image of you—for a long time. But I don't know what we'll do with, or about, each other tomorrow. Or next year."

He slid chicken into the pan, turned. "I think there's a reason you moved in next door. I think there's a reason I saw you all those years ago, but didn't meet you until now. I don't think I was ready for you until now."

He watched her, sitting at his counter with her she-lion eyes, running her finger along the etched cup of his grandmother's glass. "Maybe that means things are falling into place. Or it means something else. I don't have to know right this minute."

"You talked about potential, when you look at a new place and it pulls at you. You have the potential to make me fall in love with you. That scares me."

He felt something rush into his heart, burn there. "Because you think I'll hurt you?"

"Maybe. Or I'll hurt you. Or it'll just turn out to be some big, complicated mess."

"Or it could be something special."

She shook her head. "When I look at relationships—my relationships—the glass is half empty. And what's left in it may or may not be potable."

He picked up the wine, filled her glass to the rim. "You just haven't had the right guy doing the pouring."

"Maybe not." She glanced toward the stove. "Don't burn the chicken."

He didn't, and she had to admit she was impressed that he managed to get a full meal on the table without incident. She nursed the second glass of wine, and sampled the chicken.

"All right," she said, "this is good. This is really good. That's a serious compliment coming from someone who grew up in an atmosphere where food isn't just sustenance, isn't even merely art, but a way of life."

"The rosemary chicken gets them every time."

She laughed, continued to eat. "Tell me about your first love."

"That would be you. Okay," he added when she narrowed her eyes at him. "Tina Woolrich. Eighth grade. She had big blue eyes and little apple breasts—which she generously let me touch one sweet summer afternoon in a darkened movie theater. How about you?"

"Michael Grimaldi. I was fourteen, and desperately in love with Michael Grimaldi, who was stuck on my sister Bella. I imagined that the scales would fall from his eyes and he would understand it was me who was his destiny. But that love went unrequited."

"Foolish Michael."

"Okay. Who broke your heart the first time?"

"Back to you again. Otherwise . . . nobody."

"Me, either. I don't know if that makes us lucky or sad. Bella now, she thrived on getting her heart broken, and breaking hearts. With Fran, I remember her crying in her room because some jerk had asked another girl to the prom. Me, I never cared enough. So I guess that is sad."

"Ever get close to the M word?"

"Marriage." Something flickered in her eyes. "Depends on your point of view. I'll tell you about it sometime. I talked with Mandy today."

And with that, he assumed, the talk of relationships past was closed. "Yeah?"

"She called to apologize—again—and I asked if she'd meet me. Every now and again I pull Josh's file out of the closet. I wanted to talk to her about it. Nothing new, of course. But meeting her here struck me as one of those cosmic signs, so I wanted to follow through. In any case, I liked her. Buckets of energy, which may come from the fact that she drank a gallon of coffee in a twenty-minute period."

"Lives on it," Bo agreed. "She's never understood how I live without it."

"You don't drink coffee?"

"Never got the taste for it."

"Me, either. Strange."

"Just another check on the you're-meant-for-me balance sheet. Want more chicken?"

"No, but thanks. Bowen?"

"Catarina."

She laughed a little, took another sip of wine. "Did you sleep with Mandy when she was married?"

"No."

"Okay. That's just one of my lines. I don't have many, but that's one of them. I'll do the dishes," she said as she rose.

"We'll just pile them up for later," he began, then, catching her expression, sighed. "You're one of those. Okay, we'll do the dishes. Want dessert first?"

"I haven't decided if I'm sleeping with you yet."

"Ha ha. There goes my heart. I meant the sort you put on a plate and eat. We've got pie."

She set her plate on the counter, turned. "What kind?"

He opened the refrigerator, took out the dish.

"That's lemon meringue." She stepped closer, gave him a serious look. "That's not from the bakery either."

"Nope."

"You baked a pie?"

He tried an innocent, slightly insulted look. "Why is that so surprising?"

She leaned back on the counter, studied him. "If you can name five ingredients in that dish—other than lemon—I'll sleep with you right now."

"Flour, sugar . . . oh hell. Busted. Client baked it."

"She pays you in pie?"

"It's my bonus. I also have a bag of chocolate chip cookies, but I'm not sharing them unless you sleep with me. We can have them for breakfast."

"You can do time for attempting to bribe a police officer."

"What, you're wired?"

She laughed. And she thought, The hell with the dishes. She leaned her elbows back on the counter, tipped up her chin. "Why don't you put that pie down, Goodnight, and come over here and find out."

# 18

He moved, his eyes on hers. There was a challenge in hers and a sparkle of sexy amusement. He was already hard when he fit his body to hers. What man wouldn't be?

She kept her arms stretched out, her hands on the counter even as he took her mouth, even as he took in her quick gasp.

"You carrying your gun?" he asked with his mouth on hers.

She stiffened just a little. "In my purse. Why?"

"Because if somebody comes to the door this time, we're going to use it."

She had an instant to relax again, an instant to laugh, then he swept her into his arms. "And we're doing the dishes later."

"Ummm. Forceful."

"You ain't seen nothing yet." But his knees went weak when she clamped her teeth on his neck. Focus, he ordered himself as he carried her out of the room. Don't blow it. "And we're not doing this on the kitchen floor. Not that I'm opposed to it." He turned his head so he could see her face again. "Just not this time."

She touched his hair, and her smile went soft. "Not this time. You planning on carrying me all the way upstairs?"

"Tonight, Scarlett, you won't think of Ashley."

As he climbed, she wrapped her arms around his neck and covered his face with kisses.

He'd forgotten to leave a light on—so much for preplanning—but he knew the way. And there was just enough twilight left to guide him.

Her arms stayed around his neck as he lowered her to the bed, bringing him with her, keeping their mouths fused. And the thump of his heart was a jungle drum in his ear.

"Wait. It's too dark." Still he tasted her throat, the tender spot under her jaw. His hands burned to cover flesh. "I want to see you. Need to see you."

He peeled away, fumbled in the nightstand drawer for a book of matches to light the candle he'd bought with her in mind.

When he turned back, she was braced on her elbows, her hair a wild halo of melted amber. "You're a romantic."

"With you."

The halo shimmered as she cocked her head. "Generally, I distrust men who say just the right thing at just the right time. But I have to say, it's working for you. Think you can remember your place?"

He lowered to her, felt her sigh. "Yeah, that's it."

The fantasy of her had been with him all of his adult life. In fantasy she could be—had been—whatever he wanted. But the reality of her was more. Skin and lips, scents and sounds. All washed over him in a hot flood that was need and pleasure and bedazzlement.

It wasn't a dream that moved under him, that met his mouth with eager heat. And the woman she was rose out of that dream to surround him.

He spiked her pulse, had it hammering, had her mind blurring with movement and textures. The scrape of teeth, the glide of tongue, the mix of breath and sighs. His mouth was like a fever, yet somehow patient. As if he was content to let them both burn through kisses alone.

Then, when she thought she could bear it no longer, when her body arched up to him to offer more, he used his hands.

Hard, strong hands, brushing, tantalizing, then clamping, possessing.

Breasts, thighs, hips, with the heat still rising so she wondered her skin didn't catch flame.

He pulled her shirt over her head, and then it was his mouth on her, feasting on the rise of her breasts over cups of lace, sliding his tongue under thin fabric to sample, to tease.

On a gasp she rolled over him to tug at his shirt, to fight with buttons. She flung back her hair, straddled him as she parted the shirt, ran her hands up his chest.

"You're built, Goodnight." Her breathing was already thick, already unsteady. "Seriously built. Got yourself a few scars." She trailed her fingers over one that skated along his rib cage, felt him quiver. Then she lowered her head to skim lips, teeth, tongue over flesh.

He pushed up, shifting her so her legs hooked around his waist. The hands that ran up her back were rough with calluses, and more exciting for it. With one flick of his fingers, he unhooked her bra. She bowed back and moaned when he closed his mouth over her.

He could feel her heart beat under his lips, all but taste it. Her long body was so smooth, so agile. Narrow torso and hips, miles of leg. He wanted to spend hours exploring her—days, possibly years. But tonight, all those years of longing pressed at him to take, just take.

He pushed her back, dragged her pants down, followed them with his hands and mouth. Her body undulated, and when he once more feasted on flesh and lace, it bucked.

Her hands clamped his head, pressing him against her when she came, when she cried out and shuddered. His blood pounded in response as he stripped away the lace and drove her over again.

And she was dragging him up, her words incomprehensible now as they rolled over the bed. Her hands were quick as well, stripping him bare. Body and soul. Her mouth was hot and hungry, her body vibrating.

She stayed clamped around him when he tore open a condom, then pushed him next to madness when she took it from him to do the honors herself.

Once again she straddled him. He stared up at her. Her skin, her hair, her eyes, were all burnished gold in the candlelight.

She took him into the wet wonder of her.

Once again her body bowed back as she absorbed the quakes of pleasure. Shimmering through her, silken heat, velvet aches. She rode, taking him deeper, glorying in the desperate grip of his hands on her hips.

Flash point, she thought dimly when the orgasm ignited inside her. And her body swayed down to his.

Her head was still spinning, barely registered shock when he rolled, pinning her under him. He was deep in her, hard and deep. She heard his labored breath mix with her own.

She reached up, braced her hands on his shoulders. His eyes were so green now, she realized, like crystal, with all those mists burned out by passion.

He plunged into her, stealing even her gasp. Plunged, so that her fingers dug into his shoulders and her stunned system jolted with shock.

She thought she might have screamed. She heard some helpless sound as her blood rushed through her like a storm. Her body gathered for more, took more even when the pleasure became unspeakable.

She felt the muscles she gripped harden like iron, knew even as she imploded he was with her.

And as her hands slid limply off his shoulders, she thought, dazed, Flashover.


She was sprawled like the dead under him. Like someone killed in battle, she imagined. Sweaty and battered. Since he hadn't moved in the last several minutes, she decided it had been a war that had ended in a tie.

"Is that the phone?" she mumbled.

He stayed as he was, flat out on top of her, his face buried in the mass of her hair. "No. What?"

"Wait." She took slow breaths, concentrated. "God, it's my ears. My ears are ringing. Wow."

"I'm going to stop crushing you as soon as I regain the use of my limbs."

"No rush. You know, you were right. We weren't ready for this thirteen years ago. We'd have killed each other."

"I'm not sure we didn't. That's okay. They can bury us just like this."

"If we're dead, we can't make love again."

"Sure, we can. If heaven doesn't have lots of good sex, what's the point?"

Had she ever known a man who made her laugh so easily? she wondered. "I think saying something like that could send you to hell."

"If God didn't invent sex, who did?" He managed to brace himself on his elbows to look down at her. "And that was one hell of a religious experience."

"I did hear singing, but I'm not sure it was angels."

"That was me." He lowered his head, kissed her softly.

They ate pie in bed, and made love again with the tang of lemon on their tongues and crumbs on the sheets.

She gave him a slow, lingering kiss before rolling out of bed to find her clothes.

"You're going?"

"It's nearly two in the morning. We both work for a living."

"You could stay, sleep here. It's not like you have that far to go. And remember, I have cookies for breakfast."

"Tempting." She pulled on her pants, shirt, stuffed her underwear in her pockets. She was gloriously tired, the sort of tired, she thought, that only came after good, healthy sex. "But just how much sleep do you figure we'll manage? We're too hot for each other."

"I couldn't possibly go another round," he claimed. "I'm tapped."

She angled her head, studying his face in the candlelight. "Liar."

He grinned. "Prove it."

She laughed, shook her head. "Thanks for dinner, dessert and all the rest."

"My pleasure. Lots of my pleasure. How about tomorrow night?"

"How about it? You don't have to get up," she began when he tossed his legs over the bed and reached for his pants. "I know my way."

"I'll walk you over. How about dinner tomorrow? My place, your place, anyplace."

"Actually, I might have a line on a couple of tickets to the O's game tomorrow. Behind the dugout at third. If they come through, are you interested?"

"Is rain wet? You like baseball?" He pointed at her as he spoke.

"No." She raked her hair more or less into place with her fingers. "I *love* baseball."

"Seriously. Who won the series in . . . 2002?"

She pursed her lips a moment. "It was California's year. Angels over the Giants in the full seven. Lackey got the win."

"Oh my God." Goggling at her, he thumped a fist on his heart. "You *are* Dream Girl. Marry me, bear my children. But let's wait until after the game tomorrow."

"That'll give me time to buy a white dress. I'll let you know if the tickets come through."

"If they don't, I'll start working on some for the next home game." He took her hand as they walked downstairs.

She picked up her purse. "You don't have to walk me next door, Bo."

"Sure I do. There might be muggers. Or aliens. You just never know."

He grabbed his keys, stuffed them in his pocket as he headed out the door with her.

"See, romantic. And old-fashioned."

"Yet manly, and with panther-like reflexes."

"Which will come in handy with the aliens."

They walked down his steps, then up hers. Where she let him kiss her limp.

"Go home," she murmured.

"Maybe you should walk me back. You're the cop."

"Home." She gave him a little nudge, then unlocked her door. "Good night, Goodnight," she said, and shut the door.

. . .

*Watching her. Know how to wait, know how to plan. Never thought it would take so long, but hey, shit happens. Besides, the waiting makes it bigger. Slut's banging the guy next door now. Convenient.*

*Could kill him now. Go up, knock on the door. He's going to open it. He's going to think it's the whore. Slide a knife right into his guts. Surprise!*

*Better to wait. Wait and watch. Do him later.*

*While the city burns.*

*Light's on. Bedroom light. Her bedroom. Bet she's naked. Touching herself, where she let him touch her. Whore-bitch.*

*Have some of that, oh yeah, a good piece of that before you light her up.*

*Window goes dark. In bed now.*

*Let her fall asleep. More fun if she's asleep. Take your time, got nothing but.*

*Have a cigarette. Relax.*

*Take out the phone. Got a good picture of her in your head. Naked, in bed.*

*Wake up, bitch.*

. . .

The phone rang, shooting her out of sleep. She glanced at the clock first, noted she'd barely been down ten minutes. The Caller ID display made her frown. Local number, unfamiliar.

"Hello?"

"It's almost time for the surprise."

"Oh, for God's sake."

"Hot and bright. You'll know it's for you. Are you naked, Catarina? Are you wet?"

When he said her name, a fist hit her heart. "Who—"

She cursed when the phone clicked in her ear. Once again, she wrote down the number, the time.

First thing in the morning, she thought grimly, somebody else was getting a goddamn wake-up call.

She got out of bed, got her weapon. Checked her load. Taking it with her, she checked her doors, her windows. Then stretched out on the couch in the living room, the gun on the table beside her, and tried to get some sleep.

B oth cell phones." With O'Donnell beside her, Reena reported the calls to her captain. "Each is registered to a different party, but they're both Baltimore city numbers."

"He called you by name."

"The second call, yeah."

"You didn't recognize the voice?"

"No, sir. He may be disguising it. He's keeping it soft, a little hoarse. But it didn't ring any bells. The first time I figured it was just some jerk spinning the dial, getting off. But this was personal."

"Go check it out."

"Feel stupid, dragging you along," Reena said to her partner when they walked to the car. "I could handle something like this on personal."

"Guy makes threatening calls—"

"He didn't threaten me."

"Underlying," O'Donnell said, and pouted a little when Reena got to the driver's side before he did. "Threat's implied, and he makes it to a cop—uses the cop's name. It's official business."

"Lots of people know my name. And it looks like one of them's a crank-calling pervert." She backed out of the parking spot. "Closest is number two's work address. Phone's registered in the name of Abigail Parsons."

Abigail Parsons taught fifth grade. She was a generously sized woman of sixty who wore sturdy shoes and a bright blue dress.

In Reena's judgment, she looked a little thrilled to have been called out of class by the police.

"My cell phone?"

"Yes, ma'am. Do you have your cell phone?"

"Of course." She opened a bag the size of Rhode Island, plucked a little Nokia out of the meticulously ordered interior. "It's off. I don't turn it on during class, but I keep it with me. Is there a problem with it? I don't understand."

"Could you tell me who else has access to this phone?"

"No one. It's mine."

"Do you live alone, Ms. Parsons?" O'Donnell asked.

"Since my husband died two years ago."

"Do you remember the last time you used it?"

"I used it yesterday. Called my daughter when I left school. I was going over there for dinner, wanted to see if she wanted me to pick up anything. What's this about?"

The second number took them to a gym where the owner was leading an aerobics class. When she broke, she got the phone out of the bag in her employee's locker. She was a bubbly twenty-two, and stated she'd come home alone the night before after a girls' night out. She lived alone.

Neither phone displayed a call to Reena's number in memory.

"Cloned 'em," O'Donnell said when they were back outside.

"Yeah, and that's just weird. Who do I know who's going to take the time and trouble to clone cell phones so he can wake me up in the middle of the night?"

"Better to ask who knows you. We can go through some old case files, see if anything shakes."

"Surprise for me," she murmured. "Big and bright. Sexual overtones."

"Old boyfriend? New boyfriend?"

"I don't know." She pulled open the car door. "But he's got my attention."

She set it aside, but she was ill at ease all day. Who would clone two phones just to mess with her head? Wasn't that hard to clone, if you had the equipment and the know-how. And the know-how was easy to come by.

But it took deliberation and planning. And purpose.

She'd know it was for her. Know what was for her? Reena leaned back in her desk chair, shut her eyes. The big, bright surprise.

A personal surprise or a professional one?

She spent most of the afternoon in court, waiting, then testifying on a revenge fire that had resulted in one death. She scored the baseball tickets from a friend in the DA's office. And walked back to the station house with an itch between her shoulder blades.

If he knew her name, was he watching her? She felt watched. She felt exposed and vulnerable walking the familiar street.

If he called again—when he called again—she'd keep him on the phone. She'd already set up a recorder. She'd keep him on and she'd work him. She'd draw something out of him that would ring that bell.

Then they'd see who got a surprise.

Drawing out her phone, she called Bo's cell. He'd passed into the level of serious relationship. His numbers were now programmed.

"Hey, Blondie."

She strolled, and sang. "Take me out to the ball game. Take me out with the crowd."

"I'll buy the peanuts and Cracker Jacks," he said. "What time can you head out?"

"If nothing comes up—and let's both knock on a lot of wood—six-thirty."

"I'll be ready. What are you doing now?"

"I'm walking down the street. Great day out here. I just finished testifying in court, and believe I did my part in putting some murdering jerk away for twenty-five."

"Gee, all I'm doing is hanging trim. Not as exciting."

"You ever testify in court?"

"I was acquitted."

She laughed. "It's tedious. I'm going to be ready for those Cracker Jacks."

"I'll provide the surprise inside. Reena?" he said when she didn't respond.

"Yeah, right here. Sorry." She rolled the tension out of her shoulders. "See you later, okay?"

She flipped the phone closed, then paused outside the station house, did a deliberate scan of street traffic, pedestrians.

When the phone rang in her hand, she jolted, swore. Then breathed a sigh of relief when she read the display. "Hi, Mama. No, I haven't asked him about Sunday yet. I will."

She turned, walked into the station with her mother's voice in her ear.

P arking at Camden Yards was mayhem. Watching cars jockey along always made her feel smug that she lived close enough to walk to the ballpark.

She loved the crowds, the noise, the jams of cars and the carnival anticipation of the people heading toward that big, beautiful stadium nearly as much as she loved the game.

She wore her most comfortable jeans, a plain white T-shirt tucked into the waistband, and a black fielder's cap with the bright Oriole bird.

She watched kids riding in strollers, or bouncing along beside their parents. She'd done the same, she remembered. Though it had been the old Memorial Stadium during her childhood.

She could already smell the hot dogs and beer.

After they passed through the turnstile, Bo slung his arm around her shoulders. He was dressed much like she was, but his shirt was faded blue.

"Tell me your views on Boog's barbecue."

"As sharp as his fielding back in the day."

"Excellent. Want to hit that first?"

"Are you kidding? We're going to load up. I eat like a horse at games."

They jostled through the crowds, juggled food between them. She fought not to look over her shoulder, not to wonder and worry about every face in the crowd. Easy to blend here, she thought. Easy to tail someone in a baseball stadium. Price of a nosebleed ticket would get you in.

Because thinking she may be watched made her feel watched, she did what she could to bury the sensation. She wasn't going to let some nuisance spoil the evening.

And when they started up the ramp to their gate, Reena took a breath, held it a moment. "I always like this. The way the field comes into view, all that green, the brown of the baselines, the white of the bags, the stands rising up. And the sounds, the smells."

"You're bringing a tear to my eye, Reena."

She smiled, stopped another moment at the top, to take it in. The noise, so many voices—conversations, vendors hawking, music playing—washed over her. And the idea of trouble, nasty phone calls, hours in court, the stinging Visa bill she'd gotten in that day's mail, all slid away like fog in sunlight.

"The answer to all the questions in the universe can be found in baseball," she said.

"God's truth."

They found their seats and balanced food on their laps. "First game I remember," she began and took a hefty bite of her barbecue sandwich. "I think I was six. I don't remember the game—I mean the stats." She swallowed, studying the field. "What I remember is the sensory spike. The movement of the game, you know? The sounds so specific to it. It was the start of my love affair."

"I didn't make it down to a major league game till I was in high school. Talk about sensory spike. My whole conception was from TV. TV makes it smaller, and less spiritual."

"Well, that'll give you something to talk about with my father. They want you to come to dinner on Sunday. If you're free."

"Really?" Surprised pleasure ran across his face. "Is this like an initiation? Will there be a quiz?"

"Might be." She turned her head. "You up for that?"

"I've always tested well."

They ate, watching the stands fill and the light soften in the spring evening. They cheered when the Orioles took the field, rose for the anthem.

They each nursed a beer through the first three innings.

He liked the fact that she shouted, she cheered, she booed and swore. No ladylike applause from Reena. She pulled her hair, punched his shoulder, held a short conversation with the guy on the other side of her on the possible sexual proclivities of the third-base ump when he called their base runner out.

They agreed he was a myopic asshole.

She ate a Dove bar in the seventh—he didn't know where she put that one—and nearly creamed him with it when she leaped up at the crack of the bat to follow the path of a long ball.

"Now, *that's* what I'm talking about!" she shouted, did a celebratory boogie and dropped back down. "Want some of this?"

"Nearly had some."

She turned, grinned at him. "I love baseball."

"Oh yeah."

They lost, by one painful run, and she pinned it on the bad call by the third-base umpire.

He didn't think he'd win her heart by confessing he'd never enjoyed a loss more, or a game more. He would cheerfully consign his beloved Birds to a losing season if he could watch her rev at every game.

Outside the gate, she pushed him back against a tree, clamped her lips on his. "Know what else I like about baseball?" she whispered.

"I'm sincerely hoping you'll tell me."

"Makes me hot." She nuzzled his ear, breathed into it. "Why don't I take you to my place."

She took his hand, headed back to the sidewalk. They walked together through the crowds, taking the shortest route home.

# 19

He was so worked up by the time she unlocked her front door, he slammed it shut behind them by spinning her around, shoving her against it.

She dropped her shoulder bag, dragged his shirt over his head. Hooked her teeth in his shoulder.

"Right here. Right here." She was already pulling open the button of his jeans.

He couldn't think. He couldn't stop. The sound of her hips slapping against the wood of the door as he pounded into her was viciously arousing.

It was violent and fast and amazing, and when they'd emptied each other out, they slid to the floor like rags.

"Jesus. Jesus Christ." He stared at her ceiling, breathing like a steam engine. "What happens when they win?"

She laughed so hard she had to grab her own ribs. Somehow she managed to roll over on him. "Damn it, Bo. Damn it. You might just be perfect."

She pulled her jeans back up when her phone rang. Her head was still buzzing when she picked up the receiver.

"Surprise."

She cursed herself for being sloppy, not checking the ID, not switching on the recorder. She did both, quickly. "Hi. I've been waiting for you to call back." She held up a hand, signaling Bo to remain silent.

"Brendan Avenue. You'll see it."

"Is that where you are? Is that where you live?" She checked the time. Early for him. Not quite midnight.

"You'll see it. Better hurry."

"Shit!" She swore softly when he hung up. "I've got to go."

"Who was that?"

"I don't know." She hurried to the front closet, got her weapon from the top shelf. "Jerk's been calling me—cryptic, sexual messages," she continued as she clipped on her holster. "Cloned cell phone, most likely."

"Whoa, wait. Where are you going?"

"He said he had something for me on Brendan Avenue. I'm going to check it out."

"I'll go with you."

"No, you won't." She grabbed a jacket to cover the gun. And Bo stepped calmly in front of the door.

"You're not walking out of here to go alone to check out some weird guy. You don't want me along, fine. Call your partner."

"I'm not waking O'Donnell up over something like this."

"Okay." His tone was absolutely pleasant, and implacable. "Want me to drive?"

"Bo, I want you to get out of my way. I don't have time for this."

"Call O'Donnell, call a—what is it?—radio car, or I go with you. Otherwise, make yourself comfortable because you're not going anywhere."

Temper pricked at her throat, put her teeth on edge. "This is my job. Just because I've slept with you—"

"Don't go there." And the edge to his voice, the sudden coldness of his eyes, had her reevaluating him. "I get your job, Catarina. But it doesn't include going off alone because some creep's messing with you. So what's it going to be?"

She opened her jacket. "See this?"

He glanced at the gun. "Hard to miss. What's it going to be?" he repeated.

"Damn it, Bo, step aside. I don't want to have to hurt you."

"Same goes. And maybe you could put me down. I'm hoping we don't find out either way. But if you can, I'll brush off my sorry, humiliated ass and get in my truck and follow you. Either way, you're not going alone. If this is an ego thing with you, you might want to deal with it later. You're wasting time."

She rarely swore in Italian. It was reserved for her most intensely pissed moments. She let out a string of inventive oaths as he stood, placidly now, studying her.

"I'll drive," she snapped and stewed when he opened the door. "You don't get it. None of you ever do."

"None of you being the male of the species," he surmised as she swept by him.

"I call my *male* partner over what's most likely a trivial matter, it's because I'm a girl."

"I don't think so." He got in the passenger seat, waited for her to storm around the car. "I mean, you're a girl—no question—but seems to me it's just basic common sense not to go haring off alone."

"I know how to take care of myself."

"Bet you do. But you're not showing me that by taking unnecessary chances."

She shot him one deadly look before she squealed away from the curb. "I don't like being told what to do."

"Who does? So how many times has this guy called you? What does he say?"

She tapped her fingers on the wheel, struggled with her temper. "Third call. He's got a surprise for me. First time I took it for a random obscene. Second, he used my name, so I checked it out. The numbers he's called from are cells, and it looks like they're clones."

"If he knows your name, it's personal."

"Potentially."

"My ass." And there was nothing placid about him now. "You know it's personal, which is one of the reasons you're pissed off."

"You got in my way."

"Yeah."

She waited a beat. "In my family, we yell when we're fighting."

"I prefer the digging in, just-try-to-move-me strategy." He turned to give her a long, cool stare. "Look who won."

"This time," she shot back.

When she approached Brendan Avenue, she slowed, eyes tracking. *You'll know it when you see it.* She recalled his voice.

And her heart gave one hard skip when she did.

"Shit, shit." She grabbed her phone, hit 911. "This is Detective Catarina Hale, badge number 45391. I'm reporting a fire in progress, 2800 Brendan Avenue. Shrine of the Little Flower Elementary School. On visual, the fire is fully engaged. Notify the fire and police departments. Possible arson."

She whipped to the curb. "Stay in the car," she ordered Bo, then grabbed a flashlight. She jumped out, speed dialing O'Donnell. "We got one burning," she said without preamble, and called out the address as she dashed to the building. "He called to tell me about it. I'm on scene. I told you to stay in the car," she snapped at Bo.

"Obviously my answer was no. Are there people in there?"

"No one should be, but that doesn't mean it's empty." She shoved her phone in her pocket, drew her weapon as she moved toward the wide, ground-level doors.

His message was spray painted over them in gleaming, bloody red.

## SURPRISE!

"Son of a bitch. Keep behind me, Bo. I mean it. Don't think with your dick. Remember who's got the gun." She reached for the door, pulled, then shoved. "Locked."

She debated. She could leave him here, exposed, or take him with her while she circled the building. "Stay close," she commanded. And heard the first sirens as she rounded the building. She found the broken window. Through it, she saw the fire was streaming through a classroom, eating desks, crawling up walls and out into the hallway.

"You're not going in there."

She shook her head. No, not without gear. But she could see, the point of origin was right there, and trailers were set—crumpled waxed paper maybe—to lead out into the hall, across to other classrooms. She could smell gasoline, and see rivers of it still gleaming on the floor.

Was he watching?

She stepped back to scan and study the neighboring buildings, and something crunched under her foot. She shone her light down, then crouched.

Her fingers itched, but she didn't touch what she saw was a box of wooden matches. And her heart thudded into her throat when she shone her light and saw the familiar Sirico's logo. "Do me a favor. In the trunk of my car there's a kit, evidence bags inside. I need one."

"You're not going in," he repeated.

"No. I'm not going in."

She stayed where she was, considering the matches, then raising her eyes to scan the area. Okay, he knew her, wanted to be sure she understood that.

Did he have the need to be close, to watch the burn?

People were starting to come out now, and cars were stopping. Excited voices swept through the air, and the distant scream of sirens pierced it.

When Bo brought her a bag, she scooped the matchbox into it and sealed it.

"We wait." She hurried back to the front, hooked her badge on her waistband and began to order the gathering crowd to stay back.

"What can I do?" Bo asked her.

"Keep out of the way," she began, and locked the evidence bag in her car. "I'm going to need to fill in the unit chief when he gets here. You've got a good eye. Pay attention to the gawkers. If you see anybody who seems too interested, I want to know about it. He'll be an adult male. He'll be alone. He'll be watching me as much as the fire. Can you do that?"

"Yeah."

He'd never seen a response before, not outside of movies. Everything moved so fast, with so much color and sound and movement. Like some sort of strange sporting event, Bo thought as the trucks rolled up and firefighters leaped into action.

It made him think of the game they'd seen that evening. That same kind of intense and focused teamwork. But instead of bats and balls there were hoses and axes, oxygen tanks and masks.

These were the people who ran toward fire while the rest of the world ran from it. With helmets gleaming in the flashing lights, they walked into the smoke and the heat.

While he watched, firefighters in turnout gear broke down the door and walked inside while teammates soaked the building with great arcs of water from the hoses.

Responding police moved quickly to set up barricades, to keep the gathering crowd behind them. As Reena had asked, he studied faces, tried to find the type she was looking for. He saw flames reflected in wide, stunned eyes, the ripple of red and gold shimmering on skin, and imagined he looked very much the same. There were couples and loners, families with children in their arms, in nightclothes, in bare feet. More fully dressed who poured out of cars that stopped up and down the block.

Admittance free, he thought and glanced back at the building. And it was a hell of a show.

Fire shot out through the roof, quickening towers of it, flaming gold in the dense roll of smoke. The smell of it stung his eyes, and ash began to dance in the air. White water, geysers of it, spewed out, slashing the building with such force he wondered the structure could stand against it.

He heard the sound of breaking glass and looked up to see the jagged shower of it as a window exploded. Someone in the crowd screamed.

Even where he stood he could feel the press of heat. How did they stand it? he wondered. The force of it, the blinding storm and stench of the smoke.

Ladders rose, the men on them like flags, the hoses hefty streamers that gushed more water.

A man cut through the crowd. Bo stepped forward, ready to act—he wasn't sure how—then saw the flash of a badge, the nods of acknowledgment from cops, from firefighters. Big guy, Bo noticed, broad shoulders, wide belly, grim Irish face. He moved straight to Reena.

O'Donnell, Bo decided, and relaxed fractionally.

He might have stayed that way, but he saw the man helping Reena into gear. He pushed through the crowd, was already shoving at the barricade when uniformed cops held him back.

"Reena. Goddamn it!"

She glanced in his direction as she hefted on tanks. He could see the irritation ripple over her face, but she spoke to her partner. He stepped away, moved over to the barricade. "He's with us," he said briefly. "Goodnight? I'm O'Donnell."

"Yeah, fine. What the hell's she doing? What the hell are you doing?" he demanded of Reena, his eyes narrowed now against the fog of smoke.

"Going in. I'm trained for this." She adjusted her helmet.

"Pretty good smoke eater for a cop," one of the firefighters commented, and she smiled at him.

"Sweet talker. I'll explain later. I've got to move."

Before Bo could make another protest, O'Donnell slapped a hand on his shoulder. "Knows what she's doing," he said, lifting his chin toward Reena as she headed toward the building with two others. "She's qualified for this."

"So are the dozen or so of these guys already in there. What's the point?"

"Arson's the point." Smoke rolled over them in a wave, had O'Donnell coughing. He kept his hand on Bo's shoulder, drew him back to clearer air. "Putting out a fire can screw the evidence all to hell. She goes in now, she'll be able to see more before the damage is done. Somebody set this one for her. She's not one to walk away from that. She's worked with these guys before. Believe me, they wouldn't let her in unless they knew she could handle herself."

"Being a cop's not enough for her?" Bo muttered, and O'Donnell showed his teeth in a grin.

"Being a cop's plenty, but she's a fire cop. And she walks the line between. Knows more about the son of a bitch than anyone I've ever worked with. The fire," he explained at Bo's puzzled look. "That girl knows fire. Now, tell me what you know."

"I don't know dick. We went to a ball game, went back to her place. She got a call."

Bo kept his eyes on the building now—the hell with scouring the crowd—and while his heart drummed in his throat, strained to see her coming back out. "She filled me in some. Some guy's called her three times, used her name. Cloned cell phones. This time he told her he had something for her here. Fire was already going when we arrived."

"How'd you manage to come along?"

He flicked his eyes back toward O'Donnell. "She'd've had to shoot me otherwise, and I guess she didn't want to waste that much time."

This time O'Donnell laughed, and the slap on Bo's shoulder was friendlier.

"She tell you he wrote *surprise* on the front door?"

"Yeah, she brought me up to date." Casually, he took a pack of gum from his pocket, offered Bo a stick. "She'll be fine," he assured him and folded two in his mouth. "Why don't you tell me how long you've been going to ball games with my partner?"

Inside, Reena moved through the dense curtain of smoke. She could hear her own breath, the suck of oxygen from her tank, and the crackle of flames not yet suppressed.

The search for victims would still be under way, but so far—thank God—none had been found.

Easy pickings for him, she thought as she pushed through smoke. Plenty of time to plan and set this fire in this place. But what she was seeing was so amateurish, so simple. She might have taken it for kids or an ordinary fire setter.

He wasn't. She was sure he wasn't despite the use of basics like gas and waxed paper.

She'd find more.

Fire had gnawed its way down the steps, teased along by the use of gas and the trailers. It might've burned like a torch, but for the phone call sending her here.

So he hadn't cared about destroying the building.

The second floor took a hit. Both the temperature and the density of smoke increased, and she had no doubt she'd find another point of origin. She could see the silhouettes of men moving through the fog of smoke like heroic ghosts.

There were remnants of trailers here. She picked up the charred remains of a book of matches, fumbled it into a bag, marked the spot to document.

"Doing okay, champ?"

She gave the thumbs-up to Steve. "Burn pattern on the east wall? Second point of origin, I think." His voice and hers sounded tinny and strained. "Fire sucked into the ceiling here." She gestured up. "Flashed back down there. He was already long gone."

They moved together, documenting evidence, recording, climbing up into the still living heart of the fire.

It licked the walls, and men beat it back. It danced overhead along the charred ceiling with the guttural roar that always sent a finger of ice up her spine.

It was gorgeous, horribly gorgeous. Seductive with its light and heat, its powerful dance. She had to block out the innate fear, and her own intrinsic fascination, concentrating instead on fuel and method, on the fingerprints of style.

Gas, a stronger stench of it here, under the sharp smell of smoke, the dull odor of wet. The men who fought the leaping spirals of flame had faces blackened from the smoke, eyes blank with concentration. Water spat out of hoses and streamed in the broken windows from outside.

Another portion of the roof collapsed with a kind of shuddering glee, venting the fire, feeding it so that it spurted up in a sudden storm.

She jumped forward to assist with a hose, and thought of lion trainers slapping at a violent cat with a whip and a chair.

The effort sang in her muscles, shook down to her toes.

She saw where part of the wall had been hacked away to studs, and through the blur of water and smoke noted the char, the pattern.

He'd done that, she thought. Initial point of origin.

And knew, as her arms trembled and the fire slowly died, this hadn't been his first.

The relief was wild, a kind of stupefying release, when he saw her come out. Despite the gear and her height, Bo recognized her the instant she stepped through the dense smoke.

However casual O'Donnell'd been, whatever he'd said before, Bo heard his release of breath when Reena waded out through the smoke and wet and debris.

Her face was black with soot. As she shrugged off her tanks, ash rained off her protective gear.

"There's our girl," O'Donnell said lightly. "Why don't you wait here, pal. I'll send her over in a minute."

She took off her helmet—and there was a short spiral of dark gold as she bent from the waist, braced her hands on her knees and spat on the ground.

She stayed there, lifting only her head to acknowledge O'Donnell. Then she straightened, brushed off a paramedic. Unhooking her jacket, she made her way toward Bo.

"I have to stay, then I'm going to need to go in. I'm going to have somebody take you back home."

"You're okay?"

"Yeah. It could've been a lot worse in there. He could've made it a lot worse. No loss of life, building empty, school out for the summer. This was just for show."

"He left you that matchbox from your family's place. So the show was for you."

"I can't argue with that." She glanced over to where a couple of soaked, soot-covered firefighters were lighting cigarettes. "You notice anybody who seemed off?"

"Not really. I have to admit after you went in, I didn't pay much attention. Praying takes most of my focus."

She smiled a little, then lifted her brows when he wiped at the soot on her cheek with his thumb. "I'm not looking my best."

"I can't begin to tell you how you look. You scared the hell out of me. We'll save the buts for when you've got more time." He stuffed his hands in his pockets. "I figure we've got a lot to say to each other, and I'd rather do it without the audience."

She looked over her shoulder. They were doing a surround and drown, and the worst was over. "I'll get you a ride. Look, I'm sorry how this turned out."

"Me, too."

She walked away, arranged for his ride home. And she thought that the fire had done more than hull out a building. If she wasn't misreading the way Bo had stepped back from her, the fire had also turned a developing relationship into ash.

She went to her car for her field kit, pulled it and a bottle of water she kept there out as Steve wandered over to her. "So, is that the guy Gina said you're seeing?"

"That's the guy I've *been* seeing. I think he's just decided the whole cop, arson, fires-in-the-middle-of-the-night routine is more complicated than he likes."

"His loss, hon."

"Maybe, or maybe he just had himself a lucky escape. I am hell on men, Steve."

She slammed her trunk. Her car was coated with ash. And she stank, no question about it. She leaned on her car, opened the bottle to take a long drink of water to clear her throat.

She passed the bottle to Steve, stayed as she was while O'Donnell came to join them.

"They'll clear us to go back in, just a few minutes. What you got?"

Reena took a small tape recorder out of her kit so she'd only have to say it once. "Phone call from unidentified subject, my home residence, at twenty-three forty-five," she began, and moved through the events, her observations, the already collected evidence point by point.

She switched off the recorder, put it back in her kit. "My opinion?" she continued. "He made it look half-assed. Made it look simple. But he took the time to open the wall upstairs, set the fire in such a way that it would progress behind the walls as well as into the room. We had a broken window up there when I arrived. Maybe he did it, maybe it was already broken, but that ventilation moved the fire along. He used basic stuff. Gas, trailers of paper and matchbooks. But they're basic because in the right circumstance, they can work extremely well. It doesn't look like a pro, but it smells like one."

"Somebody we've met before?"

"I don't know, O'Donnell." Tired, she pushed at her hair. "I've been through old cases. So have you. Nothing jumps out. Maybe it's some wack job I met along the line, brushed off, and this is his way of courting me. This is the neighborhood school. My neighborhood school."

She unlocked the car, took out the bagged matchbox to show him. "From Sirico's, to tell me he knows me, and he can get close. Left where I'd find it. Not inside, where if things got out of hand it could be destroyed. Outside, where the odds were better I'd find it, outside his point of entry, or what he made look like his point of entry. It's personal."

She locked the bag back in the car. "And, okay, it's fucking spooky. It's got me wound up."

"We work the scene, we work the case. And next time he calls," O'Donnell added, "and you think about going to check out something without calling me first? Don't."

She hunched her shoulders. "He ratted me out." She blew out a breath. "And he was right. You're right. I figured it was just some creep pushing my buttons—which I can handle. Have handled. But this is more." She studied the building, hazed through smoke. "He's more. So no, you don't have to worry about me hotdogging."

"Good. Let's get to work."

# 20

It was after six in the morning when Reena left the scene. She split off from O'Donnell, hooking up with Steve to head to the fire station. O'Donnell would log in the evidence, write the initial report. She'd talk to any of the fire department team who'd been on the fire and who were awake.

She could get a shower there—finally. She always kept a change in her trunk. Besides, odds were she'd get a good meal at the firehouse, and nights like the one she'd put in stoked her appetite.

"So this guy Goodnight, what's the story?" At Reena's bland stare, Steve shrugged. "Gina's going to grill me about it. She gets pissy when I don't have details."

"She's going to grill me anyway. Just tell her I said to come straight to the source."

"Appreciate it."

"She handles what you do. I mean, it's never been an issue between the two of you."

"She worries sometimes, sure. But no, it's not a big deal. When we lost Biggs last year, that was rough. As rough on her as me. We've talked about it." He pulled on his ear. "About how that kind of risk is part of the job. You have to buy the package, you know? Doesn't always work, but Gina, she's tough. You know that. We've got the kids, another coming. She's got to be tough."

"She loves you. Love's tough." Reena pulled up at the station. "When you call her this morning, ask if she'll call my parents. Just let them know I'm on this case and everything's fine. Can you spare the details, Steve? Just for now?"

"No problem."

A couple of men were washing down the pumper. Steve loitered to talk. Reena settled for a wave as she carried her fresh clothes inside.

She washed smoke out of her hair until her arms ached, then just closed her eyes and let the water beat on her head, her neck, her back.

Her eyes felt gritty, exhausted, but that would pass. The taste of it would linger, she knew, no matter how much water she drank. The flavor of fire lingered, and even when it passed, it was something she never forgot.

She took her time, soothing her skin—herself—by rubbing in scented cream. She slathered on moisturizer. She'd walk into a burning building, but damn if she'd sacrifice her skin. Or her vanity, she thought as she carefully applied makeup.

When she was dressed, she slung her bag over her shoulder and headed to the kitchen to bum a meal.

Something, it seemed, was always cooking here. Big pots of chili or stew, a huge hunk of meat loaf, a vat of scrambled eggs. The long counters, the stove, would be scrubbed clean after every meal, but the air would always smell of coffee and hot food.

She'd trained out of this station, and volunteered here often in her free time. She'd slept in the bunks, cooked at the stove, played cards at the table or zoned out to the TV in the lounge.

No one was surprised when she walked in. She got sleepy nods, cheerful greetings. And a big plate of bacon and eggs.

She sat next to Gribley, a twelve-year man who sported a neat goatee and burn scars along his clavicle. War wounds.

"Word is the torch from last night gave you a heads-up."

"Word's right." She scooped up eggs, washed them down with the Coke she'd taken from the refrigerator. "Looks like he's got an issue with me. The structure was fully engaged when I got there. Maybe ten minutes after he called."

"Poor response time," Gribley commented.

"He didn't tell me he'd lit something up or I'd've been faster. I will be, next time."

Across the table one of the other men lifted his head. "You looking for a next time? You're thinking serial this soon out?"

"I'm prepared for it. You're going to need to be prepared for it, too. He made this one easy. A little testing move. Like when you stretch your arm up so you can coyly wrap it around a woman's shoulder. Looking for my reaction, I think. Second floor, eastmost wall first engaged?"

"Yeah." Gribley nodded. "That section was in full flashover when we got up. Part of the wall hacked out, vent holes in the ceiling."

"First floor had the same deal," Reena continued. "He took some time. We found four matchbooks, one of them didn't go off."

"Had trailers along the second floor, heading down to the first." The man across from her, Sands, picked up his coffee mug. "Hadn't fully caught when we hit them. Slop job, you ask me."

"Yeah." But was that carelessness, or craftiness?


It was almost childish." Reena sat, kicked back in her chair. O'Donnell mirrored her pose. "Gas and paper and matches. The kinds of things a kid might play with. If you discount the deliberate venting, it's kid stuff, or amateur hour. Matchbooks that didn't have time to catch—so we'd find them. So did he think we wouldn't see the venting, or did he want us to see?"

"If you're trying to psych him, I say he wanted you to see it. The rest of us are background. You're the spotlight."

"Thanks for putting my mind at rest." She sat up, hissed. "Who? Why? Where did our paths cross? Or have they only crossed in his head?"

"We go through old cases, again. And start talking to people involved. Maybe it's somebody we put away. Maybe it's somebody we didn't. Maybe it's somebody you had a thing with and doesn't like that you broke it off."

She shook her head at this. "I haven't had a serious thing. I haven't let a thing get serious since . . ." She trailed off, then rubbed the back of her neck when O'Donnell's eyes stayed steady on hers. "You keep up with current events, O'Donnell. You know I've played it loose since that business with Luke."

"Long time to play it loose."

"Maybe, but that's how I like to play it. And any ideas this might be Luke, forget it. He'd never crawl around some grimy building. He'd get his designer suit dirty."

"Maybe he wore his play clothes. He still in New York?"

"As far as I know. Okay." She lifted her hands. "I'll check. I *hate* that I have to check."

"You ever think just how bad that guy messed you up?"

"Hell, he gave me a couple of bruises. I've had worse playing touch football."

"I'm not talking about your face, Hale. Messed up your head. Shame you gave him the satisfaction. Gonna get some coffee." He rose, walked off to give her time to think about it.

Instead, she swore under her breath and turned to her computer to get current data on Luke Chambers.

Her voice was stiff when O'Donnell came back with a mug. "Luke Chambers has a New York address, and is employed by the same brokerage house which took him to Wall Street. He was married in December of 2000 to a Janine Grady. No children. He was widowed when his wife was killed on nine-eleven. She worked on the sixty-fourth floor of Tower One."

"Tough break. Something like that can twist a man. Wouldn't've happened to him if you'd gone along with his plan back in the day."

"Jesus, you're like a dog with a bone. Fine. I'll reach out to the local cops, ask them to verify he was in New York last night."

O'Donnell stepped to her desk, then put the can of Diet Pepsi he'd stuck in his pocket in front of her. "Situation was reversed, you'd push me to do the same. If I wouldn't, you'd do it for me."

"I'm tired. I'm edgy. The fact that you're right only makes me want to punch you."

With a satisfied smile, O'Donnell sat back at his desk.

It was a relief to finally get home—and all Reena wanted now was a major nap.

She went inside, hung her purse over the newel post. Then, when her mother's disapproving frown flashed into her mind, took it off and put it in the closet.

"There, happy now?"

She ignored the flash of the answering machine, went straight into the kitchen.

She tossed her mail on the table, set the file copy she'd brought home beside it. Nap first, she told herself, but gave in and punched the message retrieval on her answering machine.

As soon as the recording announced message one had been received at two-ten A.M., her heart began to pound.

"Did you like your surprise? I bet you did since you're still out there. All that fire. Gold and red and hot blue. I bet it made you wet. Bet you wanted to climb inside and let the boy next door fuck you while it burned. I'll do better than that. Just wait. Just wait."

Her breathing was too loud, and too fast. She paused the playback, closed her eyes until she could bring it under control.

He had watched. He'd known Bo was with her. Known she'd gone to the window.

He'd been close enough to watch her, but she'd missed him. Had he been one of the people coming out of neighboring buildings? One of the drivers of a passing car? One of the faces in the crowd?

Watching her. Watching her watch the flames.

She shuddered. He wanted to spook her, and she couldn't stop that. But she could control what she did about it.

She ran through the rest of the messages.

The second came through at seven-thirty.

"Still not home?" He laughed, a kind of indrawn breath. "Busy, busy, busy."

"Bold, aren't you, you bastard," she said aloud. "That's always a mistake."

The third recorded at seven forty-five.

"Reena."

She jolted, then blew out a breath at the sound of Bo's voice. Yes, indeed, she admitted, she was thoroughly spooked.

"Your car's not back, so I guess you're still working. I've got a bid to work up today, and a supply run. Sounds pretty tame after the adventures of last night. Anyway, if you're home later, give me a call."

The next came in an hour later—Gina wanting to get together so she could get the full scoop on the new guy.

"Pretty sure you're too late on that." Reena made a whooshing sound and snapped her fingers. "Here, then gone."

Then she frowned when her sister Bella's tearful voice blasted through the machine. "Why aren't you ever around when I need you?"

As that was the sum and total of the message, Reena reached for the phone. Then stopped herself. Sometimes she had to think like a cop first, then like a sister.

She deleted all the messages after the second call, took the tape out, sealed it in a bag before digging out a fresh tape.

She called O'Donnell to bring him up to speed.

"So he was there."

"Most likely. Or he was watching my house, saw me leave with Bo. He may have me staked out here, may have followed me over. I didn't make a tail, and I've been looking for one."

"We'll start another canvass in the morning," he told her. "I'll call in, have a car patrol your place tonight."

She started to object, caught herself. "Good idea. Somebody from the unit, okay? He spots a patrol car, it might push him back. Unmarked's better."

"I'll fix it. Get some rest."

She thought of the call from Bella. "Yeah." And rubbed her tired eyes. "I'll do that."

She looked at the phone. She had to call Bella back. Of course she did. The fact that the outburst could have been brought on by something as petty as a broken fingernail wasn't the point. And that was unkind—and untrue—Reena admitted. Bella wasn't quite that ridiculous. Close, but not quite.

It might be something about the kids, though it was more likely she'd have half a dozen calls from relatives if that were the case. Her parents would have called on her cell if there was an emergency.

And what did it say about her that she was dawdling this way over a simple return call to her sister?

Reena picked up the phone, hit her sister's number on memory.

She wasn't certain if she was relieved or irritated when the housekeeper informed her Bella was at the salon. Which could still mean there was a crisis, Reena thought as she hung up. Her sister shot to the salon the way other people rushed to the ER.

She was about to head upstairs but detoured at the knock on her front door. She felt the tingle along her ribs as she wondered if it was Bo. Instead she opened the door to an exuberant and six-months-pregnant Gina.

"Steve said you should be home. I just had to see how you were." She threw her arms around Reena for a huge hug. "What a night, huh? You okay? You look tired. You should take a nap."

"Now there's an idea," Reena said as Gina strolled in.

"Well, let's sit down. My mother's got the kids for a couple hours. God bless her with eternal youth and beauty." She plopped, patted a hand on her rounded belly, then grinned around the room at walls the last owners had painted a kind of strange kiwi green.

"Picked out your colors yet? You ought to get on that in this nice weather, so you can leave the windows open, cut back on the painty smell. Steve will give you a hand with the work."

"Appreciate it. I haven't really settled on anything. I'm thinking something a little more classic than this."

"Anything would be. I can help you. I love picking out colors. It's like toys. Am I cheering you up?"

"Do I look like I need it?"

"Steve tells me things, Reene. Don't worry, I haven't said anything to your family, to anyone. I won't if you don't want me to. I'll just worry about you all by myself."

"You don't have to worry."

"Of course not. Just because some fire maniac is obsessed with my best friend, enough to all but burn out our elementary school."

Reena sighed, then rose to go to the kitchen and pour them both tall glasses of San Pellegrino.

"Got anything to go with that?" Gina asked from behind her. "Something containing large quantities of sugar?"

Reena took out the remains of a coffee cake. "It's a few days old," she warned.

"Yeah, that matters." Laughing, Gina broke off a hunk. "I'd eat tree bark if it had sugar poured on it." She sat at the old butcher block Reena was using as a kitchen table. "Okay, I've been busy, you've been busy. Now it's time for me to get all the deets on this carpenter. My mother got from your mother that you knew him in college. I knew who you knew, and I don't remember some hunky guy named Goodnight."

"Because we didn't know him. Or I didn't. He saw me when we were in college. When you and I were in college."

"My mother never gets it straight." Gina broke off another piece. "Sit and spill."

She did, and the leading edge of fatigue dulled when Gina punctuated the recitation with gasps and *Oh my Gods* and dramatic slaps of her hand to her heart.

"He saw you across the room, and he never forgot you. He carried you inside him all—"

"Ick."

"Oh, shut up. This is so romantic. It's Heathcliff and Catherine romantic."

"They were crazy."

"For God's sake. Okay, it's *Sleepless in Seattle* romantic. You know how I love that movie."

"Sure, except for the fact that we don't live on opposite coasts, I'm not engaged to someone else, and he's not a widower with a kid, it's just exactly the same."

Gina jabbed a finger. "You're not going to spoil this for me. I've been married six years, I'm on my third kid. I don't get that much sappy romance these days. So, how good-looking is he?"

"Really. He's built. Some of it probably comes from the kind of work he does. All that manual labor."

"Now the grit. How's the sex?"

"Did I say I've had sex with him?"

"How long have I known you?"

"Damn. Got me there. It's off the scale."

On a blink, Gina sat back. "You've never said that before."

"Said what?"

"You always say, it's great, or it's intense. Sometimes, it's fun or it's mediocre. If I were to use a scale, I'd say you've peaked at around eight."

Reena's forehead furrowed. "I've had tens. And you're entirely too obsessed with my sex life."

"What are friends for? How is this the best sex of your young, adventurous life?"

"I didn't say . . . Okay, it is. I don't know. It's great and intense and fun, and it is romantic. Even when it's wild. And after last night, it's over."

"Why? What? I just got here."

Reena poured more fizzy water, then just sat and watched the bubbles. "Dragging a guy to a scene—one in which you're personally as well as professionally involved—having him see you running around in turnout gear, snapping out orders, some of them at him, with him knowing you've got some wack job focused on you? It takes the bloom off, Gina."

"Then he's got a really tiny dick."

With a laugh, Reena shook her head. "He doesn't. Figuratively or literally. We just started to dance, Gina. The tune changes this abruptly—it gets complicated."

With a huff, Gina sat back. "Well, if that's his attitude, I don't like him after all."

"You would like him. He's likeable. I'm not going to blame him for stepping back."

"Which means he hasn't stepped back yet."

"I got a sense of the back step last night. It's just not official."

"You know your problem, Reena? You're a pessimist. When it comes to men, you're a big pessimist. That's why—" She broke off, frowned, sipped water.

"Don't stop now."

"Okay, I won't because I love you. It's why your relationships don't last, why they don't move into any real depth. It's been that way since college. Since poor Josh. And it got worse after Luke. He was an asshole of major proportions," Gina added as Reena sputtered. "No question. But what happened there messed with your head, if you ask me, and it's blocked you from making real connections."

"That's not true." But she heard her own voice, and the lack of conviction in it.

Gina reached over, took Reena's hand. "Hon, I'm hearing you talk about this guy the way I haven't heard you talk about a guy since we were kids. I'm seeing serious connection potential, and you're ready to blow it off. Hell, you're braced to. Why don't you wait and see how it stands up before you put an X through his name?"

"Because it matters," Reena said softly, and Gina's hand squeezed hers. "Because he looks at me and it matters. I've never felt that before. Not once, not with anyone. It was all right that I didn't, or couldn't. Maybe wouldn't. It was okay. I've got plenty in my life. My family, my work. If I wanted a man, there were plenty out there. But he matters, and it's so quick, it's so *much*, I don't want to be flattened when he walks away."

"You're in love with him?"

"I'm teetering. I'm scared."

Gina's smile bloomed as she pushed herself to her feet, walked around to wrap her arms around Reena's neck. Kissed the top of her head. "Congratulations."

"I think I blew it last night, Gina."

"Stop. Wait. See. Remember what a wreck I was when things started getting serious with Steve."

Reena smiled. "It was cute."

"It was terrifying." She straightened, absently massaging Reena's shoulders. "I was going to go live in Rome for a year, have a mad affair with some struggling artist. How the hell was I going to do that when some damn firefighter had me all twisted up? And he still twists me up, still scares me. Sometimes I look at him and think what would I do if anything happened to him, if I lost him? What if he fell in love with somebody else? Give this one a chance." She eased around, laid a hand on Reena's cheek. "I haven't even met him, and I'm telling you to give this one a chance. Now, I'm going to go pick up my kids and get back to the circus that is my life. Call me tomorrow."

"I will. Gina? You cheered me up."

"Then my work is done."

She slept for three hours, and woke with her heart pounding and the dregs of a nightmare clogging her brain. Fire and smoke, terror and dark—a jumble of elements that wouldn't coalesce. That was probably best, she thought, curling up to wait for her pulse to level.

She had bad dreams now and then, especially if she was stressed or overtired. Cops were prone to them. Nobody saw what they saw, touched what they touched, smelled what they smelled.

But it would fade, as always. She could live with the images because the job meant she did something about them.

She sat up, switched on the light. She'd eat something, get a little work done. That would ward off the three A.M. spell of wakefulness and worry.

She was still muzzy-headed when she went downstairs. Gina was right, she decided as she trailed her fingers over a wall. She should get serious about paint, go pick up some chips, start making the house more hers.

Commitment phobia? she wondered. She'd dragged her feet about buying a house, even though it had been something she'd wanted for years. Now she was dragging them over putting herself into the house, making it reflect her taste and style.

Well, the first step was recognizing she had a little problem. So she'd buy some damn paint and make a stand.

She'd get through this case, close it down. Then she'd take a week off and do something for herself. Paint and paper, some trips to the antique stores, the thrift shops. She'd plant some flowers.

Without much interest, she poked around the kitchen. She didn't actually feel like eating. She felt like brooding. It wasn't her fault she was a cop and sometimes her work was unattractive and urgent. It certainly wasn't her fault he couldn't handle that.

Commitment phobic, my ass, she decided. She'd been on the verge of making one to him—her first—and he jumps off the ship at the first rocky wave.

Screw it.

He was the one who came on to her. Dreamy green eyes, sexy mouth. Son of a bitch. She got out garlic, Roma tomatoes, began to chop as she mentally ripped Bo to pieces. Dream Girl? Bullshit. She wasn't anybody's dream, and had no intention of filling the slot. She was who she was, and he could take it or leave it.

She heated olive oil in a skillet, got out red wine.

She didn't need him. Plenty of men out there if and when she wanted one. She wasn't looking for some charming, sexy, funny carpenter to fill any gaps in her life.

She didn't have gaps.

She sizzled garlic, then jolted at the knock on her back door. Wound up, she told herself, but she picked up the gun she'd set on the counter.

"Who is it?"

"It's Bo."

Breathing out, she put the gun in her junk drawer. Rolled her shoulders, then unlocked the back door.

Her chest was tight, and there was nothing she could do about it. Tight chest, dry throat, and there was a heaviness in her belly. All this was a new and unwelcome kind of dread when it came to a man.

But she opened the door, gave him a small, casual smile. "Need a cup of sugar?"

"Not so much. You get my message?"

"Oh, yeah. Sorry. I didn't get home until after four, then I had company. I caught a nap. Just got up."

"Figured. Your bedroom curtains were drawn when I got home, so I guessed you were getting some sleep. Thought I'd chance it when I saw the light back here. Something smells good—besides you."

"Oh, shit." She dashed back to the stove, saved the garlic. "I'm just fixing some pasta." She added the diced tomatoes, a dollop of the wine. Maybe she wasn't hungry, particularly, but she was glad to have something to do with her hands. She added some basil, ground in some pepper, let it all simmer.

"I guess you being good at that comes naturally. You still look tired."

"Thanks." She heard her own voice, sour as lemons. "I love hearing that."

"I was worried about you."

"Sorry, comes with the territory."

"I guess it does."

"I'm going to have a glass of wine."

"Thanks." His eyes stayed on hers. "That'd be good. Anything more you can tell me about what happened last night?"

"Illegal entry, arson with multiple points of origin, messages directed at arson investigator. No loss of life." She handed him a glass of red.

"Are you feeling bitchy because you're tired, because this asshole's complicating your life, or are you pissed at me?"

Her smile was as bitter as her tone. "Pick one."

"Okay, I get the first two. Why don't you explain door number three?"

She leaned back on the counter. "I did what I was trained to do, what I'm obliged to do, what I'm paid to do."

He waited a moment, nodded. "And?"

"And what?"

"That's what I'm saying, and what? Who's arguing?"

She could be civilized, she told herself. Civilized and mature. She got out a pot, took it to the sink to fill with water. "I've made more than enough if you're hungry."

"Sure. Reena, are you chilling me here because I got in your way last night?"

"You shouldn't have."

"When somebody I care about starts to do something reckless, something dangerous, I get in the way."

"I'm not reckless."

"Not as a rule, I wouldn't think. But he got under your guard."

"You don't know my guard." She carried the pot to the stove, turned on the burner. "You barely know me at all." And went very still when he put a hand over hers, when he turned her around to face him.

"I know you're smart. I know you're dedicated. I know you're tight with your family, and when you laugh your whole face gets into it. I know you like baseball, and where you like to be touched. That you like lemon meringue pie and don't drink coffee. I know you'll walk into a fire. Tell me something else, then I'll know that."

"Why are you here, Bo?"

"To see you, to talk to you. And I'm getting pasta out of the deal."

She stepped back, picked up her wine. "I assumed after last night you'd be uncomfortable."

"With what?"

"Don't be dense."

He lifted his hands. "Trying not to be. Uncomfortable . . . with you."

She gave a little shrug, took a small sip.

"And I'd be uncomfortable with you because . . . Okay, no multiple choice," he decided when she said nothing. "Because we had a fight about you heading out alone? No, that's not it, because I won. Because I had to stay out of the way? Can't be because I'm not with the police or fire departments. You're stumping me here."

"You didn't like that I went in."

"Into a burning building?" He made a sound, a kind of spitting laugh. "Fucking-A right. I'm supposed to like it when you run into fire? Problem there, then, because that's never going to happen. Adding to that, it was my first experience with it, I think I behaved myself. It's not like I ran after you, tackled you and dragged you away. Which did buzz briefly through my mind as a possibility. Is liking the risks you've got to take part of the requirements of us?"

She stared at him. "God. I *am* a pessimist."

"What are you talking about? Can you please translate your strange female language into words I can comprehend?"

"Do you want to be with me, Bo?"

He threw up his hands, the image of a frustrated, baffled male. "Standing right here."

She laughed, shook her head. "Yes, you are. You certainly are. I'm going to apologize."

"Good. Why?"

"For assuming you were a jerk. For assuming you were breaking things off because you didn't want to deal with what I do, with what I am. For working myself up so I wouldn't care if you did. I didn't get there, but I was putting some effort into it. For being mad at you when I was the one who wasn't dealing with it. I'm beginning to realize I have issues in this area—the relationship area."

She stepped to him, put her hands on his cheeks, pressed her lips warmly to his. "So I apologize."

"Are we over our first fight now?"

"Apparently."

"Good." He put his hands on her cheeks, kissed her back. "That one's always the tricky one. Let's talk about something completely different while we eat, which I hope is soon because all I had tonight was a peanut butter sandwich."

She turned away to get the pasta. "This is going to be a lot better."

"It already is."

# FLASHOVER

*The final stage of the process of fire growth.*

*About, about, in reel and rout*
*The death-fires danced at night.*
—SAMUEL TAYLOR COLERIDGE

# 21

I want to know more about this girl you're seeing."

Bo continued to hammer out the new garden shed Mrs. Malloy insisted she needed, pausing only to shoot her a wink. "Mrs. M., don't be jealous. You're still the love of my life."

She sniffed, set the fresh lemonade she'd made him on a sawhorse. Her hair remained a brilliant red, and she was wearing trendy amber-lensed sunglasses. And a floral bib apron.

"You got a look in your eye, boy, tells me I've been replaced. I want to know about her."

"She's beautiful."

"Tell me something I couldn't figure out for myself."

He set aside the nail gun, picked up the lemonade. "She's smart and funny and intense and sweet. Her eyes, they're like a lioness, and she's got this little mole, right here." He tapped above his lip. "She comes from a big family. They run an Italian place in my neighborhood. She grew up there. Hey, maybe your brother knows her. Isn't your brother a cop?"

"He is, these past twenty-three years. Has he arrested her?"

He laughed. "Doubtful. She's a cop. Baltimore city. Arson unit."

"So's my brother."

"Get out. I thought he was . . . I don't know what I thought. They must know each other. What's his name again? I'll ask her."

"It's O'Donnell. Michael O'Donnell."

Now he set down the lemonade, pulled off his safety goggles. "Okay, *Twilight Zone* music. He's her partner. She's Catarina Hale."

"Catarina Hale." Mrs. Malloy folded her arms. "Catarina Hale. The same one I tried to fix you up with years ago?"

"You did not. Did you?"

"My brother says he has a pretty new partner—and I say, is she single? And he says yes, and I say, I've got a nice boy, the boy who does work around the house for me. I tell him he has to ask her if she wants to go out with a nice boy. But she's seeing someone else. Turns out not to be such a nice boy, but Mick won't bring it up to her again. So."

"Wow. It's this weird circle with us, me and Reena. I mean we circled around each other for years, never quite connecting. Have you ever met her?"

"Once, when she came to a party at Mick's. Very pretty, good manners."

"I'm going to dinner tomorrow. Her parents' house. Family dinner."

"You take flowers."

"Flowers?"

"You take her mother some nice flowers, but not in a box." She shook her finger as she gave Bo instructions. "It's too formal. Nice colorful flowers you can hand her when you go in the door."

"Okay."

"You're a good boy," she pronounced, then left him to work so she could go inside, call her brother and get more inside scoop on this Catarina Hale.

Flowers, he could handle flowers. They had them at the grocery store, and he needed to pick up a few things anyway. He stopped by the store near Mrs. Malloy's house, wheeled a cart in. Milk, he was always running out of milk. Cereal. Why didn't they stock the cereal near the milk? Didn't that make sense?

Maybe he should pick up a couple of steaks, have Reena over and grill them. With that in mind, he picked up a few more things, working his way over to the florist.

He stood, thumbs in pockets, studying the selections in the refrigerated displays.

Mrs. M. had said cheerful. The big yellow ones—he thought they were lilies—looked cheerful. But didn't lilies say funeral? Nothing cheery about that.

"Harder than I thought," he muttered out loud, then glanced over, slightly embarrassed, when a man stepped up beside him.

"In the doghouse, too?"

"Sorry?"

The man gave Bo a long-suffering smile, then frowned at the flowers. "Thought maybe you were in the doghouse. That's where I lived last night. Gotta get the wife some flowers, buy my way out."

"Oh. No, dinner at my girlfriend's parents' tomorrow. I think it's roses for a doghouse pass."

"Shit. Guess so." He stepped to the counter and the clerk on duty. "Looks like I need a dozen of those roses. Red ones, I guess. Women," he said to Bo and scratched his head under his gimme cap.

"Tell me about it. I think I'm going for those." Bo glanced at the clerk. "Those different-colored things with the big heads?"

"Gerbera daisies," he was told.

"Daisies are cheerful, right?"

The clerk smiled at him as she took out the roses. "I think so."

"Cool. A big mess of those daisies then, when you're done. Just mix them up."

"Bet wives cost more than mothers," the man said mournfully.

Bo looked back at the daisies. Was he being cheap? He was going for pretty and cheerful, not cheap. Why was it so complicated? He waited until the roses were wrapped.

"See ya."

"Yeah." Bo gave the man an absent nod. "Good luck," he added, then fell on the mercy of the clerk. "Look, it's a family dinner thing—my girl-friend's family. Are the daisies the thing? Is a dozen enough? Help me."

She moved to the cold box again. "They're perfect. Major points for casual, happy flowers."

"Good. Fine. Thanks. I'm exhausted."

• • •

*Easy as pie, keeping an eye. Change of pace to follow the boy next door, check him out up close. Asshole working on Saturday.*

*Could've stuck him in the parking lot. Could've waited for him to come out with his fistful of posies and jabbed him right then and there.*

*Hey, buddy, can you give me a hand a minute? His type runs over like a frig-ging puppy. Have the knife in his gut while the son of a bitch is still grinning.*

*Toss the roses on the seat of the car. Doghouse my ass. Like you'd ever let a woman rule the day. Whores and bitches. Need to be kept in their place. Keeping them in their place was half the fun.*

*Wait and watch anyway. Watch him come out, walk to his truck with a couple of bags. Dumb-ass daisies sticking out the top. Probably a fag underneath. Probably thought of butt-fucking some other fag when he was banging her.*

*Do the world a favor and stick a knife in his gut. One less queer in the world. How would she feel if the queer she's banging bought it in the supermarket parking lot?*

*Better ways, better days.*

*Cruise on out of the lot behind him. Nice truck. There's a thought. Fun time to burn up that nice truck. More fun if he was in it. Something to think on.*

• • •

Mrs. Malloy hit the bull's-eye, Bo decided. Bianca not only smiled when he handed her the flowers at the door on Sunday afternoon, she kissed him on both cheeks.

Some of the family were already there. Xander, the brother, sprawled in a chair in the living room with the baby tucked in the crook of his arm. Jack, the brother-in-law—somebody get him a scorecard—was stretched out on the floor with one of the kids playing with cars.

Fran, the oldest sister, wandered out from the kitchen rubbing circles on her belly the way pregnant women do.

Another kid peeked out from behind Fran's legs and gave him a long, owlish stare.

Reena moved forward—hugs, kisses—like none of them had seen one another for six months. Then she scooped up the little owl. And the stare became a giggling grin.

He was offered a drink, a chair. Then the females deserted the field.

Xander turned from the game on TV, gave Bo a big, toothy smile. "So, when you marry my sister, you could take out the wall between the two houses. Give you lots of space for five, six kids."

Bo felt his mouth drop open, heard some response gurgle in his throat. Otherwise, the room was silent but for the play-by-play commentary on the ball game.

Then Xander hooted with laughter and booted his father's leg with his foot. "Told you it would be funny. He looks like he swallowed a bulb of garlic."

Gib kept watching the screen. "You got something against kids?"

"What? No." Somewhat desperately, Bo looked around the room. "Me? No."

"Good. Have mine." Xander rose, and to Bo's frozen shock, deposited the baby in Bo's lap. "Be right back."

"Oh. Well." He looked down at the baby, who stared up at him with long, dark eyes. Since he was afraid to actually move, he shifted his gaze to Gib. He knew there was panic in it, but it couldn't be helped.

"What, you never held a baby?"

"Not this small."

The kid on the floor scooted over. "They don't do much. My mama's having another baby. And it better be a brother." He turned, looked darkly at his father.

"Did my best, pal," Jack said.

"I've got a baby sister now," the boy told Bo. "She likes doll babies."

Taking his cue, Bo shook his head in pity. "That's disgusting."

Obviously sensing a kindred spirit, the boy climbed up on the arm of the chair. "I'm Anthony. I'm five and a half. I have a frog named Nemo, but Nana doesn't let me bring him to dinner."

"Girls are funny that way."

In his lap the baby squirmed and let out a cry. A bellow was more like it, in Bo's opinion. He jiggled his legs without much hope.

"You can pick him up," Ryan told him. "You just have to put your hand under his head, 'cause his neck's all floppy. Then you put him up on your shoulder and pat his back. They like that."

The baby continued to wail, and since no one came to his rescue—the sadists—Bo gingerly slid a hand under the baby's head.

"Yeah, like that," his baby expert said. "And kinda scoop the other under his butt. He's wiggly, so you gotta be careful."

Panic sweat dribbled a line down his back. Why did they make babies so damn small? And loud. Surely better arrangements could be made for the propagation of the human race.

Holding his breath, he lifted, angled, fit and let it out again when the bellows simmered down to whimpers.

In the kitchen, Fran whipped eggs in a bowl, Reena chopped vegetables while Bianca basted the chicken. It was, for Reena, one of those comfort moments. Essentially, intimately female and familial.

The back door was open to the breezy warmth, the room was full of cooking smells and perfumes. Bo's flowers were prettily arranged in a tall, clear vase, and her niece was busily banging a spoon in a big plastic bowl.

Work, and the worries of it, were in another world. Part of her was still a child in this house, and always would be. That was comfort. Part of her was woman, and that was pride.

"An will be here as soon as she's done at the clinic." Bianca straightened, shut the oven door. "Bella will be late, as usual. So, look at you." She put her hands on her hips, studied her youngest daughter. "You look happy."

"Why wouldn't I be?"

"Love sparkle," Fran said and, setting the bowl aside, leaned over the island as much as her belly would allow. "How serious is it?"

"Day at a time."

"He's hot. What?" With a shrug, Fran eased back. "I can't think he's hot? Plus he's got that puppy look in his eyes, so you've got sweet and hot, like melted man candy."

"Fran!" The name came out on a shocked laugh as Reena goggled at her sister. "Listen to you."

"It's not me. It's the hormones."

"Everywhere I look, somebody's pregnant. I just saw Gina a couple of days ago. She ate a quarter of a three-day-old coffee cake."

"With me it's olives. I could eat a vat of olives. Just lift up jar after jar and—" Fran mimed shaking them into her mouth.

"With all my babies it was potato chips." Bianca checked a pot on the stove. "Ruffles, every night. Nine months times four? Holy Mary, how many potatoes is that?" She came around the counter, caught Reena's face in her hand, shook it gently side to side. "I like that you look happy. I like this Bo. I think he's the one."

"Mama—"

"I think he's the one," Bianca continued, undaunted, "not only because he gives you a sparkle, not only because he looks at you like you're the most fascinating of women, but I think he's the one because your father gets the beady eye when he's around. That's his radar. 'So, this guy thinks he's going to take my daughter away? We'll just see about *that!*'"

"Where's he going to take me? Pluto? He lives in the neighborhood."

"He's like your father." She smiled when Reena frowned at her. "Strong and solid, hot and sweet," she added with a wink toward Fran. "And that, baby of mine, is what you've been waiting for."

Before Reena could respond, An walked in with Dillon over her shoulder. "Sorry I'm late. What are we gossiping about?"

"Reena's Bo."

"Cutie-pie. Dillon was giving him a bit of a hard time. He took it like a champ." She sat at the table, flipped open her shirt and guided the baby's seeking mouth to her breast. "Your dad's grilling him about his business," she added, then waved Reena back. "No, leave him be. He's holding his own. Mama Bee? I think you might get that back terrace on the shop you've been angling for."

"Oh really?" Bianca tapped a spoon on a pot. "I like when my kids bring useful people to dinner."

Xander poked his head in. "Hey. We're heading down to the shop for a minute."

"Dinner's in one hour. If you're not back, sitting at the table, I'll beat you all unconscious with a spatula."

"Yes, ma'am."

"Take the baby." Fran bent to pick up her daughter.

"Sure." Xander boosted his niece onto his hip where she bounced and babbled. "Reena? This guy's okay."

"Gee, thanks," she replied as her brother disappeared out the door. "We've only been dating a few weeks."

"When it's right, it's right." Bianca gathered up peppers, took them to the sink to wash them.


Down the block, Bo stood with Gib, Xander, Jack and a couple of kids. He gauged the ground in the rear of Sirico's, noted the stingy seating area that was set up for the summer season, the traffic pattern from tables to the door.

"Bianca wants more of a terrace," Gib explained. "Italian influence, maybe terra-cotta tiles. I figure pressure-treated wood would be easier, quicker, cheaper, but she keeps pushing for tile, maybe slate."

"Yeah, you could throw up a platform in lumber pretty easily. Come off the back there, angle it. Do maybe a faux paint treatment—something Italianesque—you know, a mural deal, or just paint it to look like tile or stone. Seal it up."

"Mural." Gib pursed his lips. "She might go for that."

"But."

"Uh-oh." Xander grinned, rocked back on his heels. "I hear dollar signs in that but."

"But," Bo repeated as he stepped off the rear of his imagined terrace, using his strides as an approximate measuring. "If you were going to go for it, you could add a little more, do the tile, put yourself in a kind of summer kitchen. You got that whole open-kitchen deal going inside, so you'd be mirroring it—smaller, more casual out here."

"What do you mean, 'summer kitchen'?"

He glanced back at Gib, saw he had his attention, warily. "You could put another stove out here, another cooktop deal, workstation. You lattice off those two sides, maybe you plant something viny, and do a kind of pergola, carrying the vines up and over the roof—just slats. Keeps it sunny but dappled, so it doesn't drive your customers away when it's too hot and bright."

"That's more elaborate than I had in mind."

"Okay, well, you can just extend what you've got, resurface or—"

"But keep going on it. Pergola."

Xander elbowed Jack and spoke under his breath. "Hooked him."

"Well, see . . ." Patting his pockets, Bo trailed off. "Anybody got something to write on?"

He ended up using a paper napkin, with Jack's back for a writing surface, and sketched out a rough design.

"Christ, Mama will love it. Dad, you're so screwed."

Gib rested his elbow on Xander's shoulder, leaned in closer. "How much would something like this cost me?"

"For the structure? I can work you up an estimate. I'd want to take true measurements first."

"You done back there? I want to see it." Jack turned around, studied the napkin. Then lifted his gaze to his father-in-law. "Screwed. Only way out is to make him eat the napkin, kill him and dispose of the body."

"I already thought of that, but we'd be late for dinner." Gib let out a sigh. "Better go back and show it to her." He gave Bo a slap on the back and a fierce grin. "We'll see how long he lives after the estimate."

"He's kidding, right?" Bo asked Xander as Gib started back.

"You ever watch *The Sopranos*?"

"He's not even Italian." And looked like a nice, ordinary guy, carrying his granddaughter up the sidewalk toward home.

"Don't tell him that, I think he's forgotten. Just messing with you. But this place?" He paused out front. "With my father his emotional pecking order is my mother, his kids, their kids, his family, then this place. It's not just a business. He likes you."

"How you figure?"

"If he didn't like somebody Reena brought to Sunday dinner, he'd be a lot more friendly, a lot quicker."

"And that's because?"

"If he didn't like you, you wouldn't worry him because he'd tell himself Reena wouldn't get serious about you. You wouldn't matter. If Dad's got a favorite of us, it's Reena. They've just got something . . . extra. Ah, Bella's gang just got here." He nodded up the street toward the late-model Mercedes SUV.

A willowy girl, early teens, Bo judged, got out first, flipped a shiny crop of gleaming blond hair over her shoulders and sauntered toward the Hales'.

"Princess Sophia," Xander told him. "Bella's oldest. She's going through her I'm-bored-and-beautiful stage. There's Vinny and Magdalene and Marc. Vince—corporate lawyer, lots of family dough."

"You don't like him."

"He's okay. He's given Bella what she wanted, keeps her in the style to which she always insisted she was entitled. He's a good father. Dotes on those kids. Just not the kind of guy you sit around drinking beer and shooting shit with. Last, but never least, Bella."

Bo watched Bella step out of the car when her husband opened the door for her. "You've got a crop of beautiful women in your family."

"That we do. Keeps us guys on our toes. Hey, Bella!"

He waved, dashed across the street and lifted his sister off her feet in a hug.

The noise level was huge. It was, Bo thought, like walking into a party that had been at peak for several years, and showed no signs of winding down. The floor was littered with kids of varying ages, with adults stepping over or around them.

Reena slipped up beside him, ran a hand down his arm. "You hanging in?"

"So far. They talked about killing me, but decided against it because, you know, dinner bell."

"We do have our priorities," she added. "What did you—?"

She broke off when Bianca stepped back in and shouted, "Dinner!"

It wasn't quite a stampede, but it was a kind of blur of motion. Apparently, when Bianca Hale spoke, everybody listened. He was directed to a chair between Reena and An, then was served, family style, enough food to hold him for a week.

Wine flowed, as did conversation. No one seemed to mind if they were interrupted, talked over, even ignored. Everyone had something to say, and insisted on saying it whenever they liked.

The usual rules didn't apply. If it was politics on the table, they talked politics. They talked religion, food, business. And prodded him without mercy regarding Reena.

"So . . ." Bella gestured with her glass. "Just where do you stand with Catarina, Bo?"

"Ah, about four inches taller."

She gave him a little cat smile across the table. "The last one she brought home—"

"Bella," Reena admonished.

"The last one she brought home was an actor. We decided he was able to memorize his lines because his head was so empty of anything else."

"I dated a girl like that once," Bo said lightly. "She could tell you what everyone wore to, say, the Oscars, but was a little shaky on who was actually president of the United States."

"Bella can do both," Xander said. "She's multitalented. Vince, how's your mother's arm?"

"Better, much. She'll be out of the cast next week. My mother broke her arm," he explained to Bo. "She fell off her horse."

"Sorry to hear that."

"Barely slowed her down. She's an amazing woman."

"The paragon," Bella said with a sweet, sweet smile. "How about your mother, Bo, will Reena have to compete with her, and pale in comparison?"

Tension slammed in, an angry party crasher. "Actually, I don't see much of my mother."

"Lucky Reena. Excuse me." Bella set down her napkin, strode out of the room.

Reena was up a second later and marching after her.

"Let me show you an idea Bo had for the shop." Gib took the napkin out of his pocket, smoothed it. "Just remember, I'm the father of your children, so you can't throw me over for this guy just because he's supposed to be good with a hammer. Pass this down," he said to Fran.

Bella grabbed her clutch bag and stormed out the back door with Reena on her heels.

"What the hell is the matter with you?"

"Nothing's the matter with me. I wanted a damn cigarette." She pulled out a jeweled box, slipped out a cigarette and lit it with a matching lighter. "You can't smoke in the house, remember?"

"You were needling Bo."

"No more than anyone else." She sucked in smoke, blew it out in a quick stream.

"Yes, it was, and you know it. Subtext, Bella."

"Screw your subtext. What do you care? You're just going to fuck him for a few weeks, then move on. As usual."

Temper had Reena shoving her sister back two full steps. "Even if that were true, it would be my business."

"Then mind your own business, it's what you're best at. You're only out here talking to me because you're pissed off. Otherwise, you can't be bothered."

"This is bullshit. I called you back—twice. I left two messages."

Bella took another, slower drag, and her fingers trembled. "I didn't want to talk to you."

"Then why did you call?"

"Because I wanted to talk to you then." Her voice broke as she whirled away. "I needed to talk to somebody, and you weren't there."

"I can't be there every minute of every day, anticipating one of your crises, Isabella. That one's not in the Sisters Rule Book."

"Don't be mean to me." She turned back, and there were tears. "Please don't be mean to me."

With Bella, there were often tears, Reena thought. But those who knew her understood when they were temper, show or genuine. And these were real. "Honey, what's the matter?" She moved forward, slipping an arm around Bella's waist to lead her to a bench at the edge of the patio.

"I don't know what to do, Reena. Vince is having an affair."

"Oh, Bella." Reena leaned over, drew Bella closer. "I'm sorry, so sorry. Are you sure?"

"He's been having them for years."

"What are you talking about?"

"Other women. There've been other women almost from the beginning. He just used to . . . He used to care enough to keep it from me. To be discreet. To at least pretend he loved me. Now, he doesn't bother. He goes out two, three nights a week. When I confront him, he tells me to go shopping, to get off his back."

"You don't have to tolerate this, Bella."

"And my choices are?" she asked bitterly.

"If he's sleeping with other women, if he's not honoring your marriage, you should leave him."

"And be the first in this family to divorce?"

"He's cheating on you."

"He *was* cheating on me. When you cheat, you at least try to hide it. Now he's just flaunting it, throwing it in my face. I tried to talk to his mother about it—he listens to her. And do you know what? She just shrugged it off. His father's had mistresses right along, what's the big deal? You're the wife, you have all the benefits. The home, the children, the credit cards, the social standing. The rest is just sex."

"That's just stupid. Have you talked to Mama?"

"I can't. You can't." She squeezed Reena's hand, battled back the tears. "She . . . God, Reena, I feel like such a fool, I feel like such a failure. Everyone else is so happy, and I'm so . . . not. Fran and Jack, Xander and An, and now you. I've got thirteen years invested in this marriage. I have four children. And I don't even love him."

"Oh God, Bella."

"I never did. I thought I did. I thought I did, Reena. I was twenty, and he was so handsome and smooth—and rich. I wanted all that. It's not wrong to want it. I've been faithful."

"What about counseling?"

She sighed, stared beyond the patio, away from the house where she'd grown up. "I've been in therapy for three years. There are some secrets I can keep. She says we're making progress. Funny, I don't feel like it."

"Bella." Reena kissed her hair. "Bella, you have your family. You don't have to go through this alone."

"Sometimes you do. Fran's the sweet one, you're the smart one. Even though Fran's prettier, I was the pretty one. Because I worked at it more. That's what I traded on, and this is what I got."

"You deserve better."

"Maybe I do, maybe I don't. But I don't know if I can give it up. He's a good father, Reena. The kids adore him. He's a good father, and he's a good provider."

"Listen to yourself. He's a cheating sack-of-shit adulterer."

With a watery laugh, Bella crushed out the cigarette, threw her arms around Reena. "That's why I called you when I couldn't call anyone else. Just that, Reene. Because you'd say something like that. Maybe this is partly my fault, but I don't deserve my husband rolling out of my bed into another woman's."

"Damn right you don't."

"Okay." She drew a tissue out of her bag, dried her face. "I'll talk to him again." She opened a compact, began to repair her makeup. "I'll talk to my therapist. And maybe I'll talk to a lawyer, just to test the ground."

"You can always talk to me. I might not always be there when you call, but I'll always call you back. Promise."

"I know. God, look at this mess I've made of myself." She pulled out a lipstick. "I'm sorry about before. Honestly. I'll make it up to you. To him. He's a nice guy, seems like a nice guy. That alone got me started."

"It's okay." Reena kissed her cheek. "We'll be okay."

# 22

"Tell me one thing," Bo asked as they walked home. "Did I pass the audition?"

"Sorry about that." She winced. "About the questions, the demands to perform, the request for blood tests."

"I'm getting one tomorrow."

She reached out to pat his arm. "You're a good sport, Goodnight."

"Yeah, but did I pass?"

She glanced over, decided he was serious. "I'd say your colors are flying. I'm particularly sorry about Bella at dinner."

"It wasn't that big."

"It was rude and uncalled for, but it wasn't personal. She was upset, about something entirely unrelated. She's going through a rough patch I didn't know about until tonight."

"No harm, no foul."

"My mother's not going to rest until she has her pergola."

"Is your father going to hurt me when he gets the bid?"

"Depends on the bid." She hooked her arm through his. "You know, when I was a kid, I used to dream about walking home on a warm summer night with a cute guy who claimed to be crazy about me."

"Since I can't be the first to make your dreams come true, I'll try to make this one memorable."

"You are the first."

"Get out."

"No, back when . . ." She stopped herself. "Just how many of my deep, dark secrets do I expose?"

"All of them. Back when?"

"When I was eleven, I was so sure when I got to be a teenager, everything would fall into place. My body, boys, my social skills, boys, boys. Boys. Then I got to be a teenager, and it didn't all fall into place. Part of it, I think part of it goes back to the night of the fire at Sirico's."

"I heard about that. People in the neighborhood still talk about it. Some guy had a grudge against your father and tried to burn you out."

"That's the short version. Things changed for me that summer. I studied, I badgered John—John Minger, the fire inspector who handled our case. And I hung around the fire station. By the time I got to high school, I was, well, I was fairly geeky."

"No possible way."

"Oh, so possible. I was studious, athletic, obedient, shy around boys. I was a guy's dream lab partner, his study buddy, his wailing wall, but not the girl he'd think to ask to the prom. I aced my way through high school, graduated third in my class, and could count the number of actual dates I had on one hand. And I yearned."

She laid a hand on her heart, gave an exaggerated sigh. "I yearned for the boy who plopped down beside me for help with a chem test, or to tell me about the trouble he was having with his girlfriend. I wanted to be one of those girls, the ones who knew how to stand, and talk, and flirt, and juggle four boys at once. I studied them. I was a born observer, a cataloger. I studied, documented, practiced in the privacy of my room. But I never geared up the courage to take my show on the road. Until that night with Josh, the night you saw me. I finally got there."

"He saw what the others had missed."

"That's a nice thing to say."

"Easy, because I saw it, too."

By tacit agreement, they turned at his house. "After Josh, something closed off in me, at least for a while." She stepped inside when he unlocked the door. "I didn't want a boyfriend anymore. Fire had tried to take my family's treasure, its heritage, and now it had taken the life of the first boy who'd touched me. I bore down then. For months I didn't do anything but study and work. When I was in the mood, I scooped up a boy, enjoyed him. Let him enjoy me. Moved on."

She moved into his living room, no longer sure how her light reminiscence had turned so internal, and so serious. "There weren't many, and they didn't mean anything. I didn't want them to. I wanted the work, the knowledge of how to do the work. Grad school, training, field work, lab work. Because the fire was in me, too, and it wouldn't let anyone get too close."

She let out a breath. "There was another guy I felt a little spark with. We were just circling around what we might do about it. And he was killed."

"That's a rough knock. You've had more than your share of them."

"It was. And I guess, if I think about it, it soured me. Start to get too close to having someone mean something, and I lose them."

He sat with her, picked up her hand, played with her fingers. Playing with fire, he thought. "What changed?"

"I'm afraid it was you."

"Afraid?"

"A little bit, yeah. It's only fair to tell you that because things have changed, or may be changing, what's happening between us is going to have to be exclusive. If you want to see other women, it's not going to work for me."

He lifted his gaze from her fingers, met her eyes. "The only one I'm looking at is you."

"If that changes, I expect you to tell me."

"Okay, but—"

"Okay's enough." She swung around so she straddled his lap. "Let's leave it at okay for right now."

I t looked like a typical kitchen fire. Big mess, smoke damage, minor injuries.

"Wife cooking dinner, frying up some chicken on the stove, leaves the room for a minute, grease flames up, catches the curtains." Steve nodded toward the scorched counter, the blackened walls, the charred remnants of the curtains at the windows.

"Says she thought she turned it down, but must've turned it up, went to go to the bathroom, got a phone call. Didn't think about it until she heard the alarm go off. Tried to put it out herself, burned her hands, panicked, ran out and called nine-one-one from the neighbor's."

"Uh-huh." Reena walked across the sooty floor to study the burn pattern on the backsplash, the under cabinets. "Nine-one-one came in at about four-thirty?"

"Four thirty-six."

"Early to be cooking." She looked at the counter, the nasty trail the grease fire had left on the surface. "So, what? She says she grabbed the pan, and ended up spilling the grease along her counter, dropped it." She bent closer to the skillet, and the smell of grease-soaked chicken.

"Something like that. She was pretty incoherent. Paramedics were treating her hands. Got her some second-degree burns."

"Guess she was too panicked to think of grabbing this." O'Donnell tapped the home fire extinguisher hooked on the inside wall of a broom closet.

"Lot of flame to reach those curtains," Reena commented. "Chicken's cooking away here." She stood by the stove. "That's some smart fire that leaps out of a pan and engages the curtains over a foot away. Must be a really sloppy cook." She gestured to the surface of the stove. "You've got grease running back across here, taking a turn, hitting the wall. Like it had eyes. Then gosh, oh my goodness, look at what I did! Grab the pan, haul it another foot in the opposite direction, trailing more grease before you drop it and run away."

O'Donnell smiled at her. "People do the craziest things."

"Yeah, they sure do. Crappy cabinets," she commented. "Countertop's faded, scratched up. Appliances are low-end, old. Vinyl floor's seen better days, even before our incident."

She glanced over. "Phone right there on the wall. Portable job. Where's the bathroom she used?"

"She said she used the one off the living room," Steve told her.

They walked out, wending their way. "Nice furniture in here," Reena observed. "On the new side. Everything's color-schemed and clean and tidy. Another portable phone right there, on that little table."

She stepped to the powder room door. "Coordinating guest towels, fancy little soaps, smells lemon fresh and looks like a magazine. I bet that kitchen was an eyesore."

"Pebble in her shoe," O'Donnell added.

Reena lifted the top of the toilet, saw the blue water. "Woman keeps a house this clean, this fresh and decorated, she doesn't let her stove get greasy. We on the same page here, Steve?"

"Oh, yeah."

"Guess we'd better have a talk with her."

They sat in the pretty living room with Sarah Greene's bandaged hands in her lap. Her face was swollen from crying. She was twenty-eight, with glossy brown hair pulled back in a long tail. Her husband, Sam, sat beside her.

"I don't understand why we're talking to the police," he began. "We've talked to the fire department. Sarah's had a rough time. She really ought to be getting some rest."

"We just need to ask a few questions, clear up a few things. We work with the fire department. How are your hands, Mrs. Greene?" Reena asked.

"They said they're not too bad. They gave me something for the pain."

"When I think of what could've happened." Sam rubbed her shoulder.

"I'm sorry." Her eyes went wet and shiny. "I feel so stupid."

"Fire's a scary thing. You work for Barnes and Noble, Mrs. Greene?"

"Yes." She tried to smile at O'Donnell. "I'm a manager there. This is my day off. I thought I'd surprise Sam with a home-cooked meal." Her smile twisted. "Surprise."

"Honey, don't."

"Got started on it early," Reena commented.

"I guess. Impulse, really."

No, not really, Reena thought. Since the package the chicken had come in, the one she'd dug out of the kitchen trash along with the market receipt for it, indicated it had been bought the Saturday before.

Which meant it would have been frozen for a few days, and would have taken some time to defrost. "You have a lovely house."

"Thanks. We've been working on it since we bought it two years ago."

"I just bought a row house recently. It's screaming to be updated, fixed up. Takes a lot of time, effort, not to mention the expense."

"Tell me about it." Sam rolled his eyes. "Deal with one thing, you've got six others. Like dominoes."

"I hear you. I'm starting to look at paint chips. And when I do, I realize once I do that, I'm going to have to replace curtains, deal with the floors, probably start shopping for new furniture. Then I'm going to have workers underfoot, probably for weeks at a time."

"Gets old," Sam agreed.

"But if you're going to live there, you might as well have what you want." Reena smiled at Sarah as she said it.

"Well, it's your home." Sarah pressed her lips together, avoiding meeting Reena's gaze.

"Don't get her started," Sam said with a laugh, and leaned over to kiss her cheek.

"I'm going to have to get some estimates, I suppose, at least for things I can't handle myself." Reena kept her tone casual, conversational. "Like the plumbing, some carpentry. The kitchen. I'm told the kitchen's usually the biggest chunk in the budget. What kinds of bids did you all get for yours?"

"Got one two weeks ago. Twenty-five thousand." Sam shook his head. "You go custom cabinets, solid surface, and that can double. It's ridiculous." He waved a hand. "Don't get *me* started."

"It must be hard, Mrs. Greene, to have most of your house done up just as you want it, and have an old, outdated kitchen. Sore thumb."

"I guess it's going to get done now," Sam put in. He wrapped an arm around Sarah. "Triumph through tragedy. Insurance will cover a lot of it. Not worth Sarah getting hurt." He lifted her injured hand gently at the wrist, kissed the bandage. And she began to cry again.

"Come on, baby, it's not so bad. Don't cry. Does it still hurt?"

"If you don't make the claim, Sarah," Reena said gently, "this can go away. We can make this go away, but not if you put in an insurance claim. Then it's fraud. Then it's arson. It's a crime."

"What are you talking about?" There was anger topping off Sam's question. "What the hell is this? Fraud? Arson? Is this how you treat people when they're hurt, when they're in trouble?"

"We're trying to make this easy on you," O'Donnell told him. "On both of you. We have reason to believe the fire didn't start exactly the way you've stated, Mrs. Greene. This goes to the next step, to your insurance company, we're not going to be able to help you."

"I want you to leave. My wife was *hurt*. You're sitting here trying to say she did this on purpose. You're out of your mind."

"I didn't mean it."

"Of course you didn't, honey."

"I just wanted a new kitchen."

Reena took tissues from her purse, passed them over. "So you started the fire."

"She didn't—"

"I was mad," she interrupted, and turned to her husband's stunned face. "I was just so mad at you, Sam. I hated cooking in there, or having our friends over. I told you, but you kept saying it was too much right now, and we'd have to wait, and you were sick of having the house torn up."

"Oh my God, Sarah."

"I didn't think it would be like this. I'm so sorry. And after I did it, it was so awful, and I was so scared. I really did panic," she said to Reena. "I thought it would burn the curtains, and some of the counter, but it got so much so fast, and I just panicked. And when I picked up the skillet the second time, after I put it on the counter, it was so hot, and it burned my hands. I was afraid the house would burn down, and I ran out, ran next door. I was so scared. I'm so sorry."

"Sarah, you could've been killed. You could've . . . over a kitchen?" He gathered her in when she began to sob, looked at Reena over his wife's head. "We won't put a claim in. Please, you don't have to charge her, do you?"

"It's your home, Mr. Greene." O'Donnell got to his feet. "As long as there's no attempt to defraud, there's no crime."

"Sarah, people do stupid things." Reena touched her shoulder. "But fire's very unforgiving. You don't want to test it again." She took out a card, set it on the coffee table. "You can call me if you have any questions, or need to talk about this. Ah, it's probably none of my business, but when you're ready to deal with the repairs, I know somebody who might give you a lower bid."

People," O'Donnell said as they walked to the car.

"I felt a little like I was poking at a puppy with a stick." She glanced back at the house. "They'll either be able to make a joke out of this—tragedy plus time equals comedy. Oh yeah, we love these countertops. We got them because Sarah torched the old ones. Or they'll be divorced in two years. What's your view on divorce, O'Donnell?"

"Never been there." He settled into the passenger's seat. "Wife won't let me."

Reena snickered and took the wheel. "She's so strict. We're pretty strict on it, too, in my family. It's the Catholic thing, and the family thing. Some of my cousins have been through rocky patches in their marriages, but so far, things have stuck. Makes it a little intimidating to take the step into holy wedlock. 'Cause it can mean serious lock."

"You thinking about getting hitched? The carpenter?"

"No. Well, yes, it's the carpenter, but no, not hitched. Just thinking in general." She hesitated, then thought partners were partners, and the same as family. "My sister Bella told me her husband's stepping out. Has been for years, apparently, but he's rubbing her face in it now."

"Rough."

"You ever cheat?"

"Nope. Wife won't let me."

"That bitch." Reena sighed. "I don't know what she's going to do. First off, it's a surprise to me that she didn't blab this to everyone, kept it to herself this long."

"Touchy area."

"We thrive on touchy in my family. And she's been seeing a therapist—another surprise. It just makes me think how marriage is a land mine. A really intimate land mine. Adultery to kitchen fires. Never a dull."

O'Donnell shifted in his seat to study her profile. "You're serious about this guy."

She started to blow it off, then shrugged. "Heading that way, for me. Gives me the wet palms if I think about it too hard. So I'm going to think about something else, like the fact that my fire-starter hasn't called since the night he torched the school."

"You're not figuring he's done."

"No, no, I'm not. I'm trying to figure how long he's going to make me wait. Meanwhile, you mind if we take a detour? I've got something I want to do."

"You got the wheel."

Vince's law firm was downtown, with a view of the Inner Harbor from his office. She'd been there only once before, but she remembered.

She wondered if the striking brunette who was his administrative assistant was the one he was stepping out with.

The waiting area was plush, neutral tones, very contemporary, with splashes of plum. She wasn't kept waiting in it long, but was escorted through to Vince's spacious office with its wide windows and walls of dramatic art.

He kissed both her cheeks in welcome. There was already a soft drink on ice and a tray of cheese and crackers on the coffee table in his seating area.

"Such a surprise. What brings you to my neck of the woods? Need a lawyer?"

"No. And I won't keep you long. I don't have time to sit, thanks."

He smiled, charming, handsome, smooth. "Take a minute. The city can afford it. We never get to talk, just the two of us."

"I guess we don't. You skip a lot of the family events."

His smile was full of regret. "The demands of the job."

"And of the women you play with. You're cheating on Bella, Vince, and that's between the two of you."

"Excuse me?" The charm drained out of his face.

"The fact that you've decided to rub her face in it, humiliate her, makes it my business. You want side dishes? Go ahead. You can break your marriage vows. But you won't continue to make my sister feel like a failure. She's the mother of your children, and you'll respect that."

He stayed calm. "Catarina, I don't know what Bella's told you, but—"

"Vince, you don't want to call my sister a liar." It was hard, it took vicious effort, but she stayed calm as well. "She may be a whiner, but she's not a liar. That would be you. The liar and the cheat."

There was a flash of fury. She felt it burst out of him, saw it kindle in his eyes. "You have no right to come into my office and speak to me like this, about matters that are none of your concern."

"Bella's my concern. You've been a member of the family long enough to know how we work. Respect her, or divorce her. That's your choice. Make it soon, or I'll make things very hard for you."

He let out a surprised laugh. "Are you threatening me?"

"Yes. Yes, I am. Give the mother of your children the proper respect, Vince, or I'll see other people know where you're spending your evenings instead of with your wife. My family will take my word on it," she added. "But I'll have it documented. Every time you go out to play, someone will be watching, and documenting. When I'm done, you won't be welcome in my parents' home any longer. Your children will wonder why."

"My children—"

"Deserve better from their father. Why don't you think about that? Honor your marriage, or dissolve it. Your choice."

She walked out. Not like poking a puppy with a stick this time, she thought as she strode to the elevator. No, the weight on her shoulders now was pure satisfaction.

B o walked into Sirico's carrying the briefcase he used when he wanted to impress potential clients. Or in this case, the parents of the woman he was sleeping with.

It looked to him as if the dinner shift was well under way. He probably should've chosen a less chaotic time. Still could, he decided. But since he was here, he might as well order a pizza for takeout.

Before he could turn toward the counter, Fran walked over to him, bussed both his cheeks. He wasn't quite sure what to make of that.

"Hi, how are you? Let me get you a table."

"That's okay, I was just going to—"

"Sit, sit." She took his arm, steered him toward a booth already occupied by a couple eating plates of pasta. "Bo, this is my aunt Grace and uncle Sal. This is Bo, Reena's friend. Bo, you sit with the family until we get a table cleared."

"I don't want to—"

"Sit, sit," he was ordered again, this time by Aunt Grace, who studied him with avid eyes. "We've been hearing all about you. Here, have some bread. Have some pasta. Fran! Bring Reena's boyfriend a plate. Bring him a glass."

"I was just going to—"

"So." Grace gave his arm two light slaps. "You're a carpenter."

"Yes, ma'am. Actually, I just stopped in to drop something off for Mr. Hale."

"Mr. Hale, so formal!" She batted at him again. "You're going to design Bianca's pergola."

Word did travel, he decided. "I've got some sketches for them to look over. In fact."

"In your case?" Sal spoke for the first time, jabbed his loaded fork toward Bo's briefcase.

"Yeah, I was going to—"

"Let's have a look." Sal stuffed the pasta in his mouth, gave a come-ahead gesture with his free hand.

Fran came back with a salad, set it in front of Bo. "Mama says you'll eat a nice salad, then you'll have the baked spaghetti with Italian sausage." Fran smiled winningly as she set down a red wineglass. "And you'll like it."

"Okay. Sure."

"Tell your papa to come over," Sal ordered Fran as he poured wine from his bottle into Bo's glass. "We're looking at the pergola."

"Soon as he gets a minute. Do you need anything else, Bo?"

"I seem to have it all."

When Sal cleared the center of the table, Bo took out his sketches. "You've got your straight-on, your side and your bird's-eye views," he began.

"You're an artist!" Grace exclaimed, and gestured to the charcoal sketch of Venice on the wall beside her. "Like Bianca."

"Not even close, but thanks."

"You got these columns on the ends." Sal peered over his reading glasses. "Fancy."

"More Italian."

"More money."

Bo lifted a shoulder, decided to eat the salad. "He can always go with treated posts. Either way, I'd paint them. Strong colors. Festive."

"One thing to draw pictures, another to build. You got any samples of your work?"

"I've got a portfolio."

"In the briefcase?"

Bo nodded, kept eating, and Sal made another come-ahead gesture.

"Gib's busy, but he'll be over in a minute." Bianca slid into the booth beside her brother. "Oh, the sketches. These are wonderful, Bo. You've got a lovely hand."

"An artist," Grace said with a firm nod. "Sal's browbeating him."

"Of course he is," Bianca agreed, and managed to elbow her brother and pick up a sketch at the same time. "It's more than I imagined, more than I planned."

"We can always adjust to—"

"No, no." She waved Bo's words aside. "Better than I imagined. Do you see, Sal? You and Grace could be sitting out there tonight, the pretty little lights, the vines, the warm air."

"Sweating in August."

"We'll sell more bottled water that way."

"A separate kitchen. More help, more expense, more trouble."

"More business." There was challenge on her face as she swiveled full-on to her brother. "Who's run this place for the last thirty-five years? You or me?"

His eyebrows went up and down in a facial shrug.

They argued—or so he assumed, since part of the byplay was in rapid Italian with lots of dramatic gestures. Bo played it safe and concentrated on his salad.

Moments later, it was scooped away, and a plate of baked spaghetti set in its place. Gib dragged over a chair, sat at the end of the booth. "Where's my daughter?" he asked Bo.

"Ah . . . I don't know. I haven't been home yet, but she said she'd probably be working late."

"Look, Gib. Look at what Bo is building us."

Gib took the sketches, took a pair of reading glasses out of his shirt pocket. Lips pursed, he studied them. "Columns?"

"You can go with posts."

"I want the columns," Bianca said definitely, and jabbed a finger in her brother's face when he opened his mouth. *"Basta!"*

"It's more than I thought."

"Better," Bianca said, and her eyes narrowed on Gib's face. "What, you need new glasses? You can't see what's in front of your face?"

"I don't see a price in front of my face."

Saying nothing, Bo opened his briefcase again, took out an estimate sheet. And had the pleasure of seeing Gib's eyes widen.

"This is pretty steep." He passed the sheet to Sal, who had his hand out.

"This is top-dollar labor rates."

"I'm worth top dollar," Bo said easily. "But I'm not opposed to bartering. This is great spaghetti, Bianca."

"Thank you. Enjoy."

"Bartering what?" Gib demanded.

"Meals, wine." He grinned at Bianca. "Will work for cannoli. Word of mouth. I'm just getting established in this neighborhood. I can give you the material at my cost. Plus if you provide some of the grunt work—hauling, painting—that cuts it back."

Gib breathed through his nose. "How much does that cut it back?"

Bo took a second estimate sheet out of his case, handed it to Gib.

Gib took a long look. "You must really like cannoli." Once again he passed the sheet toward Sal, but this time Bianca snatched it.

"Idiot," she said in Italian. "What he likes is your daughter."

Gib sat back, drummed his fingers on the table. "How soon can you start?" he asked. And offered his hand.

# 23

"Bo, I don't want you to feel obligated to cut your profit like this, to work for below your going rate just because it's my family."

"Hmm." He kept his eyes closed, continued to stroke his hand along her bare leg. "Did you say something? I'm in a cannoli coma complicated by a sexual haze."

Understandable, she thought, since he had had three of her mother's outrageous cannolis before they'd—finally—done justice to his kitchen floor.

"You do good work, and you deserve to get paid for it."

"I'm getting paid for it. I just ate most of my initial deposit. It's good business," he continued, anticipating her. "Sirico's is a neighborhood landmark. This job will show off my work, get people talking. Your parents are leaders in the word-of-mouth department."

"Are you saying we're blabbermouths?"

"You guys sure can talk. My ears have been ringing since dinner. In a good way," he added, and yawned. "I think I even won your uncle over by the time it was done."

"Uncle Sal, oldest son, renowned cheapskate. We love him anyway."

"So, they get a bargain, I get to do a job I'll enjoy—and reap the advertising. And, oh God, eat your mother's cooking until I die."

"You forgot the sexual bonus."

"That's personal." This time he walked his fingers up her thigh, down again. "Doesn't factor. But since I've been fiddling with some plans for your place, you could always take me upstairs and bribe me with continued sexual favors."

She rolled over on top of him, made him moan. More from excess pastry than desire. "You've been working on plans for me?"

"Fiddling. Haven't had too much time. But your dining room table's almost finished."

"I want to see. I want to see everything."

"Table'll be done in another couple days. The sketches are rough yet."

"I have to see." She rolled off, tugged his hand. "Right now. Right now."

He groaned, but sat up and reached for his pants. "Half of the plans are still in my head."

"I want to see the other half." She dragged on her own pants, grabbed her shirt. Then she grabbed his face, smacked her lips to his. "Thanks in advance."

"Thank me after." He pulled open the refrigerator for water, then frowned when the phone rang. "Who the hell's calling me at one in the morning? Better not be Brad wanting me to bail him out of jail. Though to be fair, that only happened once."

"Don't answer it yet. Wait." With her shirt half buttoned, she dashed to the phone, studied the readout. "Do you know this number?"

"Not right off." It clicked, she could see it on his face. "Shit. Shit. Do you think it's him?"

"Let me answer it." She picked it up, said, "Yes?"

"Ready for another surprise? I hate to repeat myself, but you gotta do what you gotta do."

She nodded at Bo, then gestured for him to get her paper and pen. "I wondered when you'd call again. How'd you know to reach me here?"

"Because I know you're a whore."

"Because I slept with you?" she asked, and began to write down the conversation.

"Can you remember everybody you slept with, Reena?"

"I've got a pretty good memory for that sort of thing. Why don't you give me a name, or a place? Then we'll see how memorable it was."

"Just think about it, you just think about it, about all the men you let fuck you. Right back to the first."

Her hand jerked. "A woman never forgets her first. That's not you."

"We're going to party, you and me. But right now, why don't you take a little walk? See what I left for you."

The phone clicked. "Bastard," she muttered, hunting up her cell phone. "He's done something close, within walking distance. Don't hang that up," she added, then picked up her weapon, holstered it on as she dialed from her cell.

"It's Hale. I need you to triangulate this number." She read it off. "It's going to be a cell phone, and he's probably mobile. I'm giving you the number he called, leaving that line open." She rattled out Bo's number as she walked out of the kitchen. "He may have set a fire in the vicinity of my house. I want a couple of patrols. I'm heading outside now to check it out. You can reach me . . . Son of a bitch!"

She heard Bo curse behind her, then take off running back to the kitchen. "I've got a vehicle fire, this address. Bastard. Call it in!"

Bo flew by her, armed with a fire extinguisher.

The hood of the truck was up, the engine spitting out fire. Smoke billowed out of the bed, and beneath, pools of gas shimmered with flame. The tires were smoldering and the acrid stench of burning rubber soiled the air. More flames danced over the hood, along the roof of the cab, aided by the pleasant summer breeze.

But fury turned to fear when she spotted the trailer of rags burning toward the open gas tank. Twisting out of the tank with them was a red linen napkin with the Sirico's logo folded down at the corner.

"Get back!" She leaped at Bo, yanked the extinguisher out of his hands. There was either enough left, or there wasn't, she thought dully, and aimed at the tank.

Foam spurted out. Smoke blinded her, choked her as the breeze waved it in her face. The flavor of fire filled her mouth again as, along the ground, the streams of burning gas slid closer.

"Forget the truck." Bo grabbed her on the fly, dragged her with him as he sprinted across the street.

The explosion shot the rear of the truck into the air, slammed it back down as the punch of it knocked them off their feet. There was a firestorm of blazing metal, hot shrapnel that rained onto the street, over other vehicles as he rolled with her under the cover of a parked car.

"Are you hurt? Are you burned?"

He shook his head, stared at the inferno that had been his truck. His ears rang, his eyes stung, and his arm felt flame kissed. When he ran his hand over it, it came away bloody.

"I almost had it. Another few seconds—"

"You almost got yourself blown up for a goddamn Chevy pickup."

"He played me. He timed it." Fire danced in her eyes as she slammed her fist on the asphalt. "The engine, the bed, distractions. If I'd seen the fuse sooner . . . Jesus, Bo, you're bleeding."

"Scraped up my arm some when we hit."

"Let me see it. Where's my phone? Where's my damn phone?" She crawled out, saw it lying broken on the street. "Here they come." Sirens wailed, and people poured out of neighboring houses. "Sit down over here, let me look at your arm."

"It's okay. Let's both sit down a minute."

He wasn't sure if he was shaking, or if she was. Maybe both of them, so he gave in to his weakened legs and sank to the curb, pulled her down with him.

"You've got a gash here." At the sight of his blood, she forced her mind to go cold. "You're going to need stitches."

"Maybe."

"Take off your shirt. We need to put some pressure on this. I can do a field dressing until the paramedics look at it."

Instead, he lifted his hip, pulled a bandanna out of his pocket.

"That'll do. I'm so sorry, Bo."

"Don't. Don't apologize." He stared at his truck while she bandaged his arm. The pain hadn't gotten through yet. He imagined it would soon enough. But he had plenty of rage inside him as he stared at what had been his. "That takes it off him and puts it on you."

The response team leaped off their truck, began to smother the fire.

When she was done with the field dressing, she rested her head against her updrawn knees for a moment, then sucked in a breath. "I have to go talk to these guys. I'll send a paramedic over. Unless he says different, I'll drive you to the ER, get that dealt with."

"Don't worry about it." He wasn't in the mood for hospitals. He was in the mood to kick some ass. He rose, offered a hand. "Let's go tell them what happened."

She'd barely finished giving the details when half the people she knew were crowded on the street and sidewalk. Her parents, Jack, Xander, Gina and Steve, Gina's parents, old classmates, cousins of old classmates.

She heard her father call Fran on his cell, tell her no one was hurt and ask her to relay the news to An.

Bases covered, she thought wearily, and turned when O'Donnell pulled up.

"We get a location?" she asked him.

"Working on it. You hurt?"

"No. Bruises where I hit the pavement. Bo played the hero, broke my fall." She rubbed her eyes. "He let me keep him talking, gave him time to drive around, get the party started. He'd levered up the hood, doused it, dumped a bunch of mattress wadding in the bed, got that going for the smoke. Pools of gas under and around the truck, got the tires going. Big smoky stink, which distracted me long enough."

Almost too long, she thought. If Bo hadn't dragged her off, it might have been more than his truck seriously damaged.

"By the time I spotted the fuse—he'd hung one of Sirico's dinner napkins out of the tank—we were on borrowed time. I started to deal with it, then Bo grabs me like I'm a football and he's a tight end running for the goal line. Hard to say if he screwed himself out of a truck, and God knows how much in the tools he had in those lockboxes running along the bed, or if he saved my life."

"Called you at Goodnight's. You check your machine yet—see if he tried there first?"

"No, haven't been back in yet."

"Why don't you do that now?"

"Yeah. Give me a minute."

She moved off, had a word with Xander, then walked toward her house.

"Okay, pal." Xander stepped over to Bo, gave Bo's good shoulder a rub. "Let's you and me walk on down to the clinic. I'll fix you up."

"Gee, Doc, it's only a scratch."

"Let me be the judge of that."

"You go with Xander, don't argue." Bianca laid down the law. "I'll go in, get you a clean shirt."

Bo glanced toward his house. "Door's open."

Bianca tilted her head, her eyes soft with sympathy. "Do you have your keys? I'll lock up for you."

"No. I ran out without them."

"We'll take care of it." She cupped his face. "We take care of our own. Now you go with Alexander, like a good boy. And tomorrow, when you feel better, you go see my cousin Sal."

"I thought Sal was your brother."

"This one is a cousin, and he's going to give you a good price on a new truck. A very good price. I'll write it down for you."

"Jack, give Bianca a hand, will you?" Gib gave his wife a pat as he joined Xander and Bo. "I'll walk along, make sure the patient doesn't try to run for it."

"He just likes to see me stick needles in people," Xander said, taking Bo's good arm.

"That's heartening." He looked for an escape route and found himself neatly flanked. "The paramedic said maybe a couple stitches. I can wait till the morning."

"No time like the present," Xander said cheerfully. "Hey! You had a tetanus shot lately? I love giving those."

"Last year. Stay away from me." He looked dubiously toward Gib. "I don't need an honor guard."

"Just keep walking." Gib waited until they were through the thicket of neighbors. "I caught bits and pieces back there, and it sounds like there's something going on I should know about. Somebody called Reena at your place."

"Yeah, the guy from before. The one who's been hassling her. The one who set fire to the school? And she hasn't said anything to you about any of this?"

"Now you're going to."

Not just flanked, Bo decided. Squeezed. "Better if you asked her."

"Better if I don't help Xander hold you down while he does a prostate exam."

"Now *those* are fun," Xander agreed.

"Point taken. She should've told you, and now she's going to be pissed I did. Maybe being the only child of divorced parents isn't so bad. You guys are work."

He told them what he knew as they walked the two blocks to the clinic, and inside. Xander's amusement had turned to stony silence. He gestured toward an exam table.

"When did this start?" Gib demanded.

"From what I gather, right after she moved in."

"And she says nothing." Gib spun around, began to pace.

"Steve either," Xander pointed out, and began to clean the gash.

Bo hissed in his breath at the sting. "Can't you medical sadists come up with stuff that doesn't burn down to the frigging bone?"

"You've got a nice gash here, Bo. About six stitches' worth."

"Six? Well, shit."

"Going to numb you up."

He studied the syringe Xander took from a drawer, then decided he preferred looking at Gib's livid face. "I don't know any more than that. I don't know what his game is, but he's got her on edge. She handles it, but it's working on her."

"Someone she put in prison," Gib murmured. "Someone she put in, who got out. My little girl and I are going to have a talk."

"Talk is our euphemism for yelling and swearing and occasionally throwing breakables," Xander explained. "Little prick."

"I don't think I deserve to be called a prick just because—ouch. Oh, you meant that kind of prick. Mr. Hale . . . Gib, you're her father, so you've known her longer, you know her better, but I'd say yelling and swearing and throwing breakables isn't going to change a thing."

Gib showed his teeth. "Never hurts to try."

The front door rattled open, and a moment later Jack came in with a shirt and shoes. He glanced at Bo's arm, gave a wince of sympathy. "Bianca thought you could use these. Stitches, huh?"

"Six, according to Dr. Gloom here."

"Close your eyes, and think of England," Xander said to Bo.

It could have been worse, Bo decided. He could have humiliated himself and squeaked like a girl. As it was he walked back home with his dignity fairly intact, sucking on the cherry lollipop Xander had handed him after the ordeal was over.

Most of the crowd had dispersed, with a few lingering in clutches to watch the sort of thing he imagined they only saw on TV.

Reena, O'Donnell and Steve, along with a couple of guys he figured were crime-scene people, were still swarming over the wreckage.

He wondered if his insurance had to cover the damage to the cars caused by the flying parts of his truck. Man, his rates were going to soar like a frigging eagle.

Reena broke away, crossed to him.

"How's the arm?"

"Apparently I get to keep it. And I got a lollipop."

"It made him stop crying," Xander told her. "As for the truck, that looks DOA."

"It's bad," she agreed. "Collateral damage on cars parked front and back—which includes mine. We're about done with what we can do here. You can sign off on it, Bo, so we can take it into evidence."

"What about my tools? Any of my tools make it?"

"Once we're done, I'll get what we've collected back to you. Mama's inside." She looked at her father. "She wanted to wait for you, to check on Bo."

"Fine. I'll go wait with her."

"I'm going to be a little while longer here. It's late, you should go on home."

"We'll wait."

She frowned after Gib as he walked toward her house. "What's going on?"

"Come on, Jack, I'll walk you home." Xander slung an arm around his brother-in-law's shoulders, looked at Bo. "Keep that dressing dry, use the ointment as prescribed. I'll check on you tomorrow." He caught Reena's chin in his hand, kissed her on the cheek. "Your butt's cooked. 'Night."

Jack kissed her forehead. "You take care of yourself. See you, Bo."

Reena's gaze ticked back to Bo. "What's going on?"

"You didn't tell them."

She opened her mouth, hissed out a breath. "And you did."

"You should've told them, and you put me in a spot where I had to be the bearer."

"Great." Stewing, she stared at her house. "Just great. You couldn't just keep it zipped, wait for me to deal with this."

"You know what?" he said after a moment. "It's been a crappy night, and I don't feel like going another round. Do what you do. I'm going to bed."

"Bo—" He held up a hand as he walked away, and she was left with a good mad on, and no place to put it.

By the time she dragged herself through her own front door, it was after four in the morning. She wanted a long, cool shower and her own soft bed.

Her parents were on the sofa, snuggled up like a couple of sleeping kids. Considering that a blessing, she eased back, intending to tiptoe upstairs.

"Don't even think about it."

Her father's voice stopped her, had her closing her eyes. Not once, not *once* had any of them been able to sneak into the house after curfew. The man had instincts like a snake.

"It's late. I want to catch a couple hours' sleep."

"You're old enough so your wants won't hurt you."

"Oh, I hate when you say that."

"You should be careful with your tone, Catarina." Bianca spoke without opening her eyes. "We're still your parents, and we'll be your parents a hundred years after you're dead."

"Look, I'm really tired. If we can just table this until tomorrow."

"Someone's threatening you, and you don't tell us?"

Okay, no chance for a respite. Reena dragged out the band holding her hair back as her father rose from the couch. "It's work, Dad. I don't, can't, won't tell you everything about the job."

"It's personal. He's calling you. He knows your name. He knows where you live. And tonight, he tried to kill you."

"Do I look dead?" she shot back. "Do I look hurt?"

"And what would you be if Bo hadn't acted quickly?"

"Oh, great." She threw up her hands, stormed around the room. "So he's the white knight and I'm the helpless damsel. Do you see this?" She yanked her badge out, shoved it in her father's face. "They don't give these out to helpless damsels."

"But they give them out to stubborn, selfish women who can't admit when they're wrong?"

"Selfish?"

They were shouting now, their faces inches apart. "Where do you get that? It's my job, it's my business. Do I tell you how to run your business?"

"You're my child. Your business is always my business. Somebody tried to hurt you, and now he's going to have to deal with me."

"This is just what I was trying to avoid. Why didn't I tell you all this? Play this conversation back. You are not getting into this. You are not getting into my work, into this part of my life."

"Don't you tell me what I'm going to do!"

"Back at you."

"*Basta! Basta!* Enough!" Bianca sprang off the couch. "Don't you raise your voice to your father, Catarina. Don't you yell at your daughter, Gibson. I'll yell at both of you. Imbeciles. *Stupidi!* You're both right, but that won't stop me from knocking your empty heads together to hear the crack. You—" She jabbed a finger into her husband's chest. "You go round and round and don't get to the meat. Our daughter isn't selfish, and you'll apologize. And you—" The finger stabbed out at Reena. "You have your work, and we're proud of what you do, who you are. But this is different, and you know it. This is not about someone else. This is *you*. Do we ever say, 'No, no, Catarina' when you go into a building that may fall on your head? Did we say, 'No, you can't become a police officer, and worry us every day, every night'?"

"Mama—"

"I'm not finished. You'll know when I'm finished. Who stood the tallest, who was the proudest when you became what you always wanted? And you'd stand here and tell us this isn't our business when someone wants to hurt you?"

"I just . . . I just didn't see the point in worrying everyone."

"Hah! That's our job. We're *family*."

"Okay, I should've told you, and I would have after tonight—and if Bo hadn't—"

"You're going to blame him now?" Gib broke in.

She hunched her shoulders. "He's the only one left, and since he's not here to object, sure. I like hanging this on him. And what, suddenly he's your new best friend?"

"He got hurt making sure you didn't." Gib took her face in his hands. "Xander could have been sewing you up tonight. Or worse."

"Apologize," Bianca reminded him, and had Gib casting his eyes to the ceiling.

"I'm sorry I said you were selfish. You're not. I was mad."

"It's okay. I am selfish when it comes to you. I love you. I love you," she repeated, sliding into his arms, reaching for her mother's hand. "I don't know who's doing this, or why, but I'm afraid now. At both scenes he's left something from Sirico's."

"Sirico's?" Gib repeated.

"One of the matchboxes at the school, a dinner napkin tonight. He's telling me he can walk in there, get to you. He's telling me . . ." Her voice wavered. "I'm afraid that he might try to hurt one of you. I couldn't stand it."

"Then you know how we feel about you. Go, get a little sleep. We'll lock up on our way out."

"But—"

Bianca squeezed Gib's hand before he could speak. "Get some rest," Bianca continued. "Don't worry any more tonight."

When they were alone, Gib whispered to his wife, "You're not thinking about leaving her alone."

"We're going to leave her alone. We have to believe in her, and she has to know we believe in her. It's so hard." She pressed her lips tight for a moment, steadied her voice. "It never stops being hard to step back from your babies. But you do it. Come on, let's lock up. We'll go home and worry about her."


The phone woke her at five forty-five. Reena clawed her way through the sticky syrup of exhaustion, fumbled on the light, then the recorder.

"What?" she mumbled into the receiver.

"Just weren't quick enough, were you? Not as smart as you think you are."

"But you're smart, aren't you?" She chained back her temper. "Except, you know, that was a lot of trouble, a lot of bang to take out a truck. Plenty more where that came from."

"Bet he's pissed." There was a low laugh. "Wish I'd seen his face when it blew."

"You should've stuck around. If you had balls, you'd have stuck around for the show."

"I've got balls, bitch. You'll be licking them before we're done."

"If that's all you want, tell me where and when."

"My time, my place. You don't get it, do you? Even after tonight you don't get it. You're supposed to be the smart one, but you're just a dumb whore."

Her eyes narrowed. "If that's the case, why don't you give me a couple hints. The game's no fun if I'm lagging behind. Come on," she coaxed, "let's play."

"My game, my rules. Next time."

When he hung up, she sat back. Her mind was working now, cleared of sleep and working fast.

*Don't get it, do you? Even after tonight.*

What came out of tonight? she asked herself. He uses different methods, different types of targets. He doesn't stick with the same MO, the same targets as a more typical serial arsonist would.

He leaves something from Sirico's as a signature. As a message to her.

Someone she'd taken there in the past? O'Donnell was looking at Luke, and Luke hadn't had any love for the shop. But Luke was in New York. It was possible, of course, that he drove down to Baltimore, but why would he? Why would he harass her after all these years?

And the syntax was wrong, the pattern of it. Luke could do that deliberately, to throw her off. But again, why?

Added to it, he didn't know anything about fire, about explosives. Other than having his Mercedes torched, he . . .

She sat straight up.

"Oh God!"

It wasn't the same—not exactly. Bo's truck hadn't been broken into, the interior fired, the alarm disengaged. But . . .

Gas poured on the engine, on the tires, under the chassis, the device in the gas tank.

All those years ago. Could this be the same person? Not someone who'd wanted to attack Luke, not someone with a grudge against Luke.

But her. All this time.

But so much damn time, she thought, getting up to pace herself through it. Six years? Had there been incidents between she hadn't clicked into? Fires she'd investigated that were his work?

She'd have to go through the open files, the cold cases. Anything that had come through the unit and hadn't been closed.

How far back had it started? How long had he been gearing himself up to make personal contact with her?

A cold chill squeezed her heart, had her stopping. She could feel the blood draining out of her face even before she turned and ran down the stairs.

Her hands shook as she grabbed the notes she'd brought home from Bo's kitchen. The notes of her conversation with the arsonist.

*Just think abt it,* she'd written in the bastard shorthand she used during interviews. *thk abt all the men you let fk you rgt bk to the 1st.*

"The first," she murmured, and sank slowly to the floor. "Josh. Oh, Mother of God. Josh."

# 24

At five minutes to eight, Reena banged on Bo's front door and kept banging until he answered.

His eyes were heavy, his hair pancaked on one side of his head, spiked on the other. He wore nothing but a pair of blue boxers and a sleepy scowl.

"I need to talk to you."

"Sure, sure, come on in," he muttered when she breezed right by him. "Have a seat. Want some breakfast? I'm here to serve."

"I'm sorry I had to wake you, and I know you had a bad night, but this is important."

He jerked a shoulder, cursed when his injured arm objected to the movement. Then he turned his back on her and shuffled toward his kitchen.

He got a can of Coke from the fridge, popped it. Guzzled it where he stood.

"I also know you're irritated with me," she continued. She heard her tone—prim as her first-grade teacher's—and wasn't entirely displeased. "But this isn't the time to be childish."

His bleary eyes narrowed over the can. He flicked up his middle finger. "That," he told her, "was childish."

"You want to fight, I'll pencil you in for later. This is official, and I need you to pay attention."

He dropped into a chair, gave her a careless, get-on-with-it wave.

She could see the resentment, the fatigue and, she noted, some pain lurking in his eyes. But coddling wasn't on the agenda.

"I have reason to believe the connection I have with the arsonist goes back much further than we initially thought."

He downed more Coke. "So?"

"I'm pursuing the theory based on some of the conversations I've had with him, including the one early this morning."

His hand tightened on the can enough to leave impressions. "So, he gave you a wake-up call and you decided to spread the wealth and get me out of bed."

"Bo."

"Fuck it." He said it wearily, without heat, as he pushed himself out of the chair and went to a cabinet. He pulled out a bottle of Motrin, poured a few in his palm, tossed them into his mouth like candy.

"It's hurting."

He gave her a steely stare as he washed down pills with Coke. "No, I just like Motrin and Classic Coke. Breakfast of frigging champions."

Something sank in her stomach. "You really are angry with me."

"I'm angry with you, with men and women, small children and all manner of flora and fauna on the planet Earth, possibly in the universe, where I believe other life exists, because I got about five minutes' sleep and my entire body hurts like a mother."

She'd noted the bruises, in addition to the bandaged arm. Bruises, scrapes, nicks—she'd found a number on herself as well. His were worse, no doubt. His were worse because he'd taken the brunt to shield her.

She'd intended to be quick, brisk, give him the gist without going into detail. Now, looking at his sulky eyes, his bed hair, his poor battered body, she changed her mind.

Even her strict first-grade teacher had kissed it better when she scraped her knee on the playground.

"Why don't you sit down? I'll get you something to eat, an ice pack. That knee's pretty banged up."

"I'm not hungry. There's a bag of frozen peas in there."

Having suffered through her share of sprains and bruises, she understood what the peas were for. Retrieving them from the freezer, she walked over to lay them over his knee herself.

"I'm sorry you were hurt. I'm sorry about your truck. I'm even sorry I swiped at you for telling my father something I wasn't ready to tell him myself."

She sat, propped her elbows on the table, pressed the heels of her hands to her eyes. "Bo, I'm so damn sorry."

"Don't do that. If you cry, you're going to ruin a perfectly good mad."

"I'm not going to cry." But it was a nasty internal war to keep her word. "It's bad to worse, Bo. And you're in this because of me."

"How much worse?"

"I have to make a call." She drew out her phone. "This is going to take a little longer than I planned. Is it okay if I get one of those?" she asked, nodding toward his Coke.

"Go ahead."

"O'Donnell?" She rose as she spoke. "I'm going to be another half hour. Running a little behind." She opened the fridge. There were Diet Pepsis mixed in with his Classic Cokes. Ones she knew Bo had bought for her.

Tears stung again, made her feel ridiculous.

"No, I won't. See you in thirty."

She disconnected, sat again. Opening the can, she looked at Bo. "A few years ago, I was seeing someone. We'd been seeing each other, exclusively, for a few months. Closer to four, I guess. He wasn't my usual type. A little slick, a lot demanding. I wanted a change, and he was it. Status type, drove a Mercedes, wore Italian suits, drank the right wines. We saw a lot of movies with subtitles that I'm dead sure he didn't enjoy any more than I did. I liked being with him because I got to be a girl."

"And other times you're what? A poodle?"

"Girly," she corrected. "Fussy female, accommodating." She shrugged a little, and still felt silly about it. "Change of pace for me. I let him pick the restaurants, make the plans. It was a brief relief. In my line, you've got to be on your toes, and you can't be girly. You've got to see a lot of things, do a lot of things . . . Well. Maybe I wanted the contrast."

"Can we pause it here? You think this guy's the one who's been calling you?"

"No. It's not impossible, but no, I don't. He's a financial planner who got a manicure twice a month. He lives in New York now. In any case, he was beginning to get under my skin some. I let it slide because . . . I'm not entirely sure, and it doesn't matter. The night I caught my first case as a detective with the unit we had a little argument. He hit me."

"Whoa." Bo set his can on the table. "What?"

"Wait." Get it all out, she told herself. The whole humiliating ball of it. "I thought it was an accident, which is what he claimed. It was one of those dramatic moving around, gesturing, and I moved toward him from behind, his hand came back. It could've been an accident, and I accepted it as such. Until the next time."

There were no sleepy mists in his eyes now. They were pure, hard green. "He hit you again."

"This was different. He made these elaborate dinner plans, and I was clueless. Fancy French place, champagne, flowers, the works. He tells me he's been promoted. And transferring to New York. I'm happy for him—it's kind of a jolt, but what are you going to do? Plus . . ."

She paused, sighed out a breath. "Plus, some part of me was thinking, Boy, this sure makes it easy on me. No dramatic breakup scene."

"And you say that with guilt because?"

"It seems cold, I guess. Hey, the boyfriend I'm getting a little tired of is moving out of state. Lucky me! But while I'm trying to pretend I'm not a little relieved, he says he wants me to go to New York with him, and even then it takes me a few minutes to get he means move there. That's not going to happen, and I'm trying to tell him why I can't. Won't."

"Okay, the guy you've been seeing a few months wants you to pull up stakes, leave your home, your family, your job because he gets a transfer." He drank with one hand, jabbed a finger at her with the other. "See, I told you there was life beyond our big blue ball. Obviously this guy was spawned on Planet No Way In Hell."

It made her laugh a little. "Well, it gets worse. Suddenly he's flashing this meteor-sized diamond ring, telling me we're getting married, moving to New York."

She closed her eyes because the sensations she'd experienced then came right back. "I'm sucker punched, I swear. This came out of nowhere for me, and while I'm trying to tell him thanks but no thanks, the waiter's bringing champagne over, people are applauding, and the damn ring's on my finger."

"Ambush."

"Yeah." She blew out a breath, grateful he understood. "I couldn't get into it there, in front of the whole damn restaurant, so I waited until we got back to my place. Let's say he didn't take it well. He blasted me good. I'd humiliated him, lying bitch, stupid and blah blah. I stopped feeling sorry for him and blasted back. And he nailed me. Said he was going to teach me who was in charge, and when he came up for the follow-through, I took him down, bruised his balls and kicked him out."

"I'm going to say congratulations, and add that from what you've just told me, he's a top contender for what's going on now."

He wasn't going to make her feel guilty, Reena realized. Or stupid or weak. It was an interesting experience to share a nasty and humiliating experience with a man who wouldn't let her feel soiled or humiliated.

The race going on inside her heart kicked into another gear.

"I don't think so, but I think he's connected. The next morning, early, my captain and O'Donnell are at the door. Turns out that somebody torched Luke's Mercedes, a few hours after he crawled out my door. He was pointing the finger at me for it. It didn't stick. For one thing, Gina had come over, stayed the night, and was still there. For another, they believed me."

She could see by his face he was keeping pace with her, but she filled in the last details anyway. "The method used wasn't *exactly* like last night, Bo, but there are strong similarities. And when the fire-starter called me this morning, he alluded to it."

"This Luke asshole could have torched his own car to take another jab at you. He could be doing this now for more payback."

"Possible, except . . . Last night, when he called, he said something else. Didn't click in, not completely. Everything happened pretty quick after, and it didn't gel for me until this morning. He said I should think back over the men I've been with, right back to the first."

"And?"

"The first was Josh. Josh was killed in a fire, long before I met Luke."

"Smoking in bed."

"I never believed it." Even now, her voice caught. "I had to accept it, but I never believed it. Three men now, three I've been involved with, that I know of, have been connected to serious fires. One of them's dead. I'm not going to consider it a coincidence. Not now."

He rose, limped to the fridge, got out another Coke. "Because now you're thinking Josh was murdered."

"Yes, I am. And I think the use of fire's been deliberate all along, because anyone who knew me knew I was studying and working toward becoming an arson investigator. Ever since . . ."

"Ever since the fire at your restaurant," he finished.

"Jesus. Pastorelli." It made her stomach cramp. "It all started that day. Everything started that day." She let out a breath. "All right, I'm going to check this out. Meanwhile, can you take some time off?"

"What for?"

"Bo, Josh is dead. Luke moved to New York, and I broke things off with him in any case. You're right next door. He could try for your house next, or for you."

"Or you."

"Take a couple of weeks, take a vacation, give us time to shut this down."

"Sure. Where do you want to go?"

Her hands balled into fists on the table. "I'm the fuse. I go, he stops, waits for me to come back."

"The way I see it, we're both the fuse. Unless you plan on taking up with some other guy while I'm off somewhere water-skiing. I value my skin, Reena, what's left of it. But I'm not running off and waiting for you to send me an all clear. I don't work that way."

"This isn't the time to be such a damn man."

"Until I grow breasts, I'm stuck being a man."

"You'll distract me. Worrying about you will distract me. If something happened to you—" She broke off as her throat slammed shut.

"If I said that to you, you'd tell me you can take care of yourself, that you're not stupid or reckless." He raised his eyebrows when she said nothing. "Why don't we skip the part where I say it back to you, we both toss around the same arguments."

The good nature faded from his eyes, turned them that chilly green. "The son of a bitch came at me, Reena. He blew up my goddamn truck. You think I'm walking away?"

"Please. Just a few days, then. Three days. Give me three days to . . ." Her voice began to hitch.

"No. Don't cry. It's hitting below the belt, and it won't work."

"I don't use tears to get my way, you stupid ass." She dashed at them with the backs of her hands. "I can put you in protective custody."

"Maybe."

"Don't you see, I can't handle this." She pushed away from the table, stalked to the window over the sink, stared out.

"I can see you're not handling something."

"I don't know what to do." She pressed her fist between her breasts as her heart shuddered. "I don't know how to be. I don't know how to deal with this."

"We'll figure it out."

"No, no! Are you blind, are you stupid?" she demanded as she whirled around to him. "I can handle the case. You work it, you just work it. It's a puzzle and all the pieces are there. It's just finding them and putting them in the right place. But this? I can't . . . I can't handle this." She thumped her fist between her breasts. "I'm . . . I'm . . . "

"Asthmatic?" he said when she just stood there wheezing.

She stunned them both by grabbing a mug off the counter and hurling it against the wall. "You *blithering* idiot, I'm in love with you."

He held up a hand as if to ward off another mug, though hers were empty. "Minute, okay. Just a minute."

"Oh, screw this." She started to charge out, but he grabbed her hand, locked her down.

"I said wait a damn minute."

"I hope you have a seizure, and it makes you stumble all around the room so you cut your feet to ribbons on broken glass."

"Love comes in many forms," he muttered.

"Don't make fun of me. You started this. All I did was walk out my own back door one day."

"I'm not making fun of you. I'm trying to catch my breath." His hand stayed firm on hers, and he stayed planted in the chair with a bag of frozen peas defrosting over his bruised knee.

"When you say you're in love with me, is that upper- or lowercase *L*? Don't you hit me," he warned when he saw her other hand fist.

"I have no intention of resorting to physical force." But it had been a close one. Now she forced her hand, her arm, then her body to relax. "I'd appreciate it if you'd let go of my hand."

"Fine. Then I'd appreciate it if you wouldn't go storming out of here so I have to get up and limp after you, perhaps have a seizure and cut my feet to ribbons on broken glass."

Her lips twitched. "See? Damn it, that's got to be why this happened to me. You're no pushover, Goodnight, but you make yourself so damn affable it's easy to think you're pushable. And you're accommodating, right up to a line you've drawn in your head. It would probably take dynamite to blast you over that line once you've drawn it. My mother was right. She's always right."

On a sigh, she walked to his broom closet, got out the broom and dustpan. "You're like my father."

"I am not."

She smiled and began to sweep up the shards. "I never got really serious about anyone before you because they never made the cut. They never measured up for me to the one man I admire most. My father."

"You're right. We're exactly alike. Separated at birth."

"It was lowercase, and that was disconcerting enough. Then this morning, you opened the door and it was a big, fat, shiny capital *L*. And look at you. Your hair's all stupid."

He lifted a hand in response, felt it. Grimaced. "Shit."

"And your underwear's falling apart."

He hitched at the ragged waistband. "It's got plenty of wear in it yet."

"You're all bruised up and scowly. And it doesn't matter. I'm sorry about the mug."

"Your brother mentioned you guys throw things. I've been in love with you since approximately ten-thirty P.M., May ninth, 1992."

Her smile stayed soft as she dumped the shards in his trash can. "No, you haven't."

"Easy for you to say. It was lowercase," he continued while she replaced the broom. "With a lot of fantasy sparkling over it. Took on a different kind of glow after I actually met you, but it was the lowercase deal."

"I know. I'm going to be late," she said when she looked at her watch. "I'm going to have a couple of cops assigned to you until—"

"It grew up."

She dropped her hand, said nothing.

"It grew up, Reena, so I guess we're both going to have to figure out how to handle it."

She stepped to him, laid her cheek on the top of his head. She felt, actually felt her heart settle. "This is the strangest thing," she told him. "And I can't stay. I can't stay any longer."

"It's okay. It can wait."

She bent down until her lips met his. "I'll call you later." She kissed him again. "Be careful." And again. "Be safe."

Then hurried out, dashing to the front door before he could lever out of the chair.

So he sat where he was, in the morning light coming through the windows, with a can of warm Coke on the table. And thought what a strange, strange ride life was.

He'd barely finished off the Coke when there was more banging on his door. "For God's sake."

He got up, decided the pills and the peas had helped, and headed out. He was going to have to give the woman a key, he could see that coming. And that was the next thing to living together, which was cousin to the all-powerful *M* word. And he just didn't want to think about that yet.

When he pulled open the door, his arms were immediately filled with female. But it wasn't Reena.

"Bo. God, Bo!" Mandy squeezed him hard enough to have his bruises weeping. "We came right over, as soon as we heard."

"Heard what? We who?"

"About the bomb in your truck." She jerked back and her eyes raced over him. "Oh, you poor baby! They said minor injuries. You're all banged up. You've got a bandage. And what is wrong with your hair?"

"Shut up." He scrubbed at it.

"Brad's parking. You have to go on safari for a parking place in this neighborhood. And they've got the front of your house blocked still."

"Brad."

"I didn't hear sooner because I turned off my cell by mistake and I wasn't home, so the paper couldn't reach me. We didn't know anything until this morning. Why didn't you *call*?"

"Brad?" He wasn't slow, even if he was working on about five minutes' sleep. "You and Brad? Together? My Brad?"

"Well, God, it's not like you were going to sleep with him. And it was completely unplanned. Come on, let me help you sit down."

He waved his hands like a traffic cop. "Wait, wait, wait. Am I in Bizzaro World?"

"It's not so bizzaro. We've known each other for years. We just hooked up, decided to go get something to eat, maybe see a movie, and one thing, another thing." She grinned, wide and bright. "It was *great*."

"Shut up! Don't tell me." He clamped his hands over his ears, made loud noises with his mouth to block her out. "My brain cannot withstand the data. It'll implode."

"You're not going to be one of those jerks who's like, 'I used to sleep with her so now none of my friends can be interested,' are you?"

"What? No." Was he? "No," he decided after another minute. "But—"

"Because we really connected. Now, let me help you . . ." Her face went dreamy, and when Bo followed the direction of her gaze, he spotted Brad coming down the street with the male version of dreamy on his face.

Bo turned away, hands clamped to his skull. "My head, my head. You guys, my best friends in this life, are about to finish the job that son of a bitch started last night."

"Don't be silly. And in case you haven't noticed, you're parading in the doorway in your underwear. Ratty underwear. He's okay," she called out to Brad.

"Man, scared ten years off us." Brad jogged up the steps. "You're okay? Did you see a doctor? Want us to run you in for X-rays?"

"I saw a doctor." He grunted when Brad wrapped his arms around him.

"We were worried sick, came right over. What about your truck?"

"Toast."

"Damn good truck. What can we do? Want me to leave the car for you? Or we can hang, take you anywhere you need to go."

"I don't know. I haven't pulled it together yet."

"Don't worry about it," Mandy told him. "You want to stretch out? I can make you something to eat."

Despite the fact that he saw their hands sneaking together, Bo realized they were there for him. Just like always. "I've got to take a shower, get dressed, clear my head."

"Okay, I'll make breakfast while you do. We'll both take the day off, right, Brad?"

"Sure."

"And when you come back down," she added, "we want to know what happened. Everything."

Reena rubbed her eyes to clear them, then refocused on her computer screen. "Pastorelli Senior's been swinging in and out of the system most of his life. Assaults, drunk and disorderly, assault with intent, the arson, petty larceny. There are four questioned-and-released in his file on suspicious fires. Two before the one at Sirico's, two after he was released from prison. Last known address is in the Bronx. But his wife's in Maryland, just outside D.C."

"The son's been working on following in his father's footsteps," O'Donnell told her. "A couple stints in juvie before he hit sixteen."

"I know about those. John kept up for me, when I asked him. They took him away," she told him. "Like they took his father. The night Joey killed his dog and left it burning on our steps."

She rose, walked around to sit on the corner of O'Donnell's desk so their conversation was less hampered by the backchat of the squad room. "He killed his own dog, O'Donnell. They said it was a violent acting out, a result of having his father arrested because of the fire. A troubled child, a confused child from an abusive home life. Because his father used to tune his mother up regularly. And knocked the kid around from time to time, too."

"But you're not buying that."

"No. I saw the way he ran after the car when they arrested Pastorelli. He worshipped his father. A lot of kids in that sort of atmosphere do. His mother was weak, ineffectual. His father ruled. And look at his pattern," she added, turning so she could see the readout on O'Donnell's screen. "Arrests for assault, sexual assault, vandalism, grand theft auto, parole violations. Not just following, outdoing his father."

"There's no fire on his record."

"So, maybe he's more careful, or more lucky, in that area. Maybe he and his father have some sort of tag team going. Maybe he saved his fire-starting for me. But one or both of them is behind this."

"No argument."

"One or both of them killed Josh Bolton."

"It's a big step up from what's on their sheets to murder, Hale."

She shook her head. "There might be others, and they just haven't been caught. It goes back to me. Straight back to the day Joey assaulted me. Sexual assault, that's what it was, but I was too young to get that."

But she could remember it still, and very well, the way he'd grabbed at her chest, her crotch, the names he'd called her. And his face, the wild-ness on it.

"He jumps me, and my brother, a couple of his friends hear me scream-ing—run him off. I tell my father, and he goes straight over, gets in Pastorelli Senior's face. I've never seen my father like that. If some of the neighbors, some of the people in Sirico's, hadn't come out, broken it up, it would've gotten bad. Seriously bad. My father threatened to call the cops, and people who were there, hearing what went down, were behind him."

"And that night Pastorelli torches Sirico's."

"Yeah. Get in my face, you bastard, here's what you get. Sloppy job. Drunk and sloppy, and no thought to the family who lived upstairs. The place could've burned down around them."

"But you saw the fire."

"I saw the fire. Back to me. So we had a mess on our hands, but nobody was hurt. Insurance would cover it, and the whole neighborhood ready to lend a hand. You could tip it one way and say the fire actually benefited the family. Built loyalty, gave my parents a chance to expand, renew."

"That's a pisser for somebody who wanted to make trouble."

"And gets caught. His dog barked, O'Donnell. That was one of the things I told John. The dog barked in their backyard, where he kept his shed, where they found the gas can, some of the beer he'd stolen, the shoes he'd worn."

"Kid kills the dog."

"Yeah. You could twist it so the dog played a part in the chain. Damn dog helped ruin his father."

"Dog has to die."

"Yeah, and more, the dog has to burn. Kid goes away, evaluation, juvie, in the system. He gets out and his mother pulls him up to New York. He gets in trouble up there, but he's still a kid. Hard for a kid to get from New York to Baltimore to cause me or my family any grief. And see."

She tapped the screen. "He does a short stint himself. But they were both out when Josh died. Joey's not a kid anymore. Joe's mopping floors. Hell of a comedown."

She could feel it now, feel the truth of it in her belly, in her throat. These were pieces of the puzzle.

"But Sirico's is doing fine. Our family's doing fine. And the little bitch who caused all this is in college, screwing some jerk. Joey puts hands on her and she screams, messes everything up. But she lets this guy do her, no problem. Time for payback, some serious payback. I'd been with him that night, with Josh that night, after Bella's wedding. One of them killed that boy, set him on fire. Because I'd been with him."

"All right, if we take that angle, why didn't he, or they, just deal with you? You were there. Why not kill both of you?"

"Because it wasn't enough. Kill me, it's over. But make me suffer, hurt me, use fire against me again and make me wonder. Pastorelli Senior had an alibi for that night. John checked it out. But it could've been bogus. Joey was supposed to be in New York, and there were people who said he was.

But people will. And look, three months after Josh's death, Joey goes up for the car boost. In Virginia, not New York."

"I'm not saying people don't hold on to grudges or obsessions for twenty years. But twenty is a long stretch."

"There have been shots along the way. There might've been things I passed over, didn't connect. There was an incident right after I came on the job. Firefighter I was seeing casually was killed. He was on his way to North Carolina—long weekend deal. I got hung up, so I couldn't go with him, but Steve and Gina and I were going to head down the next morning. They found him, in his car, in the woods off a back road. He'd been shot, and his car set on fire. It looked like he'd been carjacked, robbed, killed, and the fire set to cover it. It was eleven years to the day after the fire at Sirico's."

O'Donnell eased back. "Hugh Fitzgerald. I knew him some. I remember when he was killed. I didn't know you were connected."

"It was casual. We'd gone out a couple times, and he was a pal of Steve's. Steve and Gina were an item. It looked, seemed, random. And the locals put it down as such."

So had she, she thought, raking her fingers through her hair. She'd never looked beyond the surface.

"One of his tires was flat, late at night, dark country road. They figured he flagged down the wrong person, or somebody came along, tried to shake him down. Kills him. Pushes the car into the woods, lights it up, hopes the fire covers the tracks. Which, essentially, it did. The case is still open."

She drew a breath. "I never made any connection, not on the surface. Hell, my uniform buttons were still bright and shiny. Who was I to question seasoned cops just because I had a sick feeling down in the belly? We'd gone out a couple of times, and we were both thinking it might lead to more. But we weren't a couple. He was killed in North Carolina. Arrows weren't pointing at somebody who'd fired up my father's restaurant a dozen years before. I should've seen it."

"Yeah, too bad your crystal ball was on the fritz that day."

While she appreciated the sarcasm and the sentiment behind it, it didn't cool her blood. "Fire, O'Donnell. It's always fire. Josh, Hugh, Luke's car and now Bo. It's always fire. There might have been more, things I didn't focus in on. Case is still open."

"Difference is, now he wants you to know."

# 25

Laura Pastorelli worked the counter at a 7-Eleven near the Maryland/D.C. line. She was fifty-three, and carried the years poorly on a rickety frame. Lines, dug deeper by worry and sorrow than by years, scored her face. Her salt-and-pepper hair framed it without style. Around her neck was a silver cross. That and her wedding ring were her only jewelry.

She glanced up when O'Donnell and Reena came in, and her gaze passed over Reena without recognition.

"Help you?" She said it without interest, something she said by habit dozens of times a day.

"Laura Pastorelli?" O'Donnell showed his badge, and Reena saw the instinctive flinch before Laura's lips thinned.

"What do you want? I'm working. I haven't done anything wrong."

"We need to ask you a few questions regarding your husband and your son."

"My husband lives in New York. I haven't seen him for five years." Her fingers crept up her skinny chest to fondle the silver cross.

"And Joey?" Reena waited until Laura's gaze shifted to her face. "You don't remember me, Mrs. Pastorelli? I'm Catarina Hale, from the neighborhood."

Recognition crept as slowly as her fingers. When it hit, Laura averted her eyes. "I don't remember you. I haven't been back to Baltimore in years."

"You remember me," Reena said gently. "Maybe there's somewhere more comfortable where we can talk."

"I'm working. You're going to make me lose my job, and I haven't done anything. Why can't you people leave us alone?"

O'Donnell walked over to a doughy-faced man in his early twenties, who wasn't doing much to pretend he wasn't avidly listening. He was wearing a name tag that said: Dennis.

"Dennis, why don't you take over at the counter for a few, while Mrs. Pastorelli takes a little break?"

"I gotta do stock."

"Paid by the hour, aren't you? Watch the counter." O'Donnell walked back. "Why don't we step outside, Mrs. Pastorelli? It's a nice day."

"You can't make me. You can't."

"It'll be more difficult if we have to come back," Reena said quietly. "We don't want to have to speak to your supervisor, or make this any more complicated for you."

Saying nothing, Laura came out from behind the counter, walked outside with her head bowed. "He paid. Joe paid for what happened. It was an accident. He'd been drinking and it was an accident. Your father pushed him. He said lies about Joey and pushed at Joe so he got drunk, that's all. Nobody got hurt. Insurance covered everything, didn't it? We had to move away."

Her head came up now, tears glimmering in her eyes. "We had to move away, and Joe went to jail. Isn't that enough penance?"

"Joey was awfully upset, wasn't he?" Reena said.

"They took his father *away*. In handcuffs. In front of the whole neighborhood. He was just a little boy. He needed his father."

"It was a difficult time for your family."

"Difficult? It busted my family to pieces. You— Your father said terrible things about my Joey. People heard what he said. What Joe did wasn't right. 'Vengeance is mine, sayeth the Lord,' but it wasn't his fault. He'd been drinking."

"He served additional time. Got himself in some jams when he was in prison," O'Donnell pointed out.

"Had to protect himself, didn't he? Prison scarred his soul. He was never the same after."

"Your family has grievances against mine. Against me."

Laura frowned at her. "You were a child. You can't lay blame on a child."

"Some do. Do you know if either your husband or your son has been back to Baltimore recently?"

"I told you, Joe's in New York."

"Not a long trip. Maybe he wanted to see you."

"He won't talk to me. He's fallen away from the Church. I pray for him every night."

"He must still see Joey."

She lifted a shoulder, but even that small gesture seemed to take more effort than she had to expend. "Joey doesn't come around much. He's busy. He has a lot of work."

"When's the last time you heard from Joey?"

"Few months. He's busy." Her voice took on an insistent shrill, almost like weeping. Reena thought of how she'd wept into a yellow dishcloth.

"You people are always pointing the finger at him. They took his father away, they took *him* away. So, he got in some trouble, he did some wrong things. But he's okay now. He's got work."

"What kind of work?"

"He's a mechanic. He learned about cars when he was in jail. About cars and computers and all sorts of things. He's got education, and he's got good, steady work up in New York."

"At a garage?" O'Donnell prompted. "You know the name of it?"

"Something like Auto Rite. In Brooklyn. Why don't you leave him alone?"

S he didn't recognize me," Reena commented when they were back in the car. "But once she did, she wasn't surprised I was a cop. Somebody's kept her abreast of the local events from the old neighborhood."

O'Donnell nodded, acknowledging Reena as he made a call, scribbled a number. "Got an Auto Rite in Brooklyn." After a brief hesitation, he handed the page from his notebook to Reena. "You take Junior, I'll take Senior."

Back at her desk, Reena put a call through to the garage. Over the sound of the Black Crowes, and considerable clanging, she had a brief conversation with the owner.

"Joey did work at the garage," she told O'Donnell. "For about two months, a year ago. Place was broken into twice during that two months, equipment and tools stolen. Last break-in somebody drove off with a Lexus. One of the other mechanics claimed he heard Joey bragging about the easy pickings. Owner informed the cops, who questioned. Couldn't pin him, but he got fired over it. Five months later, the place is broken into again in what looks like vandalism. Cars beat to shit, graffiti all over the walls, and a wastebasket fire."

"And where was our boy when the party was going on?"

"Allegedly in Atlantic City. Had three people verify. His alibis are connected, O'Donnell. The Carbionellis. New Jersey family."

"Your childhood nemesis got himself connected?"

"It's going to be worth finding out. I'll run the three names who backed him up."

"Meanwhile, Senior's currently unemployed. Had work cleaning a couple of bars, lost it for helping himself to too much of the booze. Six weeks ago."

"One or both," Reena added. "One or both are in Baltimore."

"Oh yeah. Why don't we call our friends in New York, ask them to check it out?"

Her stomach was knotted, something she wasn't ready to share even with her partner. She offset it by concentrating on the routine of the work. Gathering data, drawing the lines, writing it up until she was ready to update both her partner and their captain.

A case. She had to think of it as a case, objectively, with just that sliver of distance. Because she couldn't actively—officially—investigate the vehicular fire, she signaled Younger and Trippley before she went with O'Donnell in to the captain.

"You two need to hear what we've got," she told them.

Captain Brant gestured them in.

"Working on a theory," O'Donnell began and nodded for Reena to take the lead.

She ran through it, from the fire at Sirico's the summer she'd been eleven, to the destruction of Bo's truck the night before.

"The younger Pastorelli is known to pal around with three members of the Carbionelli family, out of New Jersey. He did some time in Rikers with a Gino Borini—a cousin of Nick Carbionelli. It was Carbionelli, Borini and another low level who alibied Pastorelli for the night the garage was hit.

"It looked like kids," she continued. "Five months since he'd gotten the ax, and it was set up to look like a bunch of kids, or amateurs. Destruction, petty theft, a half-assed fire to cover it. They didn't look at him very hard."

"We've got the locals doing some legwork," O'Donnell added. "It's not on their priority list, but they'll send two detectives out to last known addresses."

"There was a lot of similarity between the car fire several years ago involving Luke Chambers and the one last night." She looked at Trippley. "Maybe he used the same device in the gas tanks."

"We'll look at that."

"Captain, I want to reopen Joshua Bolton's case."

"Younger can take it. Fresh eye, Detective," he said to Reena. "You've been looking at that case regularly for years. Let's get the tap on your phone. Goodnight's phone. Take another pass at the wife."

————

Laura Pastorelli's shift had ended, so they headed to her address. It was a small, tidy house on a narrow street. An old Toyota Camry sat in the drive. Reena noted the St. Christopher's magnet on the dash, and one of the trinkets called a parking angel perched on it.

When they knocked, the door was opened by a woman of about the same age as Laura, but with a lot less wear on her. Her face was round and carefully made up, her dark brown hair styled. She wore navy pants with a white camp shirt tucked neatly in the waistband.

A fluffy orange Pomeranian sat at her legs, yapping its lungs out.

"Be *quiet*, Missy, you old fool. She's an ankle nipper," the woman said. "Fair warning."

"Yes, ma'am." Reena held out her badge. "We'd like to speak with Laura Pastorelli."

"She's at church this time of day. Goes by every afternoon after work. Was there trouble at the store?"

"No, ma'am. What church would that be?"

"Saint Michael's, over on Pershing." Her eyes narrowed. "If there wasn't trouble at the store, this must be about either her worthless husband or her worthless son."

"Do you know if she's been in contact with either Joseph Pastorelli Senior or Junior?"

"Wouldn't tell me if she had. I'm her sister-in-law. Patricia Azi. Mrs. Frank Azi. You might as well come in."

O'Donnell looked dubiously at the still yapping ball of fur, and Patricia smiled thinly. "Give me a minute. God sake, Missy, will you put a lid on it!" She scooped up the dog and carried it off. They heard a door slam before she came back.

"My husband's in love with that idiot dog. We've had her eleven years now, and she's still half crazy. Come on in. You want to talk to Laura, she'll probably finish wearing her sackcloth and ashes in another half hour." She sighed heavily, gestured toward a small, cozy living room. "Sounds bitchy, sorry. It's not easy living with a martyr."

Reena gauged the ground, offered a sympathetic smile. "My grand-mother always said two women can't share a house comfortably, no matter how fond they might be of each other. It's got to be one woman's kitchen."

"She really doesn't get in the way much, and she can't afford her own place. Or barely. We've got room. Kids're grown. And she works hard, insists on paying rent. Are you going to tell me what this is about?"

"Her husband and her son may have information regarding a case we're investigating," Reena began. "When we spoke with Mrs. Pastorelli earlier today, she indicated it had been some time since she'd had contact with either of them. We're just doing a follow-up."

"Like I said, she wouldn't have told me if she'd seen or talked to either of them. She wouldn't tell Frank either, not after he laid down the law."

Part of cop work was simply picking up on someone's rhythm and going with it. So Reena smiled and said, "Oh?"

"He showed up right before Christmas last year, right out of the blue. Laura cried buckets, her-prayers-had-been-answered sort of thing." Patricia cast her eyes heavenward.

"I'm sure she was happy to see her son again."

"When a bad penny gets stuck in your shoe, it's smart to dig it out before you end up half crippled."

"You and your nephew don't get along," O'Donnell prompted.

"I'll say it straight out, he scares me. Worse than his father, sneakier, and I guess a lot smarter."

"Has he ever threatened you, Mrs. Azi?"

"Not directly—just the look in his eye. He's been in jail a few times, I guess you know. Laura likes to make excuses for him, but the fact is, he's a bad one. And here he is, on my doorstep. We didn't like it, Frank and me, but you don't turn family away. At least you don't want to. So he shows up . . . Sorry, I didn't offer you any coffee."

"We're fine," Reena assured her. "Joey came to see his mother for the holidays?"

"Maybe. I know he was full of himself. Driving a fancy car, wearing expensive clothes. Gave her a watch with diamonds around the face, and diamond earrings. Wouldn't surprise me if he'd stolen them, but I kept quiet about it. Claimed he had a big deal going, some club he and some *partners*"— she made air quotes around the word—"were going to open in New York and make piles more money. My husband asked him how he was going to open a club, could he get a liquor license because he had a record, and like that. Got under Joey's skin, I could tell, but he just got that little sneer on his face and said there were ways. Anyway, that's not important."

She waved it away. "He stayed for dinner, said he had himself a hotel suite, and spent an hour or so bragging. But every time Frank asked him a direct question about this new business of his, he got evasive and pissy with it. Things got heated, and what does Joey do? He swipes his arm over the table, broke my dishes, threw food all over the walls. Yelling and cursing at Frank, who got right up in his face. Frank's not one to back down, and you can bet he's not going to tolerate that kind of thing in his own house."

She gave a decisive nod. "He's got a right to ask questions and express opinions in his own home. Laura's taking up for Joey, grabs at Joey's arm, and what does he do? He hit her. He hit his own mother in the face!"

Patricia slapped a hand to her breast. "We've got some tempers in the family, sure, but I've never seen the like of it. Never. A man hitting his own mother? Called her a whiny bitch, or something like that."

She colored a little. "A few things worse than that, to tell the truth. I was already heading to the phone to call the police. But Laura begged me not to. Standing there with her nose bleeding, begging me not to call the cops on her son. So I didn't. He was already heading out the door, the coward. My Frank's bigger than him, and it's a lot easier to punch a skinny woman than take on a two-hundred-pound man. Marched right out behind him, told him never to come back. Said if he did, he'd kick his worthless ass back to New York."

She took a breath, as if she had to catch it after the recital. "I was proud of him, I can tell you. Then once Laura stopped being hysterical, Frank sat down with her, told her as long as she lived under his roof, she wasn't to open the door to Joey. If she did, she was on her own."

She sighed. "I've got children of my own, grandchildren, too, and I know it would break my heart if I couldn't see them. But Frank did what he had to do. A man who'd hit his own mother is the worst kind of trash."

"That was the last time you saw him?" Reena asked.

"The last time, and as far as I know that's the last Laura's seen of him. Put a cloud over the holidays, but we got through it. Things simmered down, the way things do. The most excitement we've had since is when there was a fire in the house my son's having built up in Frederick County."

"A fire?" Reena exchanged a glance with O'Donnell. "When was this?"

"Middle of March. Just got in under the roof, too. Some kids broke in, had themselves a party, hauled in some kerosene heaters to take the chill off. One of them got knocked over, somebody dropped a match and half the place burned down before the fire department put it out."

"Did they catch the kids?" O'Donnell asked her.

"No, and it's an awful shame. Months of work up in smoke."

When the front door opened, Patricia glanced at Reena, then got to her feet. "Laura—"

"Why are they here?" Laura's eyes were red-rimmed and swollen. Reena imagined she'd spent as much time crying in church as praying. "I told you I haven't seen Joe or Joey."

"We weren't able to contact your son, Mrs. Pastorelli. He's no longer employed at the garage."

"Then he found something better."

"Possibly. Mrs. Pastorelli, are you in possession of a watch and a pair of earrings given to you by your son last December?"

"I don't know what you're talking about."

"Mrs. Pastorelli." Reena kept her voice gentle, her eyes level. "You've just come from church. Don't add to your own grief by lying about these items."

"They were gifts." Tears, obviously close to the surface, dribbled down her cheeks.

"We're going to go upstairs and get them now." Still gentle, Reena put her arm around Laura's shoulder. "I'm going to give you a receipt for them. And we're going to clear this all up."

"You think he stole them. Why does everyone always think the worst of my boy?"

"Better to clear it all up," Reena continued, leading Laura up the stairs.

"He did steal them," Patricia grumbled. "I knew it."

P iaget," Reena said as she examined the watch. "Forty brilliant-cut diamonds around the bezel. Eighteen-karat gold. This is going to run about six, seven thousand retail."

"How do you know that shit?"

"I'm a woman who loves to window-shop, especially for stuff I'll never be able to afford. The earrings, probably two karats each, nice, clean square cuts in a classic setting. Our boy splurged on his mama for Christmas."

"We'll check with New York, see if any jewelry stores were hit, or residences that reported items matching these stolen."

"Yeah." She held the diamonds up to the light. "I've got a feeling some nice woman didn't get the bling bling she was supposed to from Santa last year." Idly, she flipped down the vanity mirror, held an earring next to her ear. "Nice."

"Jeez, you are a girl."

"Damn right. Came down to show off for his mother, rub some of his own into his uncle's face. Expensive car, clothes, gifts. I don't think he hit the frigging lottery. But the uncle gives him some third degree instead of being impressed, and he gets pissed. Big scene, tossed out. He's not going to let that go."

"He's patient. He's one patient son of a bitch."

"That's where he's got it over his old man. Waits, plans, figures. He knows family, too. How do you get back at the father? You screw with the son."

"We'll get the file from Frederick on the fire."

"It fits the elementary school job, and the garage in New York. Make it look like kids, or an amateur, nothing fancy—not on the surface. He's good at this, O'Donnell. He's really good at it."

. . .

*Smart, smart. Give the old lady a cell phone, a number to call when and if. Stupid bitch. Have to show her again and again how to work the thing. Just our little secret, Ma, you and me against the fucking world.*

*Laps it right up, like always.*

*And it pays off. The little whore from the neighborhood finally gets a clue! Having her remembering, that was sweet, hell of a lot sweeter.*

*It'll all turn around now. All the bad luck, all the bad breaks. It'll all turn around.*

*It'll all burn, including the little whore who started it all.*

. . .

Reena had a head full of data, theories and worries when she walked into Sirico's. It was usually what she needed to clear out the smears of a hard day. Tonight, she had the bonus of Bo meeting her there.

She didn't spot him on the first scan of the tables, but did see the redhead—Mandy, she recalled—snuggled in a booth with a man of about thirty with light brown hair. J.Crew for him, retro hippie for her.

They were drinking the house red, and plastered together at the hip.

She also spotted John at one of the two-tops. Wending through the usual waves and greetings, she aimed for his table. "Just the man I wanted to see."

"Clam sauce is good tonight."

"I'll keep that in mind." She sat across from him, waved off the waitress who headed their way. "I've got something going."

He forked up more linguini. "So I hear."

She sat back. "Dad called you."

"You think he wouldn't? Why didn't you?"

"I was going to. I need your ear, I need your brain, but not here and not now. Can we meet in the morning, hook up for breakfast? No, better, can you come to my place? I'll cook you breakfast."

"What time?"

"Can you make it early? Seven?"

"Probably work that into my schedule. Want to give me something to chew on meanwhile?"

She started to, but knew once she started he'd need it all. Just as she'd need to say it all. "I'd like to let this cook in my head overnight, organize it some."

"Seven, then."

"Thanks."

"Reena." He put a hand over hers as she started to rise. "Do I need to tell you to be careful?"

"No." She got up, bent and kissed his cheek. "No, you don't."

She walked to the kitchen, made a kissy sound at Jack as he ladled sauce on a round of dough. "Have you seen Bo? I'm supposed to meet him here."

"Back in the prep area."

Curious, she walked around the work counter and into prep. Then just stood in the doorway, watching her father give Bo a lesson in the art of pizza.

"Gotta be elastic, or it won't stretch right. You don't want to pull it, see it pop full of holes."

"Right, so I just . . ." Bo held a ball of dough from one of the oiled holding pans in the cooler. He began to stretch it, drawing it out.

"Now, use your fists like I showed you. Start shaping."

Focused on the job at hand, Bo worked his fists under the dough, gently punching, turning—not bad for a beginner, Reena thought.

"Can I toss it?"

"You break it, you bought it," Gib warned him.

"Okay, okay." Legs spread, eyes narrowed in concentration, like a man, Reena decided, about to juggle flaming torches. Bo gave the dough a toss in the air.

A little higher than was wise, in Reena's opinion, but he managed to catch it, keep turning, toss it again.

And the grin that popped out on his face had her biting back a laugh. No point in breaking his rhythm, but he looked like a boy who'd just mastered a two-wheeler for the first heady solo.

"This is so cool. But what the hell do I do with it now?"

"Use your eyeballs," Gib told him. "You got a large going there?"

"Looks like. Looks about right."

"On the board."

"God, okay. Here we go."

He flopped the dough on the board, absently wiping his hands on the short apron he wore. "It's not what we'd call exactly round."

"Not bad though, shape it up some. Give me the edges."

"How many did he drop before he managed that one?" Reena asked as she stepped in.

Bo grinned over his shoulder. "I got this down. Mangled two, but nothing hit the floor."

"He learns quick enough," Gib said as he and Reena exchanged kisses.

"Who knew there was so much involved in making a pizza? You got your big-ass dough mixer there." He nodded toward the stainless-steel machine used to mix massive amounts of flour, yeast, water. "You gotta get a couple of manly men to haul that bowl up on the counter."

"Excuse me, but I've been in on that countless times, and I'm not in the least manly."

"You can say that again. You divide it up, weigh it, stack the pans in the cooler, then you gotta cut the dough out after it rises. All that before you can start making the thing. I'm never taking pizza for granted again."

"You can finish this one out front." Gib picked up the board, carried it out to where Jack made room on the worktable.

"Ah, don't watch me," he said to Reena. "You're making me nervous. I'll clutch. Go on over and sit with Mandy and Brad." He gestured.

"Sure." She grabbed a soda, moved over to join them.

"Hey! You made it. Reena, this is Brad. Brad, Reena. I met Reena during one of my more embarrassing moments."

"Then I'll be dignified and counterbalance. Nice to meet you—in the flesh after all these years of hearing about Dream Girl."

"You, too." She sipped, smiled at Mandy. "When I was fifteen, I dropped my notebook rushing to class. It fell open and this guy—tall, nice shoulders, streaky blond hair, big blue eyes—named Chuck picked it up for me, before I could dive after it. Inside I'd filled pages with "Reena" and "Chuck," and hearts with our initials in them, or just his name over and over the way you do."

"Oh God, he saw it?"

"Hard to miss."

"That *was* embarrassing."

"I think my face went back to its normal color in about a month. So, now we're even."

# 26

She'd been right, Reena decided. The evening at Sirico's had been exactly what she'd needed. Her mind had calmed down, her stomach had smoothed out.

It had been interesting and educational to spend an hour in the company of Bo's closest friends.

Family, she thought. Those two were his family as much as her own brother and sisters were hers.

"I like your friends," she told him as she unlocked her front door.

"Good, because if you didn't, you and I would've been history." He patted her butt when they walked inside. "No, seriously, I'm glad you all hit it off. They're important to me."

"And to each other."

"Did you get that before or after they started slurping on each other?"

"Before." She stretched her back. "When I walked in. Lust vibes."

"I'm having a tough time getting around that."

"That's just because you're used to seeing them as family, or you have since you and Mandy stopped hitting the sheets. But the fact that they're now hitting them with each other doesn't make them less yours."

"I think I need to block the image of the sheets, at least for the time being." He put his hands on her arms, rubbed them up and down. "Tired?"

"Not as much as I was. Got a fresh charge." She clamped her hands on his hips. "Got something in mind as to what I should do with the energy?"

"Might. Come on out back. I've got something I want to show you."

"You want to show it to me outside?" She laughed as he pulled her along. "What are you now, Nature Boy?"

"Sex, sex, sex, that's all the woman thinks of. Thank you, Jesus." He pulled her out the back door.

There was a nice half-moon shedding sharp white light. Flowers she'd managed to grab and plant on the run were spilling out of her patio pots.

The air was warm, a little close, and heavily scented with the green smell of summer.

And there, under a leafy maple, was a glider.

"A glider! You got me a glider for the yard?"

"Got? Heresy. Guess I should've strapped on my tool belt."

"You *made* it." Her eyes misted, and now it was Reena dragging him. "You made me a glider? Oh my God, when? It's beautiful. Oh, feel how smooth." She ran her fingers over the wood. "It's like silk."

"Finished it up today, kept my mind off things. Want to try it out?"

"Are you kidding?" She sat, stretched her arms over the back and set it in motion. "It's great, it's wonderful. Another ten pounds of stress just fell off my shoulders. Bo." She reached her hand out for his. "You sweetie."

He sat beside her. "I was hoping it'd be a hit."

"Major league." She dropped her head on his shoulder. "This is fabulous. My own house, my own yard on a warm June night. And a sexy guy sitting with me on a glider he made with his own two hands. It makes everything that happened last night seem unreal."

"I guess we both needed to box that away for a few hours."

"And you spent yours building me this."

"If you love what you do, it's not really work."

She nodded. "It's satisfaction."

"That's the one. And hell, it looks like I'm going to score a new truck tomorrow." His fingers toyed with the curling tips of her hair. "Your mom's coming along. Her cousin's a Dodge dealer."

"My advice? Give her her head." Something she'd planted smelled strong and sweet. Like a splash of vanilla on the warm air. "She'll cut cousin Sal's price down to the bone. Pull her back when you see tears leaking out of his eyes, but not before."

"Check."

"You're handling this so well."

"Not much else I can do."

"Sure there is. You could rant, rave, put your fist through the wall—"

"Then I'd have to replaster."

Her laugh came easily. "You're steady, that's what you are, Bowen. I know under it you're enraged, but you've got the lid on it. You haven't asked me if there's been any progress on the whole mess."

"I figured you'll tell me."

"I will. I need to talk to someone first, but after, I'll tell you what I can. You make it easy for me."

"I've got this whole love thing going on. Why would I make it hard for you?"

She turned her face into his shoulder for a moment, let the quiet thrill of him pour through her. It was unnerving how much she'd come to love him, how quickly it had lodged in her heart and spread so that there were times, like this, she would've sworn she felt that love pulsing in her fingertips.

"Destiny," she whispered, and grazed her lips along his jaw. "I think you must be mine, Bo. I think you must be."

She shifted around, straddled his lap, linked her hands behind his neck. "It's a little bit scary," she told him. "Just enough to add a nice edge. But mostly it's sweet and it's smooth. I feel like . . ." She let her head fall back, looked up at that slice of moon, the scatter of stars. "Not like I was waiting," she continued, coming back up to look at his face. "Not like you stand and wait for a bus to come pick you up, take you where you want to go. But like I was driving myself, destination in mind, doing what I wanted. Then

I thought, Hey, why don't I take that road? That's the one I'd like to travel. And there you were."

He bent forward to press his lips to her collarbone. "Did I have my thumb out?"

"I think you were walking right along, destination in mind, too. We decided to share the wheel." She cupped his face. "This wouldn't be working if the only thing you saw when you looked at me was a girl in a pink top, across the room at a party."

"I do see her, and who she was. And I see who she is now. I'm crazy about who she is now."

She kept her hands on his face as she lowered her lips to his, as they sank into the kiss together. Into the warmth and the wet.

"You made a pizza," she murmured dreamily.

"And it was good, despite Brad's cracks about indigestion or possible ptomaine."

"You made a pizza," she repeated, brushing her lips over his cheeks, his temples, his lips, his throat. "And you built me a glider." She caught his bottom lip between her teeth, tugged, then dipped her tongue into his mouth, focusing the world in that long kiss. "I'm about to express my sincere gratitude."

"I'm about to accept it." His voice had gone thick, and his hands were roaming. "Let's go inside."

"Mmm-mmm. I want to see how well this glider is built." She tugged his shirt over his head, let it fly over her shoulder.

"Reena, we can't—"

Her mouth stopped his. Her hands slid between them to flip open the button of his jeans. "Bet we can." She bit his shoulder, tugged down his zipper. When she felt him tense, she clamped her hands on the back of the glider to keep him from lifting her up. Her eyes sparkled out of the dark.

"Relax. It's just you and me." She nipped at his jaw, seeped herself in the taste of him as she cruised her lips over his face. "We're the whole world. Let's glide," she whispered, bringing his hands to her breasts. "Touch me. Keep touching me."

He couldn't stop. His hands slid under her shirt, but it wasn't enough. Not now. He fought with buttons to find more, and take it. He cupped her, tasted her, while the glider gently rocked.

There was something witchy about it, the heavy air, the motion, the smell of grass and flowers and woman, and the taut ready feel of her under his hands.

They were the world in that moment, in the star-washed dark and the summer-scented air.

Her skin, silvered by moonlight, dappled by leaf shadow, seemed to float over his. And his belly quivered—helpless need, when she rose, when she settled. When she surrounded.

She moaned, long and low. Her eyes were half closed as they watched each other. Watching each other as their mouths met and their sighs mingled. Pleasure and excitement tangled, built, trembled. She used that pleasure and the easy motion to rock them both. Sweet and slow, slow and sweet, so release was like a lazy slide over silk.

They melted together in a contentment as gentle as the sway of the glider.

"You do good work," she whispered.

"Actually, I think you did most of it."

She chuckled, nuzzled his neck. "I meant the glider."

By seven in the morning, Reena had crisp bacon warming in the oven, coffee brewed, bagels sliced and the makings for an omelet set out.

She felt guilty about shoving Bo out the door at six-thirty with nothing but a hastily toasted bagel. But she wanted to talk to John alone.

She was already dressed for work, right down to her holster, where she would dash to as soon as her meeting with John was over.

He was prompt. She could count on him for that, as well as a hundred other things. "Thanks. Really."

At the door, she kissed his cheek.

"I know it's early, but I'm on eight-to-fours. O'Donnell's got it covered if I need to squeeze in a little more time. I'm about to make you a first-class omelet for your trouble."

"You don't have to bother with that. We can do this over coffee."

"Absolutely not." She led the way to the kitchen. "I let this perk around in my head through the night. What I'd like to do is just pour it out on you." She filled a coffee cup for him. "Okay?"

"Pour away."

"It goes back, John, all the way back to the beginning."

She made the omelet while she spoke. He didn't interrupt, but let her lay it out as it came to her.

She moved like her mother, he thought. Fluidly, with those graceful gestures to punctuate the words. And thought like a cop—but then he'd seen that in her when she was a child. Logic and observation.

"We're checking on the jewelry." She set his plate down, settled in with her own breakfast of half a bagel and a single strip of bacon. "It may not have been from New York, but we'll find where he lifted it. Getting a warrant out on him for that will help. It was a stupid move, and though he's not stupid, it was like him. He needs to show off, pump himself up. Fire-starting plays into that," she added. "A lot of the inner motivation for a fire-starter is the pump, and the showing off. But with him, it's also a statement. My father did it, and so can I. Only bigger, better."

"There's more."

"Yeah. These are vengeance fires, all of them. If I'm right, and I believe it, John. I believe it's him. Maybe working with his father, maybe alone. Their revenge against me and mine, because to him we're responsible for what happened to his father."

"He's too good at it to just have done this handful," John commented. "Too organized, too focused and prepared."

"Yeah. Maybe the New Jersey family's used him as a torch, or he might have freelanced. He's not afraid to wait. Sure, some of the gaps came about because he was inside, but he's not afraid to wait, to pick his moment. He waited three months after his uncle kicked him out of the house to retaliate by setting his cousin's house on fire. That had to be him."

"I can help you with that one. I know some people in Frederick County."

"I was hoping you did, and would. We're reopening Josh Bolton's case." She sipped some of the Diet Pepsi she'd poured herself. "It's going to be him there, John. If there's nothing else that comes out of this, nothing else, I need to nail him for that." She couldn't stop the tremor in her voice, or in her heart. "For Josh."

"You let it get personal, let it crawl in there, Reena, you're playing into his hands."

"I know it. I'm working on it. He wants me to know it's him. No matter how he set the scenes, covered his tracks, he wants me to know. But why now? Why wait all these years, then move on me so directly? Something's changed, something lit his fuse."

Nodding, John forked up more eggs. "He's kept you on his radar all this time, and slipped under yours to take hits at you. Maybe it's something you've changed. Could be as simple as you buying this house. Getting involved with the guy next door."

"Maybe, maybe." But she shook her head. "I've had big moments in my life before now. Graduating college—he got a GED in prison. Getting my shield, and he's been drifting, at least on record, from job to job. I've been involved with men before, and we can't find any serious relationships for him. He can't get into my head and know how I felt about the men I've been involved with, if I was serious. From the outside, my relationship with Luke looked serious. And yeah," she said before John could speak, "he blew up his damn car, but he didn't contact me. He didn't start a dialogue."

"Maybe it's the timing. The twenty-year thing. Anniversaries are milestones, after all. But finding his motive is going to help you work him. We want to shut him down before he gets tired of playing and comes after you. You know he will, Reena. You know how dangerous he is."

"I know he's dangerous. I know he's a violent sociopath with misogynistic tendencies. He'll never let any slight—actual or perceived—go unpunished. But he won't come after me, not for a while. This is too exciting for him, makes him important. He could, however, come after people I love. That scares me boneless, John. I'm afraid for my family, for you, for Bo."

"Playing into his hands again."

"I know that, too. I'm a good cop. Am I a good cop, John?"

"You're a good cop."

"Most of my time on the job's been concentrated on arson investigation. The puzzle of it. Working the evidence, details, observation, psychology, physiology. I'm not a street cop." She drew in a breath. "I can count the times I've had to draw my weapon in the line. I've never once had to fire it. I've subdued suspects, but only once have I ever had to subdue an armed suspect. Last month. And my hands were shaking the whole time. I had a nine millimeter, he had a pissant knife, and for God's sake, John, my hands were shaking."

"Did you subdue the suspect?"

"Yes." She dragged a hand through her hair. "Yes I did." She closed her eyes. "Okay."

She spent the day dealing with the myriad and headachy chores of the job. Reading reports, writing them, making calls, waiting for them.

The legwork took her back to her own neighborhood to question one of Joey's old friends.

Tony Borelli had been a skinny, sulky-faced boy, a year ahead of her in school. His mother, she recalled, had been a screamer. The sort of woman who stood on her steps or the sidewalk, screeching at her kids, the neighbors, her husband. The occasional total stranger.

She'd died from complications due to a stroke at the age of forty-eight.

Tony had had his share of dustups. Shoplifting, joyriding, possession, and had done a short stretch in his early twenties for his involvement in a chop-shop organization in South Baltimore.

He was still skinny, a bag of bones in grease-stained jeans and a faded red T-shirt. His hair was topped by a gray gimme cap with the name *Stenson's Auto Repair* scrolled across it.

He had a Honda Accord on a lift, and wiped oil off his hands with a bandanna that might, once, have been blue.

"Joey Pastorelli? Jesus, haven't seen him since we were kids."

"You and he were pretty tight back in the day, Tony."

"Kids." He shrugged, continued to drain oil from the Honda. "Sure, we ran together awhile. Thought we were badasses."

"You were."

Tony flicked a glance over, nearly smiled. "Guess we were. That was a long time ago, Reena." His eyes tracked over to O'Donnell, who loitered near a workbench as if fascinated by the display of parts and tools. "Gotta grow up sometime."

"I'm still friends with a lot of the kids I ran with back then. Even the ones who left the neighborhood. We keep in touch."

"Girls are different, maybe. Joey went off to New York when we were, what, twelve? Long time ago."

He continued to work, she noted, just as he continued to give O'Donnell nervous looks.

"You had some trouble along the way, Tony."

"Yeah, I had some trouble. Did some time. Once you do, some people, they never figure you can clean it up. I got a wife now, I got a kid. I got a job here. I'm a good mechanic."

"A skill that helped you get a job chopping cars."

"I was twenty, for Chrissake. Paid my debt to society. What do you want from me?"

"I want to know the last time you saw or spoke to Joey Pastorelli. He's made some trips back to Baltimore, Tony. A guy comes back to the neighborhood, he's bound to touch base with his old friends. You're holding back on me, and you keep doing it, I can make trouble for you. I wouldn't like doing it, but I would."

"This all goes back to when he knocked you around when we were kids." He pointed a grease-stained finger. "I didn't have anything to do with that, that's not on me. I don't hit girls—women. You see anything on my sheet about hitting women?"

"No. I don't see anything on your sheet about violent behavior, period. Just like I see you kept your lip zipped when you got busted for chopping. Didn't name names. You think this is about loyalty, Tony? We're looking at Joey in connection to murder. You want a piece of that, accessory after the fact?"

"Whoa, wait. Hold on." He stepped back, the wrench dangling from his hand. "Murder? I don't know what you're talking about. Swear on my life."

"Tell me about Joey."

"Okay, maybe he's breezed through a couple of times. Maybe we had a beer. There's no law against it."

"When? Where?"

"Man." He pulled off his cap, showing Reena his hair was thinning, veeing back from his forehead to form a long, sharp widow's peak. "First time I heard from him, after the fire, all that crazy shit, was right before I hooked up with the chop shop. He came back around, said he had some business to take care of. Said he knew these guys if I was looking to make some money. He took me over to the shop. That's how I got into it."

"You were busted in 1993."

"Yeah. Chopped for about a year before I got busted."

She felt the clutch in her gut. "So Joey plugged you in in 'ninety-two?"

"That'd be right."

"When? Spring, summer, winter?"

"Well, God, how'm I supposed to remember?"

"Give me a weather picture, Tony. Joey comes around, all these years since, you hit a couple of bars maybe. You walk? Was there snow?"

"No, it was nice out. I remember. I was smoking some weed, listening to the ball game. I remember now. Early in the season, but it was nice out. April or May, I guess."

It was hot in the garage, hot and close, but the sweat that had beaded on Tony's face was from more than steamy working conditions. "Look, if he killed somebody, he didn't tell me about it. I'm not saying I'm surprised he did, or could, but he didn't tell me." Tony wet his lips. "Talked about you some."

"Is that so?"

"Just bullshitting. Asked me if I still saw you around . . . if, you know, I'd ever gotten any of that."

"What else?"

"I was pretty loaded, Reena. I just remember we talked the kind of shit you talk, and he hooked me up with the operation. I did three years for that, and I got clean. Been working here since. He blew through again a few years after I got out."

"'Ninety-nine?"

"Yeah. I had a drink with him for old times' sake. He tells me he's got a lot of lines dangling, can help me out. But I wasn't going back down that road, told him. Pissed him off, and we got into it a little. Took off, left me stranded on The Block 'cause he was driving. Nearly froze my ass off trying to get a cab home."

"Cold out?"

"Witch's tit. Slid on some ice, fell on my ass. I met Tracey a few weeks later. That cleaned me up some more. She doesn't take any bullshit."

"Good for her."

"Good for me. And I know it, Reena. Next time I saw Joey I told him flat out I couldn't do that shit anymore."

"When was this?"

Tony shifted his weight. "Couple weeks ago. Maybe three. He came by the house. I don't know how he found out where we're living. It was close to midnight. Scared Tracey. Woke up the kid. He'd been drinking, wanted me to come out with him. I wouldn't let him in, and I sent him away. He didn't like it."

"Was he on foot?"

"No. Ah, I watched, to make sure he kept going. I saw him get into a Cherokee. Black Jeep Cherokee. Looked like a 'ninety-three."

"Catch the plates?"

"No, sorry. Never looked." He kneaded his cap between his hands now, but what she saw wasn't guilt nerves. It was fear. "He upset my wife and kid. Things are different now. I've got a family. If he's done murder, I don't want him coming around my family."

"He contacts you again, I want to know about it. I don't want you to tell him we've had this talk. If you can, find out where he's staying, but don't press it."

"You're scaring me some, Reena."

"Good, because he's a scary guy. If he works up a mad about you, he'll hurt you. He'll hurt your family. That's not bullshit, Tony, that's straight."

She walked out with O'Donnell, then turned when Tony came out of the garage, calling her.

"Ah, something else. Private."

"Sure. Be right with you," she said to O'Donnell, and walked around the side of the building with Tony.

"He really kill somebody?"

"We're looking at that."

"And you think he might try to hurt Tracey or the kid?"

"He deals in payback, Tony. Right now he's too busy to worry about you. But if we don't get him, he may find the time. You're going to want to stay out of his way, and contact me if he gets in touch."

"Yeah, I got that. I got a break when Tracey took a chance on me. I don't risk that, not for anything or anyone. Listen." He took his cap off again, ran his hand through what was left of his hair. "Um, when we were kids, before, well, before all hell broke loose on the block, he used to follow you."

"Follow me?"

"He used to watch you around school, around the neighborhood. He'd, ah, sneak out at night and look in the windows of your house, maybe climb that tree in the back, try to see into your bedroom. I went with him sometimes."

"See anything interesting, Tony?"

His gaze lowered to the toes of his boots. "He was going to rape you. He didn't call it that, and I'm telling you straight, Reena, I didn't think of it like that, either. I was twelve. He said he was going to do you, wanted me to come along for it. I didn't want any part of that, and, besides, I thought he was just blowing smoke. Mostly I thought it was gross. But after, well, when everybody heard how he'd knocked you down and . . . I knew what he'd been trying. I didn't say anything to anybody."

"You're saying it now."

He looked back at her. "I've got a little girl. She's just five. When I think . . . I'm sorry. I want to say I'm sorry I didn't say anything to anyone before he tried to hurt you. I want you to know, you've got my word, if he gets in touch with me again, I won't tell him you're looking for him. And I'll call you first thing."

"All right, Tony." To seal it, she took his hand, shook it. "It's nice you have a family now."

"Makes a difference."

"Yeah. Yeah, it does."


W e have confirmation Joey P. was in the area at or around the time of Josh's death, and of the vehicular fire of Luke's car. We have confirmation he was in Baltimore two to three weeks ago."

Reena briefed the arson squad, Steve as fire inspector and members of the Crime Scene Unit.

"He was reported to be driving a black Jeep Cherokee, possibly a 'ninety-three, when he left the residence of Tony Borelli. There is no vehicle registered in the name of Joseph Pastorelli, Junior. Or Senior. His mother doesn't own a car. It's possible the vehicle was borrowed from an acquaintance, or more likely stolen. We're in the process of culling through reports of stolen Cherokees. Younger?"

He shifted in his chair. "We're still piecing things together, but it looks like the device placed in Goodnight's gas tank was the same type used in the Chambers vehicular fire six years ago. Firecracker floating in a cup, soaked rags for a fuse. We're looking at like crimes, pulling them in from New York, New Jersey, Connecticut and Pennsylvania. We're also taking a closer look at the homicide and car torching in North Carolina that took out Hugh Fitzgerald. And the case, deemed accidental death, of Joshua Bolton is now reopened."

One of the other detectives nodded toward the board where both Pastorellis' mug shots were pinned, along with various crime-scene photos. "We're going on the assumption that this guy's been lighting fires for ten years or more, has killed at least two people, and never got smoke in his eyes before this?"

"That's right," Reena said. "He's careful, he's good. It's very possible he had some protection from the Carbionellis, has likely done some torch work for them. And the assumption continues that up until this point he had no motive to make himself known to me. What that motive is? He's still the only one who knows it. But he keeps coming back here. He's drawn back to Baltimore."

"You're part of the reason why," Steve pointed out.

"Me," she agreed, "his father and what happened during that August of 'eighty-five. He holds grudges, and he's not afraid to hold them for a long time. Before this, as far as we know, he came in, took his shot, backed off. This time, he's staying, he's playing it out. He'll call again. He'll light something up again."

She looked back at the mug shot. "This time he means to finish it."

At the end of shift, Reena gathered up files and notes. She'd work, she decided, but she wanted to work at home, without the background noise. And she wanted to be home the next time he called.

She balanced folders as she grabbed the phone. "Arson Unit, Hale. Yeah, thanks for getting back to me. NYPD," she told O'Donnell, and set down the files to take notes. "Yeah, yeah, I'm getting it. You've got the name of the fire and arson inspectors? The detective on the burglary case? I'd appreciate that. I'll be in touch."

She hung up, looked at O'Donnell. "The watch, the earrings, a lot of other goodies, stolen from an apartment on the Upper East Side, December fifteenth of last year. The building was evacuated due to a fire in a neighboring apartment—empty apartment as the owners were on vacation. When the fire department suppressed, let people back into the building, these people found they'd been hit. Cash, jewelry, coin collection."

"Small, portable."

"There's a doorman on the building, but one of the other tenants had a party that night. Catered. People in and out—guests, wait people, so on. Wouldn't be hard to slip through that, get into an empty apartment, set a fire."

"Cause of fire determined?"

"They're sending copies of the files overnight, but the gist was multiple points of origin. Utility closet full of cleaning supplies, sofa, bed. That place was also burgled. Small objets d'art, some jewelry that wasn't in the home safe."

"Somebody inside had a piece of it."

"No arrests, as yet, no recovery of stolen goods. NYPD's grateful for the possible lead."

"Tit for tat," O'Donnell said.

# 27

Before she went home, Reena decided she'd swing by and have an overdue sit-down with her mother.

She spotted the shiny new blue truck outside Sirico's, and put two and two together. She pulled in behind it, did a quick walk-around, and concluded Bo had gotten himself a solid piece of equipment.

Business was light—too early for dinner, too late for lunch—and she found Pete running the show, with his daughter, Rosa—home from college for the summer—waiting tables.

"Out in back," Pete called to her. "A whole gang."

"Need help in here?"

"Got it for now." He poured sauce generously over a meatball sub. "But you can tell my boy we've got a delivery, so to get his butt back in here. It's nearly ready to go."

"You got it." She moved into the prep area and out the employees' exit. Her family, including a couple of cousins, her uncle Larry, along with Gina, her mother and her two kids, were all scattered around the narrow backyard.

The fact that everyone was talking at once didn't surprise her.

There were some x's marked on the scrubby grass with orange spray paint.

Even now her father was pointing in one direction, her mother in the opposite. Bo appeared to be caught between them.

Reena stepped out, and up to the little table where Bella sat sipping fizzy water.

"What's going on?"

"Oh." Bella waved a hand. "They're measuring, marking, arguing about this summer kitchen, terrace dining deal Mama's got a wild hair over."

"Why a wild hair?"

"Don't they have enough work to do as it is? They've been shackled to this place for thirty years. More."

Reena sat, looked into Bella's eyes. Something's up, she thought. Something. "They love this place."

"I *know* that, Reena. But they're not getting any younger."

"For God's sake."

"They're not. They should be off enjoying this time of their lives, seizing the damn day or whatever, instead of making more work for themselves."

"They are enjoying this time of their lives. Not only here, working here, seeing their work rewarded every day, being with family, friends. But they travel, too."

"What if there'd never been a Sirico's?" Bella turned in her seat, lowering her voice as if she were blaspheming. "If there hadn't been, if Mama and Dad hadn't met each other so young, had this place to lock themselves to, she might have gone on to art school. She might have become a real artist. Experienced things, *seen* things. Done things before she jumped into marriage and baby making."

"Let me first state the obvious and say if she had, you wouldn't be here. And second, she could have chosen art school. She could have chosen Dad and art school. What she did was choose him, this place, this life."

Reena shifted her gaze now, studied her mother, slim and lovely with her hair slicked back in a shiny tail, laughing as she drilled a finger into her husband's chest.

"And when I look at her, Bella, I don't see a woman with regrets, a woman who asks herself what-if."

"Why can't I be happy like that, Reena? Why can't I just be happy?"

"I don't know. I'm sorry you're not."

"I know you went to talk to Vince. Oh, don't put the cop face on with me," she said impatiently. "He was angry. But he was a little shaken up, too. Wouldn't expect my little sister to get in his face. Thanks."

"You're welcome. It was impulse. I couldn't stop myself. I was afraid you might be irritated I waded in."

"I'm not. Even if it hadn't changed a thing, I wouldn't be irritated that you stood up for me. He's cut things off with his current mistress. At least as far as I can tell. Maybe it'll last, maybe it won't." She shrugged, looking back at her mother. "I'll never be like Mama, part of that kind of team with a husband who adores everything about me. I'm never going to have that."

"You have beautiful children, Bella."

"I do," she agreed, smiling a little. "I have beautiful children. And I think I'm pregnant again."

"You think—"

But Bella shook her head quickly, cutting off the conversation as one of the kids ran to the table.

"Mama! Can we have ice-cream cones? Just one scoop. Nana said to ask you. Please, can we?"

"Sure. Sure you can." She brushed her son's cheek. "Just one scoop. I love them so much," she told Reena when he ran off to spread the good news. "I can't talk about this now. Don't say anything." She popped to her feet. "Sophie! Come help me make the cones."

Bella swung into the building, with the younger kids whooping as they raced to follow. Sophia brought up the rear.

Sulking, Reena noted, but obedient. And still young enough to secretly lust after a scoop of ice cream.

"I don't see why she needs me to help. It's always me."

"Hey, what's wrong with you?" Reena demanded. "You get put on the front line, who's going to notice if you have two scoops instead of just one?"

Sophia's lips twitched. "Want one?"

"There's lemon gelato in there. What do you think?" Reena reached over, pinched Sophia's cheek. "Be kind to your mother. Don't roll your eyes at me. Just do it. Just twenty-four hours of kindness. I think she could use it."

She gave the cheek she'd pinched a kiss, then walked to her own mother. Bianca wrapped an arm around Reena's waist. "You're just in time. Your father has realized what was obvious. That I was right."

Reena watched, as her mother did, Bo, Gib, Larry and some of the others as they walked to the corner of the building. Bo gestured with the spray paint, got a shrug from Gib, and began to spray a gently serpentine line on the grass.

"What's he doing?" Reena asked.

"Laying out the idea for my walkway from the corner. People will be able to stroll around from the sidewalk out front and come right back to my pergola. Maybe they don't want to walk through the restaurant like they have to now if they want an outside table. Maybe they're out for a walk, hear the music—"

"Music?"

"I'm putting in speakers. There'll be music when we have the pergola. And lights along the path. And big pots of flowers." She slapped her hands on her hips as she circled around, the gesture of a satisfied woman who knows how to take charge. "Ornamental trees. Lemon trees. And in the back corner there. A little play area so the children won't be bored. And—"

"Mama." With a laugh, Reena tapped her hands to her own temples. "My head's spinning."

"It's a good plan."

"Yes, it's a good plan. A big one."

"I like big." She smiled as Bo began to gesture, tick points of some sort off on his fingers while Gib frowned. "I like your Bo. We had fun today. I brought tears to cousin Sal's eyes, so that was fun, and Bo bought me a hydrangea."

"He . . . he bought you a bush?"

"And planted it for me. Either you marry him or I adopt him, because I'm not letting him get away."

The kids came running out with ice-cream cones, Gina and her mother wandered over, and Bo caught Reena's eye and grinned at her.

It wasn't the time to talk about serial arson and murder.

She couldn't stay, though her excuses to go home were met with protests.

"I just want to lay as much of this out as I can for your parents," Bo told her. "So they can hash it out overnight, be sure this is what they want. If you can wait a half hour, I'll go with you."

"You've got your own ride. Big burly one, too. I've got files I need to read over. An hour of quiet and thinking time's just what I want."

"Want me to bring you dinner?"

"That'd be great. Anything. Just surprise me."

Xander caught up with her as she followed, for curiosity's sake, the path between the curvy orange lines. "I'll walk you around." He tugged her hair, an old habit.

She poked an elbow in his ribs in the same spirit.

"Why don't I go home with you," he began, "hang out awhile? We never get to—"

"No. I'm working, and I don't need my little brother playing guard."

"I'm taller than you."

"Barely."

"Which means I can be the younger brother, but not the little brother. Either way. Catarina, he could come to your house."

"Yes, he could. He knows where I live. I'm prepared for that, Xand. I can't have someone with me twenty-four hours a day. I want you to be careful." She turned to him, laid her hands on his shoulders. "Joey Pastorelli. If I'm right, he wants payback. You—nearly three years younger—took him on, beat him back. I can promise you he hasn't forgotten that. I want you to be careful, to take care of your wife and baby. Don't worry about me, and I won't have to worry about you. Deal?"

"The son of a bitch comes anywhere near An or Dillon—"

"That's right." Her eyes held his in perfect understanding. "That's exactly right. Keep them close for now. You and Jack, you look out for Fran and Bella, the kids. Mama and Dad. I've got some extra patrols, but nobody knows the neighborhood, the feel of it, like we do. Anything, *anything* seems off, you call me. Promise me."

"You don't even have to ask."

"It's hot," she said after a moment. "It's going to be a hot night. Summer's starting to kick."

She got in her car and drove home. But when she got there, she sat, studying the house, the street, the block. She knew several people who lived on this row, had known them all or most of her life.

She knew this place, had chosen to live here. She could walk in any direction and pass half a dozen people who knew her name.

Now neither she nor they were safe.

Gathering her files, she got out, locked her car. She studied the dents and scars pocking it, little reminders of how much worse the explosion on Bo's truck could have been.

How long would it take him to light up her car? she wondered. Two minutes, three? He could do it while she slept, while she showered, fixed a meal.

But that would just be a poke in the ribs. She thought he'd go up a level now.

She walked to her door, waved to Mary Kate Leoni, who was washing the white marble steps three doors down. Housekeeping, she thought.

Life went on with simple things like housekeeping, waiting tables, eating ice-cream cones.

She unlocked her door, set the files aside. And unholstered her weapon. Whatever she'd said, or told herself, about handling things, wanting an hour of quiet and solitude, she was jittery enough to do a full walk-through of her own house. With her gun in her hand.

Satisfied, if not settled, she went downstairs for the files and a cold drink. It was time she made good use of the office she'd only begun to set up on the third floor. Time she did what she did best: organize, study and dissect.

She booted up her computer, then turned to the board and easel she'd hauled up shortly after she moved in. From the files she selected photographs, newspaper clippings, copies of reports. She brought up and printed out copies of photos and reports from her own computer.

When they were arranged, she stepped back, looked at the board as a whole. Then she sat at the keyboard and wrote out the sequence of events beginning with that day in August when she'd been eleven.

It took longer than the hour, but she barely noticed the passing of time. When the phone rang, she swore, and was so deep in what had been she nearly forgot what was. Her fingers were an inch away from snatching up the phone when she stopped herself. Looked at the readout.

She let it ring a second time as she drew herself in. Though she knew the phone was tapped, and there was a cop somewhere with recording and tracking equipment, she engaged her own recorder before she answered.

"Hello, Joey."

"Hey, Reena. Took you long enough."

"Oh, I don't know, I think I did pretty well, considering I haven't given you a thought in twenty years."

"Thinking of me now, aren't you?"

"Sure. I'm remembering what a little asshole you were when you lived on the row. Looks like you're a big asshole these days."

"Always had a mouth on you. I'm going to make use of that mouth, real soon."

"What's the matter, Joey? Can't you get a woman? Is your method still knock them around and rape them?"

"You'll find out. We've got a lot to settle, you and me. Got another surprise coming. It's all picked out for you."

"Why don't we ditch the crap, Joey? Why don't we hook up? Give me the when, give me the where, and we'll get down to business."

"You always thought I was stupid, always thought I was less than you, and your holy family. Who's still living in the neighborhood, slinging greasy pizzas?"

"Oh now, Joey, there's nothing greasy about a Sirico's. Come on, meet me there—I'll buy you a large."

"Too bad the guy banging you now wasn't in that truck when it blew." His breath came quicker now, puffing out the words.

Getting under his skin, Reena thought. Poking at a cobra with a stick.

"Maybe next time. Or maybe he'll have an accident at home, in bed. Shit happens, right? He smelled like pig cooking. The first one. Remember him, Reena? I could smell you where you'd come on the sheets I used to fire him up."

"You son of a bitch." She doubled over when the pain hit her belly. "You son of a bitch."

He laughed, and his voice dropped to a whisper. "Someone's going to burn tonight."

It took Bo closer to two hours than one to pull away from Sirico's. The job was going to be an interesting one, to say the least. In addition, he'd fielded a half dozen other inquiries about repair, remodeling, cabinetry from people who'd wandered out while he was measuring the site. He'd given out twice that many cards before he'd gotten the takeout chicken Parmesan.

If even a third of those turned into actual work, he was going to have to seriously consider hiring a full-time laborer.

Big step, he decided. Big, giant step from taking on a part-time helper, or just shanghaiing Brad when a job was too big for one man or he was in a time crunch.

This would be commitment time for a man who'd been perfectly content to work alone. He'd be cutting someone a regular paycheck—someone who'd depend on him for that paycheck. Every week.

Definitely needed to think about it.

He ran a hand over the hood of the truck as he skirted it. A nice piece of machinery, he admitted. And he'd gotten it for a better price than anyone could expect. Bianca had all but stolen it for him.

But damn, he was going to miss his old horse.

He reached for his keys, glanced across the street, up the block a little when he heard a quick, signaling whistle.

He saw the man standing with his thumbs in his front pockets. Ball cap, jeans, sunglasses, hard grin. Something about him was familiar enough to have Bo lifting his hand, keys in it.

Then it clicked. Flower guy, buying supermarket roses to get out of the doghouse.

"Hey," he called out, opening the door of the truck. "How's it going?"

With that tooth-baring grin still in place, the man walked to a car, got in. He rolled down the window, leaned out. He mimed shooting a gun with his index finger. Bo heard him say *bang* as he drove by.

"Weird." With a shake of his head, Bo slid the takeout bag onto the seat, climbed in behind the wheel. He glanced up the street, down, then pulled out, making a quick U-turn to drive to Reena's.

He let himself in, called out to let her know he was back, then took the bag into the kitchen. Because he caught a whiff of something other than the chicken, he decided a nice, cool shower was the first thing on his agenda.

So he'd bop home and get one, and grab the sketches and designs he'd drawn up for Reena. Going over those would keep both their minds off more serious matters for a few hours.

He headed back out of the kitchen, up the stairs, calling out again.

"Hey, I hunted and gathered. Just going next door to grab a shower, and apparently I'm talking to myself," he decided when he saw no sign of her in the bedroom.

He heard a door open overhead and climbed to the third floor.

"Hey, Reene, why do people like you and me buy houses where you have to climb . . . Hey, what's the matter?"

She was standing just outside of what he knew was a small bathroom. Her face was pale as glass.

"You need to sit down." Even as she shook her head, he was taking her arm, taking her weight and guiding her back into her office. "He called again."

This time she nodded. "I need a minute."

"I'll get you some water."

"No, I had some. I'm okay. Yeah, he called again, and he got to me. I had control, I was pushing the buttons, then he got to me, and I lost it."

She'd barely been able to get through the follow-up call to O'Donnell before she'd been sick. Horribly sick.

"I saw you pull up." She'd had her head out the window, just trying to breathe.

"What did he say?"

Rather than repeat it, she gestured to the tape recorder. "Play it back. You should hear it for yourself."

While he did, she rose to go to the window. She opened that one, too, though the air outside was hot and weighty.

"Not exactly what you signed on for," she commented and kept her back to him.

"No, I guess it's not."

"Nobody's going to think less of you if you decide to back off from all this, Bo. He'll hurt you if he can. He's already hurt you."

"So, it's okay with you if I take off for a couple weeks. Maybe go visit some national parks, or do some snorkeling in Jamaica."

"Yes."

"Good Catholic girl like you's going to have to go to confession with that big, fat lie."

"It's not a lie."

"Then you've got pretty low standards in men."

"It has nothing to do with standards." She pulled the window back down with an impatient snap. "I don't want anything to happen to you. I'm scared."

"Me, too."

She turned around, looked him dead in the eye. "I want to marry you."

His mouth opened and closed twice, and definitely lost a few shades of color. "Well. Wow. Wow, there's a lot of stuff flying around in this room. I'm just going to sit down before a piece of it crashes into my skull."

"What do you think, Goodnight? I *am* a good Catholic girl at the core. Look at my family. Look at me. What do you think I'd want when I finally found someone I love and respect and enjoy?"

"I don't know. I don't know. The whole, let's say 'institution' isn't something—"

"It's a sacrament to me. Marriage is sacred, and you're the only man I've ever wanted to take vows with."

"I . . . I—I—I. Shit, now I'm stuttering. I think something did crash into my skull."

"I didn't care if I ever got married and had kids because there was no one I wanted to marry and have kids with. You changed that, and now you have to deal with the consequences."

"Are you trying to scare me so I'll go visit those national parks?"

She walked to him, bent down, gripped his face hard in her hands and kissed him, firmly. "I love you."

"Oh, boy. Oh, boy."

"Say 'I love you, too, Reena.' If you mean it."

"I do mean it. I do love you."

His eyes stayed on hers, and the fact that there was a trace of fear in them made her smile.

"It's just . . . I never completed this part of the plan in my head. You know, there's the whole we're-having-a-really-good-time-with-each-other part—despite fear and mayhem. Then there's the maybe-we-should-move-in-together part. After a while there's the where-should-we-go-from-here? part."

"That doesn't work for me. I'm thirty-one. I want children, your children. I want to make a life, our life. You told me once you knew because the music stopped. I'm telling you I know, because the music started. Take some time." She kissed him again. "Think about it. There's enough going on right now."

"A lot going on."

"I'd still marry you if you went away for a while, somewhere out of all this."

"I'm not going anywhere. And I don't know how you could . . ." He couldn't quite form the word *marry*. "How you could be with someone who'd leave you to save his own skin."

"Your skin's pretty important to me." She let out a breath. "Well, all this detouring has settled me down a little. So there's that. We'll get him, maybe not in time to stop whatever he has planned for tonight or tomorrow. But we'll get him."

"Confidence is good."

"I believe good overcomes evil, especially if good works its ass off. Just like I believe in the sacrament of marriage, and the poetry of baseball. These are constants for me, Bo. Unassailable."

She looked away, felt steadier. "He knows me better than I know him, and that's his advantage. He's had years to study me, to explore my weaknesses. But I'm learning. I want to know why now, why he feels he can or must show me who he is, what he's done. He's got cops up and down the eastern seaboard on his tail. He could have taken me out, or tried, without anyone knowing who or why."

"It wouldn't be as important? He wouldn't be as important?"

"Yes, that's part of it. This is the big bang, what he's been building up to for twenty years. God, what kind of person obsesses over a woman for twenty years? I can't understand it."

"I can." He stayed where he was when she turned back to him. "It's not the same, but I know what it is to have someone get inside you, against all reason, and just get stuck in there. For me, it was magic. For him, it's a sickness. But in a way, for both of us it was a kind of fantasy. It just grew in different directions."

She considered, studied the board. "His was rooted in childhood. His and mine. Rape isn't sexual, it's violence. It's power and control. The fact that he earmarked me, focused on me, tried to rape me wasn't so much about me but about who I was. The youngest daughter—and likely pretty pampered—of the Hale family."

She walked around the board as if to study it from different angles. "Holy family, that's what he said. We were happy, respected, crowded with friends. His family was violent, isolated, and he was the only child. There were others like ours in the neighborhood, but we were more in the forefront because of Sirico's. Everyone knew us. No one really knew them. And I was the closest to his age. His father abused his mother—he in turn learns abuse, directed at women. But his attempt to take power over me, to do violence to me, wasn't just thwarted—and by my younger brother, at that—but its consequences affected the rest of his life. My fault, as he sees it."

She circled the board once more. "But it still doesn't speak to why now, and what next. He's a sociopath. No conscience, no remorse, but he's also self-serving. When something kicks him, he doesn't just kick back, he burns. Something kicked him. Something triggered this. Something pushed him into coming back here and letting me know who he is."

He'd stopped listening. Bo had risen, stepped to the board, and her last few words were just buzzes in his head. "This is him? This is Pastorelli?"

"Junior, yeah."

"I saw him. Twice. I've seen him twice. The first time he was as close as you are."

"When?" she snapped. "Where?"

"The first time it was the Saturday before I had the family dinner deal. I went into the grocery store near a client's to pick up the flowers for your mother. He stood right beside me. Goddamn, I'm stupid!"

"No. Stop. Just tell me what happened. Did he talk to you?"

"Yeah." His hands had balled into fists, but he released them now, went back in his head and told her about the incident as best he remembered.

"Son of a bitch bought red roses."

"He's followed you. Taking the time to surveil. Client's house, grocery store. He'd have gotten a thrill out of talking to you. Made him feel superior, powerful. I need a chalkboard in here. Why didn't I think to buy a chalkboard?"

Instead she dug out a map, pinned it to the back of her corkboard. "Show me the client's house, the store."

She grabbed pushpins, stuck red ones in the two locations he pointed out. "Good. Let me mark where else we know he's been seen." She stuck another red pin into the map on Tony Borelli's street. "Where did you see him the second time?"

"About twenty minutes ago," Bo told her. "Diagonal from Sirico's."

She nearly fumbled the box of pins. "Was he going there?"

"No." He clamped a hand on her shoulder. "He drove off. He was across the street, few houses up the block. When he saw I'd seen him, recognized him from before, he got in his car."

"Make, model."

"Ah . . ." He had to close his eyes, work to bring it back. "Toyota. One of the 4Runners, I think. Dark blue, maybe black. It impinges my masculinity, but I don't actually know every make and model of every available car out there. I made this one because I dated someone who had one. So anyway, I'd sort of half-waved, like you do if you see someone familiar. He drove by, gave me one of these out the window." He made a gun out of his thumb and forefinger. "Said bang, and drove off."

"Ballsy bastard." Her throat was hot and dry at the thought there might have been a gun. "He must've been standing out in front of his own house, watching the shop. He said he's got another surprise planned for me tonight. He's plank stupid if he thinks I'll give him a chance to hit Sirico's."

She stabbed a pin into the map. Temper steadied her nerves. "I need to make some calls."

# 28

There were cops posted at Sirico's, in position to watch the restaurant and the apartment above. There were two more who'd be enjoying her parents' hospitality, and yet others keeping watch on Fran's home. And though Vince had objected, and pointed out his home was protected by state-of-the-art security systems, Reena had men patrolling their grounds.

"He could try for any one of them. Or none of them." She paced the living room. She stopped, stared at her map. "He's going to light a match somewhere tonight."

Bo had hauled her board downstairs at her request. So much for keeping the job and her life separate, she thought, even symbolically. Right now, the job was her life.

Her cell rang in her pocket. She yanked it out. "Hale. Wait." She grabbed a notebook. "Go." And scribbled. "Yeah, yeah, okay. We need to send a unit out to BWI, check long term there. Most logical place for him to ditch one, grab another. Good. Thanks."

She flipped the phone back in her pocket, moved back to the map and used a yellow pin to mark the airport. "Family just got back from a big vacation in Europe. Shuttle out to long-term parking at Kennedy, and their

Jeep Cherokee's gone. Boost that to make the trip south, go see an old pal and get the bum's rush. Maybe you keep it awhile. Going to take a while for them to track it all the way to Maryland. Then you drive it to BWI— maybe Dulles, maybe National, but probably BWI, pick another, do the switch, drive away. You like SUVs. Plenty of room to hold your toys."

"I'm going to go next door and shower, it was hot out there today."

Distracted, she frowned over at Bo. "What?"

"I said I need to go clean up."

"Would you mind cleaning up here? Don't you watch movies? The bad guy always breaks into the house when you're in the shower. Look what happened to Janet Leigh in *Psycho*."

"Janet Leigh's a woman."

"Regardless. I'd appreciate it if you'd grab that shower here. You've got a clean shirt in the laundry room."

"I do?"

"You left one here. It got washed. So, do me a favor, okay?"

"Sure." He put his hands on her shoulders and understood what people meant when they talked of someone coiled like a spring. "Any point in telling you to try to relax?"

"Not one."

"Then I'll go clean up. Look, if some guy dressed in his mother's clothes breaks in, fight him off until I get my pants back on."

"There's a deal."

Alone, she went into the kitchen to get another bottle of water to off-set her intake of caffeine. She saw the bag of takeout he'd set on the counter. No, she couldn't relax, she thought, but she could be grateful. Grateful to have someone who fit so truly into her life.

She was definitely going to marry him, she decided as she took out the plastic containers. He could wriggle on the hook for a while—he was entitled—but she was reeling him in.

It made her laugh to remember buying red shoes with Gina at the mall, and having Gina tell her she was marrying Steve. He just didn't know it yet.

All these years later, she finally understood.

She put the chicken in the oven on warm. A meal would keep her energy up more productively than nerves.

She took the water back into the living room to study the map. "Where are you, Joey?" she asked aloud. "Where are you now?"

T hey look over there, you work over here. It wasn't just timing that counted. It was planning.

Rattled now, sure she was. Thinks I'll come after her mommy and daddy.

Not yet.

Nice little spot, Fells Point. Be nicer yet when it starts to burn.

Cops were so stupid. How many times had he proven that? Maybe they'd tripped him up a couple of times, but he'd been younger then. Besides, he'd learned from it. Lots of time to learn in the joint. Time to plan and imagine, read, study.

He'd honed his computer skills inside. Nothing handier in today's world than strong computer skills. Hacking, searching, cloning phones.

Or finding out where a certain cop's widow lived.

Too bad the other one moved to Florida. He'd deal with that one of these days, but it would've been nice to take out both of the bastards who hauled his father away. Who pulled the man out of his own home, humiliated him.

Humiliated both of them.

It didn't matter that the other cop bastard had already bought it. His widow would do just fine.

He left the car—another Cherokee this time—a block south and walked briskly up the sidewalk like a man with things to do.

He was still wearing jeans, but he'd changed into a blue button-down shirt, sleeves rolled up. He wore Nikes and a black O's fielder's cap. He carried a small backpack and a glossy white florist's box.

She lived alone, Mrs. Thomas bastard Umberio. Deb to her friends. Her daughter lived in Seattle, so was out of the zone for game time. Her son lived in Rockville. He'd been closer to Baltimore, Joey thought, he'd have taken the son instead of the widow. But this was a hometown show, after all.

He knew Deb was fifty-six, taught high school math, drove a 1997 Honda Civic, went to some cunt-gym three times a week after school and closed her bedroom curtains most nights at ten.

Probably so she could masturbate, he thought and strolled into the apartment building, chose the stairs rather than the elevator to take him to the third floor.

There were four apartments to a floor. He'd already done his scope. Not much to worry about, and the old coots directly across the hall went out to dinner early every Wednesday night.

Pays to do your homework, right, teacher? he thought, and knocked cheerfully on Deborah Umberio's door.

She opened the door, keeping the security chain in place so he caught only a slice of her. Brown hair, pointy face, careful eyes.

"Deborah Umberio?"

"That's right."

"Got flowers for you."

"Flowers?" Pink came into her cheeks. Women were so predictable. "Who's sending me flowers?"

"Ah . . ." He turned the box as if reading a label on the side. "Sharon McMasters. Seattle?"

"That's my daughter. Well, what a surprise. Wait just a minute." She shut the door, rattled the chain off, pulled it back open. "What a nice surprise," she repeated, reaching for the box.

He rammed his right fist into her face. As she fell backward, he nipped inside, closed the door, flipped the lock, set the chain.

"It is, isn't it?" he said.

He had plenty to do. Hauling her into the bedroom, stripping her down, tying her up, gagging her. She was out cold, but he punched her again, just to keep her that way for a while longer.

The bedroom curtains were closed a little early tonight, but he didn't think anyone would notice. Or give a rat's ass.

He left her TV going. She'd had the Discovery Channel on—for God's sake—while she worked in the kitchen.

Looked like she'd been making herself a salad. Too lazy to cook, he decided as he poked inside her refrigerator. Well, something would be cooking soon.

He found a bottle of white wine. Cheap shit, but sometimes you had to make do.

He'd learned to like finer wines while working for the Carbionellis. He'd learned a hell of a lot working for the Carbionellis.

He drank the wine with the hard-boiled eggs she'd set out for the salad. Though he had surgical gloves in his backpack, he wasn't worried about fingerprints any longer.

They'd moved past that part of the game.

He riffled through her cupboards, in her freezer. He found several frozen dinners. His initial reaction was disgust, but the picture on the box of the meat loaf and mashed potatoes didn't look half bad.

He popped it in the oven, dumped some Italian dressing on the salad.

While he waited, he surfed channels. Couldn't the stupid bitch spring for more than basic cable? He kept the sound low in case some nosy neighbor came to the door and settled on *Jeopardy!*

*Jeopardy!* ended, *Wheel of Fortune* began while he ate the meat loaf and potatoes.

There was a lot to do, but plenty of time to do it. He caught the low, muffled moaning from the bedroom.

Ignoring it, Joey drank some wine with *Wheel*. "Buy a vowel, you asshole."

He got a sudden, vivid image of his father, kicked back in the living room recliner, drinking a beer and telling some stranger on the game show to *buy a vowel, you asshole.*

It pushed him up, pushed the fury through him, fresh and bright.

He wanted to punch his fist through the TV, slam his foot into it. Nearly did as his brain screamed with the rage.

*Buy a vowel, you asshole,* his father had said, and sometimes, sometimes had shot his son a wide grin.

"When are you gonna get on the show, Joey? When you gonna get on and win us some money? You got more brains in half your head than these cocksuckers."

He murmured the words, remembered the words as he paced the tiny living area, calming himself again.

They'd've been all right, he thought. They'd've come out of the slump and been all right. They'd just needed a little more time. Why didn't they get the time?

Because that little bitch had gone crying to her old man and ruined everything.

It shook his body for a moment. The fury and the grief stormed through him so that his body vibrated and hummed until he got it under control once more.

He picked up the wine, took another long sip.

"All right. Time for work."

A man who loved his work was a prince among men, Joey thought as he flashed on the lights in the darkened bedroom. He smiled at the woman in the bed whose eyes blinked, then widened with terror.

His pal Nick mouthed off about never taking it personally, about remembering it was just business, but he didn't buy that crap. He *always* took it personally. Otherwise, what was the damn point?

He strolled up to the bed while her eyes wheeled toward him. "Hiya, Deb. How's it going? Just want to say that for a woman pushing toward sixty, you're not in bad shape. That's going to make this more pleasant for me."

She was shaking, her body jerking with shudders as if with small electric shocks. Her arms and legs pulled and twisted against the clothesline he'd used to bind her. He was tempted to rip off the duct tape from her mouth, pull the wadding out, just to hear that first bubbling scream.

But there was no point in disturbing the neighbors.

"Well, why don't we get started?" He put his hands on the button of his jeans, watched her head shake frantically, her eyes fill with tears.

God, he *loved* this part.

"Oh, wait, where are my manners? Let me introduce myself. Joseph Francis Pastorelli Junior. You can call me Joey. Your cocksucking husband dragged my father out of our home, put handcuffs on him and pulled him out in front of all the neighbors. Put him in jail for five to seven."

He unbuttoned his jeans now. She was rubbing her wrists raw with the struggles. There'd be some blood in a minute, and that was always satisfying.

"That was twenty years ago. Now, some people might say that's a long time to hold a grudge, but you know something, Deb, some people are assholes. The longer you hold it, the better it feels when you make the fuckers pay."

He unzipped, released himself. Stroked. The sounds she made now were tinny, high-pitched shrieks held in by the wadding and the tape. "The cocksucker you married? He's got to bear part of the blame for all this. Since he's dead—oh, condolences, by the way—you're going to get what was coming to him."

He sat on the side of the bed, making her leg jerk and twist when he patted it. He removed his shoes. "I'm going to rape you, Deb. But you've figured that out already. I'm going to hurt you when I do." He boosted up his hips, pulled down his jeans. "That really adds to it for me, and I'm the one in charge here."

She struggled and wept and bled. He watched her face as long as he could, the bruises and bleeding he'd caused. He saw Reena's face. He always did.

He came hard, with that tinny shriek in his ear.

She was down to mewling whimpers when he rolled away. He used her bathroom, emptied his bladder, cleaned himself up. He didn't care for the smell of sex, that whore smell women coated on a man.

He went out, drank a little more wine, surfed around, found the ball game and watched an inning while he snacked on some Wheat Thins.

Goddamn O's, he thought as they went down in order. Couldn't find the ball if you rammed it up their ass.

When he went back into the bedroom, she was struggling weakly against the bonds. "Okay, Deb, I'm refreshed. Time for round two."

This time he sodomized her.

Her eyes were dull and distant when he was finished. She'd stopped fighting and lay limp. He could probably perk her up for another go, but a man had a schedule to keep, after all.

He showered, humming to himself and using her lime-scented body gel. Dressed, he lined up what he could use from her own kitchen.

Cleaning fluid, rags, candles, waxed paper. No need to make it look like an accident, but no point in being sloppy. A man should take pride in his work.

He snapped on the surgical gloves from his backpack. While he was soaking rags, the phone rang. He paused, waiting, listened to the bright, female voice that came on after the answering machine picked up.

"Hi, Mom. It's just me, checking in. I guess you're out on a hot date." There was a tinkle of laughter. "Give me a call if you don't get home too late. Otherwise, I'll talk to you tomorrow. Love you. Bye."

"Isn't that sweet?" Joey whined as he continued to work. "Yeah, your mom's got a hot one tonight."

He chipped up some of the vinyl tile to expose the subflooring, used the electric screwdriver out of his pack to remove some of the cupboard doors to tent into funnels for flame. He cracked the window for ventilation, set his trailers of rags and loosely crumpled waxed paper.

Satisfied, he carried candles and rags into the bedroom.

She was only half conscious now, but he saw what was left of her go on alert, the fear that leaped into her eyes.

"Sorry, Deb, just don't have time for a third round, so we're going to move straight to the grand finale. Your cocksucking husband ever bring his work home?" he asked, and pulled out a knife.

She went wild—still some life in the old girl yet—when he turned the blade in the light.

"You ever have discussions about how he spent his workday? He ever bring pictures home so you could see what happens to people who burn in bed?"

He brought the knife down, viciously, an inch from her hip. Those hips reared up, and she began to struggle madly, gurgling, air wheezing out her nose, her eyes so wide he wondered they didn't just pop out of her skull like a couple of olives.

He scored the mattress, pulling stuffing free. After replacing his knife, he took a container out of his pack. "I used some of your kitchen supplies in the other room. Hope you don't mind. But in here, I brought my own. A little methyl alcohol. Goes a long way."

He soaked the scattered stuffing, rags, the sheets she'd soiled in terror, drawing them onto the floor, using them and the rags, the rest of the waxed paper as a trailer to her curtains.

He set her lamp on the floor, and whistled between his teeth as he dismantled her bedside table. "Just like making a campfire," he told her as he arranged tepees of wood over the trailers. "See the methyl alcohol, it's got a flash point below a hundred degrees. The pine oil I used in the kitchen, it'll take a lot more heat, closer to two hundred—that's Fahrenheit. But you set it all up right, it'll burn pretty good once it gets going. Out there, that's what we're calling my second wave. What they call a point of origin. In here's the main show, and, Deb, you're the star. Just a couple more details, first."

He picked up her little desk chair and stood on it to open the casing of the bedroom smoke alarm. Unhooked the battery.

Since it was handy, he broke the chair apart, used it to arrange another tent on the mattress.

He stepped back, nodded. "Not bad, not bad at all, if I do say so myself. Damn, getting another woody here." He rubbed his crotch. "Wish I could give you one more taste of it, honey, but I've got places to go."

He arranged books of matches along the trailers, inside the tents, smiled—coolly now—while she twisted, beat her heels against the mattress, strained to scream through the gag.

"Sometimes the smoke gets you first. Sometimes it doesn't. The way I've set this up, you're going to hear your own skin crackling. You're going to smell yourself roasting."

His eyes went flat as a shark's, and just as cold. "They won't get to you in time, Deb. No point in false hope, right? And when you see that cocksucking husband of yours in hell, tell him Joseph Francis Pastorelli Junior sends his best."

He used a long, slim butane lighter—let her see the flame spurt out of it before he set mattress wadding, matchbooks, rags on fire.

He watched it start to smolder and leap, watched it slyly sneak its way along the path he'd provided for it.

He gathered his pack, strolled out and lit his stage in the kitchen. Then he turned on the gas stove, extinguished the pilot and left the door open.

The fire was edging toward her, crawling over the bed like a lover. Smoke rose in sluggish plumes. He stepped around it, opened the window two inches.

For a moment he stood there, watching it circle him, daring him.

He'd loved nothing in his life the way he loved the dance of flame. It tempted him to stay, to watch, to admire, just another minute. Just one more minute.

But he stepped back. The fire was already starting to sing.

"Hear it, Deb? She's alive now. Excited and hungry. Feel her heat? I almost envy you. Almost envy you what you're about to experience. Almost," he said.

And hitching his pack, he picked up the florist's box and slipped out the door.

It was dark now, and fires burned brighter in the dark. This one would. He took a Sirico's takeout menu, dropped it at the front edge of the building.

When he reached his car, he stowed his backpack, the empty florist's box in the cargo area. He checked his watch, calculated the time, then took a leisurely drive around the block.

He could see the whiffs of smoke finding their escape from the window he'd opened, and the sparkle of flame just rising up, seeking the air he'd provided.

He dialed Reena's number. He kept it short this time, simply rattled off the address. He tossed the phone out the window and drove toward home.

He had work to do.

The war was being fought when Reena arrived. Arcs of water hurled against the building, battled the bright flames that shot out of windows. Firefighters carried people out of the building while still others dragged hoses in.

She grabbed a helmet out of her trunk and shouted at Bo over the sounds of battle. "Stay back. Stay way back until I get a handle on the situation."

"There are people in there this time."

"They'll get them out. That's what they do." She raced over, around barricades that were still being set up. Through the haze of smoke, she spotted the company commander barking into a two-way.

"Detective Hale, arson unit. I called it in. Give me the status."

"Third floor, southeast corner. Evacuation and suppression. Black smoke, active flames on arrival. Three of my men just went in the door of the involved unit. We've got—"

The explosion blasted out, punching through the wall of noise. Glass and brick rained down, lethal missiles battering cars, the street, people.

She threw up an arm to shield her face and saw the sword of fire stab through the roof.

Men rushed the building, charging into the holocaust.

"I'm certified," Reena shouted. "I'm going in."

The commander shook his head. "One more civilian reported inside. Nobody else goes in until I know the status of my men." He held her off, snapping orders, questions into his two-way.

The voice that crackled on reported two men down.

The night was full of the fire, the power of it, the terrible beauty. She stood, as mesmerized as she was horrified as it danced out of wood and brick, toward the sky.

She knew how it capered inside that wood and brick, flying, consuming, lashing back at those who tried to kill it. It roared and it whispered, it slithered and it flashed.

How much would it destroy? Flesh and bone as well as wood and brick, before it was tamed. This time.

The third floor collapsed with a sound like thunder and opened the gateway for the fire to soar.

Men stumbled out of the building with their fallen comrades on their backs. And paramedics dashed forward.

She moved forward with the commander toward one of the men taking long hits of oxygen through a mask. The man shook his head.

"Bitch was in flashover. We got in. Victim on the bed. Gone. Already gone. We laid down a line of suppression, and it blew. Carter took the worst. He took the worst. Jesus, I think he's dead. Brittle's bad, but I think Carter's dead."

Reena looked up at the sound of more thunder. More of the roof going, she thought dully. And most of the floor under the apartment he'd chosen.

Who had he killed tonight? Who had he burned to death?

She crouched down, touched a hand to the shoulder of the firefighter who dropped his head to his knees. "I'm Reena," she said. "Reena Hale. Arson unit. What's your name?"

"Bleen. Jerry Bleen."

"Jerry, I need you to tell me what you saw in there while it's fresh in your mind. Give me everything you can."

"I can tell you somebody set that bitch." He lifted his head. "Somebody set her."

"Okay. You went in the southeastern apartment, third floor."

"Through the door. Brittle, Carter, me."

"Was the door closed?"

He nodded. "Unlocked, hot to the touch."

"Could you tell if there'd been forced entry?"

"No sign, none I saw. We hit the room with a stream. Bedroom on the . . . the left, fully engaged, kitchen straight back, thick black smoke. He'd set chimneys."

"Where?"

"I saw one in the kitchen, maybe two. Window was open. Me and Brittle, we swung toward the bedroom. The whole room was going. I could see the body on the bed. Crisped. Then it blew. From the kitchen. I smelled the gas, and it blew. And Carter . . ."

She closed a hand over his. And, sitting with him, watched the men surround and drown the lethal beauty of the fire.

Her shoes crunched broken glass when she rose, walked over to meet O'Donnell. "He killed two this time. One civilian inside the apartment he used as point of origin, and a firefighter who was killed in the explosion, probably gas from the stove. He timed it, timed it to call me so by the time the fire department arrived on scene, it would already be fully involved."

"Reena." He waited until she turned away from the belching smoke, the stubborn tongues of flame. "Deb Umberio lives at this address."

"Who?" She rubbed the back of her neck, struggled to place the name. When it hit, her heart slammed her ribs. "Umberio? Relation to Detective Umberio?"

"His widow. Tom died a couple years ago. Car wreck. That was Deb's apartment."

"God. Oh God." She pressed her hands to her eyes. "Alistar? What about his partner, Detective Alistar?"

"In Florida. Retired, moved there six months ago. I've put a call in to him, gave him a heads-up."

"Good, okay, good, then we . . . Oh sweet Jesus. John."

She was already fumbling out her phone when O'Donnell clamped her arm. "He's okay. I got him on his cell. Some lucky bug crawled up his butt and told him to drive to New York tonight, check up on Pastorelli in person. He's okay, Hale, and since he's already on the turnpike, he's going to follow this through. We've got a unit going by his place, just in case. Check it out."

"We'll want to put a net over his social worker from back then, the court psychologist, hell, the family court judge. Anybody who had a piece of this. But I think he'll be concentrating on those who had any part in taking his father down. I need my family protected."

"We've got that. We'll stay on that until we've got him."

"I'm going to call home—I mean my parents and the rest—just clear that out of my head first."

"You do that. I'll talk to some of the tenants, see who saw what."

Once she'd made her calls, she walked back to where Bo waited. "He killed two people tonight."

"I saw them take that firefighter away." In a body bag, he thought. "I'm sorry."

"The woman he killed was the widow of one of the detectives who arrested his father for the fire at Sirico's. He's made his big move now, he's opened the field. It doesn't matter that we know who's done this. It doesn't matter to him that we know why. It just matters that he can do it. I'm going to ask you to do me a favor."

"Name it."

"Don't go home. Call Brad, stay with him tonight. Or Mandy. Or my parents."

"How about a compromise? I won't go home. I'll wait for you."

"This is going to take hours, and you can't help me here. You can take my car. I'll ride with O'Donnell. Do me a favor, okay?"

"One condition. When you're done, you don't go home either. Not without calling me first so I can meet you there."

"All right, that's fair."

She leaned against him for a moment, let herself be held.

An ambulance whizzed by, sirens screaming. On its way to take someone toward help, maybe comfort. She walked back through the smoke and into the weeping.

# 29

The heat hung, a curtain soaked in sweat, when John threaded through the unfamiliar streets of the Bronx. The call from O'Donnell had changed his plans to find a motel off the turnpike, get some sleep and track down Joe Pastorelli in the morning.

Even with the map he'd printed off the Internet, he'd made a couple of wrong turns. His own fault, he admitted, shifting to find comfort behind the wheel after four hours in the car.

Getting old, he mused. Old and creaky. His eyes weren't as good for driving at night—and when the hell had that happened?

Used to be he could work forty-eight hours straight on a couple of catnaps and coffee. Used to be he *had* work that could keep him going two days straight, he reminded himself. Those days were gone.

Retirement wasn't a reward at the end of a well-run career, not in his mind. In his mind, it was a void surrounded by endless dull hours, haunted by memories of the work.

It was probably foolish to have driven all this way, but Reena had come to him, asked for help. That was a hell of a lot more to him than a gold watch and a pension.

Still, his eyes were gritty from the strain by the time he found the right street, and his head was aching when he searched out a parking lot.

The walk from the lot to the address he had on Pastorelli worked out the kinks in his legs, but did nothing for the dull pain in his lower back. Sweat clung to him like a second skin. He stopped at a Korean grocer's, bought a bottle of water and a pack of Excedrin. He downed two on the sidewalk, watched a hooker on the corner come to terms with a john and slide into his car. Wanting to avoid the others still hawking their wares, he cut across the street.

Pastorelli's building was a low-rise, its bricks scarred and smoked from time and generations of exhaust. His name was printed beside a first-floor apartment. John pushed buttons for third- and fourth-floor apartments, then opened the door when some cooperative soul buzzed him in.

If the air outside had been a steam bath, inside was a closed box baked in a high oven. The headache traveled from the back of his eyes up into his skull.

He could hear the TV through Pastorelli's door clearly enough to make out some dialogue. He recognized *Law & Order,* and had the sudden, uncomfortable flash that if he hadn't taken this impulsive trip north, he'd be sitting alone in a darkened room watching the same damn thing.

If it was Pastorelli watching justice climb the slippery rope of the law, he sure as hell hadn't been in Maryland playing with fire ninety minutes before.

He balled his fist, thumped the side of it on the door.

He'd thumped a second, then a third time before the door creaked open on the chain.

Wouldn't have recognized you, Joe, he thought. Would've passed you on the street without a glance. The tough, handsome face had devolved into a hollow-eyed, jaundiced skull with skin bagging at the jowls as if it had melted off the bone and pooled there.

He smelled cigarettes and beer, with something soft, like rotted fruit, underlying it.

"What the hell you want?"

"Want to talk to you, Joe. I'm John Minger, from Baltimore."

"Baltimore." A dim light bloomed in those sunken eyes. "Joey sent you?"

"Yeah, you could say that."

The door shut, the chain rattled. "He send money?" Pastorelli asked when he opened the door. "He's supposed to send some money."

"Not this time."

A couple of fans stirred the stale heat and spread the smell of smoke and beer, and that underlying stench.

John recognized it now. Not just old man, not just old, sick man. It was old, dying man.

A black leather recliner sat like a man in a tuxedo at a homeless shelter. The rickety TV tray beside it held a can of Miller, an overflowing ashtray, the remote for the TV that looked as shiny and out of place as the recliner. With them were bottles of medication.

A sofa held together by dust and duct tape was pushed against the wall. The counters in the kitchenette were spotted with grease and layered with boxes from various takeout and deliveries. John could see the menu for the last few days had included Chinese, pizza, Subway.

A roach strolled across the pizza box, obviously at home.

"How do you know Joey?" Pastorelli demanded.

"You don't remember me, Joe? Why don't we sit down?"

The man looked like he needed to, John thought. He wasn't sure how he managed to move the bag of bones he'd become without rattling. John took the single chair—a metal folding type—and pulled it opposite the recliner.

"Joey's supposed to send money. I gotta have money, pay the rent." He sat, picked up a pack of cigarettes. John watched the bony fingers fish one out, fight to light a match.

"When did you see him last?"

"Couple months maybe. Bought me a new TV. That's a thirty-six-inch, flat screen. Fucking Sony. He don't buy cheap."

"Nice."

"Got me this chair last Christmas. Son of a bitch vibrates, you want it to." Those dead eyes latched on to John's face. "He's supposed to send money."

"I haven't seen him, Joe. Fact is, I'm looking for him. Talk to him lately?"

"What's this about? You a cop?" He shook his head slowly. "You ain't no cop."

"No, I'm not a cop. It's about fire, Joe. Joey's got himself in a real fix down in Baltimore. That keeps up, he won't be sending you any money."

"You looking to get my boy in trouble?"

"Your boy's in trouble. He's been lighting fires back home, back in the neighborhood. He killed somebody tonight, Joe. He killed the widow of one of the arson investigators who helped put you away for the Sirico fire."

"Bastards dragged me out of my own house." He blew out smoke, hacked until his sunken eyes watered. "Out of my own house." He picked up the beer, sipped and hacked some more.

"How long did they give you, Joe? How long do you have left?"

When he grinned, he looked like a nightmare. "Asshole doctors said I'd be dead already. Here I am, so what the fuck do they know? I beat 'em."

"Joey know you're sick?"

"Took me to the doctor a couple times. They wanted to put poison in me. Screw that. Cancer, pancreas. Said the cancer's eating up my liver and shit now, too, and how I can't drink, can't smoke." Still grinning with that death's head, he sucked on the cigarette. "Fuck them, fuck them all."

"Joey went back to clean things up, finish things off for you."

"Don't know what you're talking about."

"Take care of the people who screwed with you. Especially Catarina Hale."

"Little slut. Sashaying around the neighborhood like she's better than anybody else. Teasing my boy. So he tried to get a piece, so what? That asshole Hale thinks he can mess with me and mine? Showed him."

"You paid for it."

"Ruined my life." The grin melted away. "That asshole Hale ruined my life. Couldn't get a decent job after. Mopping up other people's puke, for chrissake. Took my dignity's what he did. Took my life away. I got sick 'cause of being in prison, no matter what the fuckhead doctors say. Probably pass this on to Joey, good chance of it. All because of that little whore."

John decided not to point out you couldn't catch pancreatic cancer in prison. And if you could, you couldn't pass it on to your son.

"Pisser, all right. I guess Joey felt that way, too."

"He's my son, isn't he? He respects his father. Knows it's not my fault he maybe got the cancer genes offa me. He's got brains. Joey's always had brains. He didn't get them from his stupid bitch of a mother. He's going to send me some money, maybe take me on a trip so I can get out of this godforsaken heat."

He closed his eyes a moment as he turned his face toward one of the fans. His wispy hair stirred in the stale breeze. "Going to Italy, up north, in the mountains where it's cool. He's got something going, the cops'll never take him for it. He's too smart."

"He burned a woman to death in her own bed tonight."

"Maybe he did, maybe he didn't." But the sudden light in those eyes showed a father's horrible pride. "If he did, she must've had it coming."

"If he gets in touch with you, Joe, do yourself a favor." John took out a notebook, wrote down his name and number. "Give me a call. You help me find him, it'll be better for him. Cops do, I can't promise what'll happen. He killed a cop's wife. You call me, Joe, and maybe I can fix it so you get a little money."

"How much money?"

"Couple hundred," John said as his gut roiled with disgust. "Maybe more."

He rose, put the number on the tray table. "He's pushing his luck, I promise you."

"You got brains, you don't need luck."

While John was driving out of the Bronx, Joey picked the lock on the rear door of his row house. A couple of stops along the way, and he was right on schedule.

He imagined the cop's wife roasting like a suckling pig, and the image made him smile as he finessed the locks.

Places to go, he'd told her. Yeah, he had places to go. And people to burn. Big-nosed John Minger was on his short list.

He slipped in the back, took the snub-nosed .22 out of his pack. He'd shoot him first. Kneecap him. Then they'd have a little talk while he set the fire.

Going to keep the city's heroes busy tonight, he thought and worked his way carefully through the darkened house.

Old man was probably in bed already. Already sawing them off this time of night.

He'd rather be dead than old.

Age wouldn't be a problem for Minger much longer. He'd be dead, the whole fucking slew of them would be dead before his father bought it. That was justice.

They'd killed his father sure as if they'd carved him open with a knife. Every mother's son of them was going to pay for it.

He made his way upstairs, excitement and pleasure building. In the knees, he thought again. Pop, pop! See how he liked it.

See how he liked watching the fire claw across the bed toward him. See how he liked having it eat at him the way the cancer was eating at his father.

He wasn't going down that way. No fucking way. Joseph Pastorelli's boy, Joey, wasn't going by cancer.

Things to do, he thought again, a lot of things to do before he walked into the fire and ended it.

When Minger was done, it'd be time to move on to the main attractions. The night was young yet.

But he slipped into and searched every room, and didn't find his prey.

His finger vibrated on the trigger, his hand shook with the effort of resisting the urge to fire into the empty bed.

Went out to watch the cop's bitch burn, that's what he did. People like to watch. Reena probably called crying to him, so he went to hold her hand.

Probably banged her plenty over the years.

He could wait a little bit. Yeah, the night was young, so he could spare a little time. Get him when he got home. Just wait like a cat at the rat hole.

He'd just put the wait time to good use and set things up.

Smoke still curtained the room, and her boots squished in the wet of the bedroom carpet as Reena looked down on the remains of Deborah Umberio.

The sodden remains of the charred mattress told the tale.

"She burned where she lay," O'Donnell said. "Right into the padding."

Peterson, the ME in a short-sleeved shirt and khakis, waited while Reena took digitals. "Could have been dead before he lit the room. Or unconscious. I'll let you know what we find. We'll move on this right away."

"She wouldn't have been dead, or unconscious." Reena lowered the camera. "He'd have wanted her alive and aware. He'd want her to know what was coming. To feel it. That would feed him. He'd have tortured her first, he'd need to. He'd have made her suffer first."

She drew a breath. "Because she was a woman, he'd have taken his time with her. It makes him feel more important, more virile. With his history of sexual assault, he probably raped her."

"Traces of what looks like cloth inside her mouth." Peterson leaned over the body, close. "Indicate she was gagged."

"She opened the door to him." Like Josh, she thought. "Why? She was a cop's wife for what, thirty years, and she opens the door to a strange man? He had a pass—delivery, maintenance. Someone had to see him come into the building. Canvass has to turn up something, someone."

"We'll start working through the layers here," O'Donnell told her, and she nodded.

"You can see what he did. Used a flammable, focused on the bed, then set trailers around the room, built his chimneys to punch it all up. He didn't need the other point of origin in the kitchen to kill her. That was for us. That was for the firefighters who responded. Why not take out a couple of them, too? More bang for the buck."

She stepped carefully through and around debris, looked toward the kitchen. A pot lid protruded from a wall. Wet dripped down it, and from the jags of ceiling that remained. The street-facing wall was all but gone. Some of the charred remains of cupboards were missing doors. Moving in, crouching down, she used a light and magnifying glass.

"These doors didn't burn, or blow, O'Donnell. He unscrewed them, used them for his chimneys, for fuel. He's inventive." Frowning, she looked back at her partner. "But would he come in empty-handed, trust that she had everything he'd need for the job? He'd need rope, an inflammable of his choice, matches, maybe a weapon. Means a bag, a briefcase, a duffel. Something."

She straightened, pulled out her ringing phone.

"It's John," she told O'Donnell.

"Go ahead. I'll get the team started in here."

They started the grids and the photographs.

"Pastorelli's dying." Reena pinched the bridge of her nose. "Pancreatic cancer. He told John he hasn't seen Joey for a couple of months, that he's supposed to send money. Something about them taking a trip soon, to Italy."

"That's why he's escalated."

"His father's dying. He can't let that go unsung. And from what John got out of the interview, Senior may have convinced his boy that he's going to face the same fate. Joey wants me to know who's doing this, who's coming for me because it's a tribute to his father—and Jesus, maybe a kind of suicide mission. He's still the boy running after the police car, after his father."

"So he figures if they live, he can get them both out of the country after he's done here? Take his revenge, pay his tribute, whatever he wants to call it, then hide out in Italy?"

"Not hide out. He wouldn't think of it as hiding out. That would make him weak." She rubbed at her stinging eyes. "Getting away with it, that's different. Enjoying the high life somewhere—for the time he thinks they have left—thumbing his nose at what he's left behind. He had money last December. He could have used some of that for fake passports, for transportation, for a place overseas. He might have friends or a connection there. Pastorelli said northern Italy, up in the mountains. We can start working that. But he's not going to get that far."

She looked around at the steam and the rubble, the ruin. "I'm not going to let him get that far."

"Is John looking to stay on Pastorelli in New York?"

"No, he doesn't think he can get more there. He's heading home. I nagged at him to get a room for the night instead of trying to drive all the way back. He sounded beat."

He waited until midnight, then thought, What the fuck. He could come back for the old bastard another time. He could leave him a nice surprise, then take him out some other time.

He'd seen the cops come to the front and back doors, and he'd seen them drive away. Doing a check, getting a lay of the land. So maybe it was best to do a little work, and move on to the next.

He'd already primed the bedroom, the one where he'd found clothes in the closet. He used some of them to make trailers. Mattress stuffing—something he thought of as a trademark now. Waxed paper, methyl alcohol. Might as well sign the portrait, he thought.

Though it would be fun to spread things out through the house, it was quicker—and just as effective—to concentrate on the one room.

He'd found family photographs. These he broke out of their frames and scattered. Maybe he'd move on the real thing one of these days. You take my family, I take yours.

But for now, he struck flame, watched it come to life.

On the way out, he laid a paper takeout napkin with Sirico's cheerful logo on the kitchen counter.

Reena worked in the bedroom, teasing out liquid that had pooled in the cracks of the floor, settled under the remains of the baseboard. She bagged traces of trailers that hadn't burned to ash, took samples of the ash itself.

Trippley came and crouched beside her. "We found some hair in the shower drain. Might be his."

"Good. Good. We get his DNA on scene, it'll wrap him like a bow."

"We've got glass fragments from a wine bottle in the living area. Might get prints."

There was something else, Reena thought as she paused. Something in his tone. "What is it?"

"They found a Sirico's takeout menu outside."

Her fingers curled, then released. "I wondered where he'd put it." Eyes grim, she got back to work. "Delivery. Could've posed as a delivery guy. Not food. She wouldn't let him in. Package? She'd have to have ordered something. What would . . ." Flowers, she decided, remembering Bo's brush with him at the supermarket. "Maybe flowers."

She tilted her head back. "Why does a veteran cop's wife open the door to a stranger? Because he's delivering flowers. We need to ask the neighbors, the people in neighboring buildings if they saw a guy carrying a florist's box in addition to the duffel or briefcase idea."

"I'll get that going."

They both looked as O'Donnell moved into the room. "He hit again. Engines are responding to a fire at John Minger's."

"He's not there." Reena got shakily to her feet. "He can't be there yet, even if he drove straight back."

"Go," Trippley told her. "We'll stay with this."

She moved quickly, stripping off her protective gloves on the way out. "If he's trying to push this through tonight, he may go for my parents, my brother or sisters."

"They're covered, Hale."

"Yeah." But she made a rapid series of calls anyway.

"Don't leave the house," she told her father. "Nobody leaves the house. I'm on my way to John's now. I don't want anyone stepping foot out of the house until I say different. I'm going to get back to you as soon as I can."

She hung up before he could argue. "He isn't staying around here. Maybe in the county, but not in the city. Maybe down in D.C."

"We've got cops flashing his picture at hotels, motels. It's a lot to cover."

"He'd go for high end. He's not tapped out, and he thinks ahead. He's got ID, he's got a credit card to match it. Playing the traveling exec, maybe. A few days at one location, move to another."

She popped out of the car when O'Donnell braked behind the engine. There was a clenched fist in place of her heart, though she could see the fire was contained, nearly suppressed.

She moved quickly toward Steve. "Gas lines?"

"No leaks. Word is the fire was contained in the bedroom. Smoke alarm deactivated. Woman out walking her dog saw the smoke, called it in."

"Where is she?"

"Right over there. Nancy Long."

"Nancy? Gina and I went to school with her." Finding her in the crowd, Reena walked over. Nancy held her excited terrier on a leash with one hand and her husband's arm with the other.

"Nancy."

"Reena. God this is awful! But they said Mr. Minger wasn't home. Nobody was inside. I saw smoke. Susie was making such a fuss I gave up and took her for a walk. She was just peeing when I looked up. Maybe I smelled it, I don't know, but I looked up and I saw smoke coming out of the window. I didn't know what to do, I guess I panicked. I ran over and beat on Mr. Minger's door, shouted for him. Then I ran home. I couldn't even dial nine-one-one my hands were shaking so hard. I had to yell for Ed to do it."

"You might have saved John's house. And if he had been inside, you might have saved his life."

"I don't know. I'm just sick about it."

"Did you see anyone else? Someone out walking, someone driving away?"

"No. I didn't see anyone, not then."

"Not then?"

"I mean, there was nobody out walking around except me."

"Maybe you saw someone earlier?"

"Housetraining a new puppy means you're outside a lot. Before we went to bed I took Susie for what I thought was our last walk of the night. I was just opening the door to go in, and I saw this guy walk by. But that was earlier, near to midnight, I think."

"You didn't recognize him?"

"No. I wouldn't have paid any attention, except he glanced over when I spoke to Susie, and he kind of waved. And I thought, I wonder who's getting lucky tonight?"

"Lucky?"

"He had one of those long white flower boxes, and I thought how Ed never brings me flowers anymore."

"This was around midnight?"

"Right around."

"I'm going to show you a picture, Nancy."

Reena stood in John's kitchen, stared at the Sirico's takeout napkin on the counter. She put the evidence marker in its place, then bagged it.

"John's on his way back." O'Donnell closed his phone. "It'll take him two, three hours. You want to get started on this or wait until he gets here?"

"Can you handle this for now? I want to check on my family, then get the samples we've got so far in."

"Take a uniform."

"That's my plan. He could've waited on this. Given it another day or two, made sure John was home. Having us scramble tonight was more important. He was just waiting for me to click to who he is."

"There's a unit sitting on your house now, men front and back."

She managed a smile. "That's going to piss him off." Her belly tightened when her phone rang. "Hale."

"Too bad he wasn't home. He'd be frying now."

She signaled O'Donnell. "That must've been a disappointment to you, Joey."

"Hell, the cop's bitch was enough for tonight. I thought of you when I was doing her, Reena. Every time I raped her, I was thinking of you. You get your messages?"

"Yeah, I got them."

"That's your dad's face in the lame chef's hat, isn't it? Your sexy old lady drew it." He laughed when she said nothing. "There's another one waiting for you. At your brother's clinic. Better hurry."

"God. Goddamn it." She cleared the call, hit 911. "The clinic where my brother and his wife work. Two blocks away."

"I'll drive." O'Donnell rushed out the door with her.

The Sirico's wine list was in the gutter, and the building up in flames.

"I'm suiting up." She popped the trunk, pulled out her gear. "Help with suppression."

"Reena."

The surprise of hearing him use her first name stopped her. "You've been going what, closing on eighteen hours? Let the engine company handle it."

"He's running us in circles, spreading us thin." She slammed the trunk. "He can't hit Sirico's or me or my family directly, so he does this. Just pissing on me."

She stood, the helmet dangling from her fingers and the fire dancing in front of her. "He's caught now," she stated firmly. "He's caught in it. He can't stop, how can he stop? It's hypnotizing. It's so compelling."

"What else is there for him to hit? Everything left is under guard."

Smoke brought tears to her eyes. "The school, then Bo—but Bo was just, I think, a moment of opportunity. Giving me a little tune-up. Umberio's wife, then John. Now Xander."

"Working his way to you."

"I'm the finish line. It's all payback, but it's not in order. Xander should've come after the school. Xander was the next step, then my father, then the restaurant, and so on. So he's bouncing, but it's still a pattern."

"His old house. It plays," O'Donnell added when Reena turned to stare at him. "They come to get his father there, he never comes back. He gets pulled out of the house himself by his mother."

She tossed the helmet into the car. "This time I'll drive."

# 30

Flames licked out of the windows on the second and third floors of the house that had once been the Pastorellis'. There were no alarms, no screams, no crowds. There was only the fire, torching in the dark.

"Call it in!" she shouted to O'Donnell, and grabbed her helmet, raced to the trunk for gear. "There are people in there. Two—probably second-floor bedroom. I'm going in."

"Wait for the squad."

She pulled on turnout gear. "I've got to try. They could be alive, restrained. I'm not going to let someone else burn to death tonight."

She grabbed a fire extinguisher, heard in some part of her brain O'Donnell's voice clipping out the situation and address. He was right behind her as she raced up the steps.

"He could be in there." O'Donnell's weapon was in his hand. "I've got your back."

"Take the first floor," she snapped back. "I'm going up."

He'd left the door off the latch, she saw. Like an invitation to come on in, make yourself at home. She locked eyes with O'Donnell, nodded, then shoved through the door.

There was light, the backwash from the street, silver slivers of moon. Shadows and silhouettes that were furniture and doorways, all swept with eyes and weapons while her heart galloped at the base of her throat.

And there was ice in her belly as she raced up the steps where smoke bloomed along the ceiling.

It gathered, that smoke, thickened and boiled in a filthy brew as she climbed. The sound of the fire was like a roll of raging surf that she knew could become a tidal wave. She tested a closed door for heat, found it cool. After a quick sweep, she continued down the hall.

Fire danced on the ceiling over her head, surrounded the door like a golden frame. It licked slyly at her boots.

She heard her own muffled cry of fear as she swept foam over flame. There were screams now, but of sirens. No one answered her shouts. She gathered her courage, her breath, and ran through the wall of fire.

The room was blazing, a small mouth of hell. Fire plumed from the floor, clawed up the dresser where a vase of flowers was already engulfed. For a heartbeat she stood surrounded by it, its brilliance and fantastic heat, the colors and movement and power.

Her weapons were so small, pathetic she knew, against the sheer passion of it. And she was already, pitifully, too late.

He hadn't lit the bed. He'd saved that for her, had wanted her to see.

He'd arranged them, of course. After he'd shot them, he propped them both up so they seemed to be watching. A captive audience to the fire's majesty.

She moved. Part of her mind stayed rooted to the spot, appalled and fascinated. But she moved, rushing the bed, risking the burn. She had to be sure. Had to be sure she was too late.

"Get back! Get clear!"

She turned at O'Donnell's shout. Part of her mind registered him standing in the doorway, framed by the violent dance of flames. His face was stained with sweat and smoke, but his eyes were clear and hard.

He'd holstered his gun and held instead a home fire extinguisher.

"They're dead." She shouted it over the roar and spit of flame, but heard the dullness in her own voice. "He killed them in their own bed."

His eyes held hers another moment, that flash of understanding that was rage and disgust. "We save what we can." He lifted the tank. "That's the job." And pulled the pin.

The explosion knocked her off her feet, kicked her onto the bed so she lay across the dead. For an instant her mind was stunned, unable to comprehend.

Then she was screaming her partner's name, dragging the bloody sheet from the bed and rolling through the fire, through the door.

She knew he was gone, knew it, even as she threw the sheet and her own body over the fire that buried him.

Water gushed behind her, drowning fire, as others ran into her personal hell.


He knew I'd go up first." Reena sat on the curb. She'd shoved aside the oxygen mask Xander had pushed on her. "Those people up there, they were nothing to him. That's why he shot them instead of giving them to the fire. They meant nothing. But he knew I'd go up first."

"There was nothing you could do, Reena. Nothing you could change."

"He killed my partner." She squeezed her eyes shut, pressed her face to her knees. She would always, always, see him burning, his torn body engulfed.

*That's the job.* The last words he'd spoken. Now she wondered if she had it in her to do the work that had killed him. Grief and guilt filled her belly.

"The bastard knew I'd go up first, to the fire. He rigged that home extinguisher, figuring O'Donnell—or someone—would grab it, use it. In the kitchen, probably in the kitchen. Plain sight. You go with instinct. You grab it, you use it. If I'd waited to go in—"

"You know better than that." Xander gripped her shoulders, lifted until their eyes met. "You know better than *if*, Catarina. You did what you had to do, and so did O'Donnell. There's only one person to blame here."

She looked back toward the house. The war still raged, but she was just one more casualty. She'd lost her partner up in that room. She'd lost her heart, and she was afraid she'd lost her nerve there as well.

"He only killed them to show me he could. He only killed them so I would see. O'Donnell, he was just icing. Fucking bastard."

"You need rest, Reena. You need sleep. I'm going to take you to Mama's, give you a sedative."

"No, you're not." She rested her forehead on her knees again, struggled with tears she was afraid would never stop if she shed the first of them. She wanted her anger, wanted to feel it burn through her blood, but could only struggle with an awful, demoralizing grief.

They were young, she thought. Younger than she. He'd killed them cold and quick in their own bed, then posed them like dolls.

The image of it would haunt her for the rest of her life. Just as the image of a good man, a good cop, a good friend, covered with flames would haunt her.

She lifted her head again, looked into her brother's eyes. "I told you to stay inside. I told you it was important you stay inside."

It could've been her brother, she thought. Her mother, sister, father. That was Joey's message to her with O'Donnell's death. He could have chosen anyone, and still could.

"I'm the least of your worries." Xander cupped her cheek. "One of the cops took An and the baby to Mama's. We've got our own personal police force at this point."

He'd touched her face then, too, she remembered. Twenty years before, when she'd lain stunned and crying after Joey's attack. Her brother had touched her face. He'd smelled of grape Popsicle.

The grief in her heart poured out into her throat, her eyes. "Xander. He burned your clinic."

He lowered his brow to hers now, and her arms went around him. "It's okay. It's going to be okay."

"Oh God, Xander. He burned you out. He'll come after you, after all of you if we don't stop him. O'Donnell was the next thing to family. He knew that. He had no part in what happened twenty years ago. His connection to me, not revenge, is why he's dead. I don't know how to stop this. I'm scared to death."

The shaking started in her toes, worked its way up so she gripped his hands as if to keep herself from shaking to pieces. "I don't know what to do. Xander, I don't know what to do next."

"We need to go home. We just need—"

He broke off, and both of them looked over as Bo pushed and shoved his way through people and barricades, shouting for her. She gained her feet, teetered a bit until Xander steadied her.

"Wait here. I'll get him."

"No." Reena trained her eyes on Bo. "I can't just sit anymore."

She moved as quickly as she could, but it was like swimming through syrup as Bo struggled with two uniformed cops who restrained him.

"He's with me. It's okay. He's with—"

Bo broke free, smothering the rest of her words as he grabbed her up. "They said you went in." His arms locked around her, stole her air. "They said you went inside. They said a cop went down. Are you hurt?" He yanked her back, his hands running over her. "Are you hurt?"

"No. O'Donnell." Her vision blurred with tears. "He . . . he's dead. He's dead. Joey rigged an extinguisher, it blew up in his hands. It blew up, and the fire . . . I couldn't save him."

"O'Donnell?" She saw the fear in his eyes go to grief. "Oh Jesus. Jesus, Reena." He dragged her close, held hard. "I'm sorry, I'm sorry. Oh God, Mrs. M."

"What?"

"His sister." He rocked her as they stood there, in the street, with death and smoke everywhere. "Reena, I'm sorry. I'm sick and I'm sorry." And so glad it wasn't you. Relief tangled with grief had him clutching her tighter. "What can I do?"

"There's nothing." The dullness was creeping back. The empty sorrow. "He's gone."

"You're not." He drew her back to look at her face. "You're alive. You're here."

"I can't think. I don't even know if I can feel. I'm just—"

He cut her off again, this time blocking words with his mouth on hers. "Yes, you can. You'll think and you'll feel, and you'll do what you have to do." He pressed his lips to her forehead. "That's all there is."

We save what we can, she thought. And with that, she found her balance.

"You level me out, Goodnight," she murmured.

"What?"

She shook her head. "What are you doing out here? Running down the street like a crazy person. Doesn't anyone listen to me?"

He kept touching her, her hair, her face, her hands. "I'm younger and faster than your father. I got by the cops at the house. He didn't."

"Hell." She turned, studied the scene.

The fire would take the top two floors. It would nibble at the neighboring houses, scar lives. But it wouldn't take any more tonight, not here. And it was done with her, for now.

That's the job, O'Donnell had said. It was her job to *do* something. To study, observe, dissect. To find the why and the who, not to sit on the curb and shake with shock and grief.

"Give me a minute." She squeezed Bo's arm, walked back to Younger, who'd come when the news of O'Donnell's death had hit. "I'm going to go reassure my family, check in there. If he calls again, I'll let you know."

"Took one of ours now." His face was cold as winter. "Took a cop. A good cop." He looked up at the sky. "He's walking dead now."

"Yeah. But he may not be done with us. We've covered everything. I want to clean up." She unfastened her jacket. "Clean up, clear my head. If you want to do the same, stay close, you can use the facilities at my parents'."

"I may take you up on it. Captain's on his way. I'll update him, post guards."

"Appreciate it."

He put a hand on her arm as she turned. "He was a step ahead of us, Hale. He, by God, won't stay that way."

Couldn't he? Reena thought. He was a fucking cobra, just as patient, just as lethal. He could go under, go into the wind for years and slither back out whenever he wanted.

She took a last look at the house as she walked away. No, that was wrong thinking, that was exhaustion and discouragement thinking. He'd gone too far to stop now, to wait now. He was too close to the goal for a frigging time-out.

She locked her things in the trunk.

"Detective Younger may come up when he's finished here. John's on his way back from New York."

"What was he doing in New York?" Bo reached for her hand, linked fingers.

"Looking up Joe Pastorelli. He's got pancreatic cancer. He's terminal."

"Hard way to go." Xander flanked her other side. "Is he in treatment?"

"Didn't sound like it, and it may be Joey figures he's got tumors ticking away like little time bombs inside himself."

"Is it genetic?" Bo asked.

"I don't know." Fatigue weighed on her like a cairn. "I don't know. Xander?"

"Under ten percent of the cases are hereditary. Smoking's the leading cause."

"There's some irony for you. Smoke, fire, death. In any case, I'll get the details when John gets back. What it tells us is this is most likely what set Joey off, pushed him to finish things up. Look, I'm going to run home, get some fresh clothes."

"I'll go with you."

"There are cops on the house, Bo."

"I'll go with you," he repeated and walked around to get in her car.

She rolled her eyes. "Get in," she ordered her brother. "I'll drop you at Mama's. Nobody walks around alone tonight. Tell them I'm fine," she added as she started the car. "That I'll be there in a few minutes."

The lights were on, she saw, all over the house. She got out for a moment to speak to the two cops parked at the curb. Head cocked, she walked back to Xander.

"Fran, Jack, the kids, Bella, her kids. You didn't mention everyone congregated over here."

"It's what we do."

She kissed both his cheeks. "Go in, smooth everyone's nerves. Ask . . . ask Mama to say a rosary for O'Donnell. I'll be back in fifteen minutes."

She got back in the car before someone inside spotted her. She'd never get home for clothes if they started streaming outside.

"They hold together," Bo said when she pulled away. "You've got granite for a base there, Catarina. They're scared, they're sick with worry, but they don't come apart."

"He wants to hurt them. I'm afraid knowing that will make me come apart."

"It won't. I guess if I'm going to do the married thing—hey, I said 'married' right out loud. If I'm going to do the married-and-kids thing, I'd want to build that on a good, solid base."

"Well, the timing's odd, but if that's a proposal—"

"Uh-uh. You proposed, I'm just giving you an answer."

"I see."

"Don't see a ring, though. It's not official until you buy me a ring."

She stopped, just braked in the middle of the street, laid her head on the steering wheel. And wept.

"Oh hey, oh God, don't cry." He yanked at his seat belt, swiveled over to try to take her in his arms.

"I have to, just for a minute. I thought I would lose it in the house, first in that bedroom. Seeing what he did to them. He shot them, then sat them up in bed like puppets."

"What?"

"Carla and Don Dimarco. I didn't know them well. They only bought the house a few months ago. Young couple, first house. Her mother and

Gina's mom went to school together." She sat up, wiped at tears. "He didn't fire the bed. I could see them. I could see the pillows he used to muffle the shots. I was standing there, the fire's all around and I could see how he came in while they slept, put the pillows over their faces . . . low caliber. Little hole. Just a little hole."

Bo said nothing, only took her hand.

"It's all around. The fire. The heat, the smoke, the light. It talks. You can hear it mutter, sing, roar. It has speech. It fascinates me. It pulls at me. It always has, since the night I stood on the sidewalk with a glass of ginger ale and watched it dance behind the glass at Sirico's. I understand his . . . attachment to it," she said and turned to look at Bo.

"I understand why he chooses it, or it chooses him. I can see the steps that brought us here, all of us. But now, after O'Donnell, I feel as though I'm standing on the edge of them. I lost my balance up in that room, looking at people who did nothing except buy a nice house in a nice neighborhood. Looking at them and feeling the fire, I lost it, then my partner's standing in the doorway, pulling me back from that edge, reminding me we had a job to do. And dying for it."

She shuddered out a breath. "I can see what he's doing, why. More, why he *has* to do it. The fire fascinates him, too."

"Have you got some screwy idea that you and this crazy bastard have something in common?"

"We do, more than one thing in common. But I've got that granite base, and thank God for it. And now I have you. I said you level me out, Bo. If I lose my balance, you're going to steady me again. Why else would you sit here on this hellish night and talk about marriage and children?"

"You want to know?" He hitched up a hip, pulled out a bandanna and used it to mop at her wet cheeks himself. "I've spent a good part of tonight sitting, standing, pacing in your parents' house. Watching your family sit, stand, pace. And I realized if you love someone, when it's the most real, the most important thing in your life, it's not enough to coast. You need to dig in those footers, start building on that base. You want something to last, you put your back into it." He kissed her hand. "I've got a strong back."

"Me, too." She kissed his hand in turn, then, pushing back her hair, started the car again. "What kind of ring do you want?"

"Something gaudy that I can show off to my friends to their envy and avarice."

Her laugh felt rusty in her throat.

She pulled up behind the police unit in front of her house. "I'm going to talk to these guys a minute, then run in and get some things. Why don't you wait here and start planning your dream wedding? You're going to look amazing in a long white dress."

"That may be going a little too far. It's not really appropriate for me to wear white."

She had her badge out, then recognized the officer who stepped out of the radio car. "Officer Derrick."

"Detective. Bastard killed O'Donnell."

"Yeah." She steadied herself again. "How long have you been on?"

"Since two. Another unit was doing circular patrols, but since it looked like he might be working his way here, we pulled off the clinic fire to do the sit and watch. Two officers are covering the back. Check-in's every fifteen."

"Status?"

"Quiet. Some people came out when they heard sirens. Had some milling on the sidewalk. We dispersed."

"I'm going in to get some fresh clothes. My—" She started to say "friend," then gave herself a lift. "My fiancé's in the car. Appreciate the duty, Officer."

"No problem. Want me to walk you in, stand by?"

"It's okay. I'll be quick. Alert the rear team that I'm entering the premises."

"Will do."

Jingling her keys, she crossed the sidewalk, started up the steps.

Four fires set in under six hours, she thought. Was he going for the record book, looking for fame as well as revenge?

He knew the neighborhood, so that was to his advantage, but still it was fast work. Damn fast.

She unlocked the door, flipped on the lights as she stepped in. She set her keys down as she brought the map back into her head.

From Fells Point, entering around six-thirty. Exiting between nine-fifteen and nine-thirty. Plenty of time to get to John's, set the fire. Had to leave that location after midnight. Cutting it close there, barely enough time to get to the other locations. Fire was hot, fully involved when they'd arrived at the clinic, minutes after he'd called her.

Minutes, she thought on her way upstairs. And only minutes after that—five?—she and O'Donnell had raced to the old Pastorelli house.

Not just one step ahead. Nobody was that good, nobody was that fast. An accomplice? Didn't fit, just didn't fit. This was his mission, his obsession. He wouldn't share.

But he'd fired the clinic, gone two blocks, broken into his old house, shot two people, planted the rigged extinguisher and set another fire. One that had been fully involved before she'd gotten there.

Because he'd killed Carla and Don first. Before the clinic. Because he'd set both fires, used timers. Very likely set the clinic to burn before he'd gone to John's. That's the pattern, she thought. Xander then John.

She'd missed it. Missed it because she'd been running around, just as he'd wanted. Because he'd had everyone scrambling to put out blazes that were as much distraction as they were points on his scoreboard.

Missed more, she realized, because she'd been grieving.

*Since two.* That's what Derrick had said. They'd been on since two.

Her palms went damp. She spun, reaching for her weapon, poised to run down and out.

He stepped out of the doorway in front of her, wearing a Sirico's T-shirt. And holding a .22.

"Time for the big surprise. You're going to want to take that gun out slow, Reena. Drop it on the floor."

She raised both hands. Don't surrender your weapon, she thought. Never give up your weapon. "There are cops all around the house, Joey."

"Yeah, I've seen them. Two front, two back. Got here about ten minutes after me. Had a busy night, haven't you? You got soot on your face. You went into my house, didn't you? I knew you would. I've done quite a study on you. Did you get to them before the fire did?"

"Yeah."

He grinned hugely. "Hey, where's your partner?"

Gleeful, that's what he was. And she would see him in hell for it, whatever the cost. "You've killed a cop now, Joey. You're done. Every cop in Baltimore will come after you. You're not going to get out of this."

"I think I will. But if I don't, I'll have finished what the hell I started. The gun, Reena."

"You use yours, the cops'll be in here before I drop. That's not the way you want to finish this. That's not the point, is it? Fire's the point. There's no satisfaction unless I burn."

"And you will. Bet your partner burned good."

The image flashed back, and she suppressed it. But it left a sparking wire in her blood.

Oh, she could feel, and she could think. And he'd misjudged her. "I know about your father, the cancer."

Fury flamed into his face. "You don't talk about my father. You don't say his name."

"Maybe you think you have it, too. That it came into you from him. But that's a small chance, Joey. Single digits."

"What the fuck do you know about it? It's eating him from the inside. You can watch it eating him, smell it. I'm not going that way, and neither's he. I'm going to take care of him before it finishes him. Fire purifies."

Fresh horror struck her. He meant to burn his own father to death. "You can't help him, can't purify him if you die here."

"Maybe not. But he taught me to look out for number one. And I think I'll get out. You'll burn, they'll come running, and I'll slip out. Like smoke."

He stepped forward; she stepped back. "Belly shot probably won't kill you—at least not right away. But it'll hurt like hell. They might hear it. Little gun like this doesn't make much of a bang, so maybe not. Either way, I'll have just enough time. I got everything set up for you."

He shoved her back, into the bedroom, hit the lights.

Trailers and chimneys were set over the floor, over the bed.

He grabbed her hair, yanked her down to her knees with the gun pressed to her temple. "One sound, one move, I put it in your brain, then burn what's left of you."

Stay alive, she ordered herself. She couldn't shut him down if she was dead. "You'll burn, too."

"That happens, I can't think of a better way to go out. I've been waiting to find out what it's like since I was twelve." He wrenched her police issue out of her holster, tossed it aside. "Too big a bang," he told her. "You've wondered what it was like, too. To go into it, to let the fire take you. You're going to find out. Here's what we're going to do. You're going to call your old man, tell him to come on down. You want to talk to him, in private."

Doesn't know I just came in for clothes. Doesn't know they're waiting for me. "Why?"

"He burns, you burn, and that ends it. Circle closes."

"Do you think I'd bring my father to you?"

"He killed mine. He's got a price to pay. You got a choice. You call him, you sacrifice him, or I take them all. Your whole family." He wrapped her hair around his fist, yanked until stars exploded in front of her eyes. "Mother, brother, sisters. All those little brats. Every single one. So you choose. Your father, or all of them."

"All he did was defend me, the way fathers are supposed to."

"He humiliated mine. He had him dragged off, locked in a cell."

"Your father did that to himself the minute he lit the match inside Sirico's."

"He didn't do it alone. Didn't know that, did you?" His grin spread until his whole face was alight with it. "He took me with him that night. He showed me the fire, how to create it. He showed me what you do to people who *get in your face!*" He backhanded her, straddled her.

"You're shaking." His voice trembled with laughter now. "You're shaking, just like you did that day. When your father gets here, I'm going to do you in front of him. I'm going to show him what a whore his precious daughter is." He tore her shirt open, pressed the gun under her jaw.

She heard herself whimper, fought the need to struggle.

"Remember when I did that on the playground? You got tits now though." He squeezed her breast with his hand, pursed his lips in mock approval. "Nice ones. You don't cooperate, I'm going to do the same to your mother, to your sisters, even that Asian tramp your brother married. Then there's that slutty little niece of yours. The young ones are the tastiest."

"I'll kill you." She was cold and hard as stone inside. She hadn't had to find her anger. It had been there, waiting, all along. "I'll kill you first."

"Who's holding the gun, Reena?" He traced the barrel down her throat. "Who's got the power?" Rammed the barrel hard under her jaw. "Who's in fucking *charge*?"

"You are." She kept her eyes on his, built her courage on that rock of anger. Do the job. "You are, Joey."

"Goddamn right. Your father for mine, bitch. Lose him, I let the rest of them live."

"I'll call him." She let the tears come, let herself shake—let him see what he expected to see. Weakness and fear. "He'd rather die than have you touch any of them."

"Good for him."

He shifted his weight. She counted her own breaths. Slowly sat up, keeping her teary eyes on his, hoping he saw only pleas and defeat.

With tears dripping, she lifted a hand as if to draw her ripped shirt together. She swung out with her forearm, slapping away his gun hand, punched out with her other fist toward his face. She heard the gun clatter on the floor, then saw more stars as he fell on her.

In the car, Bo drummed his fingers. What the hell was taking her so long? He rechecked her bedroom window, saw the light burning. Checked his watch—again.

She took much longer, he thought, the relief, the inactivity, the fact that it was four in the morning was going to put him to sleep.

He got out, walked over to the cop on the passenger side. "I'm going to go in, okay? She must be packing a trunk instead of grabbing a clean shirt."

"Women."

"Whatcha gonna do?"

He fished out his keys. They were going to have to think about the houses, he thought, studying the look of them as he walked to the steps. Sell one—which? Keep both and combine them? Might be an interesting job, but they'd end up with some big-ass house.

He stifled a yawn, unlocked the door. "Hey, Reene, did you decide we should elope so you're packing a trousseau? What exactly is a trousseau anyway?"

He'd shut the door behind him, had gotten to the base of the stairs, when he heard her shout his name.

Her nose was bleeding. She could taste blood in her mouth as she fought viciously. He'd kicked her—she thought he'd kicked her—but she couldn't feel anything but rage and terror. She'd raked his face, gone for his eyes.

She wasn't the only one bleeding.

But he was stronger, and he was winning.

The sound of Bo's voice wrenched a scream from her.

"Bo! Get out. Get the cops!"

Joey dived away from her. After the gun, oh God, the gun.

Her vision was blurred, her lungs all but shut down. Tears spilled through the blood on her face as she crawled toward the doorway and her own weapon.

Feet pounded. Or was it her heart? She rolled, the weapon gripped in both hands. And saw with dull horror that he hadn't dived for the gun.

"Don't. For God's sake. Can't you smell it? You'll go up like a torch."

"You, too." He held the flaming match in the air. "Let's see what it's like."

He dropped the match into the pool on the floor. Fire burst, a quick roar of freedom. He flew onto the flames.

She rolled as it leaped toward her. Screamed as it snatched at her legs. Bo was dragging her away from it, smothering flames with his hands, his body.

"Linen closet, blankets." Panting, she dragged off her smoldering pants. "Don't touch the extinguisher, he might have rigged it. Go. Hurry!"

She crab-walked back, teeth chattering.

He was screaming now—horrible, inhuman sounds as he spun around the room. Fire embraced him.

She saw, thought she saw, and would always see, his eyes locked on hers through the flames that consumed his face.

Somehow he walked toward her. One step, then two, toward the doorway.

Then he fell, with fire rolling over him like a molten sea.

They were coming. Cops battering down the door. Sirens would be close behind. The trucks, the hoses, the heroes in turnout suits.

She braced her back against the wall and watched the burn.

"Put him out," she murmured when Bo rushed back. "For God's pity, put him out."

# EPILOGUE

She sat at her mother's kitchen table, sipping chilled wine with a blanket over her shoulders. She didn't need her brother the doctor to tell her she was shocky. She didn't want the ER, or sedatives.

She needed to be here, to just be.

The salve An dabbed on the burns was like heaven.

"Ribs are bruised, nothing broken that I can tell." Xander frowned at her battered face. "You need X-rays, damn it, Reena."

"Later, Doc."

"Second degree." An gently bandaged her ankles. "You're lucky."

"I know." She reached behind her for Bo's hand, smiled at her father. "I know it."

"She's going to eat, and she's going to rest. She's not going to do cop work right now." Bianca spoke straight to Younger.

"No, ma'am. We'll deal with it in the morning," he said to Reena.

"When we go through the layers, we'll find the timers. I don't think he meant to die, not until the end. He just . . . he couldn't be humiliated. Beaten, like his father. He couldn't face it, or the idea of a slow death. So he chose."

"You're going to eat. I'm going to fix eggs, and everyone's going to eat." Bianca yanked open the refrigerator, then just covered her face with her hands and began to sob.

Gib moved to her, but Reena patted his arm, shook her head. "Let me."

Her breath caught on a shock of pain as she got to her feet, but she went to her mother, slid her arms around her. "Mama. It's okay. We're all okay."

"My baby. My baby girl. *Bella bambina.*"

"*Ti amo, Mama.* And I'm fine. But I'm hungry."

"*Va bene.* Okay." She mopped at her cheeks with her hands, then kissed Reena's. "Sit down. I'll cook."

"I'll help you, Mama." Bella blinked at her own tears when Bianca raised eyebrows at her. "I still remember how to make breakfast."

Yes, this is what she needed, Reena thought. The noise, the movement, the sounds and scents of her mother's kitchen. She ate what was put in front of her with an appetite that surprised and pleased her.

Later, she found her father and John sitting on the front steps, sipping coffee. Dawn broke over the neighborhood, a pearly haze that promised another day of drenching heat.

She was sure she'd never seen anything more beautiful.

"Been a long time since we first sat out here," John said.

"It was beer then."

"Will be again sometime."

"I was having myself a sulk. I'm not sure what I'm having this morning. You told me what a lucky man I was. Beautiful wife and kids. You were right. You said what a bright one I had in Reena. You were right about that, too. I almost lost her, John. I almost lost my little girl last night."

"You didn't. And you're still a lucky man."

"Room for one more out here?" Reena stepped out. "Going to be a hot one. I used to love hot summer days when I was a kid. They lasted forever, all the way into the night. I could lie in bed and listen to them. Fran coming in from a date, old Mr. Franco out walking his dog. Johnnie Russo driving by with those glasspack mufflers. You used to give him such a hard time about that, Dad."

She bent down, kissed the top of his head. "Mornings like this, people'll start coming out early, before the heat hits. Walk down to the park or the market, gab over the fence in the back, or across the front steps. Head off to work. Water their flowers, catch up on the news, if they have the day off. We're all pretty lucky, if you ask me."

They sat for a while in silence, watching the light come into the morning, then John patted her gently on the knee. "Going to get on home, see what needs to be done."

"I'm sorry about your house, John."

"Sorry about yours, honey."

"We've got a lot of hands to help you put it back together," she told him. "And I know a good carpenter."

Then he bent, kissed the top of her head. "Your partner would be proud of you. I'll be in touch. You take care, Gib."

"Thanks, John. For everything."

Reena watched him drive away. "He helped make me what I am. I hope you're okay with that."

"Seeing what you are, I'm fine with that." There were tears in his eyes. She could see the glimmer of them as he stared out across the row. "Your mom and I may be shaky for a day or two, but we'll settle down."

"I know you will." She leaned against him a moment, just sitting on the front steps, watching the light grow. "You helped make me what I am, too," she told him. "You and Mama. *Vi amo. Molto.*" She leaned just a little harder against him. "*Molto.*"

He slid an arm around her. Then his lips brushed her hair. "Are you going to marry that carpenter?"

"Yes. Yes, I am."

"Good choice."

"I think so. Now, I'm going to go in, say good-bye to everyone and see if I can push them along. You and Mama should get some sleep, too."

"I could use it."

She found Bella alone in the kitchen. "Cooking and cleaning up?"

"Fran's having some contractions. Mama took her upstairs."

"She's in labor?"

"Maybe. Maybe just some Braxton-Hicks. She's got two doctors, her mother and her husband hovering. She's fine." Bella lifted a hand, shook her head. "I don't mean to sound like that." She tossed down a dish towel. "I can't seem to help myself."

"We're all tired, Bella. You're entitled."

"I envy her. Not just that serenity she wears like a custom-made suit, but the way Jack looks at her. You could just melt. I don't not want her to have it. I just wish I had a little of it myself."

"I'm sorry."

"No point. I made this bed." She laid a hand on her belly.

"You're sure?"

"You can find out so soon, practically before you are. I'm pregnant. I got pregnant on purpose. Stupid, maybe selfish, but it's done. I'm not sorry about the baby."

"Have you told Vince?"

"He's thrilled. He does love children, even if he doesn't love me the way I want. He'll be sweet and attentive for a bit, and he'll take a little more care to hide his next affair—if he dares to have one after you blasted him."

"Will you be happy, Bella?"

"Working on it. I'm not going to divorce him. I'm not going to give up what I've got, so I'll make what I can of what I have. Don't tell the family yet. Fran ought to have this baby without another one in progress taking any shine off it."

Reena smiled. "You're okay, Isabella. You always were."

She studied the neighborhood as Bo drove them home. As she'd predicted, people were out early. Heading to the park to walk or jog, strolling with pets and kids. Hurrying off to work. She could smell fresh baked bread wafting from the bakery.

Even when she smelled the lingering traces of smoke and wet, it didn't dampen her.

She nodded to the cops left on duty.

"I need a little sleep, then I want to go to church, light a candle for O'Donnell," she told Bo. "You're going to want to go see your Mrs. M., O'Donnell's sister."

"Yeah." He rubbed a hand down her arm. "Later today."

"I'll go with you, and I'd like you to go with me when I visit his wife. But first, I need to go in."

"I'll tuck you into my bed, and later we'll go to church, we'll light a candle, we'll go see his family. But you should go to the hospital, get checked out."

"Nothing broken, second degree. Not that I don't intend to hit Xander up for some lovely drugs, but what I want most after this is a bed, and yours is just fine. But I have to go in first. I have to see it."

She unlocked the door. She smelled the smoke, studied where it had stained the walls. In silence, she walked up the stairs. Her belly clenched.

Fire had charred her bedroom door frame, flashed over the floor. Her dresser was scorched, the wood buckled, the burn pattern on the walls showing the fire's greedy reach up.

And she saw where Joey's body had fallen, and smothered the flames under it.

"He wasn't crazy when this started, not the way he was when it ended. It ate at him, at his mind, maybe his soul. Like fire eats fuel. Like cancer's eating his father. So it consumed him."

"You weren't the reason, and never were. You were an excuse."

Surprised, she turned her head, looked at Bo. "You're right. My God, you're right. And that feels like, well, absolution."

She leaned her head on his shoulder. "I'm lucky, and I know it. A few bumps, bruises and burns. But I feel sad when I look at this room. It wasn't perfect, I know. But it was mine."

"It still is." He slipped an arm gently around her waist. "I can fix it."

She laughed a little, and her body relaxed against his. "Yes. Yes, you can."

She turned away from it, and went home with the boy next door.